$17.95

Daring to Dream

Utopianism and Communitarianism
Lyman Tower Sargent and Gregory Claeys
Series Editors

*D*aring *to* Dream

UTOPIAN FICTION BY UNITED STATES WOMEN BEFORE 1950

Second Edition

Edited by

CAROL FARLEY KESSLER

SYRACUSE UNIVERSITY PRESS

Second Edition
95 96 97 98 99 00   6 5 4 3 2 1

The first edition of this book was originally published as *Daring to Dream: Utopian Stories by United States Women, 1836–1919* by Pandora Press of Routledge and Kegan Paul, London, in 1984.

The paper used in this publication meets the minimum requirements of American National Standard for Information Sciences—Permanence of Paper for Printed Library Materials, ANSI Z39.48-1984.♾™

Library of Congress Cataloging-in-Publication Data
Daring to dream : Utopian fiction by United States women before 1950
/ edited by Carol Farley Kessler. — 2nd ed.
    p.   cm. — (Utopianism and communitarianism)
    Includes bibliographical references (p.   ).
    ISBN 0-8156-2654-1 (acid-free paper).—ISBN 0-8156-2655-X (pbk.
: acid-free paper)
    1. Utopias—Fiction.   2. Feminism—Fiction.   3. American
fiction—19th century.   4. American fiction—20th century.
5. Women—Social life and customs—Fiction.   I. Kessler, Carol
Farley.   II. Series.
PS648U85.D37   1995
813.008′0372—dc20   95-2298

For Cora Robin,
with loving wishes
for the brightest of all possible futures

Carol Farley Kessler is professor of English, American Studies, and Women's Studies at Penn State's Delaware County Campus in Media, Pennsylvania. She has written *Elizabeth Stuart Phelps* (1982) and *Charlotte Perkins Gilman: Her Progress Toward Utopia* (1994), edited *The Story of Avis* (1877) by Elizabeth Stuart Phelps and a special issue on utopias of *Journal of General Education* (1985), and contributed numerous articles to journals, collections, and reference works. She is a contributor to *The Heath Anthology of American Literature,* a member of the editorial board of *Utopian Studies,* and a consultant for *Legacy: A Journal of American Women Writers.*

Contents

Preface

This collection spans 1870–1949, recovering for readers three full-length utopias never before reprinted as a whole, four short utopian stories, and significant excerpts from five utopian novels, each carefully selected to maintain the integrity of the original. This book provides an overview of utopias written by women in the United States from texts not otherwise easily available. As a group, they provide a foreground for, and feminist revision of, Edward Bellamy's popular and influential *Looking Backward: 2000–1887* (1888), as well as the imaginative underpinnings for the late-twentieth century outpouring of feminist utopias.

The collection, limited to feminist fiction by United States women, demonstrates themes common to this period and mode of writing. All selections have inherent dramatic interest. Their forms vary widely, including dream vision, satiric dialogue, alternative future, communitarian romance, and science fiction. Titles recently reprinted or in widely available library editions do not appear. In addition whole texts or complete units comprise the selections.

Several titles appearing in the 1984 edition do not reappear here. Arthur O. Lewis included the entire texts of Mary Griffith, "Three Hundred Years Hence" (1836), and Jane Sophia Appleton, "Sequel to the 'Vision of Bangor in the Twentieth Century' " (1848) in *American Utopias: Selected Short Fiction* (New York: Arno, 1971). In 1985, New Society Publishers of Philadelphia reprinted Lois Nichols Waisbrooker, *A Sex Revolution* (1894), with an introduction by Pam McAllister. And Syracuse University Press, in the Utopianism and Communitarianism series, which includes this book, has published in 1991 Alice Ilgenfritz Jones and Ella Merchant, *Unveiling a Parallel: A Romance* (1893), introduced by Carol A. Kolmerten; and in 1993 Claire Myers Spotswood, *The Unpredictable Adventure: A Comedy of Woman's Independence* (1935), introduced by Miriam Kalman Harris.

All of the selections have literary and historical interest in their own right. The collection constitutes an overview of utopian literary types and spans the nineteenth-century women's movement from post–Civil War to post–World War II. Thus the collection traces the imaginative roots of United States feminism. The selections delineate the social arrangements women wanted and demonstrate the feminist thread in United States utopian fiction.

The fictional materials, plus accompanying introduction, are relevant to a variety of contexts: cross-disciplinary courses in American studies, peace studies, utopian studies, and women's studies; classes in American literature, popular culture, and United States history (reform, communitarianism); discussion of political theory of ideal social structure, such as introductory courses in political science or philosophy could entail. Thus the anthology could be used at a variety of educational levels —from advanced high school pupils to graduate students.

The introduction discusses predominantly feminist utopias, being more than half of a sample of 148 titles. Nonfeminist utopias seem to fit what has been a major trend in Western utopian writing from Plato to the present, namely, the subordination of women to men—even in utopia—and the treatment of sexuality as negatively disruptive. The countertrend in this tradition, which encompasses the feminist thread in United States utopias, emerged in the nineteenth century. It values both women as full citizens of utopia and sexuality as a positively energized social force. This feminist utopian thread receives an overview, its broad outlines sketched. The overview is not meant to be definitive or exhaustive but rather suggestive. Its endnotes can be used as a guide to supplementary reading.

Headnotes to the selections include, where available, biographical information about the author, historical background or sources for themes she stresses, but not detailed literary analysis, which is the burden of the reader. If a selection is an excerpt, its relation to the rest of the work receives clarification. In addition, a list of references appears with each selection as well as the source for the text and listing of pages excerpted. In addition, editorial notes provide explanations for allusions or topical references within the reprinted texts.

The annotated bibliography, which originally appeared in the first edition, was revised for publication in *Utopian Studies* 1, no. 1 (1990): 1–58. A headnote explains its parameters. A brief list of criticism on United States women and utopia appears in References. It is that unrevised bibliography that is reprinted, with permission, in this edition.

No one bibliographer, no matter how diligent, can hope to cover all possibilities. The research for a project such as this gathers numerous debts in the process of completion. The book and its compiler seem to me the mere apex of a supporting pyramid, an essential foundation permitting her work. Thus may I acknowledge most heartily and gratefully everyone who has contributed. The research upon which this collection is based has been supported by funds from the Institute for Arts and Humanistic Studies, the Faculty Scholarship Support Fund, and the Liberal Arts College Fund for Research, all at the Pennsylvania State University, as well as by a Fellowship for College Teachers and Independent Scholars from the National Endowment for the Humanities, 1988–89. I wish to thank all of the foregoing for this invaluable support.

My campus administrators, Edward S. J. Tomezsko, Campus Executive Officer, and Madlyn L. Hanes, Director of Academic Affairs, have unfailingly supported my research, as have English Department Head Robert Secor and Associate Head Kenneth Thigpen.

Charles Mann, Curator, and Sandy Stelts of the Rare Book Room, Pattee Library, Penn State University, provided both advice and books. Jean Sphar, Theresa Arndt, Susan Ware, and Sara Whildin, Head, at Penn State's Delaware County Campus Library, ordered interlibrary loan and reference materials from what must have seemed an interminable stream of requests. May I thank them all for their boundless patience.

In addition fellow researchers and bibliographers, both in published work, personal correspondence, and conversation, have made a mountainous task more easily scalable. To each for helpful advice, I thank Nan Bowman Albinski, Marleen S. Barr, Phyllis Cole, Jane Donawerth, Libby Falk Jones, Lee Cullen Khanna, Carol A. Kolmerten, Helen Kuryllo, Darby Lewes, Arthur O. Lewis, Daphne Patai, Janice A. Radway, Kenneth M. Roemer, Stephen Ross, and Lyman Tower Sargent.

I thank Delaware Campus typist Loretto Catanzaro, who transcribed onto disk nearly indecipherable copy, and University Park computer specialist, Chet Smith, who made the process of scanning text to disk as painless as possible.

At Syracuse University Press, the unfailing good sense of Cynthia Maude-Gembler has eased my work immeasurably.

And my family participated as well: I thank mother, daughter, son, daughter-in-law, and now granddaughter, for loving interest and support.

For any remaining errors or oversights, I apologize and ask not your forbearance but your information!

Merion Station, Pennsylvania　　　　　　　　　　Carol Farley Kessler
May 1994

Introduction

"Pretty plain to see," I went on. "We men, having all human power in our hands, have used it to warp and check the growth of women. We, by choice and selection, by law and religion, by enforced ignorance, by heavy overcultivation of sex, have made the kind of woman we so made by nature, that that is what it was to be a woman. Then we heaped our scornful abuse upon her, ages and ages of it, the majority of men in all nations still looking down on women. And then, as if that was not enough—really, my dear, I'm not joking, I'm ashamed, as if I'd done it myself—we, in our superior freedom, in our monopoly of education, with the law in our hands, both to make and execute, with every conceivable advantage—we have blamed women for the sins of the world!"

"Put yourself in my place for a moment, Van. Suppose in Herland we had a lot of—subject men. Blame us all you want to for doing it, but look at the men. Little creatures, undersized and generally feeble. Cowardly and not ashamed of it. Kept for sex purposes only or as servants; or both, usually both. I confess I'm asking something difficult of your imagination, but try to think of Herland women, each with a soft man she kept to cook for her, to wait upon her and to—'love' when she pleased. Ignorant men mostly. Poor men, almost all, having to ask their owners for money and tell what they wanted it for. Some of them utterly degraded creatures, kept in houses for common use—as women are kept here. Some of them quite gay and happy—pet men, with pet names and presents showered upon them. Most of them contented, piously accepting kitchen work as their duty, living by the religion and laws and customs the women made. Some of them left out and made fun of for being left—not owned at all—and envying those who were! Allow for a surprising percentage of mutual love and happiness, even under these conditions; but also for ghastly depths of misery and a general low level of mere submission to the inevitable. Then in this state of degradation fancy these men for the most part quite content to make monkeys of themselves by wearing the most ridiculous

xiii

clothes. Fancy them, men, with men's bodies, though enfeebled, wearing open-work lace underclothing, with little ribbons all strung through it; wearing dresses never twice alike and almost always foolish; wearing hats—" she fixed me with a steady eye in which a growing laughter twinkled—"wearing such hats as your women wear!"

—Charlotte Perkins Gilman
With Her in Ourland (1916)[1]

Many with an interest in utópias have read Gilman's *Herland* (1915), one of the few recovered feminist classics. The foregoing segments of a conversation from its sequel, *With Her in Ourland,* suggest how both women and men can learn from reading utopias by and about women. Let's look more closely.

"I" of the first sentence is Vandyck Jennings, sociologist and husband of Herlander Ellador; the two are making a tour of Ourland (Earth) at the time of World War 1. With satiric results, Gilman shows Ourland as seen through the eyes of a visitor from an all-female society, where crime, poverty, and war never existed. Ellador—whose innocent eye and rational mind inform Van, and incidentally us readers, too—has just exclaimed with regard to stereotypic gender differences, "I call it 'The Great Divergence.' There is no other such catastrophic change in all nature—as far as I've been able to gather" (291). Realizing that Ellador can hardly in good grace complain to him about men's role in women's degradation, Van gallantly begins as above to explain the "worst result" of men's conduct: "the petted women, the contented women, the 'happy' women" (292). His inventory of wrongs receives amplification in the selections that follow, as do those Ellador mischievously enumerates. But Gilman does not stop here. Ellador then points out to Van that a women's movement has achieved the availability of education and money for women, that although the "woman man made" is deplorable, she could have—but hasn't—objected or changed very greatly. Note then that in Gilman's view, all of us share some responsibility for being where we are. Elsewhere Gilman observed satirically, "The woman is narrowed by the home, and the man is narrowed by the woman," her home—the quoted passage implies—having been narrowed by the man![2] A defeating circularity, to be sure. And only all of us together, each feeling his or her responsibility for doing so, can stop this cycle.

Historians contend that those who do not know the past are doomed to repeat it. Literary utopias are not of course "the past" in the sense intended. But if we understand that utopias usually index—however obliquely—the wrongs, the lacks, and the needs experienced or recognized by authors of the past, then by reading these utopias we obtain a sense of history-as-experienced that statistics or political documents cannot provide.[3] From these utopias we can learn what the wrongs have been. Knowing them, we can seek to change. No one of us is an island: if circumstances diminish any of us, we all stand deprived of enjoying the accomplishments any diminished person might have attained. Hence the recovery of woman's past is imperative, that we may no longer be deprived of her potential. Hence the reading of utopias, those visions of better worlds to inspire us to greater efforts in our own. As Gilman notes, "How to make the best kind of people and how to keep them at their best and growing better—surely that is what we are here for" (297).

The word *utopia* was coined by Sir Thomas More to name his 1516 fiction of a nonexistent, ideal society (from the Greek *ou* = no, *topos* = place). A fictional society, of course, is not real, but an ideal nowhere. More's *Utopia,* however, contains a pun or deliberate ambiguity, deriving from the word's etymology: an ideal nowhere appears a good society compared to what writer or author has experienced (from the Greek *eu* = good). More recently, by analogy to More's *Utopia,* a depiction of a bad society is called dystopia (from the Greek *dys* = bad). Utopia, using the metaphor of the city or the society, can convey a state of mind (not a geographical territory), or a world view. Jung considers the city or society to be a metaphor of the female principle, of a woman sheltering inhabitants as if children.[4] (Since today we would not wish to restrict the capacity to shelter to women only, we might call this a "nurturing" principle, and thus render the term free of gender bias.) Utopia then becomes a refuge or shelter wherein we may safely envision a changed society. And although mere metaphor located in no real place, utopia nonetheless has power—utopian ideals or ideas change minds: changed minds then change worlds. A critic of feminist utopias, Lee Cullen Khanna (1981), notes that we find "utopia in the process of experiencing a convincing fiction . . . not 'out there' in another time and place—but within the self."[5] In this power to change, convert, renew, utopias can be spiritual or religious in their effect.

The view of literature expressed here is unashamedly didactic, a tradition encompassing such diversity as the classical Aesop's *Fables* and the medieval morality play *Everyman,* as well as much United States fiction written during the nineteenth century, lately decried by many twentieth-century critics as sentimental, moralistic, or didactic. Jane Tompkins (1985), however, in discussing nineteenth-century women's "sensational designs" for accomplishing "cultural work," reminds us that women fully expected their fiction to effect social evolution, if not revolution. The utopian writing discussed here presents "sensational designs" for cultural adjustments just as did the "woman's fiction" depicting a heroine's "trials and triumphs," as delineated by Nina Baym (1993). Perhaps, given the outpouring of utopian writing during the 1970s, we need to reconsider the label *didactic* as a pejorative. Recent didactic fiction—of which the utopia and bildungsroman are two genres currently in evidence—again receives serious discussion.[6]

In a 1979 discussion of women's utopias, feminist critic Rachel Blau DuPlessis revived the label *apologue* (from the Greek *apologos* = "story") for the utopias these authors have written. Such novels, DuPlessis explains, "contain embedded elements from 'assertive discourse'—genres like sermon, manifesto, tract, fable," including speech or marriage contract also. Such genres usually "guide or inform the action." Although occurring in a variety of tones or moods, the speculation they provide is central to the action within the text. The source of interest in these texts is not the typical plot or character, but "speculative and didactic discourse." Plot and character in apologues embody "philosophical propositions or moral arguments," in order to persuade readers to believe them.

"Second," DuPlessis continues, "these teaching fictions often contain an analysis of the past and a projection into the future—both within one work. . . . [W]hen a novel travels through the present into the future, as these can do, social or character development can no longer be felt as complete, nor [can] our 'space' as readers (beyond the ending) [be] perceived as untrammeled. If the future is no longer a resolved place, then in the same way, the past—history itself—no longer has fixity or authority. These future visions are visions of the past as well. . . ."

"Third," DuPlessis notes, "characters in a teaching story are not the classic 'well-rounded' personages with whom one identifies and who seem to take on a life of their own." Rather they may be flat because they represent a cluster of typical traits. Further they embody "Socratic questions: that is, ideas, not characters, are well-rounded. Socratic questions, it must be remembered, are questions to which Socrates already had an answer": in an apologue, characters exist to act out an author's answers to questions or to illustrate her ideals or speculations, but not to act out lives as characters. Also the action of such books may include "speculative, fantasy, or 'science fiction' elements such as time travel or sex changes." Such "unreal elements . . . estrange the reader from the rules of the known world," thereby loosening the mind and rendering it more receptive to the stories' revelations of needed changes in values and institutions. "An ethical art moves the reader beyond acceptance of existing values and institutions."[7]

To the foregoing condensation of DuPlessis's informative extended definition of the apologue, I would add a first warning footnote: no utopia, a type of apologue, should be taken as a social blueprint, ready for implementation. Rather utopias, as apologues, foment speculation, offer alternative vicarious experience, spur us as readers to reevaluate and act upon our own world—create new consensus, establish new community. Utopias are spiritual guides, demonstrations of values, experiences of societies that, while not perfect, are in some ways better than our own. And Elizabeth Janeway would add a second cautionary note—that we beware of the utopist's occupational hazard of fastening too narrowly upon goals: even more significant is the choice of means to a goal. She prefers to focus upon process, upon techniques. At the conclusion of *Powers of the Weak* (1980), she writes, "I believe that we may accomplish so much more than we can yet imagine that laying down goals is a bad idea: it limits us and it may misdirect our energies."[8] So long as we keep in mind these two cautions, apologues as utopias can inspire potential re-vision and subsequent revolution. If we recall sociologist Karl Mannheim's understanding of utopianism as revolutionary social innovation "that breaks the bonds of the existing order," and if we recall that bonds enslave, then the study of utopia must have a liberating effect.[9] And if we see in feminism the expression of holistic and communitarian values missing from the present order, then feminism itself is a type of utopianism. Literary critic Annette Kolodny (1981) claims that feminists attempt "a revolution in consciousness so thorough going as to truly dislodge, not simply alter or reform, reigning belief systems."[10] Hence feminist utopian visions help us frame a new consciousness permitting the exploration of a more complete range of human possibilities. Apologues are fables toward our future, infinitely evolving, ever "unfinalized."[11]

Such feminist utopias constitute a persistent vision, the vision of a critical outsider wondering at the folly of the crowd. Their American Dream is different—less ruggedly individualistic, more responsibly communitarian.[12] And because theirs are dreams experienced by outsiders and thus always entail risk of censure by insiders, the dreams require that a dreamer be daring to express them.[13] The anthology title *Daring to Dream* is a variation upon a line from an 1880 poem by Elizabeth Stuart Phelps, a well-known utopian author of the nineteenth-century (see selection 2). The line—"Ideal of ourselves! We dream and dare."—effectively expresses thought becoming act, utopia realized in life.[14] The word *dare* has not varied from its Greek meaning, "to be courageous," but *dream* has lost earlier significance: in Old English "joy" or "music"; in Old Frisian, "shout of joy." This earlier meaning seems embedded still in the expression "a dream come true!" Interestingly a Malay tribe, the Senoi, take dreams so much more seriously than those of us shaped by Western cultural systems that they have incorporated dreams into daily routine. They use dreams to stimulate creative life: they teach children to remember dreams, to direct those dreams (this is possible), and to retain from dreams a dance, poem, or other creative act or idea. The dreamer then shares the dream and its creative outcome with the rest of the tribe the following morning. The Senoi are reportedly "the most democratic group in anthropological literature" and experience "no violent crime or intercommunal conflict," an actual utopia if these traits are among the indices of an ideal society.[15]

When studying or imagining a utopia, we pursue a rite of passage to a better future. As we dare to dream of the not yet known, we change our mindset concerning the possible.[16] As we try to imagine the unimaginable—namely, where we're going before we're there, we move ourselves toward new and as yet unrealized ends. In a 1971 poem "for two voices, female and male" called "Councils," Marge Piercy notes,

> "The women must learn to dare to speak. . . .
> "The women must learn to say, I think this is so. . . .[17]

Much has been said and written about men's visions of utopia; we know far less about women's.

Women's dreams of a good society, a utopia—not necessarily perfect, but simply superior to an author's experience—do have a different focus from men's. Women more than men imagine utopias where the intangible features of human existence receive more prominent consideration. Consequently, where United States utopias by men stress as ends in themselves matters of public policy, be they political, economic, or technological, women's utopias are more likely to include these matters primarily as they provide a means to the social end of fully developed human capacity in all people.[18] Typically, women make issues of family, sexuality, and marriage more central than do men. From 1836, the earliest known utopia written by a United States woman, to the present, a major thematic break occurs. Before 1970, women's autonomy is more often viewed negatively as freedom from domination, especially in marriage where women typically exchange services for economic support. The 1960s mark a transition period hinting at a changed version of the theme. Since the 1970s women's autonomy is more often viewed positively, as freedom for the development and expression of potential, especially within the context of a supportive community, occasionally composed of women only. Before 1970, marriage typically appears as the center of woman's experience: marriage reform, rather than suffrage, is the change more frequently called for in utopias by women. For example, between 1836 and 1920 where about three-quarters of over 100 examples treated marriage as a problem, less than a quarter presented suffrage as part of a solution to women's place in society.[19] Here is vindication for words of Elizabeth Cady Stanton, who in 1853 wrote Susan B. Anthony, "I feel this whole question of women's rights turns on the point of the marriage relation, and sooner or later it will be the question for discussion."[20] Since 1970, utopian society-at-large becomes woman's arena at last; it, rather than marriage, is the new locus for change.

Over the century-and-a-half time span, utopias by United States women frequently mirror what women lacked and what women wanted at the time when the books were published. They also show the same range of contradictory or ambivalent positions as the women's movement, with the difference that the communitarian dimension may be larger in fiction than in history: nearly half of the utopias before 1950 include some degree of cooperative practice. A probable source of the ambivalence in both the fiction and the social movement is feminism's divided intellectual roots. Olive Banks, in *Faces of Feminism: A Study of Feminism as a Social Movement* (1980), finds three intellectual sources informing feminist thought and accounting for the range and divergence among positions considered "feminist."[21] She cites three eighteenth-century sources, whose principles continue to the present. First is evangelical Christianity, which led to moral and social reform activism as well as to the ideology of women's moral guardianship of society. In the present, radical feminists continue to believe in women's moral superiority. Second is Enlightenment philosophy with its stress upon reason, environmental influence, and natural rights. This philosophy is also the intellectual source of the feminist emphasis upon liberation, self-realization, and autonomy. Current expression of the former resides with equal-rights advocates; of the latter, with liberationists. Third is communitarian socialism, with its economic, political, and social innovations. Especially important for women are changes in the family such as communal child care, and changes in marriage, such as less restrictive sexual relationships. This third set of principles has had the smallest following of the three, but gains adherents among current radical feminists and has always been more prominent in utopian practice and fiction than in the women's movement in general.

The current expression of feminism seems to divide between equal rights advocates and liberationists, but lines are hardly clear. This general division can focus our backward look toward the imaginative roots of the women's movement as well as toward the literary tradition of which the current flood of feminist utopias is simply the most recent example: educational, political, and economic rights are one branch of concern while social conditions in marriage and family as well as concern for cooperative or communitarian experiments constitute a second branch. The 1970s and early 1980s seemed to be moving toward a consensus that rights can only exist within a supportive community, that the existence of these rights will change society as we now know it, that autarchy or autonomy for women can exist only when society itself changes substantially. The later 1980s unleashed fresh backlash against women's gains. The mid-1990s seem again to be more affirming of women, but with restriction and reservation. [22]

The discussion that follows will concentrate upon feminist utopias, a majority of the 148 utopias covered in this study. [23] Thus this introductory survey provides a context and reference point for the selections that follow. United States women's utopias fall into three periods, divided according to events in women's history and rate of output. The first two periods parallel this volume. The first extends for over eighty years from the first 1836 utopia, including the 1848 Declaration of Sentiments, to the ratification of Constitutional Amendment 19, granting suffrage to women in 1920; about half of the United States utopias by women, 1836–1920, were feminist. [24] A second period, 1921–1960, includes the Depression and World War II; almost one-quarter of the period's output were feminist, but none appeared during the 1950s. A third period, 1960 to the present, includes the transitional decade of the 1960s, about one-third of 13 having feminist values. The five-year span 1975 to 1979 astonishes; at least 50 works were published, achieving a consensus over a wide range of feminist concerns, a contrast to earlier less feminist visions. During these five years more utopias were written by United States women than during any previous period. The 1970s feminist utopias appear to be one of many indicators suggesting that a cultural paradigm shift is in process and that feminist values are central to the emerging paradigm. [25]

With respect to form, these utopias exist as one (or a blend) of several possibilities: as a description of an ideal society; as a dream from which a dreamer wakes to reveal the wonders of another world; as a voyage to an exotic land or distant planet, which the visitor observes for a later report; as a pioneering expedition to a frontier where an ideal or experimental society can be created untainted by established practices; as a long sleep, from which a reporter wakes in an ideal future society and which may later be dissolved into a dream; as the future of one's own society explained by a future resident; as an outsider's view of one's own society; as a visitor's description of a utopian homeland markedly superior to the author's country. Before 1920, utopias are typically set somewhere in then-contemporary United States, a fact revealing the effect of literary realism upon even so romantic a genre as the utopia. The next two sections survey 1836–1950 utopias by U.S. women.

1836–1920

The first known utopia by a woman writing in the United States appeared in 1836: "Three Hundred Years Hence," a technological utopia included in *Camperdown: or, News from Our Neighborhood,* exemplifies the proposition, set forth by Mary Griffith (d. 1877) in an 1831 lecture "Women": "*We are persuaded that all the misery in this world, which is dependent on vice, arises from the limited sphere of action in which woman is compelled to move*" (283, italics original). This essay antedates Margaret Fuller's (1810–50) views on nineteenth-century women by twelve years.[26] In 1868, one of the century's most popular books appeared: Elizabeth Stuart Phelps succeeded in publishing the first of her immensely popular heavenly utopias, *The Gates Ajar,* which offered bereaved women the solace of reunion with Civil War dead. Each of these utopias addressed the general issue of women's place in society—as shaper and as shaped.

A more specific concern at the time was women's labor. In 1853, Sarah Josepha Hale (1788–1879) editor of *Godey's Lady's Book,* intended to depict an African utopia in *Liberia: or, Mr. Peyton's Experiments,* the only known utopia by a U.S. woman before 1900 to consider race. Hale shows black female labor in the person of Keziah serving white male ideology as Mr. Peyton: she oversees his experiments to provide his "servants" with an economic basis for living outside slavery. Even the modes of address reveal subservience. For its time Hale's novel shows an effort in the direction of cross-cultural awareness, but by 1990s standards, it is racist. In 1866, Rebecca Harding Davis (1831–1910) in "The Harmonists" depicting the Rappite community of Economy, Pennsylvania, decries one man's power to maintain in a "communist village" a "utopia of prophets and poets," who appear to a visitor as "gross men" and "poor withered women" with "faded and tired" faces showing a "curious vacancy" (*Atlantic* 17:531, 533, 535, 537). In her 1873 semiautobiographical narrative "Transcendental Wild Oats," depicting her father Bronson Alcott's Fruitlands, Louisa May Alcott (1832–88) wryly describes "the most ideal of all these castles in Spain." To the question posed by Mrs. Lamb, "Are there any beasts of burden on the place?" seeing how overworked she was, another responded, "Only one woman!" Fruitlands fails: "The world was not ready for Utopia yet" and Mrs. Lamb wonders to her disappointed husband, "Don't you think Apple Slump would be a better name for it, dear?" (*Independent* 25:1570, 1571).[27] In each selection, women supply the labor to achieve a man's ideal, and the ideal fails to materialize as anticipated. All of the foregoing stress the hegemony of patriarchal ideology, particularly in the control of women's labor. In addition, each author subscribes to the concept of women's moral guardianship of society. Charlotte Perkins Gilman, however, as quoted above from *With Her in Ourland,* saw both women and men as degenerate and remediable.

Central in these utopias are the wrongs women experience in marriage, especially as social regulation of woman's sexuality works to her disadvantage. First, the marriage "bargain" is shown to be corrupt, as in *Life and Labor in the Spirit World, Being a Description of the Localities, Employments, Surroundings, and Conditions of the Spheres* (1884) by Mary Theresa Shelhamer (n.d.), "The man wants a housekeeper, the woman a home" (12); or as in *The God of Civilization: A Romance* (1890) by Mrs. M. A. Weeks Pittock (n.d.), he married her to "be stunning," she him for money, called "the god of civilization" (chap. 22). Both exchange of services and exchange of objects—especially when one object is a person —do not work. Second, such corrupt marriages set utopian sexual arrangements in relief: the freedom of exotic bronze-skinned women to select their sexual partners on a tropic island where mates "strive to please each other" make a "civilized" mate's demand to be pleased the more objectionable (Pittock, chap. 12, 60). Third, the children resulting from such corrupt marriages receive inadequate financial support: as in *Other Worlds: A Story Concerning the Wealth Earned by American Citizens and Showing How It Can Be Secured To Them Instead to the Trusts* (1905) by Lena Jane Fry (n.d.), a deserted mother of three small children tries taking in borders as a livelihood, but crying infants drive boarders away. Then her husband abducts her son (chaps. 12–15).

To correct men's control of women's labor and sexuality, feminist utopias of this period suggest four possible solutions: paid work, education, suffrage, and cooperation. In "A New Society" (1841), envisioned by Lowell "mill girl" Betsey Chamberlain (n.d.), an employee receives equal wages regardless of sex, works a day limited to eight hours, and enjoys a required three hours daily of mental or manual labor, whichever was not a person's means of livelihood. In general, both women and men work with access to the full range of jobs (Shelhamer, 1884; Fry, 1905; Gilman, Selection 8). A short story called "Friend Island" (1918) by Gertrude Barrows Bennett (1884–1939?) boasts a sea-captain heroine: "a true sea-woman of that elder time when woman's superiority to man had not been so long recognized (126). The story is her reminiscence of a sentient island, an early science-fiction tale that anticipates 1970s strategies for demonstrating interrelationships among human, animal, plant, and earth.[28]

A second strategy for avoiding control is education—for daughters as well as sons (Chamberlain, 1841), especially to make "an honorable living" instead of submitting to "the best we can get" in a marriage (Shelhamer, 1884). And such self-sufficient women would of course keep their own names when they married (Fry, 1905, chap. 28; Gilman, *Herland,* 1915, 118).

A third strategy, suffrage, is far more emphasized in subsequent histories of women than in utopias by women: of over 100 utopias appearing before 1920, nearly one-quarter favor suffrage, though more consider political issues, including general activity and office holding. Typical of a feminist viewpoint is a passage from Shelhamer's *Life and Labors in the Spirit World:*

> She should have a voice in the affairs of the country under whose laws she lives and educates her children . . . Some people pretend to fear that when women vote they will have no time for domestic affairs, and the institution of the home itself will be destroyed. . . . From the fuss made . . . one would think it took a week to put a small slip of paper into a medium-sized box. Why, we have known of men who could put in half a dozen in less than half that time, and no one suspects women to be less clever than men (13).

The passage is interesting for its acknowledgment of popular fears that women would no longer perform traditional domestic roles once they were admitted to the political sphere reserved for men. Many accepted the view that women, family, and home were the calm center in a raging storm of social flux, that to permit change there would ensure complete social chaos. One antifeminist utopia, *Pantaletta: A Romance of Sheheland* (1882) by Mrs. J. Wood (n.d.), showed women's political control to be a comedy of error. Shelhamer ridicules this popular fear at the same time that she assumes the sexes to be equally clever, such equality of intelligence more readily assumed, however, in utopian fiction than by the public at large. Women utopists ignore woman's traditional restriction to the home and thereby imply that integrating the public and private spheres for women will be no more disastrous than for men.[29]

More important than suffrage in feminist utopias are cooperative or communitarian solutions to social control: over half for this period include such solutions. They take two forms—cooperative services or self-sufficient experimental communities. After Howland (selection 3), one of the earliest communitarian novels is *Hiero-Salem: The Vision of Peace* (1889) by Eveleen Laura Knaggs Mason (1838–1914), in which "dualized" (that is, androgynous) citizens actualize their full human capacities, unlimited by gender stereotypes: these and other values emanate from one household to become the Eloiheem (meaning "male and female aspects of the divine") Commonwealth, founded in Wisconsin upon peace, cooperation, and diversity of population. Another by Alice Elinor Bowen Bartlett (1848–1920) is *A New Aristocracy* (1891) of "brain and heart," to be established in Idlewild, New York, upon a Parisian suburban model. As in works by Marie Howland and Rosa Graul (selections 3 and 6), independent wealth makes possible the establishment of a factory, with workers' cottages and cultural buildings (306–9). Child nurture is the major focus of *Reinstern* (1900; "pure star"), by Eloise O. Randall Richberg (n.d.), "a planet as yet undiscovered by your astronomers, who waste lifetimes searching with telescopes for what inner vision will readily disclose when you allow the real self to predominate" (10). This utopia presents an apprentice system to educate young adults for shared parenting, such training believed prerequisite to marriage (19–20). Parents of each sex receive "equal honors, salaries, and privileges," (23–24), but biological parents are not solely responsible for children and systematically receive support appropriate to their children's ages. Gilman's *Moving the Mountain* (1911), a 1940s utopia having cooperative services, also includes detailed nursery and child-garden arrangements, apartment residences for the many self-supporting women in the United States, designed with facilities to provide food hygienically and knowledgeably (chap. 4). Gilman was particularly outraged by "the waste of private housekeeping" and devoted the novel *What Diantha Did* (1910) to demonstrating an alternative.[30] Seeds for each of these utopias exist in Gilman's "A Woman's Utopia" (1907, selection 8).

Two points emerging from this group are especially salient for the concerns of utopias during the 1970s. First, the observation that the "nowhere" of utopia can be the "somewhere" of inner vision marks the 1970s recognition of utopia as a state of mind showing a spiritual or religious motive to underlie utopia. Nineteenth-century utopists called this visionary "nowhere" by more theological names: the "heaven" of Phelps' *Beyond the Gates* (1883) or the "spirit world" of Shelhamer (1884). Several recent analysts of current utopias by women consider these to be intrinsically spiritual.[31] In fact some would see women's liberation itself as a spiritual quest, in a basically religious sense of overtly binding women to the whole of humanity (from the Latin *re* = back, *ligare* = to bind or fasten).[32] Second, on a more mundane level, the domestic labor typically a concern of these communitarian utopias before 1920 currently receives broadly based investigation in research, as well as visionary alternative solution in utopia. Economists, historians, and anthropologists provide studies of women's triple labor load: unpaid childcare and housekeeping work added to underpaid salaried work.[33] That 1970s utopias completely restructure society to remove from women this triple burden should not surprise us. The particular domestic solutions envisioned in utopias before 1920 have not come to pass, but the domestic problems that we now seek to address were accurately forecast. Utopias, though not blueprints, can be harbingers.

1921–1960

After 1920, women's writing of utopias declined until 1960. Although the passage of Amendment 19 apparently lulled women into thinking that all needs could now be met, history has shown suffrage to be a more limited achievement than predicted for improving women's position in society: changes in values must accompany institutional changes. But for only eight of thirty-five utopias published during this period can feminist values be argued. Of these eight, three focus upon the relationship between women and men as the central feature of a woman's life. This narrowing of focus after the wide-ranging visionary alternatives appearing before 1920 reflects the times: all nonfeminist utopias enclose women in marriages and families that subordinate women's needs to those of the social unit.

The three feminist novels each recommend a different strategy for improving the heterosexual love bond. First, the earliest emphasizes sexual communication, as taught to an Earth woman by two Venusian, space-traveling experts in Rena Oldfield Pettersen's (n.d.) *Venus* (1924). Here love is the universal utopian condition, with the innovation that women initiate its highest expression in mating with men. A second,

World Without Raiment, A Fantasy (1943) by Louise Dardenelle (n.d.), stresses a nudist existence, occurring after technological disaster results in a warmer climate. This utopia depicts a California nudist colony, where both sexes enjoy freely given, nonexclusive love. And third, Gaile Churchill McElhiney's (n.d.) *Into the Dawn* (1945) relies upon astral means from an Island of Heaven somewhere in the Pacific—a stage of consciousness where death is absent. Here aviator Jeanne Wallace, re-united with her lover, sets a goal of loving contribution to the world's welfare. (This denial of death's finality during wartime repeats Phelps's post-Civil War *Gates Ajar*.)

Although male-female relationship receives positive treatment in these utopias, its excess centrality suggests Freudian influence. And the consistent appearance of marriage may be reflective not only of social possibilities, but also of a need for self-realization missing from the traditional institution. As current research has shown, women enjoying a marriage they claim is "happy" can exhibit paradoxically disturbing symptoms—ill health, both mental and physical—the claim to "happiness" perhaps more accurately labelled "reconciliation."[34]

Thus only five of thirty-five works do not present relationships with men as women's central concern in life. These broader utopias suggest the diversity of both the earlier and the later periods. Gilman in her 1920 essay "Applepieville" imagines a rural town laid out with farms radiating like pie-wedges from its center, where cultural activities and domestic services may be concentrated (*Independent* 103, [25 Sept.]: 365, 393–95). Sarah Norcliffe Cleghorn (1876–1959) in her 1924 "Utopia Interpreted" offers four varied explanations for social evolution by 1995 into a non-hierarchical, nonracist, egalitarian society (*Atlantic* 134:56–57, 216–24). Lilith Loraine's [pseud. Mary Maude Dunn Wright, 1894–1967] 1930 science fiction, "Into the 28th Century," describes Nirvania, whose one-world government practices sex egalitarianism (*Science Wonder Quarterly* 1, no. 2: 250–67, 276). Fourth, *The Unpredictable Adventure: A Comedy of Women's Independence,* a 1935 satiric utopia by Claire Myers Spotswood (1896–1983), depicts heroine Tellectina traveling from Smug Harbor in the Land of Err to scale the heights of Nithking. Along her path is the Colony of the New Chimera, where free women worship the Goddess Frewo, but the "free love" they revere as the Priestess Frelo turns out to be a deception—a critique of the 1920s Flapper (chap. 5). Fifth, Gertrude Short's 1949 *A Visitor from Venus* (selection 12), with its critique of World War II, resembles 1970s utopias or Herlander's view of Ourland (Gilman 1915, 1916). Thus five candles glimmer between the slats of a bushel basket stretching over four decades.

The decade of the 1920s—when Freud and the Flapper reigned—also firmly established that "wifehood and womanhood are the normal status of women," the words in 1923 of Gilman, appalled at what she called "sex mania."[35] Where previously feminists had wanted to reconcile work, marriage, and family, suddenly only the last two needs remained, with a new need added—to avoid at all costs the unnatural status of not-married. A single woman as "spinster" or "old maid" was a social reject. Women's solidarity in a social movement was dispersed into numerous individual households by requiring that the indication of her normalcy and maturity be attractiveness to a male sexual partner—whose home she would keep and whose children she would bear and rear.[36] In addition to such social mythology, two post-World War decades added momentum to a return to traditional practices; a 1930s Depression decreased women's access to the labor market. Only the need during the 1940s to fill jobs vacated by enlisted men sent to fight World War II momentarily raised women's hope for pecuniary recognition. But women were never again to stay home as before World War II: historians demonstrate women's steady march toward paid labor outside the home.[37]

The effort to change social values to female affirmation is central to the feminist utopia, whether it depicts two sexes fully integrated, or all-female separation (selections 4 and 12). At first glance it might seem that women-only utopias like Mary E. Bradley Lane's (n.d.) 1881 *Mizora: A Prophecy* or Gilman's 1915 *Herland* could polarize readers. But the "wild zone" concept explicated by critic Elaine Showalter can lead to ultimate integration. This wild zone is an area peripheral to mainstream (male-centered or androcentric) culture, a veritable no-man's-land where women's culture and women's reality exist apart. Although subordinate groups must know about the range of dominant culture, a dominant group need not know what lies beyond the pale of their definition of society. This wild zone provides the content of all-female utopias, which then have the possible social function of moving the wild zone within the realm of shared, rather than gender-specific, reality. Thus the insistence upon utopia-from-a-female viewpoint effects not separation, but communication.[38]

New possibilities exist for both men and women—for men to learn to value what our culture has labeled as female, that unknown wild zone whose practices may be crucial to the survival of humankind, and for women to reclaim the values of the wild zone across a complete range of human activity from private living to the pinnacles of public power. The tradition of utopian writing by United States feminists provides a record of dreams from this wild zone of women's culture—where power enables and constructs, where experience not dogma informs behavior, where support comes from varied social groupings, where sensuality and bodily expression share communicative primacy with the word, where feeling as well as mind inform human knowledge, where holism and integration—rather than fragmentation and alienation—guide a group's way.

We have returned to the starting point, utopia as a call to action. As apologues, these novels teach. They persuade us to act. In *The Anatomy of Freedom,* Robin Morgan quotes nineteenth-century poet Adelaide Proctor, "Dreams grow holy when put into action."[39] Can we together become "ideals of ourselves" who dare to dream, and dreaming, dare to act?[40]

Selections

1

Man's Rights;
or, How Would You Like It?
1870

ANNIE DENTON CRIDGE
?–by 1884

During the 1860s, Annie Denton Cridge and her husband Alfred were reform-
ers in Washington, D.C., where they advocated cooperative kitchens and work-
*shops, as her essay on "The Society of Co-Workers" indicates (*Boston
Investigator, *1 April 1868). Also in 1868 she published a children's book*
called The Crumb-Basket. *Her brother, a professor of geology, William Den-*
ton (1823–1883) of Wellesley, Massachusetts, wrote His Garrison in Heaven
(1884) and published Man's Rights. *Apparently at the time of publication, she*
herself resided in Pennsylvania. She was believed to be a psychometer, a person
having the power "to see all that has ever happened" to any piece of matter
placed in contact with her. She had died by 1884 when her son Alfred Denton
Cridge advertised himself as son of "the late" Mrs. Cridge and as author of
Utopia: or, The History of an Extinct Planet. *The son's utopia shows his*
mother's feminist influence in that women's equality characterizes those societies
evolving to a high level.

Cridge, in writing a dream vision, followed the lead of her predecessors,
Mary Griffith (d. 1877) and Jane Sophia Appleton (d. 1884). Griffith's
"Three Hundred Years Hence" (1836) is a dream vision of the United States,
realistically projected three centuries into the future. The male narrator Edgar
Hastings receives information from an alleged male descendent of the same name.
Though women's rights receive central focus, women characters strangely do not
(a situation Cridge would firmly change). Except for the omission of political

3

rights, a female version of Jacksonian democracy emerges—a spirit of expanded possibilities for the common woman. Appleton also couched her utopia as a dream vision focused upon women but set only one century into the future—"Sequel to 'The Vision of Bangor [Maine] in the Twentieth Century' " (1848). Appleton was directly responding to "Vision of Bangor" by then-governor Edward Kent (also in American Utopias, ed. A. O. Lewis; see Appleton citation in bibliography). "Sequel" depicts a society more rewarding to women than Kent's, correcting his myopic and misogynist male error in viewpoint.

Man's Rights consists of nine satiric dreams, in which a female narrator-author imagines a gender-role reversal. The work anticipates an 1893 novel, Unveiling a Parallel: A Romance by Alice Ilgenfritz Jones and Ella Merchant, also reversing and thereby satirizing gender-role expectations (reprint, Syracuse Univ. Press, 1991). Man's Rights depicts a society on Mars, where men are confined to house keeping and baby tending, while women run the government and enjoy all privileges. Cridge ridicules the cult of domesticity by exposing its contradictions, made especially glaring when enacted by men. Criticism of marital practices continues the concerns of both Griffith and Appleton. Comparable satire currently appears in Egalia's Daughters: A Satire of the Sexes by the Norwegian Gerd Brantenberg (Seattle: Seal, 1994).

References: Allibone's Supplement (Philadelphia: Lippincott, 1892); Encyclopedia of Occultism & Parapsychology, ed. L. Shepard (Detroit: Gale, 1979); Barbara Quissell, "The New World That Eve Made," in America as Utopia, ed. Kenneth M. Roemer (New York: Franklin, 1981), 153–54, 171; Carol A. Kolmerten, Introduction to Unveiling a Parallel: A Romance (Syracuse: Syracuse Univ. Press, 1991).

Text: Annie Denton Cridge, Man's Rights; or, How Would You Like It?, Woodhull & Claflin's Weekly 1:17–25, 27, Sept. 3–Nov. 19, 1870, text for dreams 6–9; Boston: William Denton, 1870, text for dreams 1–5. The 1870 serial publication of the dreams is as follows: Dream 1, 1, no. 17, Sept. 3; Dream 2, 1, no. 18, Sept. 10; Dream 3, 1, no. 19, Sept. 17; Dream 4, 1, no. 20, Oct. 1; Dream 5, 1, no. 21, Oct. 8; Dream 6, 1, no. 22, Oct. 15; Dream 7, 1, no. 23, Oct. 22; Dream 8, 1, no. 24, Oct. 29; Dream 9, 1, no. 25, Nov. 5; Conc., 1, no. 27 [2, no. 1], Nov. 19.

Dream Number One

Last night I had a dream, which may have a meaning.

I stood on a high hill that overlooked a large city. The proud spires of many churches rose high, here and there; and round about the city were beautiful, sloping hills, stretching away, away into the distance: while a broad river wound here and there, extending a kindly arm toward the city.

As I stood there, wondering what manner of city it was, its name, and the character of its inhabitants, all at once I found myself in its very midst. From house to house I flitted; from kitchen to kitchen: and lo! everywhere the respective duties of man and woman were reversed; for in every household I found the men in aprons, superintending the affairs of the kitchen. Everywhere men, and only men, were the Bridgets[1] and housekeepers. I thought that those gentleman-housekeepers looked very pale, and somewhat nervous; and, when I looked into their spirits (for it seemed in my dream that I had the power), I saw anxiety and unrest, a constant feeling of unpleasant expectancy,—the result of a long and weary battling with the cares of the household.

As I looked at those men-Bridgets and gentleman-house-keepers, I said to myself, "This is very strange! Why, these men seem unsexed! How stoop-shouldered they are! how weak and complaining their voices."

I found, too, that not only was the kitchen exclusively man's, but also the nursery: in fact, all the housework was directed and done by men. I felt a sad pity for these men, as I flitted from house to house, from kitchen to kitchen, from nursery to nursery.

I saw them in the houses of the door, where the "man did his own work." I saw him in the morning arise early, light the fire, and begin to prepare the breakfast, his face pale and haggard. "No wonder!" I thought, when I saw how he hurried, hurried, while in his spirit was a constant fear that the baby would awake. Very soon I heard the sharp cry of the baby; and away while in his spirit was a constant fear that the baby ran the poor father, soon returning with baby in his arms, carrying it around with him, while he raked the fire, fried the meat, and set the table for breakfast. When all was ready, down came two or three un-washed, unkept children, who must be attended to: and, when all this was done, I observed that the poor gentleman's appetite was gone; and, pale and nervous, he sat down in the rocking-chair, with the baby in his arms. But what greatly astonished me was to see how quietly and composedly the lady of the house drank her coffee and read the morning paper; apparently oblivious of the trials of her poor husband, and of all he had to endure in connection with his household cares.

It was wash-day, and I watched him through that long and weary day. First at the wash-tub, while baby slept; then rocking the cradle and washing at the same time; then preparing dinner, running and hurrying here and there about the house: while in his poor, disturbed mind revolved the thought of the sewing that ought to be done, and only his own hands to do it.

Evening came, and the lady of the house returned to dinner. The children came to meet her; and as she lifted up one, and then another, and kissed them, I thought! "Why, how beautiful is that woman!" Then in my dream I seemed to behold every woman of that strange city; and, ah! the marvellous beauty of those women! Eye hath not seen, neither hath it entered into the heart of man to conceive; for a beauty almost angelic was so charmingly combined with intellect, and health brooded so divinely over all, that, at the *tout ensemble,*[2] I was profoundly astonished and intensely delighted.

Then I turned myself about, and was again in the home I had left. It was evening: the lamp on the table was lighted, and there sat the poor husband I have described, in his rocking-chair, darning stockings and mending the children's clothes after the hard day's washing. I saw that it had rained; that the clothesline had broken, and dropped the clothes in the dirty yard; and the poor man had had a terrible time rinsing some and washing others over again; and that he had finally put them down in wash-tubs, and covered them with water he had brought from a square distant. But the day's work was over; and there he moved to and fro, while his wife, in comfortable slippers, sat by the fire reading.

"Well," I said to myself, "such is the home of the lowly; but how is it where one or more servants can be kept?" Then, as by magic, I saw how it was: for I found myself in a kitchen where a male Bridget was at work, his hair uncombed, his face and hands unwashed, and his clothes torn and soiled. Bridget was cooking breakfast, a knife in his hand, while he was bending over the cooking-stove, moodily talking to himself. The gentleman-housekeeper, pale and unhappy, opened the door, looked at Bridget, but said nothing, and soon went into the dining-room. As soon as his back was turned, Bridget turned around, lifted the arm that held the knife, and, with a fiendish look, whispered to himself, "I would like to strike you with this."

Breakfast on the table, I looked, and beheld bad coffee, burned meat, and heavy biscuits; and I heard the lady of the house, who sat in a morning-robe and spangled slippers, say to the poor gentleman,—

"My dear, this breakfast is bad, very bad: you ought to attend to things better."

I observed how sad he felt at these words; and I did pity the poor fellow. It seemed to me that I staid a whole day with this poor gentleman. His health was very feeble: he was suffering from dyspepsia. I saw him attending the children, saw him sewing, saw him go nervously into the kitchen, and sadly and wearily attend to things there, while the dark glances of the male Bridget followed him viciously everywhere. I saw the waste and thieving of that man-Bridget, and saw how completely that poor gentleman felt crushed and held by his help. My heart yearned toward that poor, feeble housekeeper, unable to do his own work, and so much at the mercy of that terrible Bridget; and I ceased to wonder at the pale faces of the men everywhere.

The homes of the wealthy I visited; and almost everywhere I found those gentleman-housekeepers anxious and worried, no matter how many servants were kept. There was trouble about washing, trouble about ironing, trouble about children: there was waste, there was thieving; and, oh! the number of poor, sickly gentlemen I found made me very sad.

And while, in my dream, my heart was going out in pity and commiseration toward those gentleman-housekeepers, I found myself in the midst of a large assembly, composed exclusively of these men. Here almost every man in the city had congregated to hold an indignation-meeting,—a housekeeper's indignation-meeting. Every man wore a white kitchen-apron, and some I noticed whose sleeves were white with flour, while others had pieces of dough here and there stuck on their clothes: others, again, had hanging on their arms dish-cloths and towels. Very many, too, had babies in their arms, and one or more children at their side.

Then I listened to some of their speeches. One gentleman said,—

"I have kept house sixteen years; and I know what it is to be poor and do my own work; and I know what it is to have servants: and I tell you, gentlemen, the whole system of housekeeping, as now conducted, is a bad one. It is, in the first place, wasteful and extravagant; and, in the next place, it wears out our bodies and souls. See how pale and feeble we are! It is time there was a change."

"We don't each of us make our own shoes," said another speaker; "we don't each of us spin our own yarn, or weave our own cloth: the hand-loom has departed, and it is now done by machinery, which has so far come to our rescue. It is not so bad for us as for our grandfathers, who had to weave on a hand-loom all the muslin and cloth for the family; but it is bad enough. Here we are kept every day of our lives over the cook-stove, wash-tub, or ironing-table, or thinking about them. Can nothing be done to remedy this? Can not all the domestic work be done by machinery? Can not it be done on wholesale principles? I say it can: there is no more need for a kitchen to any house than for a spindle or a loom."

Then followed many more speeches about the extravagance of the present system, whereby one or two persons, and often more, were employed in doing the work of a small family, when it might be done at much less expense for one-fourth the labor, were the wholesale principle applied to that as it is to other things.

One man remarked that the kitchen was a small retail shop to every house: another called it a dirt-producing establishment for every family, sending its fumes and filth to every room. Another gentleman said that the fine pictures painted about the domestic hearth, happy homes, &c., were all moonshine, and would continue so just as long as the present state of things continued.

"I protest against the present state of things," said a tall, delicate man, with a large, active brain. "We have this matter in our own hands; and let us here and now begin something practical. Instead of forty little extravagant cooking-stoves, with each a Bridget, and so many gentlemen employed as housekeepers, let us have one large stove, and do our cooking, washing, and ironing on a large scale."

Well, I thought in my dream that I listened to hundreds of speeches and protests and denunciations.

Then the scene changed; and forthwith there sprang up large cooking-establishments in different parts of the city, that could, as if by magic, supply hundreds of families with their regular meals. I looked, and lo! what machinery had done in the weaving of cloth, above and beyond what had been effected by the handloom, was accomplished here. The inventive genius of the age had been at work; and the result was a wondrous machine that could cook, wash, and iron for hundreds of people at once.

"I must see the workings of that establishment," I said in my dream; and forthwith a polite gentleman, who said that he had been a housekeeper twenty-five years, and knew all the petty annoyances of the old system, kindly proposed to show me the various doings of the machinery.

"We are going to cook dinner now," he said, as he walked toward a monster machine. He touched a handle, and then about fifty bushels of potatoes were quietly let down into a large cistern, where they were washed, and then moved forward into a machine for peeling; which operation was accomplished in a minute or two by its hundreds of knives, and the potatoes came out all ready to be cooked. Turnips went through the same process, and other vegetables were prepared and made ready for the huge cooking apparatus. All was done by machinery: there was no lifting, no hauling, no confusion; but the machines, like things of life, lifted, prepared, and transferred as desired.

I saw what was called a "self-feeding pie-maker," that reminded me of a steam printing-press, where the paper goes in blank at one end and comes out printed at the other. So the flour, shortening, and fruit were taken in all at once at three separate receptacles, and came out at the other end pies ready for the oven, to which they were at once, over a small tramway, transferred by machinery. Another machine made cakes and pies.

Meal-time came: the dinner was to be served. Two large wooden doors opened by means of a spring which the gentleman touched with his foot. Through them came filing past us, one after another, small, curiously constructed steam-wagons, the motion of which caused but little noise, as the wheels were tired with vulcanized India-rubber: those wagons were so arranged as to travel on common roads, and much resembled caravans. They moved past machines which were called "servers," where meals were dished and transferred to the steam cara- vans, which latter were termed "waiters." All this was done systemati- cally, quietly, yet rapidly, by a few persons in charge of the machines by which meals were prepared for and distributed to hundreds of families. I saw that there were hundreds of these "servers," as well as hundreds of "waiters"; so that the dinner was dished and served almost simultane- ously, in double-tin cases, containing all requisites for the table.

Then away went the steam "waiters," delivering the meals almost simultaneously at the houses, which, by the by, were rapidly being "reconstructed" to meet the new state of things, with dining-rooms to accommodate hundreds at once, in blocks, or hollow squares, with cook-houses, laundries, &c., at the center, or in circles similarly ar- ranged, combining, in a most inconceivable degree, economy with beauty.

To return to the steam waiters: At a time understood they called for the tin cases containing dishes and *débris,* and then wended their way back to head-quarters, where all the dishes were washed and transferred to their places by steam-power.

The washing and ironing, I discovered, was done in the same expeditious manner, by machinery; several hundred pieces going in at one part of the machine dirty, and coming out at the other end a few minutes afterward, rinsed and ready to dry. The ironing was as rapid as it was perfect,—smooth, glossy, uncreased unspecked; all done by machinery.

Then I looked once more into this strange city, and, behold! an emancipated class! The pale, sickly faces of the men were giving place to ruddy health. Anxiety, once so marked in their features, was departing. No Bridget to dread now; no washing-day any more; no sad faces nor neglected children: for now the poor gentleman-housekeepers had time to attend to the children, and to the cultivation of their own minds; and I saw that the dream of the poet and of the seer was realized: for husband and wife sat side by side, each sharing the joys of the other. Science and philosophy, home and children, were cemented together; for peace, sweet peace, had descended like a dove on every household.

I awoke: it was all a dream. My husband stood at my bedside. "Annie, Annie!" he said: "awake, Annie! that new girl of yours is good for nothing. You will have to rise and attend to her, else l shall have no breakfast. I have been late at the office for several days past, and I fear l shall be late again."

I arose: and, as my husband ate his breakfast, I pondered over my strange dream. As soon as he was gone, I transferred it to paper, feeling that it really did mean something, and is intended as a prophecy of the "good time coming," when woman will be rid of the kitchen and cook-stove, and the possibilities of the age actualize for woman that which I have dreamed for man.

Dream Number Two

Once again I have visited that strange city in dream-land, where men, and only men, were the housekeepers and Bridgets.

It is midnight: I have just awakened from my dream, and risen to pen it down, lest in the morning I should find my memory treacherous. My good husband has protested against writing by gas-light, and very gravely given his opinion on midnight writing; and—ah, well! he is sound asleep now, I see; and so at once to my dream.

I thought my husband and I were walking along some beautiful streets, when all at once I exclaimed, "Why, husband! here we are together in that very city I told you about, where the men are the house-keepers and kitchen-girls. Oh, I'm glad! Let us find out every thing about these inhabitants, both men and women."

While we were talking together, several gentlemen, pale and delicate in appearance, passed us. Some were dressed in calico suits, trimmed with little ruffles—ruffles round the bottom of the pants, ruffles down the front and round the tails of the coats; and on both sides of the button-holes of their vests were rows of small ruffles. From some of their little flat hats flowed ribbon-streamers; while on others were placed, jauntily and conspicuously, feathers and flowers.

More and more gentlemen passed us. What a variety of costume! I was almost bewildered; gentlemen in red, green, yellow, drab, and black suits, trimmed in such elaborate and fanciful styles! Some suits were parti-colored; that is to say, the pants perhaps yellow or red, the vest blue, the coat green, crimson, or drab. Some of these suits were trimmed with lace: lace down the sides of the pants and round the bottoms; lace round the edges of the coat, and beautifully curving hither and thither as a vine, over the backs and down the fronts of the coats; and also over the fronts of the vests. Some suits were almost covered with elaborate embroidery, or satin folds, or piping, or ribbon, while bows and stream-ers of the same or contrasting colors, according to taste, were placed on the backs of the coats, shoulders, and, here and there, on the vest and pants. It really makes me laugh at this moment to think of that comical sight. Their head-dresses, too, were most fantastic; flowers, bits of lace, tulle or blonde, feathers, and even birds, were mixed in endless profusion with ribbon, tinsel, glitter, and *(ad libitum)*[3] grease. Many of these gen-tlemen carried little portemonnaies,[4] which hung on their jewelled fin-gers by tiny chains. Others carried fans, some edged with feathers, or covered with pictures, or inlaid with pearl, &c., varying, I suppose, according to the purse.

Each of these gentlemen seemed particularly interested in every other gentleman's costume; for they turned and looked at each other, while several exclamations reached my ear; such as, "What a superb suit!" "What a splendid coat!" "What a darling vest!" "What a love of a hat!"

These gentlemen had a swinging ga[it], something like that of a sailor, that made their coat-tails move to and fro as they walked. I noticed, too, that they were very careful of their pants, which were decidedly wide; for on passing over a gutter or soiled part of the pave-ment, they carefully and daintily raised the legs of the pants with the finger and thumb. This impressed me favorably as to their love of clean-liness; for otherwise the laces, ribbons, embroidery, or ruffles which graced the bottoms of their pants, would have come in contact with the mud of the streets.

As we stood looking at those strange gentlemen, my husband suggested the idea of a masquerade. Then suddenly I found myself alone, and flirting from dwelling to dwelling, from home to home; and everywhere the gentlemen were dressed in flimsy materials, and all more or less decked with trimmings.

I found the majority of gentlemen busy with needlework, some doing the sewing of the family; but many, very many, with their sons, dressed in delicate morning suits, doing fancy-work. Some were working little cats and dogs on footstools; others were busy with embroidery, fancy knitting, and all the delicate nothings that interest only ladies in this waking world of ours.

As I listened to their conversation, which was generally composed of gossip, fashion, or love-matters,—for the male sex took the fashion-books, and not ladies, and these I found in the majority of homes, headed "Gentlemen's Magazine of Fashions,"—as I listened to their conversation, I repeat, and observed all this, my soul was filled with unutterable sadness. "Alas! alas!" I said: "what means this degradation? Why have the lords of creation[5] become mere puppets or dolls? Where is the loftiness and intellectuality of *man—noble man!"*

Just then I was aroused from my reverie by an aspiring young gentleman who was sewing some ruffles on the legs of his pants, saying to his father, "I don't see, papa, why men can not earn money as well as women: I want to learn a business."

"That is all nonsense," replied his father: "your business is to get married. There is no necessity for a *boy* to learn a *business:* what you have to do is to learn to be a good housekeeper; for you will be married some day, and will have to attend to your children and your wife; and that is enough business for any man."

"But I may not marry," said the boy; "and I know I will not, unless I can get a woman with money, that can give me a good home."

Then they talked about Mr. Some-one—I could not catch the name —that had married well: his wife was worth over fifty thousand dollars, and was very kind to him, taking him to theaters and concerts, and wherever he wanted to go: she let him, too, have all the dress he wanted. She had only one fault: she would not allow him to go anywhere unless she accompanied him.

Oh! my soul was sick with sympathy and pity for that race of poor degraded men! "What does it mean?" I asked myself: "why are they in this pitiable condition?"

Then, for the first time, l realized that this city was the capital of a great nation; that women, and only women, were the lawmakers, judges, executive officers, &c., of the nation; that every office of honor and emolument was filled by women; that all colleges and literary institutions, with very few exceptions, were all built for women, and only open to women, and that men were all excluded. I went from school to school, from college to college; and, ah! the beauty, the dignity, of those women! Science and art had truly crowned them with their own best gifts: their faces seemed to me almost divine; and, ah! what a contrast to the vain, silly, half-educated men who staid at home, or paraded the streets, thinking principally of fashion and dress! for these women were everywhere dressed in plain, substantial clothing, which lent to them such a charm that I realized instinctively there was something about them far more beautiful than beauty.

As I looked upon these women in the colleges, as students and professors, as lawyers, judges, and jurors, as I looked upon them in the lecture-room and the pulpit, the house of representatives and the senate-chamber,—yea, everywhere,—I observed their quiet dignity, clothed in their plain flowing robes; and I was almost tempted to believe that Nature had intended—in this part of the world at least—that woman, and only woman, should legislate and govern; and that here, if nowhere else, woman should be superior to man.

In the galleries of the legislative bodies were hundreds of gentlemen, young and old, looking on, and listening to the speeches made by the lady members. How they fluttered and fanned and whispered and smiled!

"Alas, for fallen man!" I said. Then, in an instant, I had, as by one glance, looked into the pockets of every lady and gentleman present, and also into the acquisitive pockets of the brain of each; and the result proved to me, that, as man held the purse with us, so woman held the purse in that wonderful dream-land. To obtain money from their wives, those weak, silly men would often resort to cajolery and deceit. Only from their wives could they obtain money for dress or any thing else; and so, as by common consent, nearly all the husbands had seemingly decided that they had a right to get all they could out of their wives, with out any reference to the question whether the wife could afford it or not. Thus I found, that the woman being the purse-holder, she the giver and he the receiver, worked most disastrously; for it made the interests of wife and husband separate: the interest of the wife was not the interest of the husband, his greatest care being to get all he could, and spend all he could get.

I left those buildings, and took the street-cars. Here those noble-looking, stately women escorted the gentlemen to the cars, stood while the gentlemen walked in first, then demurely stepped on board, and paid the car-fare for both. What impressed me as much as any thing I saw was, with what matter-of-course style the gentlemen, in their dainty, flimsy, flying garments, occupied the seats of the cars, while the ladies stood; or, if a lady had a seat, with what noble demeanor she rose and gave it up if a gentleman stepped on board. I saw that those ladies took gentlemen to theaters and places of amusement; ladies took those gentlemen to church, and very kindly saw them safely home; ladies told those gentlemen how beautiful they looked, how prettily they were dressed, &c.; and I saw that it gave these poor, weak-minded men much pleasure.

In ice-cream saloons and other places of refreshment, these gentlemen were as kindly and as gallantly taken by the ladies, who, in all cases, paid for the refreshments.

I looked into the churches, which were principally filled with elegantly-dressed gentlemen. "Ah!" I said to myself, "in religion these down-trodden men find some consolation;" but, in an instant, I was shocked by realizing that more than half went from custom, or to show their dress and see the fashions.

I looked into the prayer-meetings, and (being, of course, all the time invisible) was also present at the confessionals; and in both, the excess of men who attended was a remarkable fact.

Men got up sewing-societies and mite-societies;[6] and, in these, many sad, sorrowful men found a few moments, sometimes, of happy, useful existence.

Occasionally, in those public places I found a man who had risen above his fellows, who had become famous in literature. I met with some male poets, and several conversant with science in a degree equal to the best of women. And I said to myself, "If these *few* men have proved themselves equal to the best of women, then is it not strong presumptive evidence that *all* these men would be equal to women, were they equally educated?"

Then I seemed in my dream to grasp the *cause* of all this difference between the sexes; and that these beautiful, noble women might have been in the same deplorable condition had they been trained and educated as these degraded men,—without a motive in life, limited in education and culture, shut out of every path to honor or emolument, and reduced to the condition of paupers on the bounty of the opposite sex. I saw that the disadvantages under which one sex thus labored constituted a curse that extended to both; and that, though the drudgery of the kitchen had been removed, it was not the millennium, by any means, as I had supposed in my last dream, but only the beginning of the millennium. Man was not the only sufferer, but the wrong done to man acted and re-acted on woman; for men, being defrauded in their education, and nearly all avenues to pecuniary independence closed to them, marriage, with those half-educated, dependent creatures called men, was necessarily their highest ambition. There was no other way for them to obtain wealth or a home; hence they devoted all their powers to the one grand object of catching a woman with money; hence woman became also the sufferer, being often trapped into marriage by one of these silly, worthless men, who had learned well the arts and schemes of wife-catching.

I looked into the thought-cells of these ladies' brains, and found stored therein, in almost every instance, a decided belief that men constituted the inferior, and woman the superior sex.

There is a bright side, however, to every picture; and even my dream had its bright side. For instance: I had dreamed that I looked in on the gentleman with pale face and haggard countenance, of whom I spoke in my first dream as a man that "did his own work;" and now, instead of toil and anxiety about meals, washing, ironing, &c., he was in the garden with his children, planting vegetable-seeds and flower-seeds; and as I with pleasure noted his returning health and strength, I listened to his talk with the children, whom he was interesting with a story.

How I lingered with that gentleman! I accompanied him to the house, and saw him reading; I looked over his book, and was delighted to find that he was studying physiology. By and by he began to talk with the children about the nerves, which he called electric wires carrying messages to the brain; which delighted the children: and I said in deep reverence, "Thank God, that man has been emancipated from the kitchen! he will work out his own salvation: the golden key of the universe has he grasped with his own right hand, and it will open to him every door in the arcana of Nature. Not for ever will man be considered woman's inferior."

Then, like a flash, came to me the mental and moral status of every man in that great country: and I realized that with emancipation from the kitchen had come a hungering and thirsting for education, for mental aliment.

Then I turned; and, lo! I stood in the street, where great posters caught my eye:—

"MAN'S RIGHTS!
a lecture on man's rights,"

I read.

Fain would I have attended a lecture on man's rights; but, in my eagerness to do so, I awoke.

P.S.—It is morning; and, to my great joy, I have had another dream. As I retired to my bed after writing the above, instantly Dreamland was present, and the thread taken up where it was dropped. I have attended lectures on *Man's Rights,* and Man's Rights Conventions; all of which I must write down at once, even if my husband has to go without his breakfast; for dreams so often take to themselves wings and fly away!

Dream Number Three

Who can divine the philosophy of dreams? Who can account for the fact that persons visit again and again places they have never beheld by physical eyes, and talk with people they have only known in Dreamland? How real become to us the places and the people we have repeatedly visited in our dreams! Who have not experienced something of this reality in their own dreaming?

But it does seem especially remarkable to me, that, after having penned down at midnight one dream, I should, on returning to my pillow, have found myself in the very spot where my late dream ended; again in that strange city, again looking at the large posters headed,—

"MAN'S RIGHTS!!
Mr. Sammie Smiley, Mr. Johnnie Smith and others,
Will address the meeting on the
RIGHTS OF MAN!"

I was pleased on coming to these words: "Discussion is invited." "I will go," I said, and turned to follow the crowd; but, as by magic, was transferred to one of the large cooking-establishments which I saw in my first dream, and soon recognized it to be the same.

There were the huge machines at work cooking dinner, while in a comfortable rocking-chair sat the same gentleman who had in that same dream showed me over the establishment. He was reading a newspaper.

"Ah!" he said, as he looked up from his paper, "glad to see you, madam. You see I have time to read while the dinner is cooking. All goes on well. We supply one-eighth of the city with meals, and everybody is satisfied, nay, more than satisfied: they are delighted with the arrangement; for every poor man is relieved of washing, ironing, and cooking. And yet all this is done at less cost than when every house had its little selfish, dirty kitchen."

"And what is this about 'man's rights'?" I asked. "I see posters all over your city, headed, 'Man's Rights!' "

He smiled as he replied, "Well, madam, emancipating man from the drudgery of the kitchen has given him leisure for thought; and, in his thinking, he has discovered that he labors under many wrongs, and is deprived of quite as many rights. The idea of men lecturing, men voting, men holding office, &c., excites considerable ridicule; but ridicule proves nothing."

"Are you going to the lecture?" I asked.

"I will go if I have company," he replied; "but it would not look well for me to go alone: besides, I would be afraid to go home so late."

I made no answer; but I thought musingly, "Afraid! afraid of what? of what can these men be afraid? I wonder if there are any wild beasts prowling around this strange city at night. Perhaps there are wolves or mad dogs; but then he is a man, and could carry a revolver and protect himself." But, as by a flash, the truth came to me, and I wondered I had not thought of it before. In this land, *woman,* is the natural protector; and so, of course, he was afraid to go without a lady to take care of him.

I had scarcely arrived at this conclusion, when I found myself *en rapport* [Fr.: in accord] with every husband in that city. "I would like to go to the lecture on 'men's rights,' " I heard one man say to his wife very timidly.

"I shall go to no such place," replied his wife loftily; "neither will you. 'Man's rights,' indeed!"

"Let us go to the lecture," said another husband to his wife, with a pleasant smile on his face.

"No, no, my dear," replied the lady; "I like you just as you are; and I don't admire womanish men. Nothing is more disgusting than feminine men. We don't want men running to the polls, and electioneering; what would become of the babies at such times?"

Then I looked in on a bevy of young boys ranging in age from sixteen to twenty. How they did laugh at the very mention of "man's rights," as they put on their pretty coats and hats, looking in the mirror, and turning half round to see how their coat-tails looked!

"Man's rights!" said one. "I have all the rights I want."

"So have I," said a young boy of nineteen. "I don't want any more rights."

"We'll have rights enough, I presume, when we get married," said a tall boy of seventeen, as he touched up the flowers in his pretty hat, and perched it carefully on his head.

"Are you all ready?" said a lady, looking into the room. "Come, I want you all to learn your rights to-night. I warrant that after to-night you will want to carry the purse, don the long robes, and send us ladies into the nursery to take care of the babies!"

Hundreds of ladies and gentlemen were on their way to the meeting; and it rejoiced me greatly to find in the hearts of many of the ladies a profound respect for the rights of man, and a sincere desire that man should enjoy every right equally with themselves.

Then I found myself in the lecture-room, which was well filled with ladies and gentlemen, many of whom seemed greatly amused as they whispered and smiled to each other. Very soon three little gentlemen and one rather tall, thin, pale-faced gentleman walked to the platform, and were received with great demonstrations of applause and suppressed laughter. The audience were evidently not accustomed to hear *gentlemen* lecture.

"How ridiculous those men look!" I heard one elderly lady say. "What does it look like to see a parcel of men pretending to make speeches, in their tawdry pants and fly-away coat-tails, covered with finery and furbelows?"

"They sadly lack the dignity," said another female, "that belongs to ladies and long robes."

"They are decidedly out of their sphere," I heard another remark.

The meeting was opened by the tall gentleman being nominated as president, who at once introduced Mr. Sammie Smiley to the audience, remarking that Mr. Sammie Smiley, with whom they were probably all acquainted by reputation, would address the audience on the all-important subject of *Man's Rights.*

"*Sammie Smiley!*" said a young lady contemptuously. "Suppose we should call ourselves *Lizzie* instead of Elizabeth, or *Maggie* instead of Margaret. Their very names lack dignity."

Mr. Sammie Smiley stepped to the front of the platform with remarkable self-possession for one of the gentleman of that Dreamland. He wore a suit of black silk,—coat, vest, and pants all alike, bordered with broad black lace. He wore no ornaments, except ear-rings, a plain breastpin, and one or two rings on the fingers. Very good taste, I thought.

"Ladies and gentlemen," he said, "our subject this evening is the *Rights of Man;* but to properly understand this question, it would be well, before considering man's *rights,* to define his *wrongs.*"[7]

"Hear, hear!" applauded the audience.

"Education," he continued, "commences with childhood; and men's wrongs also commence with childhood, inasmuch as they are restricted from healthful physical exercise. The merry, active boy, that would romp and play like his sister, is told that it would be improper for a boy. How often your little son has to be reminded that a *boy* must not do so and so; he must be a dear little gentleman, and not rough and boisterous like a girl.

"He is kept in over-heated rooms; seldom breathes the pure air of heaven; and when he is taken out, how different his dress from that of the girl! Look at his flimsy pants of white muslin; look at his flimsy jacket and paper shoes; and contrast them with the warm cloth dress, the substantial over-garments, and thick shoes of the girl! Think how seldom the boy is permitted to inhale the life-giving, open atmosphere! The girl may romp and play in the snow, climb fences and trees, and thus strengthen every muscle; while the little pale-faced boy presses his nose against the window-pane, and wishes—alas! vainly—that he, too, had been a girl.

"The course of training for our boys causes weakness and disease in after-life, and more than a natural degree of muscular inferiority. The pale faces of boys are a sad contrast to the rosy-cheeked girls in the same family. In our boys is laid, not by Nature, but by ignorance and custom, the foundation for bodily weakness, consequently dependence and mental imbecility: in our girls, muscular strength and their accompaniments, independence and vivacity, both of body and mind. Were boys subject to the same physical training as girls (and no valid reason can be given why they should not be), the result would prove that no natural inferiority exists.

"True education I conceive to be the harmonious development of the whole being, both physical and mental. The natural or physical is before the intellectual. First the stalk, then the ear, and then the full corn in the ear. Through ignorance of these primary truths, many well-intentioned fathers hurry their children to premature graves.

"Why is it that, of all the children born, one-fifth die annually? Can not this large mortality be traced to the present ignorance of *males?* Can it not be traced to their flimsy and imperfect educational training? If men had their rights, were all literary institutions as free to one sex as to the other, our young men would be taught what is of the utmost importance for them to know, but what is kept sedulously from them; viz., a knowledge of mental and physical science.

"Let man be educated as liberally as woman; let him be made to feel the value of a sound mind, and that the brightest ornament to man, as well as woman, is intellect: then, and not until then, will he stand forth in all his beauty.

"We frequently hear that woman's mind is superior to man's; and therefore he ought not to have equal educational facilities. If, as is stated by the opponents of man's rights, men are naturally and necessarily inferior to women, it must follow that they should have superior opportunities for mental culture. If, on the other hand, men are by nature mentally equal to women, no reason can, be given why they should not have equal educational facilities."

In the midst of the audience, a beautiful, stately woman rose, and said, that, if it was not out of order, she would like to ask a question: Did not the literature written expressly for men—gentlemen's magazines, gentlemen's fashion-books, &c.,—prove their inferiority? This question caused a laugh, and round after round of applause; but the little gentleman-speaker smilingly replied, that many gentlemen never read the trash prepared for them just as simple reading is prepared for children: but the works written for *women* to read, they study and digest, feeling that they were as much for them as for women. The lecturer then continued by stating the appreciative estimates of the truths of science and philosophy evinced by men as well as women, which would be the case to a still greater extent as the *opportunities* for culture were increased, when gentlemen's books and their flimsy trash would disappear; that even were man weaker in judgment than woman, it did not follow that he should never use it; and, if women did all the reasoning for man, it would not be surprising if he had lost the power to reason.

"Pretty good, Mr. Sammie Smiley," said a lady near me.

"Smiley can reason pretty well: that is pretty good logic," remarked another. Then applause after applause arose, accompanied by stamping and clapping of hands, while some young folks in the back of the hall crowed like roosters.

It was really very funny; but Mr. Sammie Smiley took no notice of the proceeding. He referred to the exclusion of men from nearly all occupations, from governing States to measuring tape; also that men were paid only one-third of the wages of women, even for the same work, their occupations being mainly restricted to sewing and teaching; while women could do both these, and whatever else they chose. He urged the gentlemen to push their way into the employment and professions of women, and be equal sharers in the rights of humanity.

Mr. Johnnie Smith then made an excellent speech on man's civil and political rights; but the discussion that followed so interested me that I can not at this moment recall it. When he sat down, a lady arose, and said, that, as discussions were allowed, she desired to make a few remarks.

"Take the platform! take the platform!" said several voices, which she accordingly did.

"What ease! what dignity!" said I mentally, as she stood there in her long, flowing robes. "Ah, woman! thou art verily transfigured."

Then I looked around on that audience, and am compelled to say that the comparison between the sexes was any thing but flattery to the gentlemen. Woman as I am, I love above all things to behold the beautiful face of a woman; but here was womanly beauty exceeding our highest conceptions; and in profound reverence I said, "Our Father in heaven, I thank thee for human beauty. Teach us the laws of beauty, that we, thy children, may people this earth with beautiful beings. Homeliness is akin to ignorance and sin; while beauty of form and beauty of intellect constitute God's best gifts to mortals."

"Those two gentlemen," said the lady, "have given us many good things to-night. There are very few persons who do not know that our sons and husbands ought to be better educated and better paid for their labor; but shall we, for this reason, make them presidents and senators? How would they look in the senate-chamber in their style of dress, so lacking in dignity? Why, we should have them quarreling and pulling hair very soon!"

"Ha, ha!" laughed the audience.

"No, no, gentlemen! you can discuss fashion and money-spending far better than national affairs. Besides, what would become of the babies? Do you propose that we, the women, shall take these your duties upon us? Depend upon it you are wrong, gentlemen: the sphere of man is *home;* and I am decidedly opposed to taking man out of his sphere. Let us for a moment see what Nature teaches on this subject; let us look at man divested of his embroidery and trimming; look at his angular, long form; look at his hairy face. Is he not in his outward structure and appearance more allied to the lower animals? Look at him, and do you not at once think of the monkey? [Hear, hear!] Now turn to woman. Look at her! Does not Nature delight in curves as in lines of beauty?

"See how the planets as they revolve in their orbits delight in curves? It is Nature's perfect method of form and motion. Now look at woman's beautifully curved faced and bust, and compare her form in its curved outlines with the angular outlines of man's form, and tell me if Nature herself has not put the stamp of inferiority on man! Ah, woman's face is enough! No mask of hair does she wear; but clear as the sun and fair as the moon shines clearly every feature, thus conclusively attesting her superiority. Again: how well Nature knows the superiority of woman and the inferiority of man, inasmuch as she has chosen woman for maternity. Ah! Nature knew where to find the perfect mould for her handiwork; Nature knew which is the superior sex:—

> " 'Very near to the infinite nature,
>   Very near to the hand of God,
> More rich than the hills of Beulah,
>   Which the white feet of angels trod,
> Is the sacred heart of woman;
>   The nature by which alone
> The divine can become embodied,
>   And the spirit reach its home.'

"Let us look at this matter from another stand-point. Nature is harmonious in all her parts. If, as I have proved, woman is physically superior, then she is mentally superior; and as man is physically inferior, so, as he must be harmonious in all his parts, he is necessarily and unmistakably inferior in all other respects."

I thought in my dream that I was greatly dissatisfied with the lady's speech, and I did pity the little gentlemen on the platform who were forced to hear so much about their inferiority.

"One more argument," said the lady, "and l am done; and this argument is also drawn from Nature. Woman has phrenologically a larger organ of language than man. Now, what does this teach us? It teaches us this (and it ought to teach every man the same truth): *that women is the natural orator;* that it is she who should be the lecturer, the speech-maker, the orator, and not man. It teaches us that women as senators and representatives, as lecturers and orators, are where they belong, where Nature intended they should be. It teaches us more than this: that, as man has smaller language than woman, his sphere is the domestic; is the quiet, the silent, the unobtrusive; is one of *silent* influences, not public and demonstrative like that of woman."

She sat down, and I was really glad. "Woman superior to man!" I exclaimed to myself. "Well, some people can prove any thing. I do hope that little gentleman will demolish their sophistry." But, just as Mr. Sammie Smiley arose to reply, I awoke; and, behold! it was all a dream; and I gladly realized, that, in this waking world of ours, man is not considered the inferior of woman, neither is he deprived of his just rights; and I wish sincerely that I could transfer our men to their Dreamland, and that there, at least, in God's universe, there might be one spot where men and women could stand side by side as equals.

Dream Number Four

It is said that much dreaming is the result of much eating late at night. However this may accord with the experience of others, very confident am I that *my* dreaming is not thus caused.

When quite a child, I used to visit, in my dreams, a mountain region in which some excavations were going on; but, being there only at night, I never saw any one at work. An old man leaning on a staff, however, invariably met me, and would show me the progress made since a previous visit. Sometimes he would walk with me up a mountain, then down into a valley, where he had a rough log-cabin. This region of Dreamland has been visited by me hundreds of times in my sleep, all those years from childhood to the present time. I meet the same old gentleman, take walks with him in various parts of this same mountain, converse with him on the progress of the excavation, improvements made, &c.

But now to my fourth dream of that strange land where women are considered superior to men.

I dreamed: and, lo! I stood in the same hall where I had attended the meeting on "Man's Rights;" but every seat was vacant. Then I heard the murmur of voices; and, very soon, people began to pour into the hall. Into the minds of those people I had the power to look; and in nearly all was a profound belief in the *rights of men.* Then I turned me about, and looked; and, lo! the capacious hall was filled to overflowing. Several ladies and gentlemen were on the platform; but what did it mean?—there were the veritable Mr. Sammie Smiley and Mr. Johnnie Smith; but they looked fifteen or sixteen years older than when I saw them before, their hair being liberally sprinkled with gray.

To an old lady near me I remarked how strange it was that their hair should have thus turned gray in a few days. She looked at me wonderingly, and then smilingly replied, "You are probably a stranger: those two gentlemen have been gray for some years."

"But," I rejoined, "the last time I saw them, they were young, and had not a gray hair."

"Ah!" said the lady pleasantly; "but time will make us all gray.

When those gentlemen commenced the agitation of man's rights, they were young; but twenty years has made a difference."

Twenty years! what did it mean? I had just begun to rub my eyes to see if I was asleep, as I have a habit of doing when dreaming any thing unpleasant, when Mr. Johnnie Smith came forward to speak. He demanded the franchise for men forthwith. He was clad in black velvet, but without trappings of any kind. While he was speaking, it seemed to me that I had the power of passing, unseen by the audience, from one speaker to the other, and looking into their thoughts. Some of them were so beautifully true and earnest, that I was delighted. Others were full of parade; and I saw written in their souls the word FASHIONABLE in large letters. In vain I asked myself, What does this mean? I could see no connection between this word and man's rights. But just then Mr. Johnnie Smith finished his speech by saying, "We are going to make man's rights FASHIONABLE!"

Then, in the twinkling of an eye, I seemed to see those gentlemen speakers stand up; and lo! how the majority were tricked off in finery! One, I remember, was dressed in pants of green-silk velvet, with little flounces of the same material from the foot to above the knees, a blue-velvet vest, with little-flounces of green up to the pockets, and at a corresponding distance each side of the button-holes and buttons; a blue-velvet swallow-tailed coat, trimmed with green flounces and fringe down the front, round the sleeves, and round the coat-tails, which, under the influence of a "Grecian bend,"[8] were duly projected in the most fashionable style: the whole attitude, I am almost ashamed to say, suggesting that of a monkey standing on two feet, that had been accustomed to use four for that purpose. I must have laughed aloud in my sleep at this, so greatly did I feel amused. One glance around the platform showed that every gentleman on the platform attitudinized in a similar manner, except Mr. Sammie Smiley and Mr. Johnnie Smith.

But I must finish the description of this exquisitely fashionable young gentleman, whose name was Master Willie Sandy. Well, Master Willie's little head was graced with a little green velvet cap in which were four blue feathers, pointing east, west, north, and south. In Master Willie's hands, which were covered by red gloves, was a tiny porte-monnaie [see note 4], with the little chains of which his tapering fingers toyed while he spoke. On coming forward to address the audience, the projection of his coat-tails, in connection with his fashionable stoop, imparted the appearance of his being about to fly. But he talked very prettily on man's rights generally and particularly, even saying something in derogation of that fashionable life, which, as the poor boy had been taught, was the alpha and omega [Gk.: first and last letters of alphabet] of existence. He concluded by stating that he was engaged in the study of engineering and of the higher branches of mathematics, and that he found nothing very difficult in either; at which remark some savan[t]s [Fr.: scholars] in the audience were vastly amused. He retired amidst loud applause, much of which was decidedly ironical. I was pained to hear such remarks as, "Willie better take off his Grecian bend;" "He had better take off his fashionable gear before he pretends to talk about the dignity of men, men's rights," &c.

Then another gentleman came to the front of the platform. He was tall for a man, dressed in gold and black,—black satin; suit trimmed with gold-colored satin folds, with a Grecian bend of enormous size, so that his coat-tails projected yet more than those of Mr. Willie Sandy. He read a speech, or essay, on man's rights, which was very dry and uninteresting. Then followed a little gentleman dressed in black, without trimming of any kind. I saw he had a gold watch hung round his neck by a gold chain: a plain linen collar and cuffs completed his toilet. He remarked, that many colleges were now open to men, and that thousands and tens of thousands of young men educated therein had proved themselves equal to women; that governments should not be upheld merely to honor or create big-bugs, but more for the benefit of the governed, all of whom had a right to participate in making the laws. This was not a question as to whether men or women should be the governing class; but it was a question of *human* rights, *universal* rights, the rights of humanity.

"That is good," said several, as I moved again among the audience: "that was a sensible dress and a sensible speech." "What," asked another, "brings these fantastically dressed men on the platform?"

"Don't you know?" replied another: "why, Mr. Johnnie Smith and some others are resolved to make man's rights fashionable."

Then I thought in my dream that Mr. Sammie Smiley commenced to address the meeting; and I was so pleased that I can remember most of what he said. He began,—

"Friends, twenty years have passed away since we inaugurated this movement: many of us have grown gray in the cause. Allow me to give you an outline of its history. Almost simultaneously with its inauguration, a few of us came together, and, being desirous to begin at the beginning of man's wrongs, and save the generation of young children that were growing up around us, we commenced a 'Children's Rights Society.' We held meetings everywhere on this subject; gentlemen and ladies joined us, giving their time and money to the cause. Small were the beginnings; but thousands joined our ranks who were not, they said, believers in men's rights: man's rights brought in thousands, but children's rights its tens of thousands. Children's rights are the foundation of both man's and woman's rights; for we are laboring for the rights of humanity as a whole. In the first place, lectures were given to fathers and mothers on physiology. Halls were rented. We moved slowly, but surely. On every Saturday afternoon, lectures on scientific subjects were given to children. Science was simplified and illustrated by appropriate apparatus, and the children instructed in Nature's own method, not by *pouring in,* but by bringing out their own inherent powers. By degrees, halls were built in every large city, and devoted to the rights of children; and so successful were the methods of instruction adopted, that, in many places, they almost superseded our common schools.

"Allow me to specify a few examples. You all know the miserable method of teaching that not long since were nearly universal: how science was fenced in by big words and obscure phraseology; you know how our children were confined six or seven hours daily in a dreary, miserable school-house, and how, as a general thing, the children hated the very idea of school. Now look into one of our large halls devoted to the rights of children. Observe the chemical room. A number of pneumatic troughs meet your eye, at each of which is a child making chemical experiments, with the aid and under the supervision of skillful professors.

"The geological room is furnished with large assortments of specimens. To every fifty children a tutor is assigned: they ramble through the country to collect specimens and observe the various formations, —excursion-trains being frequently engaged in taking them to distant localities to see for themselves hot springs, mountains, canyons, stalactites, stalagmites, &c. Ask those children if they like to study. In an instant they exclaim, 'Why, yes! it is delightful!'

"Physiology has been taught on the same principles: nothing has been held back. The uses of every organ of the body have been so explained, that, in relation thereto, the idea of vulgarity has disappeared, and secret vices [e.g. masturbation] have departed; for knowledge is power,—power to do right. Instead of the leaden eyes and feeble brain, our young men are vigorous, both in mind and body.

"Along with all this have been given lectures and lessons to adults; and, from morning to night, there are thousands in every city being educated in all that pertains to the laws of life.

"Twenty years have passed: those who were little children when we began have now grown to manhood and womanhood, and the majority of our young boys are now ready advantageously to exercise the franchise whenever they obtain it.

"Do you talk to me of the fashionable class, the moneyed class, who have all the time been either passive on-lookers or active opponents? Do you talk *now* of making man's rights *fashionable;* tricking out its advocates in the senseless gewgaws of fashionable society, and investing our reform with its weakness and folly?

"It can not be done. We have built our temple with divine corner-stones. While physiology has broken the physical bonds and bands with which fashion has bound us, enabling our boys and girls to be dressed in loose and comfortable clothing, our thoughts have been unbound and purified by corresponding mental training. Children of both sexes can be safely trusted to study together, play together, and when they grow to men and women, mingle together in all business relations, to the advantage of each and all.

"Though despised at first by some of the friends of man's rights, and regarded as a 'side issue,' having little or nothing to do with the main question, it having been held that we should confine ourselves to the advocacy of the franchise for men (which obtained, it was claimed that all the rest must follow), yet the movement for children's rights has been proved, by twenty years' experience, to have been the most powerful engine of success; for to-day there are millions of young men fully prepared judiciously to exercise the franchise, and millions of young women who have studied side by side with these young men, and are thus able, from personal knowledge, to realize the capacity of men, to acknowledge their rights, and to desire, that, in business, in politics, and in the household, they should continue to walk side by side.

"Children's rights—a branch, if you so please, of the man's rights movement—are, in fact, its foundation, while the right of franchise is the crown, the summit, the top-stone."

Round after round of applause followed the conclusion of his speech: so loud and so continued were the cheers, that I awoke, and lo! it was a dream.

Dream Number Five

I have just awakened from another visit to the land of dreams. So vivid is my recollection of every thing I saw and heard, that I am greatly inclined to the belief that I have visited one of the planets; and have been asking myself a number of questions, such as these: If time and space are almost nothing to the spirit, if spirit can travel more quickly than light,

—yea, almost as quickly as thought,—may I not have visited one of the planets? And as the physical condition of the world so greatly resembled that of our own as to seem to me identical, and as the people were, in both physical and mental structure, so like ourselves, except that the women were superior to the men, I am more inclined to that idea than ever. On this, my last visit, I observed one or two very important facts: First, there was frost and snow; and second, the days and nights did not perceptibly differ in length from those of this earth. Hence, though I may subject myself to ridicule, though I may be laughed at as a visionary, I must own that I am inclined to believe that I have visited in my dream the planet Mars.

Another fact tends to substantiate this idea. I distinctly remember standing by my bedside as the dream terminated, and then awaking to the consciousness that my spirit stood there looking at my body asleep. It was but a moment certainly; but this double consciousness, in connection with the circumstances above mentioned, and others even more decisive, that will be hereafter specified, are such as to give a strong probability to the hypothesis, that, in this instance, the impossible (or what is currently deemed such) has been achieved, and even spectrum analysis (which embodies the latest developments in astronomical science) is outdone.

In this my last dream I found myself in a large public library; and who should enter but Mr. Sammie Smiley and Mr. Johnnie Smith, accompanied by two beautiful women. Then followed several ladies and gentlemen, whom I at once recognized as those I had seen at the meeting on man's rights. There, too, was the lady who had so amused and delighted the audience by her speech on man's inferiority. Then followed several introductions, from which I learned that said lady's name was Christiana Thistlewaite. She took from her pocket a newspaper, in which was a report (which she read) of a lecture delivered by an old woman who was on the editorial staff of a leading metropolitan paper. The lecturer considered that the recent extensive employment of men in stores in a neighboring city had proved detrimental to the morals of the sex; inasmuch as by opening up to them a prospect of support by their own labor, instead of being entirely dependent for a maintenance on their ability to secure a well-to-do wife, they became careless of their reputations, their independence, thus tending to licentiousness. Mrs. Thistlewaite remarked, that, although she (Mrs. T.) was decidedly opposed to men transcending their legitimate sphere, she considered the lecturer's position highly absurd. "Poor old woman!" she added: "she has done good service in her day; always, until within a year or two, working for the poor and down-trodden, against the rich and powerful. She was especially useful in introducing co-operative households; but she is now evidently in her dotage. The paper cannot afford to carry her many years longer, if it means to continue first-class."

While they talked together and looked at the books, some of them reclining in easy-chairs or on lounges, with books in their hands, I opened a very large, handsome book, which I found to be a Bible. "Well," I said, "this is just what I want;" so I opened it, and began to look over the passages of Scripture which referred to woman. I was astonished—nay, shocked—to find, at the very commencement, that the whole history of the fall of man was reversed as to the sexes. *Adam* was tempted by the serpent, and gave the forbidden fruit to his wife; for which reason it was said to the man that "she [the woman—ADC] shall rule over thee," and "in sorrow thou [the man—ADC] shall attend the children;" that a virtuous man was a crown to his wife, and his price above rubies; "he layeth his hands to the spindle, and his hands hold the distaff;" his *wife* being known in the gates, when *she* sat among the elders of the land, &c. Farther on it was stated that husbands should obey their wives as the head of the man was the woman, even as Christ was the head of the church; that it was not becoming that a man should speak in the church; but, if they would know any thing, let them ask their wives at home. "Why, I said to myself, "this Bible has certainly been translated and probably compiled by women; for no *man* in this land would have so interpreted the Scriptures against his sex. Thus the women have strengthened themselves behind the Bible; and so the poor down-trodden men are held in slavery by means of this book, thus interpreted!"[9]

While turning over the leaves, Mrs. Christiana Thistlewaite came to my side, to whom I said, "Are all your Bibles like this, madam?" at the same time pointing to some of the preceding passages. She smiled as she replied, "Certainly; they are all alike. Our Bible is translated from the languages in which it was originally written: wise, good women were the translators; and I would like Mr. Sammie Smiley and Mr. Johnnie Smith to see those passages of Scripture."

"Those passages," rejoined the former gentlemen, "were never intended to be used to keep men in an inferior position, or to deprive them of their just rights. Those who wrote the books in the Bible, like you, did not believe in man's rights; and they wrote as they believed. God never said those men were inferior to women; for in Christ there was neither bond nor free, male nor female (Gal. iii. 28); but all were one. God, in his works, never utters the word *inferior;* the sun shines and the flowers grow for all; the earth brings forth enough of its fruits for all, the varied diversities of manifestation beautifully blending into one unity of design: and as the varied contrasts and diversities of manifestation beautifully blending into one unity of design; and as the varied contrasts and diversities and blending of color in a painting produce a unity of expression, no *color* being inferior or superior to any other, so Nature and art alike belie any written word implying *inferiority* of one sex to another, whatever may be the *diversities*. Who says that God has made one sex inferior to another utters a blasphemy."

Here several ladies gathered around Mr. Sammie Smiley and Mrs. Christiana Thistlewaite.

"We," continued the gentleman, "have only to ask our own common sense what is right or wrong with respect to man or woman, even as was asked by an ancient reformer, once abhorred, now adored (nominally), 'Why even yourselves judge ye not what is right?' (Luke xii. 57). You, ladies, have made the laws, and you have made them to suit yourselves; think you, that, if men as well as women had the making of the laws, in marriage the man would have no control over property previously belonging to him, unless secured to him by a special deed? Realize, ladies, if you can, what would be your condition were the legal status of the sexes reversed! If a man owns property or has a store, he is wronged by having no voice in the laws or regulations of the town or city in which he resides. If the wife die, the husband has the *use* only during life of *one-third* of their joint property. If the *husband* die, however, the wife takes *absolute possession* of the *whole*. Man is thus wronged by being denied the right of franchise; even the *children* of widower being in many cases subjected to the control of strange women appointed by a court, instead of that of the remaining parent."

Mrs. Susan Thistlewaite then said to Mr. Johnnie Smith, "Allow me, sir, to ask a question. Why do gentlemen, when they meet each other, occupy the time entirely in frivolous conversation about love, marriage, &c.?"

"Admitting," replied Mr. Smith, "the generality and absurdity of the practice, it must be considered as an unavoidable result of the conditions inaugurated and upheld by those who would circumscribe man's sphere, and limit his faculties to affairs, that, when exclusively followed, tend to dwarf the faculties, and make people narrow and gossiping. You, ladies, would do the same were you in our position. Close to you, ladies, as you have closed to us, all avenues to honor and emolument; deprive you of education and pecuniary independence, making you dependent on the bounty of man; and would not the most important subject to you be marriage?"

"Mr. Johnnie Smith is right," I replied, as I stepped into the very midst of them. "In the land where I reside, *men* have all the rights which you ladies have in this country: men make the laws and oppress women, just as, in this land of yours, women make the laws and oppress men."

"Oh, oh! astonishing!" exclaimed several. "Do tell us something about things there."

"Well," I continued, "ladies are the housekeepers."

"Ridiculous!" interjected two or three ladies.

"Ladies do all the sewing and knitting."

How they laughed!

"The men hold the colleges, and are educated therein, only a few being open to women: the majority of ladies are educated at common schools, and a few at boarding-schools."

"Ha, ha! oh, ho! boarding-schools for ladies! fine education that must be for women!"

"Go on, go on!" called out several; "I never heard of any thing so ridiculous! Ha, ha, ha!"

"Men hold the purse, pay car-fares, pay for refreshments, and stand when the cars are crowded, while the ladies sit. Men dress in plain clothes, while women are walking advertisements of dry goods; men wear their hair generally short and clean, while women not only wear their own hair, but add to it quantities of horse-hair, grease, and other materials, making of the whole a putrid, uncomfortable, disgusting mass. Our women decorate themselves, too, with ribbons, as do your men, and have their fashion-books; their dresses far excelling in absurd ugliness and unhealthfulness any thing worn by your men."

"Is it possible? how outrageously absurd and repulsive!" they exclaimed; while a ringing laugh filled the library, and more ladies entered. "Go on, go on!" said several.

"Men, and only men, make the laws, as senators, representative, judges, &c. No women vote or legislate: in short, the whole matter is reversed."

"How are the women intellectually?" asked a lady.

"As a general rule," I replied, "they are just in the condition that men are here. By a singular coincidence, an old man who edits a leading metropolitan journal in my country recently delivered a lecture (at a place called Bethlehem, I think), in which he took the same position, as regards the employment of women in stores, and their morals, that your old-woman editor is reported to have taken in regard to the employment of men in stores here. The objection is probably equally well founded in both cases; and the parallelism is so far complete, that our editor is getting to be termed an old woman or old granny; those terms with us being used to designate weakness in intellectual or executive operation."

Then Mr. Sammie Smiley stepped on a chair, and began: "Friends, you have heard what the stranger has told us. What do you think of it? Does it not prove my position that those ladies would be no wiser or better than we are, were they in our position? And does it not prove conclusively that not sex, but *condition,* is the root of the matter?"

"I do not believe the story told us by the stranger," said Mrs. Thistlewaite. "Man superior to woman! men legislate! Oh! it won't bear the light of day for an instant!"

"Where is that stranger?" said several voices. I had entered a large room opening from the library, and was looking at several portraits of distinguished stateswomen; for no man's face was among them. When I heard the inquiry, I returned to the library. Then the crowd gathered around me in great curiosity. "So you live in a land," said one lady, "where men have their rights, do you?"

"Yes," I said.

"And do you mean to say that you were never permitted to vote?"

"I never was permitted; but I have protested against the exclusion."

"What is the name of your land?" asked several.

"The United States of North America."

"Where is that?"

"Do you ask where it is?" I replied; "why, look at your maps."

"Here is the map of the world," said Christiana Thistlewaite.

I went up to the map and looked it over; and, lo! it was not like our maps at all. There were the frigid zones, the equator and the ecliptic, the parallels of longitude and latitude, the tropics and the poles, to which were even added many isothermal lines; but the distribution of the land and water was very different in many parts, though in others maintaining something of a general resemblance.

"This map is not correct," I said.

Then arose a general derisive laugh. "I am very sorry," said Mrs. Christiana Thistlewaite. "It would have given me great gratification to see that land of man's rights, my friend; but it has vanished! it is not to be found on the map! Ah!" she continued in bitter sarcasm, "it is too bad that the beautiful land where men are the lords of creation,[10] where men are the superior race, and women the inferior, can not be found."

Confused and astonished by the map, confused and astonished by these puzzling remarks, I awoke. The map, however, had made such an impression on my mind, that I drew an outline of it at once; then I consulted a friend of mine versed in astronomy, to whom I showed the diagram. He took down a strange book containing some excellent engravings of the planet as viewed through telescopes of the highest magnifying powers, and one of them corresponded, in the distribution of land and water, exactly to my diagram. Yes, there was my Dreamland, there my planet,—the planet MARS!

Dream Number Six

I have just awoke. What a bad night! How it rains! Why, it is pouring down.

Once again I have been to my dreamland, where the respective conditions of men and women are reversed. My watch lies on the table and its pointers tell me it is five minutes past two o'clock. My husband is sound asleep. Sleep on, my dear, good fellow! Don't open your eyes until my dream is written down. But I must write down the two headings at once, before they are forgotten:

THE DELIRIUM PROTEST AND THE
SHEEPMAN-YELLOW-GREEN PROTEST.

There! I am glad they are down before my memory has any chance to prove treacherous. Dear me! my husband awakes.

"Why, Annie, what are you doing at midnight, with that gas burning? You know I cannot sleep with a light in the room. Writing! What in the world are you doing writing at midnight?"

"I have had another dream," I replied; "so please don't say another word. Just turn on the other side, then the gas will not shine in your face." There—he has done so; good, obliging fellow! So now to my dream, in which it seemed to me I had the power of hovering in the atmosphere. Below me was the city which I had so often visited, and there, as heretofore, were the gentlemen parading the streets, their elaborately trimmed coats, pants and vests emulating the colors of the rainbow. With astonishment I beheld that beneath every coat-tail was a Grecian bend, which caused said caudalities to project at an angle of forty-five degrees. Many of these "well dressed" gentlemen were accompanied by dignified ladies, whose beauty, dress and carriage all denoted that women were there decidedly the superior sex. "Oh, sad sight!" I said to myself. "Oh, terrible condition for man!" Then, as my heart went out to them in pity and commiseration, I found myself walking in the broad, beautiful avenue of that city; and it seemed to me, as it had often seemed before, that I had the power to look into the minds of these poor men, and also into the minds of those grand, beautiful women. I found that many of those degraded men were planning cajolery and deceit, by means of which they expected to extract money from their wives for the purchase of costly suits of clothing. As they occasionally lingered to observe the beautifully-embroidered vests, the elegantly-trimmed coats and other extravagant paraphernalia peculiar to man's wardrobe there, I saw that in many instances, their mental structure was essentially inferior to that of women, and that this was a necessary result of inherited degradation. I then thought of Darwin's observations and experiments, proving that in certain species of ants and other animals, peculiarities of sexes are transmitted, so that what one sex inherits the other does not; and I said to myself, "Here is a terrible exemplification of this principle in the *genus homo,* for this inferiority has even permeated cerebral tissues."

But at that moment I remembered the Man's Rights meeting which I had attended, the noble men I had seen there, and the great speech of Mr. Sammy Smiley, which proved that many men were, and many men might be, equal to the best of women, and I inwardly exclaimed, "Thank God for man's rights!" Then my attention was called to large posters on the walls, around which troops of little, fantastically-dressed gentlemen had gathered. "SHEEPMAN–YELLOW–GREEN PROTEST" met my eye in one place, while on the opposite corner, in yet larger head letters, I saw

DELIRIUM PROTEST.

The little darling gentlemen tittered and laughed as they read. "That is good, that is excellent for those men's rights folks!" exclaimed one of them. "I will certainly sign that."

Just then a young girl came along with an armful of papers which she began to distribute to these gentlemen and also to the passers-by. One found its way into my hands, and lo, it was the Sheepman-Yellow-Green Protest. I put on my spectacles and read about as follows:

"The petition of the undersigned gentlemen to the Congress of the United Republics protesting against the extension of the suffrage to men.

"We, the undersigned gentlemen, do most respectfully appeal to your honorable body against the extension of the suffrage to men. We shrink from notoriety, and would fain hide ourselves from woman's eye, well knowing that it is man's place to be modest and shame-faced; but we are deeply and powerfully impressed by the grave facts which threaten our happiness in view of the proposed granting of the franchise to men.

"Because the Bible says that woman was made first, then man, proving conclusively that woman was superior to man.

[This reminded me of the idea enunciated by Burns,[11] that Nature "tried her 'prentice hand on man, and then she mad the lasses, O!" but read on:]

"Because as men we find enough care and responsibility in taking care of our homes, our children, our sewing and knitting, and other *et ceteras* [*sic*] of man's life, and we don't feel strong enough, mentally or physically, to assume other and heavier burdens such as an extension of suffrage to man would bring.

"Because the possession of the franchise would be detrimental to the workingmen of our country, especially sewing men, creating among them a discontent and dissatisfaction which would never be assuaged until they should find their way to offices of honor and emolument, which, we all know, belong exclusively to women.

"Because the extension of the franchise to man would be terribly detrimental to the marriage relation, resulting in two heads to a family instead of one and causing married persons who, by reason of mutual unfitness, should never have formed that relation to each other, to seek for its dissolution though bound to each other by the holy ties of matrimony.

"Because no general law affecting the condition of all men should be enacted to meet the exceptional discontent of workingmen who are needed to perform the labor and drudgery of the world, nor of bachelors, who ought, like ourselves, to have married honorable and respectable women, well able to provide for them comfortable homes and all the luxuries of life.

"For these any many other equally important reasons do we beg of your wisdom that no law extending the franchise to the men of our country may be passed."

[Signed,] Mr. Jemima D. Hykoelorum, Mr. Josephine Rooster-Schmidt, Mr. Rev. Doctor Martha Manton, Mr. Rev. Dr. Jerusha Bottler, Mr. Rev. Dr. Patience Rankskin, Mr. Betsy B. English, Master Johnnie Carrott, Mr. Catherine V. Morecold, Mr. Sarah McCowlick, Mr. Senator Mary Shearman, Mr. Senator Jane Tocsin, Mr. Senator Caroline Telrock, Mr. Lucretia T. Troppick, Mr. Cynthia Walksome, Master Charlie E. Birching."

As I finished the names I looked up, and there was Christiana Thistlethwaite [see note 14] before me. "Good morning, my friend," she

said; "I am glad to see you perusing that document. As you have probably perceived, the Sheepman-Yellow-Green Protest is signed by the husbands of the most honorable and respectable women in our country—
husbands of Senators and clergymen. Come, walk with me to the Senate," she added; and in an instant I found myself in the reception room
of that body.

With the "Delirium Protest" in my hand, I took a chair, readjusted
my spectacles and began to look it over. I found it was signed by one
hundred and forty-one men (oh, these poor deluded men) of a *Dorain* or
Norain county—I have forgotten the exact name. The following paragraphs caught my eye.

"We men acknowledge no inferiority to women."

Pretty good! I said to myself; pretty good! You one hundred and
forty-one men are in a very hopeful condition. But I will give, as nearly
as I can render it, the DELIRIUM PROTEST.

"We believe that God has wisely made men to be husbands, to stay
at home, to take care of the children, to look after and keep in repair the
wardrobes of the family and attend to all the little etcetras the sum of
which makes home comfortable and attractive, these duties being even
implied in the very construction and derivation of the word, HOUSEBAND.

"We believe that God has made woman to legislate, to govern and
to fill every department of lucrative labor, and that each sex is well
adapted to the duties of each.

"We believe that God has ordained that every man who has not a
wife to provide for him is an outcast, and unworthy of our consideration. [Well done, Podsnap.]

"We feel that our domestic cares, our homes, our children, making
and receiving calls, studying the fashions and so arranging our households and clothing that the apparent effect is that of having twice or
thrice the income really received, fill up the whole measure of our time,
abilities and needs.

"We believe that our duties, as above-defined, are as sacred as any
upon earth.

"We feel that those duties are such as no woman could perform,
constituting *prima facie* evidence that God has wisely adapted each sex to
its special duties.

"The importance of our duties, as above-defined, urge [*sic*] us to
protest against being compelled to accept the franchise, or any of its
resultant duties, which could not be performed without sacrificing some
duties exclusively appertaining to our sex, and which we therefore feel
under obligations to perform.

"Our mothers, sisters, wives and daughters represent us at the ballot-box; our mothers and sisters love us; our wives are our choice— [happy souls!]—and are with us; our daughters are what we made them, and we are content [oh, bliss supreme!] We are content that they represent us at the ballot-box, in scientific pursuits, in the lecture-room and in the world of business and legislation—in short, in everything that would divert us from our home and domestic duties as above defined. We are content to represent them in our primary schools, at our firesides, telling stories and amusing the children, warming our wives' slippers and preparing the dressing-robes for their return home; and we well know that in this way, by the influence we thus gain over our wives, we are better represented, even at the ballot-box, than we possibly could be were all men allowed to vote."

"Happy one hundred and forty-one!" I said to myself, as I took off my spectacles; "peace be to your ashes."

Then I looked about the large reception room of the Senate; there were young men and old men, in all their finery and frivolity—ribbons and ruffles, frills and flounces—whispering and tittering, swinging and prancing on their little toes, every motion giving perspicuity to Grecian bends and long coat tails; their hands were squeezed into small gloves, which gave them a cats-paw appearance. As they walked to and fro, or stood in groups, their little gossamer fans fluttered like the wings of as many butterflies.

The pages of the Senate were young girls, whose countenances bloomed with health and intelligence; and I observed that they were busily engaged carrying to Senators in the Senate chamber dainty, perfumed cards of these delicate little gentlemen. Never had I witnessed so sad a sight. Never for an instant did I cease sorrowing for those poor downtrodden men, whom I well knew were capable of filling every department here monopolized by women.

As I sat there watching the visitors at the reception room, a Senator, in her stately robes of plain black, without any ornaments, entered from the Senate chamber; then three or four of those frivolous [*sic*] creatures I have described minced and bowed, fluttered and chattered, while she, like a superior being, graciously listened, occasionally making a remark. Two rows of parchment, tied with blue ribbon, were handed her by one of those little gents. As she unfolded first one and then the other, her eyes rapidly scanning their contents, I saw in large letters on one, "Sheepman-yellow-green protest," and on the other "Delirium Protest."

"But I believe in Man's Right," I heard the Senator say.

"O, blessed moment!" I said to myself, as a tear rolled down my face; "there is one noble, beautiful soul, brave enough to say she believes in the rights of these poor, degraded men, who in my world are considered the lords of creation."

Then I reflected, as I sat there on my chair, on the similarity in names, in sentiments and logic [?] between those protests and some that whilom[12] appeared in the papers here, signed by the wives of divers high mightinesses in Washington, Elyria and elsewhere, denouncing *woman's* rights, and I concluded that this remarkable parrallelion [*sic*] must be, and the manifestation of that general law of correspondences under which certain changes in the sun are said by savan[t]s to be concurrent with magnetic and meteoric terrestrial disturbances; and might also have a bearing on the theory of a Parisian bachelor who devoted his life to the investigation of humps, and who, from numerous facts which he had ascertained in all quarters of the globe, concluded that the forms of such protuberances corresponded with the more or less hilly character of the countries in which they respectively originated.

While intensely occupied in these philosophical comparisons, and endeavoring to apply them to reformatory operations in both worlds, I became so bewildered that I awoke.

Why, it has taken me over an hour to write this dream; the rain is still pouring. I am sleepy, and must retire.

Dream Number Seven

My noble husband has just delivered himself of the following speech:

"There you are! Up again at midnight! Another dream, I suppose! Well, this is becoming quite a serious matter! You will forget your dreams if you don't write them down at once! Indeed! These are Woman's Rights times with a vengeance, and no mistake, when I cannot rest in my bed at night without being disturbed by my wife in this manner!

"Now I will give you a little of my mind: You are a dreamer, and nothing but a dreamer, and henceforth you may rise fifty times in the night, or you may sit up all night to write your dreams if you choose; *but you shall not do it at my cost.* I believe in Individual Sovereignty. You shall go to some other room."

"All right, all right, my dear, amiable husband," I replied, with a good-natured laugh, at the same time taking up my paper, pen and ink, putting out the gas and quietly making my way to the sitting room. So here I am, all alone. Henceforth if I should have any more need to write in the night here I will come at once; my dear, good, abused husband rest in peace!

But I must relate my dream in which I again found myself in the before-mentioned city, and in a gentleman's dressing room. Before a large mirror, which appeared to be let into the walls, and which reached from the top of the room to the floor, stood a little gentleman in his long night-dress, his hair full of curl-papers, for the quantity of paper greatly exceeded that of the hair. As I was noting the beautiful needlework that profusely trimmed his night-dress, and which, I perceived, had been done by his own delicate fingers, like the strange incongruity of dreams, there began to move into the room, one after another, a great number of gentlemen in their long night-dresses and abundant curl-papers. As I stood on one side, I found that they were entering a large assembly dressing-room, as large as the reception-room of the White House. I observed, too, that on every side and down the center of this room were arranged, side by side, all necessary articles for a gentlemen's dressing-room, as if the contents of a few score of small ones such as I had just seen had been consolidated and rearranged with reference to the maximum of convenience and minimum of labor. What elegant night dreams, I said to myself as they passed! And yet, though I admired them in the abstract, I felt something I am sorry to say, akin to contempt for these gentlemen whose forms they covered.

One fat gentleman so loaded down with avoirdupoise [Fr.: weight] as to suggest by his breathing a little steam engine, the wonder of my childhood days, named "Puffing Billy," came waddling down in a night-gown having four ruffles around the lower portion and tucks innumerable. He had very little hair. I then confidently believe that in half an hour every hair on his little head could have been counted!

Each gentleman as he passed me, and seemed to be in his accustomed place, carried in his hand a pair of corsets and a long, black *something* that looked to me very like a horse's tail. The corsets I could comprehend; but what were they going to do with those horses' tails? Then another puzzling feature of this strange scene was that where they did not carry these appendages they carried an armful of tow, or sheep's wool, or what looked to me very like these substances.

By-and-by all seemed to have entered; for the doors were closed and those night-gowned gentlemen, attended by young men whom they called their servant boys, or dressing boys, prepared to dress.

There was a something in the countenances of these gentlemen that impressed me very disagreeably. Almost invariably their skin was spotted with yellow, and, as a whole, looked dark, dried and unnaturally shrivelled. Two exceptions to this rule were so grateful to my love of the beautiful that I lingered round about these two gentlemen some time. These two I had observed on entering the room, as they carried no corsets in their hands; and the diameter of their waists suggested the idea that they would form models for the men of that world as excellent as the Venus de Medici[13] does for the women of this world.

But what a scene that dressing room! what a medley! what a confusion of odors as the dressing progressed—of perfumes, grease, pomatum, powders, rouge, hair-dye, and I know not what other substances for cleanliness and hygiene!

A servant boy whom I had seen standing at the head of the room with a something in his hand—I had not observed what—here sounded a gong; and in an instant the hair-dressing commenced. Then I perceived for what were designed the supposed horses' tails, also the tow, sheep's wool and several other strange, dark masses which had seemed wholly inappropriate, for anything connected with the toilet; for lo, all these were mounted on the tops and backs of their little heads, making them look as if they had exchanged their own heads for those of horses, minus the dignity usually appertaining to those animals. Oh, sad sight! said I to myself; oh, terrible result of man's degradation!

This gear on the head and its adjustment consumed considerable time; and as it progressed I felt a strange, stifled sensation, caused, I presume, by the numerous odors of that assembly dressing-room.

Then twelve men entered the room carrying before them on waiters a number of small white cups, some containing white, others red or pink powder; also, several small, broad silvered knives and sundry tiny brushes. "Ah, here comes the porcelainists! Here are the porcelainists!" I heard several voices exclaim with a pleased flutter, as with small brushes they were painting their eyebrows.

Simultaneously as they entered twelve gentlemen took seats together in the center of the room—twelve blotched, wrinkled, yellow faces! I looked at them, then at the twelve porcelainists, and then at the cups, into which was being poured some liquid from a bottle. What can be the meaning of all this? I asked myself in astonishment; but the mystery was soon explained; for like magic the small knives in the hands of the porcelainists transferred the contents of the cups to the faces of the twelve gentlemen sitting in a row. Over the forehead and cheeks, over and round about the nose and close to the corner of the mouth went the knives, covering up ugliness instanter [sic]. In ten minutes the twelve faces reminded me of the little porcelain dolls sold in our stores.

"You must not laugh, or romp, dear gentlemen," said one of the operators; "you will mar your faces; guard against all emotions, as well as against any other agency causing sudden and extreme movements of the features; for by allowing such movements or emotions you would cause the porcelain to crack and spoil it completely. Don't move, please, for a few minutes; it takes a little time for the porcelain, after being laid on the face, to dry thoroughly." Ver[y] obediently the twelve faces kept exactly in one position. During the operation quite a circle of half dressed gentlemen had gathered round.

"Beautiful! beautiful!" I heard them exclaim; "Sweet! pretty!" said one; "Delightful!" said another; but I thought contemptuously, "I would like to suspend you twelve between heaven and earth as a spectacle to gods, to angels and to men!"

One of the beautiful (!) twelve, who evidently was suffering from a bad cold, here began to sneeze. Dear, dear! how he did sneeze! and as he sneezed the porcelain began to crack in several places, and small pieces fell to the floor. Oh, hideous sight!

But hark! the gong sounds again. (How I do hate a gong), and then a hundred corsets, embracing as many gentlemen's bodies (including the elect twelve, who were prudently conserving their new faces) were subjected to superlative pressure. Tight, tighter and yet tighter were they compressed until not only the faces of the attendant servant boys, but those of the gentlemen being laced were red with the effort. As the lacing progressed the respiration became more difficult.

But what next? The gong sounds again! "Dressing the feet!" Why, the man calls out this as he might the figures of a dance! [What absurdity there is in dreams!]

Then I thought I was greatly puzzled while I wondered I had not previously observed that some of these gentlemen wore on their feet what (for want of a better name) I shall call a *foot-vice*. This was a curious apparatus, with straps and buckles, worn on the feet during the night for the purpose of moulding the foot into a rounded form. This result had, in a few instances, been so completely obtained that the sides of the foot were rounded over and almost met on the under part of the foot. Of course those who had servant boys required them when dressing their feet; and when the *foot-vice* had been used two servant boys were brought into requisition, one of whom kept the foot in its rolled condition while the other commenced to introduce the foot into the gaiter. This was a difficult feat, for it required a long time and several trials before completion.

But I am weary; perhaps sleepy; so I shall not attempt to describe the numerous divisions of the toilet indicated by that terrible gong; the putting on of "Grecian bends" was one. May I never see such a sight again! No wonder that when dressed their coat tails projected at an angle of forty-five degrees!

Never shall I forget when the gong sounded for the false teeth to be introduced into the mouth; for it seemed in my dream that there came to me at the same moment the power to see and examine the internal organs of every gentleman present. In all who wore corsets (and there were only two gentlemen who did not), I saw that the five lower ribs were contracted, and in some cases over-lapped; that the air-cells in the lower part of the lungs were rendered inactive by compression, and that in consequence of the sympathy existing between all organs of the body, there was very observable either positive indications of disease or great weakness. One young gentleman, who had been originally healthy, I perceived was paralyzed on one side of the body from the use of the foot-vice; and that the waist, though originally of proper circumference, was gradually approaching that of the wasp.

Then, as previously in a former dream, I looked into the spirit, saw the links connecting the body with the spirit, and as by a glance was enabled to go back in time by means of these links through several generations of ancestors. Carefully and accurately *past* ancestral endowment—physical, moral and mental—were compared with those before me, especially were the co-relations of parts observed; and I perceived that it had come to be a fact, indeed, that *these* gentlemen, at least, were inferior to woman.

Oh, saddening realization! Oh, poor, silly butterfly men! Verily in this land man is inferior to woman!

Thus was I sadly meditating when the scene changed and I found myself in the home of Mrs. Christiana Thistlewaite, and Mr. Johnny Smith and Mr. Sammy Smiley as her guests.[14]

"Dear friend," she said, taking my hand; "I am very glad to see you; do you know that I am a convert to "Man's Rights?"

"You!" I exclaimed, with great astonishment.

"Yes; I am convinced that the demand of the Man's Rights Society are founded in nature."

"But how has this come to pass?" I inquired.

"I will tell you, dear friend," she replied, as she took a chair near me, still retaining my hand in her own. "You remember the *Sheepman-Yellow-Green Protest;* also the *Delirium Protest?*"

"Certainly."

"Very well; I read them over carefully, and was dissatisfied. I saw that they would not bear the light of day for an instant; then I tried to find better reasons for denying to men their claimed rights. I gave my best thoughts and attention to the subject; and to make a long story short, as a result of that thought, here I am a thorough believer in *Man's Rights*. So you see the SHEEPMAN–YELLOW–GREEN PROTEST and DELIRIUM PROTEST have done more good, in one case, at least, than the silly men who penned it ever conceived."

I commenced to express my delight at the change in her sentiments, when she remarked: "But you are very sad, my friend; you show it in every lineament of your face." Then I thought in my dream that I related all I had witnessed in the assembly dressing-room, dwelling very minutely on the peculiar and diversified ancestral endowments handed down from generation to generation, and the culture or expression these had received in each, and finally the conclusions forced upon me of the real inferiority of man to woman.

"Don't be cast down, dear friend," replied Christiana Thistlewaite; "you have only chanced to meet some of the worst specimens of our men. This class of men does not represent more than one-fiftieth of the male sex. You must know that this is a large country, composed of many races, some inferior, but many superior. These you have visited are only one race, and a very small race—the *fashionable* race; and I am glad, truly glad, of their *foot-vices,* their waist-vices, their cosmetics, paints, powders and porcelain, for they all form such powerful *brain*-vices and life-annihilators that in less than a century every one of their descendants will be swept from the face of our planet. Inferior races must give place to superior; and I thank our Father for this beautiful law." As she finished, she led me into a large, handsome room in which were gathered probably two hundred persons of both sexes. "Now use your '*soul-gift,*' dear friend," she said, "and tell me of *this* race of men and women." I did so. I comprehended the capacities of each brain, of each spirit, and then walked down the aisles of time for many generations of ancestors; divined the physical, mental and spiritual heritage that had passed from generation to generation with the added culture or repression of such heritage, and contrasted these results in the male sex with the results obtained by the same means in the female sex; and I followed from cause to effect, from added growth to added growth, there came to my own spirit a blessed peace. Here was no inferiority, no retrogression; but in characters ineffaceable were written, for both man and woman, possibilities and capabilities as far transcending the present as those of the present transcended those of the long ago, even a million of [a]ges.

Dream Number Eight

Not to the planet Mars did my dream take me this time, but on board a sailing vessel just entering New York bay. Very foggy it had been for days; but the clouds having just lifted, to my delightful eyes were revealed the shores of Staten Island and the other components of the brilliant *tout ensemble* [see note 2] greeting the voyager as he [*sic*] approached the metropolitan cities which bounded the distance.

My husband and I had for years been in some remote corner of the earth, where we had never received any news either of home, friends or country; but where the out-of-the-way place could have been situated, impenetrable not only to telegraph and post, but beyond the reach even of "our own correspondent," I could not remember. In vain I tried to recall its name and locality or even the least incident which had befallen us in our long exile—the years we had spent there were all a blank. However, I did know that our home was in New York city, and that very soon we should be there. In vain did I interrogate my husband as to where we had been; he only looked wonderingly in my face, laughed heartily several times, and said: "I really cannot remember. All I know is that we have been gone from the United States ten years, and that shortly we shall be again in New York city. Yonder is a tug-boat," he continued, pointing to one evidently making for us; "I am very anxious to hear the news. Oh, to get the sight of a New York paper once more!"

How vividly do I remember this part of my dream!—how recall every moment of time, and every feature of the beautiful scene before us. Land, land once more, bringing thoughts of home, joyous expectations of meeting dear friends from whom we had been long separated, and all the updating expectancy that seemed to make my whole being throb with delight.

By-and-by the tug-boat reached us, and my husband realized his millennium by feasting his eyes on a New York paper, in his haste to obtain which he came very near falling overboard. A newspaper man to his very bones, his existing for so many years without access to that seeming necessary of life had been to me a mystery almost as great as would have been a fish living a like period without water.

"*Der teufel! sacre tonnerre! was ist? place aux dames?*"[15] exclaimed he facetiously, as his eye scanned the contents; "what changes ten years have brought about! A lady president three months in office, and yet the world goes around as usual! I rather expect to see, when we get to the city, that the people are walking on their heads; the world must be turned upside down!"

"You mean that ten years has turned the world "right side up, with care?"

"Just as you like," he replied, with a good-natured smile, "But I was never more astonished in my life."

"There must be Congresswomen, then," I said, as a feeling of wholesome pride was born into my soul; women were something after all. How distinctly I remember the feeling of importance that leaped into existence within me, and that remains with me at this moment, though I now know that it was only a dream.

Then my husband handed me the paper. "Read for yourself," he said, "nearly one half of the United States Senate, and fully, one half of the House, are women." Then he laughed, rubbed his hands, stood on his feet, lifted his hat and said to me, as he bowed profoundly, "I salute you, dear madame, in deference to the glorious achievement of woman. May she never descend from the height to [*sic*] which she has attained!"

"I thank you," I replied, "in the name of every woman. Oh, I no more want to be a man, but rejoice that I am a woman."

"Hurrah for our side of the house," replied my merry husband. Then he looked around, saying, "How I wish that tug-boat would hurry up; no more ten years spent in—confound it! what IS the name of that place? Strange that I can't recollect, when I was always so ready with names and locations. Is my brain softening, or what *can* be the trouble? Well, no matter what it is, we will live henceforth in the United States, and die there too, when it comes to that. "Better fifty years of Europe than a cycle of Cathay." We reach here just in time to enjoy the woman government and observe its constituent parts."

All in my dream was very consistent until we landed on the wharf, and then, like the crazyness of dreams, no surprise was expressed or felt on finding it suddenly midnight, and myself and husband just afterward walking up Broadway as leisurely as if it had been a pleasant afternoon in October.

By-and-by we looked up and saw a number of men approaching; they filled the sidewalk, so we stepped aside under a lamp and saw them pass. All were evidently in charge of policemen; several were handcuffed and acting like madmen. More, and yet more, passed us, so that we could hardly walk a block without being compelled to step aside, which we always did near a lamp post.

"What does this mean?" I asked my husband.

"It means, I suppose, woman's government."

"Oh, stop your nonsense," I replied, laughing; adding, "I believe the inmates of some lunatic asylum are being removed, perhaps to another asylum."

All this time we were scanning the faces of the gentlemen (for they were all gentlemen) as they passed under the gaslight. Then my husband recognized several whom he had formerly known, one of whom, Mr.—— was a senator when we left, ten years previously. I almost gave his name, but that won't do. There were two reverend gentlemen, but I must be still more circumspect in regard to names, because, in case of an action for slander, their congregations could fee so many lawyers, that I should certainly get the worst of it; besides which, I should lose the good opinion of the religious press, which to me is very dear! Besides, I might even be suspected of heterodoxy, which would be terrible!!

But, *revenons à nos moutons,*[16] even if they are black sheep, with possibly a sprinkling of goats. It was a strange scene, for all classes of men appeared to be represented. Not only the lowest, or those on whose countenances the mark of the beast was distinctly imprinted, but also the respectable, the religious, and even the intellectual and cultivated. Men were there with fine countenances, and with heads the phrenologists would have declared those of statesmen and philosophers. Why were such men accompanied by policemen? Why these wholesale arrests?

All at once I exclaimed, "Oh, dear! see! a policeman has him handcuffed; save, save him, husband!" I did not, however, wait for my husband to do anything, but rushed into the crowd. "There is some mistake," I exclaimed: "O, dear, dear Elder Stiggins!" taking his hand in my own; but the crown pushed on, and with difficulty did I make my escape.

Then my dream, without any connecting link, landed me in a comfortable room in a large hotel. On a table near my husband was a large collection of newspapers, evidently a file extending back some years. He was greedily devouring them, scanning one after another, and then throwing them on the floor to make way for their successors. By-and-by he began to laugh—how he did laugh!

"What is the matter?" I asked; "tell me, what is it?"

"Excellent! good! first rate! happy thought!"

"Well, tell me! what is it?" Then he tried to smooth his face and answer:

"Why, it appears that one of the first acts of both Houses of Congress, after the inauguration of President—was to pass a law providing that henceforth, in the District of Columbia, no woman prostitute should be arrested, fined, imprisoned, sent to Magdalen asylums[17] for reformation(?) or otherwise molested, but that all laws punishing prostitution in women should, from and after the passage of the Act, be enforced against their male companions. A similar law was soon afterward passed in the State of New York. The Washington authorities, however, regarded it only as a huge joke intended by Congressmen for electioneering effect among their lady constituents. I have not yet reached any information as to its enforcement in this State."

Then he again vigorously betook himself to a fresh instalment [*sic*] of newspapers, and having ground up a dozen or so in his mental mill, fastened on another. "They intend the law to go into effect here," he remarked. "Three large houses for the reformation of prostitute men are being built." As he said this he handed me the newspaper, and pointed out the heading:

THREE LARGE HOUSES BEING BUILT FOR THE
REFORMATION OF PROSTITUTE MEN!!
MALE MAGDALENS!!!

"We laugh, my dear," I said, "because it is novel; but there is justice and wisdom in the law."

"Yes," he replied, "that is obvious; but why do they not execute the law? I observe that other papers characterize the article in question as purely sensational, and utterly without foundation, in fact."

"I see it all; I know it all now," I exclaimed; for, as a flash of lightning, did the whole dawn on my understanding. The law had been put in force that night, and we had seen some of the victims. Instantly my spirit was *en rapport* [Fr.: in agreement] with the whole machinery and its operation. The mayor of the city of New York was a lady; the Common Council was largely composed of ladies; the Board of Aldermen was no more, for it was Alder*women* now; and in the city detective service the ability of women to *keep* secrets as well as to find them out had been extensively tested. This first descent had been planned for some days, but even the press had been kept ignorant of the proposed measure, with the exception above mentioned. To-night the police had pounced on the *sinners* and not, as of yore, the sinned *against*—and the surprise was complete. What a simpleton I had been to rush to the police when I saw Mr. Stiggins in their custody, I thought; but, then, why be ashamed of a good impulse?

From police station to police station, all over the city, I seemed to go without the fatigue usually attendant on locomotion. What sights I beheld, and what sounds I heard! Coaxing and bribery of policemen were attempted without result; cursing, swearing and threatening were equally futile. The law enacted that the name of every man thus taken should be advertised in the newspapers of the town, city or county in which the arrests should be made; also, that a large black-board should be hung daily on the outside of every police station, whereon should be conspicuously recorded the names of the culprits brought to such station. This, I saw, was the lash that cut them, in anticipation of which the majority whined like whipped curs.

One stout, handsome gentleman with his hands in his pockets, and looking up from a sort of brown study, seemingly of the floor or of his book, but really of his situation said: "Well gentlemen, we are finely sold; it is an unpleasant piece of business; d----d smart; women's wits have outwitted us, every one; that paper was right, if the others did call it sensational: WOODHULL & CLAFLIN'S WEEKLY was right; it took women to keep it quiet and women to find it out—diamond cut diamond. I wonder how many and who of us will be sent to those houses for the reformation of prostitute men?"

The majority of his hearers laughed, but were nevertheless greatly perplexed and annoyed. "Just think," he continued, "of our names being in every paper to-morrow morning! Oh ye gods and little fishes! Our wives, our lady loves, our families! Think, gentlemen, of the long list of names that will tomorrow ornament every police station! Show yourselves appreciative of the loving kindness of the corporation in supplying us with so large an amount of gratuitous advertising! Perhaps for a trifling fee they would also allow us to exhibit our business cards on the black-board, in juxtaposition with our respective names. We are in for it gentlemen, and no mistake, and seeing we *must* advertise, willy nilly, let us get all we can for the money; we can, after all, make this thing pay if we work it right."

"Confound the women!" exclaimed an old grey-headed gentlemen who was standing on the right hand of the speaker; "we might have known how it would be if ever the women got the law into their own hands."

"I beg the gentlemen's pardon," said a third gentleman, "but I don't see how we could have known that women would have turned the tables on us so nicely; but I suppose it is all right; we have got free so far, while the poor women were made to suffer all the shame and disgrace; to-night we have chanced to see how *we* like it."

"That is so with a vengeance," said another. "Yes, we are caught in a fine trap," exclaimed a fifth.

In one station-house seventeen gentlemen had just arrived, one of whom was bitterly denouncing petticoat government. "We were fools ever to give the wretches any power; finely are we paid off for our chivalry!"

"It seems to me," said a young fellow on whose face was a reckless, don't-care expression, "that to-night against our wills, we were made to *act* a little of our chivalry." Some laughed aloud, but more imprecated interiorly. Then the voice I first heard of the seventeen resumed: "Here we are tonight, looking like a set of whipped curs. Oh, the cunning, crafty women! I tell you, gentlemen, a woman in craft equals the old gentlemen below with horns and hoofs. See how astutely they have worked the machine—the law a dead letter until to-day, as we confidingly trusted that it would so remain; then, as in a steel trap, we are secured in its iron grasp. Oh, nothing can equal a woman! Serves us right, gentlemen, for giving them power."

Some cursed and swore for very madness, while others said they did not care, as their names were of no consequence. "But," remarked another, "perhaps the houses for the reformation of male prostitutes may be of consequence," shrugging his shoulders suggestively.

Then again in my dream there was a chasm of time not bridged over, either by events or memory. It was morning—early morning—and the newsboys were calling out, "The Prostitute Act enforced! one thousand arrests!" They reaped, as might well be supposed, a most liberal harvest. What crowds gathered around the police station to read the names! There came to me at that moment not only the power to float from house to house, from building to building, but a sort of omnipresence that enabled me to see the whole effect of the late movement, and what, in that respect, was being said and done in every part of the city.

At one station I was amused to hear a man with a deep, strong voice calling out the names as he read them from the blackboard for the edification of the crowd. Occasionally a name was greeted with a general laugh or exclamation of surprise; while, as I passed through the crowd, I heard—or, shall I say *saw!*—exclamations unuttered, such as, "Is it possible?" "*That* name!" "Astonishing!" "Surprising!" etc., etc. Around the newspaper offices were such large crowds that to keep order the policemen placed them in a double file. Those in the rear or outside would frequently offer large prices for the place of some one in front, so as to make sure of the coveted intelligence and avoid delay, the presses being quite unable to keep pace with the unusual demand. All were eager to see the names of the suddenly famous one thousand, and the telegraph operators had been busy ever since two in the morning transmitting names and other particulars of the enforcement of the law.

I beheld, too, the astonishment of heads of families when the morning paper was looked over, and headings like these met the eye:

THE PROSTITUTE ACT ENFORCED!
over one thousand arrests!
Preachers and Publicans, Pharisees and Pugilists,
DIVES AND LAZARUS,
All in a heap!!!
Saints and Sinners, Senators and Slop-Sellers!!!!

————

"Black spirits and white, blue spirits and gray,[18]
Mingle, mingle, mingle, ye that mingle may!"
And now there's the devil to pay!!

————

I perceived, too, in the minds of almost everyone, men as well as women, the *justice* of the proceeding was recognized. "It needed women to administer justice", I heard a gentleman say to his wife at the breakfast table; "the late act," he continued, "has attracted the attention of thousands of earnest and influential people to this subject who have never before seriously thought on it. These poor women were liable at any time to be pounced on by policemen, dragged to the station-house, sent to prison, or houses of reformation, perhaps heavily fined, and there was no one to help them or save them from disgrace. To avoid these arrests they were compelled to bribe the police and others, to pay very high prices for board, in order to compensate those who boarded them for the risk incurred of police descents, etc. To meet those enhanced expenses and avoid arrest, these women were compelled to prostitute themselves far more, and sink into deeper degradation. Thus the practical working of the law tended to greatly increase the evil, while its real supporters—the men—were scarcely ever molested."

"Poor things!" said the wife—oh, so tenderly! "and perhaps the majority of them were let into their life of shame because corrupt men caused their ruin in the first place."

This dream of mine includes such a long period of time, so great a variety of incident, and has already taken so much space for its narration, that I must hasten to the close. Imagination must fill up the scenes enacted in the court-rooms to which the prisoners were brought for examination and disposal. There was no sham about it—no half-way measures; the character and history of each prisoner was thoroughly investigated, and those proved to be habitually licentious were duly sent to the houses of reformation for such characters. Into these houses women's shrewdness and good sense had entered; for they were not prisons, nor were their inmates told that they were lost, degraded, sinful, polluted beings, but they were instructed in physiology—in the consequences of use and abuse of every organ of the body, on the holiness of love, and sanctification of the coming together of the sexes when legitimatized by holy and god-like motives. In my dream I visited four of those houses, which had been built and furnished at public expense. They were, in deed and in truth, *Houses of Reformation,* and their inmates were treated as diseased patients not as miserable sinners.

Then my spirit realized how much more efficient for good, in this instance, had been woman's wisdom that man's much-boasted intellect; and while thus thinking, thinking, thinking, how woman had cut the Gordian knot of the social evil—the knot which man feared even to touch—I awoke, and, to my astonishment, found it was all a dream; that we had no woman President, no woman legislators, and that the *"Social evil"* remained as heretofore, the great moral ulcer of the nineteenth century; that the very laws enacted under a pretence of suppressing it were really aggravating its worst evils, inflicting the greatest curse on man in the very act of perpetrating the greatest injustice on unfortunate and defenceless women. And I said, would that our legislators had the wisdom thus to grapple with the vexed question, or our women the power, as they had in my dream, to strike at the root of the evil by shielding the victim and enlightening the wrong doer!

Dream Number Nine

If a woman grow a cabbage and take it to the market, she sells it for just as much money as would a man had he grown the cabbage.

This I said to myself as I passed through the market yesterday and saw a woman selling cabbages. I bought one of her for fifteen cents. "Are you from the country?" I asked.

"Yes, indeed," she replied pleasantly; "I am a widow; but I have a nice garden spot where I grow my cabbages, potatoes and other things for market."

"You spade your garden, plant your seed and do all the work yourself?"

"Yes indeed."

"Have you children?"

"I have two little fellows, but they are not old enough to help me any."

"You are a farmer then, eh?"

"Not exactly," she replied, laughing; "but I have two cows; I have customers for my butter here in the city; then I have an apple orchard— only a little one. I have rented just now three acres of land near my place; so next year I will have potatoes—a good many—to sell."

"And," I said, "you sell your vegetables for just as much money as would a man?"

"Oh, yes!" she replied.

"And so you have WOMAN'S RIGHTS?"

"That is so, that is so!" she said with a laugh; "yes, yes! Woman's Rights!"

I walked away meditating; I meditated all the way home; and now I have had a dream which I believe was the result of that woman, her cabbages and my meditations thereupon. I am compelled, however, to confess that this dream which I am about to relate was not given to me in the night-time. It came to pass that when I arrived at home with my cabbage and marketing, I was so tired and sleepy that I laid down on the sofa in the parlor and went sound asleep. Yes, I have slept three hours; have just awoke, and must now make haste and write my dream before my husband comes home from the office.

I dreamed that I was flying—or rather floating—through the air. Is it not a delightful feeling? How happy it makes one feel to dream of flying! Well, it seemed to me that I was high in the air and moving rapidly. Hamlets, villages, towns and cities, also the vast expanse of field, meadow, wood, river and lake were spread out as a map to my delighted gaze. But, oh, the smoking, dirty cities! As I passed over them something drew me to descend, not that I so desired, but that the collective magnetic forces of the human beings therein immured deprived me not only of the power, but, in a great degree, of the disposition to resist. So I came near enough to the surface to view the dark alleys, the narrow streets, the dark, brick walls of houses huddled together, and I longed to fly from them and again behold the beautiful country; but I was compelled to linger in each city and visit hundreds of places of which I had heard but had never seen—every garret, cellar, workshop or workroom in which poor half-paid working women toiled. But I found very few, indeed, of such individuals. What could this mean? Then millinery stores, fancy stores and all other stores were visited but the number of women employed was really very small; and those few had not that pallid, under-paid, over-worked look usually characteristic of women in such positions.

Mystery of mysteries! I said to myself; who does all the slop-work of those great cities? Who make the shirts, drawers, etc.? Who does the tailor-work we have heard so much about women doing for a mere pittance? Then with a rapidity much greater that of flying I seemed to visit the homes and places of business of those who did that work; but lo, it was principally done by men and boys! There were women, certainly; but few—very few—compared with the number which I supposed were employed on such work. What has become of the women? I asked myself. Has the race of woman tailors died out? Are they all married, and so have husbands to provide for them? No answer came. So into hotels, jewelry stores, telegraph offices, paint shops where I knew that the advocates of woman's rights should be almost exclusively employed, I looked but found scarcely any women there. Into counting-houses, broker's offices and banks I looked; and though in these latter I found some women looking quite vigorous and contented, women were by no means in the majority.

Well, perhaps they had all gone into "law, physic and divinity!" So, after considerable search, I found a few doctors' and lawyers' offices scattered here and there; but the occupation of that class of people seemed to be gone to a considerable extent—there were not one-tenth the number I expected to find; but about half the lawyers, and three-fourths of the few doctors remaining, were women. As to the pulpit, I couldn't exactly understand it, for many of the churches had been turned into lecture rooms; others had been fitted up as unitary homes; some had become polytechnic institutions and schools of science; and many of the tall steeples were transformed into observatories for the people. In about half of the churches, however, preachers were grinding away as usual, and about one-fourth of these were women.

It rejoiced me greatly to find banks wholly conducted by women, who were also, to a large extent, proprietors of stores; and seemed not to be excluded from any occupation. Still, the majority of business people were men; it was evident that but a small proportion of women were employed in business, and that the number of persons employed in what are called the professions was so few that the disappearance of women from so many employments could not be accounted for in that way. What had become of the great surplus population of poor working-women? Was it possible that their work had been taken from them and given to the men and boys who seemed to fill their places?

Then sorrow came into my soul, and I said, "Alas, alas! it would seem that tens of thousands of women must be out of employment—must be starving—who did manage to live, if ever so poorly, by the labor of their hands; at least seventy-five or ninety percent of these women must be starving!" Then I remembered a book entitled "Apoca-tastasis," or Progress backwards. How I had laughed at the idea of progress backwards! But did not this look very much like "Apocatas-tasis?"

It would take too much space to detail all my wanderings through that and many other cities all over the Continent. It will be sufficient to state that from Maine to Texas, and from Florida to Alaska, what is now woman's usual work in cities was nearly all done by me. Had the women all become wealthy? It was evident that they had not taken all the lucra-tive employments once monopolized by men.

Then the scene changed, and I found myself walking along the side-walk of that city, like other mortals. I was pondering on what I had learned, and was feeling very sad. By-and-by I lifted my eyes which, in my gloom, had been cast on the sidewalk, and lo, in every direction, large bills met my eye, headed with the words, "Fifty years ago!" "Semi-centenarian festival!" Across the street were large banners, as we see on election days, in commemoration of some great event. On these were the same words, with appropriate emblems and devices. Flags of all sizes were hung out of the windows, and carried by little boys and girls in the streets, all having the same or similar mottoes. On one of these large banners was represented, on the left, a sickly, starving woman, sewing and shivering in a garret; beside her was a coffin containing a dead infant; the pointers of the clock indicated midnight. Under this were the words, "Fifty years ago!" On the right of the banner were represented groups of beautiful, healthy, intelligent women and children, gathering fruit and flowers in the bright sunlight. This picture was entitled "To-day."

Most of the banners and flags were graced by the faces of two noble, earnest, beautiful ladies; but no names were given and only the words "Fifty years ago!" replied to my many questions as to the meaning. The bells rang joyously, and bands of music were in almost every street, but neither drum nor cannon brought back memories of war. The beautiful and joyous and the free were manifested in every countenance. Maidens and matrons, boys and girls, gentlemen and intelligent women, all par-ticipated in this celebration. But I could not learn from any of them what was its meaning, all seemed so fully occupied with their destination.

By-and-by the street cars came along, fluttering all over with small flags, on which were these same words, "Fifty years ago!" The cars were labelled, "For the Festival!" Then rattled along the street two carriages, in which were seen the beaming faces of ladies and gentlemen, and smiling children, and flags fluttering, with the same words, "Fifty years ago!"

Slowly, patiently, with the crowd of pedestrians, I moved along in the same direction as the carriages and cars, which frequently passed me, decked out with those magic words. All at once I found myself approaching a magnificent pavilion, large enough to hold tens of thousands of people. What large and beautiful flags were unfurled to the breeze! Leaves and flowers were everywhere made to repeat, in wreaths, those predominant words, and it seemed as if the very atmosphere multiplied and repeated, in each constituent action, the words, "Fifty years ago!"

Dream Number Nine (concluded)

I entered the pavilion and beheld a sight, which, for beauty and magnificence, I never saw equalled. Never, while life may last, shall I forget this part of my dream. Verily, it was a paradise far surpassing any that Adam and Eve ever beheld. Here was gathered all the beauty belonging to the vegetable kingdom. Here fruits, flowers, spreading branches and crossing vines were woven into a thousand floral arches over our heads—formed into summer bowers, grottoes, shady walks, secluded retreats. There were miniature lakes, waterfalls, fountains, fish ponds, that surprised and delighted my eyes. Here were gathered specimens of all flowers, edible fruits, grains and vegetables grown in the United States. Ladies—only ladies—presided over all this wealth of beauty. Then I looked up and beheld in letters of living flowers and vines these words: WOMEN'S AGRICULTURAL FAIR.

I looked at the beautifully-executed design, and many times repeated to myself the words, "Women's Agricultural Fair."

"This is a most beautiful place," I remarked to an old gentleman who was leaning on his staff, looking up and about him, evidently feasting his eyes.

"Yes, grand, grand!" observed the old man.

"Will you inform me," I asked, "what is the meaning of this festival, or how it originated?"

He appeared astonished at my question, but soon showed by his countenance that he had decided me to be in earnest.

"You are a stranger, I see," he replied. "Well, this is called the 'Women's Agricultural Fair' because everything you behold here—no matter what—has been grown by women agriculturists. It is this year combined with a semi-centennial festival for the following reasons: Fifty years ago a large surplus population of poor, toiling women, crowded our cities, while the land was not one quarter cultivated, causing, on the one hand, high prices for provisions, and, on the other, low prices for labor: 'From him that hath not shall be taken away even that which he hath.' To-day that large class of women who have no family duties and no husbands to provide for them are in the country; and they are no longer poor but are saving money. Besides these unmarried women and widows there are large numbers of married women[19] in the country, many of them with families, carrying on farms, their husbands remaining in the city for a few years, in order to get money to pay for and improve their farms and furnish their homes with requisites for comfort, culture and refinement. In this way our cities are but little overstocked either by workingmen or workingwomen; for just as soon as their farms are paid for and sufficiently improved, the men, too, go to their farms and remain there."

Before us played a fountain of water in the center of a miniature lake, in the depths of which beautiful salmon sported, and on its surface water-fowl were swimming and diving. From its banks were reflected orange and fig trees, lemon trees and grape vines, all laden with fruit, and kindly shading the old man as he sat in a rustic chair.

"Take a seat," he said, pointing to one near him; "take a seat. We may as well rest while we talk." How at this moment I recall that spot! What beauty, what wide-spreading branches, what luscious fruit hung all about us!

"Now," said the old man, as he rested his two hands on his stick, "let me tell you how all this has come to pass."

"I would like it, if you please."

"Fifty years ago to-day the first Womans' [sic] Agricultural Convention was held. The call was made by two brave, beautiful women, who had made a business of Agriculture for ten years. There are their portraits," he said, as he pointed with his stick through an avenue of trees; "by-and-by you can go and take a near view; they will bear close criticism; one of them has passed to the farther shore, but the other is still in the physical body. Ah, you ought to see her! She is very old, but beautiful, so beautiful! She seems to have absorbed into herself the essence of the fruits and flowers and natural beauties which she so devotedly loves. Her eyes are blue and her face beams with goodness and intelligence. She can make a speech as well as ever, though she is now eighty-seven years of age. Well, these two ladies, as I said, had made agriculture a business for ten years. Having tested the matter to their own satisfaction, they resolved to urge others, particularly women, to adopt the same business. Every winter both of them left their farms, for a month or two, to lecture on *Agriculture* FOR WOMAN. Thus others joined them, and in a few years numbers of women had secured land for themselves and had engaged in its culture to great advantage.

"To make a long story short, it came to pass that just fifty years ago to-day the first *Womans'* [*sic*] *Agricultural Convention* was held. I was there. The best hall in the city was secured, and there was a large attendance. Many women were on the platform who owned their farms and houses, and they really made some excellent speeches, abounding with eloquence and logic; for they were both experienced and earnest in their plans for redeeming woman from poverty and privation.

"How well I remember some of the ideas advanced on one of them. 'We tillers of the soil,' she said, 'have discovered the great royal road to wealth—wealth and independence for woman. On this platform are thirty-five ladies who have demonstrated in their own lives that agriculture is woman's work just as much as it is man's work. Those ladies own farms and houses, cows and horses, of their own;' then, turning round, 'and I believe every one of you has money in the bank. You are healthy, you are happy; and this has been done not in your miserable cities, not in garrets, not for cheating slop-shops, but each person in independence.' How she did urge poor workingwomen to go into the country if they only had just enough to take them there! 'Farming,' she continued, 'with the machinery now at command, is far easier and lighter than it was when we were children, and it is only habit and tradition that causes it to be regarded as requiring great muscular power. In general, it is much easier work, and far less exhaustive, than cooking, washing, ironing or sewing, especially in view of the accompaniments of fresh air and abundant food, in the one case, contrasted with foul air and semi-starvation in the other. At any rate, if it is not easier, we can do it, as it pays better and fills our pockets; and money is a great stimulant, as well as country air, beautiful scenery, fruits, flowers and singing birds.'

"I really believe I could remember most of her speech. However, she concluded by informing the audience that she had purchased a large tract of land, on which she could immediately employ twenty-five women, and hoped that number would volunteer to go, as she would pay them more wages than they could earn at any sort of sewing until they could purchase some of her land themselves, after which she would rent to them, at a low price, various farming machinery, so that they could work to the utmost advantage. Fifty-seven volunteered at once; twenty-five were selected, all of whom succeeded—a wonderful success, I think. The callers of the Convention were so encouraged that more were held in various parts of the country, and the movement rapidly grew into a power, and its adherents were numbered by hundreds of thousands. All did not go into heavy farming; many concentrated on grain culture, as machinery enabled them to perform most of the labor with ease; many made a specialty of fruit; some of poultry, and others grew rapidly rich by pisciculture. Some settled in Southern California, cultivating oranges, lemons, nuts, grapes, peaches, etc., or raising silk-worms, while other profitably raised berries in the immediate vicinity of large cities. Finely they were caricatured by reckless, half-starved, half-intoxicated 'Bohemians' always ready to sell their birthright of brains for a very small mess of pottage, and too lazy to work at any useful calling! Editorial wiseacres wrote labored articles to prove the utter futility and demoralizing tendency of any attempt by women to live by cultivating the soil. The popular lecturer said that a woman might as well attempt to keep a livery stable or a bowling alley, or pre-empt 160 acres of land in the moon, as to try to carry on farming; that, by at-tempting it, women would become rough, uncouth and masculine, and no man, who loved refinement and delicacy in woman, would ever marry such, etc, etc, etc.

"I have two sisters who were left widows when quite young; both with children. After the deaths of their husbands they came home to father's house. One had a little over a thousand and the other but three or four hundred dollars. After many long talks as to what was best to be done (for it was really a serious question with so many children), they finally purchased for a thousand dollars ten acres of land, on which was a small house; they planted trees, or rather paid a man to plant their fruit trees, and then went to work to raise vegetables for the city market. Their children became, every year, more and more useful. In ten years their success was complete; they had a fine orchard of choice fruit, a comfortable house and commodious family carriage; their boys are grown, and all of them farmers. My sisters taught the girls the impor-tance of being self-sustaining, paid them for all work done by them in the garden or orchard, and at twenty each girl owned a piece of land. One of them, however, is now in the city with her husband, and to-gether they carry on a large mercantile business. But," he remarked, "I am afraid I shall tire you; old age, it is said, tends to induce garrulity."

"Not at all; I am glad to hear you," I replied.

"Oh, it amuses me," he continued, "to see how the women have stolen a march on the men. Yes, yes, they have outwitted them. You see we have a numerous race of dandies and would-be do-nothings who prefer a good fit, morocco shoes, gloved hands, sidewalks and high brick houses to anything else in the world. This race of men had fashionable mothers and equally silly fathers as thousands of children have to-day, who are taught by their fathers and mothers that the proceeding requisites are indispensable to respectability."

"Yes," I rejoined, "and I am thinking of the little boys of whom mothers are saying to-day, 'Willie or Johnny is going to be a lawyer, a doctor, a preacher or a fine gentleman, or he is going into business' (meaning the business of trying all the time to outwit somebody else, and persuade somebody to put money in his pocket without an equivalent)."

"Yes," replied the old man, "and thus the supply of would-be do nothings exceeds the demand, and hence the surplus of empty-headed, little-brained dandies afraid of any business that would bring them within the class of mechanics. These, by the pressure of want, are necessitated to fill the places once filled, but now vacated, by the very women who are now far removed from cities, from poverty and from toil, with the birds, the flowers, the tree and the beautiful of which they are a part; and those shams of men fill their places in garrets and cellars."

"Nature has taken her children to her home and heart," I remarked.

"Just so, my friend," he replied; "birds, flowers, hills, rivers, mountains, running brooks and women should never be separated. There is," he continued, "a feature of this Agriculture for women that I should mention; it is this: You probably know that in all our large cities we had a superabundance of honest mechanics. These, having seen what women could do in the country, concluded to try what *men* could do. The experiment succeeded to that extent that the only surplus population in our large cities to-day are the miserable weaklings I have before mentioned as having fashionable mothers, who have little ability and less disposition to perform useful labor."

Then I thought in my dream that I arose to leave, and, shaking hands with the old man, thanked him for the pleasure his conversation had afforded; then directed my steps to the portraits of the two noble women who were the first to originate any extensive movement for placing women on the land. My whole being throbbed with happiness as I walked through the long avenue of trees, fruits and flowers and noted the hundreds of healthy, happy women who presided over the specimens of their own culture. Verily, woman has worked out her own salvation! I said to myself; the good time coming has surely come; woman has planted herself on the soil. She has health, she has wealth, and with these she has power. Self-salvation—this is the rock on which she has built; and not all the powers of hell shall prevail against it.

Then I found myself in front of the two portraits which the old gentleman had pointed out to me. While admiring them he came and introduced me to the surviving original—a dear old lady, whose hand I grasped with feelings akin to devotion. With her hand yet grasped in mine I awoke. A dream! I said in astonishment; but may not this dream, after all, be a prophecy?

2

"A Dream Within a Dream"
1874

ELIZABETH STUART PHELPS [Ward]
(1844–1911)

Author of some fifty-six books, Elizabeth Stuart Phelps grew up and lived in the Greater Boston region. She was educated in Andover, the daughter of popular author Elizabeth Stuart Phelps, and Andover Theological Seminary President Austin Phelps. Her mother died only three years into a writing career when daughter Elizabeth was eight. Christened "Mary Gray" after a maternal friend, the daughter assumed her mother's name, and apparently her career, too. An early regional writer, the mother Phelps had depicted women's domestic constraints in The Sunny Side *(1851) and* A Peep at "Number Five" *(1853). From these and from her mother's overburdened life, the daughter early gained an awareness of women's wrongs and rights. She commented upon them more outspokenly than had her mother. Her pen was her pulpit. She established herself as both a popular and a serious writer in 1868.* The Gates Ajar *gained her widespread popular acclaim for its message—consolatory to post–Civil War bereaved women—that they could believe in a utopian heaven. An* Atlantic Monthly *story "The Tenth of January"—inspired by Rebecca Harding Davis's* Life in the Iron Mills *(1861), an exposé of industrialists' unconcern for workers' needs—received critical approval from Thomas Wentworth Higginson and John Greenleaf Whittier.*

Thus established, Phelps continued to write "for truth's sake." Hedged In (1870) criticized a double sexual standard while A Silent Partner *(1871) faulted a double occupational standard. Also in 1871 a series of essays on a range of women's issues appeared first in* The Independent *and then in* The Woman's Journal: *one of these is an exposé of "that dummy 'the true woman.' " After a period of ill health, from which Phelps was never free, she published her masterwork* The Story of Avis *(1877), a revelation of a woman's artistic talent being drained by the necessities of daily living.* Old Maids and Burglars in Paradise *(1879, 1886) in comic vein shows women vacationing in a summer cottage named "Paradise" without much use for "male protection."* Friends: A Duet *(1881) stresses the impossibility of friendship between the sexes: passion inevitably takes over.* Doctor Zay *(1882) demonstrates a woman capably pursuing the typically male vocation of medicine.* Beyond the Gates (1883) *depicts a heavenly utopia where women receive compensation for earth's deficits, whether in education, health, or affection, and where a father keeps house awaiting his family.* The Gates Between *(1887) develops a different facet of heaven: a father must learn to care for his son. This book was offered as a subscription premium by* The Woman's Journal. *In 1888 she married Herbert Dickinson Ward, a man seventeen years younger. After this she continued to write, but the only substantial work to emerge was* A Singular Life *(1895), a novel showing a man killed for his attempt to live according to a Social Gospel.*

Phelps' utopian writing thus occurred within a lifetime of writing to raise awareness of women's needs. Although she lived most of her adulthood outside of marriage, she never gave up her hope that woman and man could live equitably together. In the meanwhile she found solid friendship with women. Her "Gates" books, read in isolation, might appear mere consolation for lost lives, but rather they depict as heaven a utopian world in which women no longer exist in want. So popular were these books that as late as 1916 Edith Wharton in "The Bunner Sisters" includes a "Gates Ajar" funeral wreath, which her characters admire. The popularity of the "Gates" books makes a provocative statement concerning the malaise in women's lives. Both the 1883 and 1887 books suggest death as escape from desolation:

> To be dead was to be dead to fear. To be dead was to be alive to a sense of assured good chance that nothing in the universe could shake (1883, 72).

> ". . . They call this death. Why, I never knew what it was to be *alive* before!" (1887, 152)

Phelps's "Gates" books stress her hope, couched in nineteenth-century religious language, for a future better relation between the sexes and in 1883, for mutually beneficial relations between women of different social classes: a working woman in heaven helps her former benefactress. For her audience, heavenly utopias served much as science fiction utopias do for us today—as imaginative transcendence of contemporary dystopia. The essay reprinted offers one of several utopian suggestions for improving the institution of marriage.

References: Ann Douglas, *The Feminization of American Culture* (New York: Knopf, 1977) and "Heaven Our Home: Consolation Literature in the Northern United States, 1830–1880," *American Quarterly* 26 (1974): 496–515; James D. Hart, *The Popular Book* (New York: Oxford Univ. Press, 1950), chap. 7; Carol Farley Kessler, *Elizabeth Stuart Phelps* (Boston: G. K. Hall, 1982) and "The Heavenly Utopia of Elizabeth Stuart Phelps" in *Women and Utopia,* ed. Marleen Barr and Nicholas Smith (Lanham, Md.: Univ. Press of America, 1983); Helen Sootin Smith, Introduction to *The Gates Ajar* (Cambridge, Mass.: Harvard Univ. Press, 1964); Elmer F. Suderman, "Elizabeth Stuart Phelps and *The Gates Ajar* Novels," *Journal of Popular Culture* 3 (1969): 91–105; Barbara Welter, "Defenders of the Faith" in *Dimity Convictions* (Athens: Ohio Univ. Press, 1976), 111–20.

Text: Elizabeth Stuart Phelps [Ward], "A Dream Within a Dream," *The Independent* 26, no. 1316 (19 Feb. 1874): 1.

It is a little singular to reflect upon that there should not be in existence a fully appropriate marriage service for the uses of either the church or the world.

The Episcopal service—that most hallowed by churchly associations and most full of excellences—has yet egregious faults. Bad taste, bad grammar, and perjury may have their places; but a marriage service would not seem to be the place for them.

"I take thee *to* my wedded wife [or husband—author's note] . . . to have and to hold" is an awkwardness for which only long-inculcated reverence could feel so much rhetorical respect as not to mar a matrimonial ecstasy. "Till Death us do part" is a dislocation in which the most devout Churchwoman must feel a pang. The inquiry "Who *giveth* this woman to be married to this man?" is, to say the least of it, an anachronism. "I pronounce you *man* and *wife*" flavors somewhat of the tenement-house patois, as of a couple henceforth to say, "My man is abroad to-day," or "My woman is getting dinner."

"With all my worldly goods I thee endow" is a fiction so stupendous as to be more amusing than impressive.

"Do you promise to obey him and serve him? The woman shall say, I will." Herein we have the spectacle of a priest at the altar offering the most solemn and binding of vows to a woman who has not the least intention of keeping it; who will not keep it, if she has; and who ought not to keep it, whether she has or not.

The Church service was written in a bygone age, for a bygone type of society. Its real beauties cannot save it intact to the future. The Marriage To-be will demand a pledge for which this is neither speech nor language.

Outside of the apostolic succession we fare scarcely better. Most of the forms of marriage ceremony current among our pastors are mere abridgments and modifications of the old Church service. One of great beauty has, indeed, been written and circulated in private ministerial circles, with much acceptance. But even this, inimitable as a literary master-piece, must something fail of reaching the temper in which many men and women nowadays find themselves moved, to exchange the marriage vows. Nor does the short, slippery formula of the civil justice help the matter much.

Musing thus, the other evening, Mr. Editor, I fell into a dream.

Epictetus[1] advised his students never to tell their dreams. As a general thing, nothing could induce me to depart from the advice of Epictetus; but I am convinced that Epictetus himself, had he been a contributor to the columns of THE INDEPENDENT,[2] and had he dreamed the dream, would have straightway converted it into "copy" and sent it INDEPENDENT-ward by the earliest possible post.

For I dreamed that behold! I was invited to succeed the Rev. Mr. Murray as pastor of Park-street church;[3] and that, having accepted the call, upon conditions not to the purpose to specify; and that, having been duly (I doubled the l in that word; but discovered the superfluity just in time)—duly ordained, settled, discussed, made in every respect as self-conscious and wretched as it is quite proper to make a somewhat bashful new pastor in a perfectly self-possessed old church; having delivered my inaugural, and received my first pair of working slippers, and declined my first donation party, and denied my first ten or fifteen enlargements, and quite become used to selecting housekeepers and conducting funerals, it fell to my lot, on a New Year's Eve, to marry my first couple.

Now, fifteen engagements is a small matter, and it is pure enjoyment to murder a donation party, and funerals and housekeepers have no effect upon my peace of mind, and it has been the one ungratified wish of my life that a young lady should work me a pair of slippers; but when it came to the wedding, I saw in my dream that my heart within me was troubled, for I doubted of the manner of the language in which I should perform this most difficult and delicate of duties satisfactorily to the young people and honorably to myself and my profession.

But I saw in my dream, and behold when the youth and the maiden came before me, there were given unto me the words which I should speak, and that I married them according to the meaning of the words.

When I awoke, all particulars of that wedding had vanished from me. Whether there were cake and cards I know not; what the bride wore I cannot say; if there were bridesmaids or favors ask me not; but the words which I spoke remained unto me.

So, while they were yet fresh in my remembrance, I transcribed them, and, if you will have them, Mr. Editor, here they are. I will not stipulate that they shall be immediately adopted as the marriage formula of the Orthodox Congregational Church. I am only inclined to claim (on the privilege of the dreamer) that they will be found not without interest as a psychological study to a certain class of minds.

MARRIAGE SERVICE

Which beginneth with the words "Let us pray."

(At the close of a brief prayer the minister shall say):

"In the presence of God and of these witnesses, we are now come to solemnize the covenant of this man and woman in marriage. Are you, Charles True, prepared, of your own free will's inclining and whole heart's desire, to take upon yourself the vows which shall make and keep you the husband of this woman as long as Death shall spare you one to the other?"

(He shall say): "I am."

"Are you, Charlotte Tender, prepared, of your own free will's inclining and whole heart's desire, to take upon yourself the vows which shall make and keep you the wife of this man as long as Death shall spare you one to the other?"

(She shall say): "I am."

"Is there to your inmost consciousness any hidden reason why you should not charge your lips with the utterances of these vows? Does the voice of your secret soul cry to you—by any reproach of memory, by any uncertainty of hope—to forbid these banns? If there be such a reason, if there be such a voice, in the presence of God and of these witnesses, regard it, before it be too late."

(Both): "There is none such."

(Unto the man he shall say): "If you feel within your honest heart that any other woman ought to hold—or, in the sweet mood of your affection, that any other could hold—the place which this woman occupies to-day, for your soul's sake and for her soul's sake, acknowledge it before it be too late."

(Unto the woman he shall say): "If you feel within your honest heart that any other man ought to hold—or, in the sweet mood of your affections, that any other could hold—the place which this man occupies to-day, for your soul's sake and for his soul's sake, acknowledge it before it be too late."

(Receiving no responses, the minister shall proceed):

"Then reverently do I offer you and loyally may you take upon yourselves the covenant of true marriage.

"Do you, Charles True, take this woman whose hand you hold to be your lawfully wedded wife?"

(He shall say): "I do."

"Do you, Charlotte Tender, take this man whose hand you hold to be your lawfully wedded husband?"

(She shall say): "I do."

"You promise to cleave onto each other in sickness and in health, in prosperity and in adversity, through trial and triumph, in temptation, peril, joy, sorrow, through life, unto death. You promise to be faithful each to the other in deed, word, and truth. You promise to be considerate each of the other's happiness, above all other earthly claims. You promise to assist each other in your mutual and individual life's work, rendering each to each such tender thoughtfulness and such large estimate of the other's nature that neither shall absorb in petty exactions or in selfish blindness the other's subject life. You recognize it to be the duty of every man and of every woman to live a life of individual service to an individual God, and you hold it to be the especial aim of marriage to assist men and women in the pursuance of such a service by a union which brings mutual responsibility, mutual forbearance, and mutual comfort, to replace solitary labors and lonely failures and unshared successes. You, therefore, promise to regard each the other's preference in all your plans of life, and to consider any claim of one to legislate for the other, as foreign to the spirit of a righteous marriage and to the letter of your vows. You believe that the sweet restraints and large liberty of mutual love shall serve you in the settlement of all difference of opinion, and that your happiness will be increased by your recognition each of the other's freedom of personal judgment and action. You promise to reverence in each other all that is essentially different in your natures, and to meet generously upon all that is common, and to elevate, each for the other and each in the other, your ideals of manhood, of woman-hood and of marriage. Do you thus believe and promise?"

(Both shall say): "I do."

"Then do I pronounce you to be husband and wife. The great neces-sity of love is laid upon you. Love is no longer its own, but another's. You are not any more your own, but each other's. You have set your-selves to learn the longest lesson of human experience. You have entered upon a condition of the highest duties, as well as of the deepest joys. As earnestly as you have come to it may it come to you. As solemnly as you have chosen each other may God's blessing choose out you. Even as tenderly as you are drawn to each other may his heart be drawn onto you. As sacredly as you cherish each other may his protection cherish you.

" 'Love,' we read, 'is stronger than Death.' Of whatever there shall be in human love which outlives human life, may the love of this man and woman be found worthy to partake!"

"For all that the love of man and woman may mean, in a world where they neither marry nor are given in marriage, God grant that this earthly marriage may fit these two Heaven-born souls!

"Amen."

3

Papa's Own Girl
1874

MARIE [STEVENS CASE] HOWLAND
1836–1921

*B*orn *in Lebanon, New Hampshire, Marie Stevens moved in her teens to Lowell, Massachusetts, where she became a millworker to support younger twin sisters after her father's death. From living in Lowell boarding houses, she learned both independence and cooperation. In 1857, she became a New York City school principal and in the same year married radical lawyer Lyman W. Case. They had met at The Club, a meeting place for feminists, anarchists, free-love advocates, and other social reformers. In the early 1860s with Lyman's approval, Marie Case and Edward Howland (b. 1832) traveled to Guise, France, probably residing for the year 1864 at the Familistère, or Social Palace, constructed from 1859 to 1888 by Jean-Baptiste André Godin (1817–1888). Influenced by Owen, Saint-Simon, Cabet, and Fourier, Godin established a cooperative community. As a financial basis, he set up an ironworks that manufactured stoves. Resident workers enjoyed the educational and health facilities, residences and shops provided. (Later in 1886 Marie would publish her translation of Godin's writings as* Social Solutions.*) Both Marie and Edward reported their impressions to the United States press; they returned as a married couple. During the late 1870s, the Howlands bought a farm, Casa Tonti, in Hammonton, New Jersey, where they helped establish the Grange. Also at this time, they were part of a group writing for* [Victoria] Woodhull *and* [Tennessee] Claflin's Weekly, *a periodical advocating in addition to women's rights, such heretical subjects as spiritualism and sexual freedom for women and men. This* *free-love group became Section 12 of the International Workingmen's Association (IWA). But in July 1872, Section 12 was expelled from IWA for its overt support of women's emancipation. By the mid-1870s the Howlands were involved in developing plans for Pacific City (1886–1894), a cooperative community also called the Credit Foncier Colony, in Topolobampo, Mexico, where Marie lived from 1888 until 1893: Edward died in 1890. She likely wrote a substantial portion of* Integral Co-operation *(1885), an explanation of the principles guiding the Topolobampo colony, published over the name of Albert Kimsey Owen (1848–1916), the colony's chief promoter. Inspired by Fourier, Godin, and the Familistère, Howland designed quarters reforming domestic work through cooperation—domestic reform advocated as well by Charlotte Perkins Gilman, whom Howland influenced (though Gilman advocated reforming domestic work by removing it from the home and creating business services). Howland's ideal designs were never to materialize. About 1893, before the colony failed, she moved to the Fairhope Single Tax Colony (1894–1954) in Alabama, where she worked as its librarian until her death.*

Howland's visit to Godin's Familistère inspired her novel Papa's Own Girl, *which appeared in France in 1880 as* La Fille de Son Père. *Her living and her writing made a continuous whole:* Papa's Own Girl *accurately reflects the range of her concerns—from individual autonomy to community responsibility for the general welfare. Her communitarian romance reveals her admiration for Godin's Familistère, her concern for the whole of workers' lives, her advocacy of one standard to govern relations between the sexes, and her dedication to women's rights, revealed as the convictions of men and the practice of women.*

The novel takes its title Papa's Own Girl *from the signature Clara Forest uses on letters written from Stonybrook College to her father Dr. Forest, a physician in L—, Massachusetts. He is one of two male characters advocating women's rights. He educates his daughter; takes into his household young Susie Dykes, pregnant from his son's heartless folly; finances Susie's florist business (Mary Griffith, author of "Three Hundred Years' Hence" [1836], was a member of two horticultural societies); and welcomes home a daughter who divorces her philandering husband, Dr. Albert Delano. (Delano's sister Charlotte becomes a good friend of Clara.) The second spokesperson for Howland's views is Count von Frauenstein ("Ladies' Rock" in German), a wealthy advocate of social experimentation. He also invests in the florist business, adopts in order to educate Susie's daughter Minnie (called "Min"), and in his person provides a spouse worthy for Clara—although in so doing he removes her need to be economically independent, a condition he has claimed essential to women's happiness. They join their lives with a simple marriage contract—after the example of Godin (Gage, 172)—and rejoice in the birth of a son, as the Social Palace, which he has financed and where she works to right social wrongs, provides a new community, an experiment in cooperative living, equitable to both sexes.*

Chapters reprinted illustrate Howland's dual stress upon women's rights and social reform. They reveal how destructive for women and how hypocritical typical heterosexual and marital relationships can be. The plans for a Social Palace suggest how changed community arrangements might facilitate less confining and more authentic living.

Note that the amelioration of marriage occurs only when the whole social system becomes equitable for women, that woman living with woman is a strongly approved alternative. Susie and Clara are crucial to each other's well-being—emotionally and financially. Howland does bow to the conventional "happy" ending of marriage, but with the requirement that to woman belongs her own body and labor. The novel, as is so often the case in feminist fiction of the period, ends with only the promise, and not the practice, of marital well-being. The depicted happiness for women in Papa's Own Girl *occurs in the business and household run by Mmes Susie and Clara, an example of the "female world of love and ritual," documented by Carroll Smith-Rosenberg* (Disorderly Conduct: Visions of Gender in Victorian America, *1985). Adrienne Rich's concept of a sexual continuum extending between hetero- and homosexual limits, explained in "Compulsory Heterosexuality and Lesbian Existence" (1980) is suggestive* (Blood, Bread, and Poetry: Selected Prose 1979–1985).

References: Robert S. Fogarty, Introduction to *The Familistère* (Philadelphia: Porcupine Press, 1975); Matilda Joslyn Gage, *Woman, Church & State* (1893; reprint, Watertown, Mass.: Persephone, 1980); Paul M. Gaston, *Women of Fairhope* (Athens: Univ. of Georgia Press, 1984), chap. 2 ("The Odyssey of Marie Howland"); Jean-Baptiste André Godin, *Social Solutions,* trans. Marie Howland (New York: John W. Lovell, 1886); Dolores Hayden, *The Grand Domestic Revolution* (Cambridge, Mass.: MIT Press, 1981), chap. 5; Vicki Lynn Hill, "Marie Howland," in *American Women Writers,* ed. Lina Mainero (New York: Ungar, 1980), 2:345–47; Carol Farley Kessler, "The Grand Marital Revolution: Two Feminist Utopias (1874, 1919)," in *Feminism, Utopia, and Narrative,* ed. Sarah Webster Goodwin and Libby Jones (Knoxville: Univ. of Tennessee Press, 1990; Albert Kimsey Owen, *Integral Co-operation: Its Practical Application* (New York: Lovell, 1885); Barbara Quissell, "The New World That Eve Made," in *America as Utopia,* ed. Kenneth M. Roemer (New York: Franklin, 1981), 161–63, 173; Thomas A. Robertson, *A Southwestern Utopia* (Los Angeles: Ward Ritchie, 1964).

Text: Marie [Stevens Case] Howland, *Papa's Own Girl: A Novel* (New York: Jewett, 1874); reprint (microfilm coll.) in *American Fiction 1851–1875,* ed. Lyle H. Wright (New Haven: Research Publications, 1971), 2, no. 1290; reprint, *The Familistère; A Novel* (Boston: Christopher, 1918); reprint, Philadelphia: Porcupine, 1975. The source is the 1874 edition, chaps. 32, 33, and 43:533–37.

Chapter 32
The Distinguished Visitor

Another year has passed—a busy and prosperous year for the firm of "Dykes & Delano, Florists." Miss Galway, the modiste, still continued to dispose of the small bouquets, and for two years, finding the supply constant and the demand certain, she had devoted one of her windows exclusively to them, furnished it with a little fountain, and given it into the hands of the little girl, her sister, who sold a part of Susie's first installment on the Common. On the promise of Miss Galway to devote the whole proceeds of this window to the education of the little girl, our florists had agreed to continue the supply two years more, though they now had their own show-room and order department in the city, conducted by Annie, now Mrs. Storrs, assisted by another woman as bookkeeper; for the firm of Dykes & Delano were "sworn," as the doctor declared, to never employ a man when a woman could be found to do the work required. The conservatory had been extended and supplied with new heating apparatus. The wedding of Annie and George had taken place as the doctor predicted, and Min had a lion's share of the wedding-cake, having munched it at intervals for a month after the event. She was now nearly five and a half years old, for it was April, and somewhat more than a year since Annie found her new and better world through the good and great heart of Dr. Forest. George had kept his promise to the doctor, to enter the lists as the champion of women, and under the influence of his reading and the society of Annie's friends, he had greatly improved. His secret ambition was to become an author; and though he continued to gain his bread as a compositor, and was expert in the art, he spent all his spare time writing or studying. Annie proved in every way a treasure to him, and had implicit faith in his success. She wrote every week to "Madame Susie," as she called her, or to Clara, giving the most careful and minute account of the progress of her wing of the business. Orders came in constantly, after the first six months; and although the firm had opened business relations with a great English nursery establishment in another part of the State, which supplied them with young shade-trees, shrubs, and ever-greens from rare foreign invoices, they could hardly supply the demand. Ten acres of Minnie's legacy from Mrs. Buzzell had been put in order as a nursery, and the propagation of shrubs and trees was progressing finely. Clara and Susie became more and more enterprising and ambitious. The taste in Oakdale and neighboring towns for lawn and park cultivation, was rapidly increasing, and the young firm looked forward to getting their supplies directly from England, instead of receiving them at second hand. One man was now constantly employed in the nursery, and other help indoors and out, when the busier part of the season demanded more hands.

One morning, as Clara was busy in the conservatory, Susie brought her the card of a gentleman who was waiting in the sitting-room.

"Frauenstein?" said Clara, looking at the card, on which was written, in pencil underneath the name, "sends his compliments to Mrs. Delano and her partner, and would esteem it a favor to be admitted into her conservatories."

"Bring him in, Susie. I cannot present myself in the drawing-room in this rig. Don't you think I shall make an impression on his countship?" she asked, glancing at her looped-up dress and bibbed apron.

"Why not? You are beautiful in any dress."

"You wicked little flatterer! Well, send in his Exalted Highness, the Count Von Frauenstein."

Before Clara had scarcely glanced at the face of the count, she was strongly impressed with the distinguished air of the man. He wore a dark-blue circular, reaching nearly to the knee, and as he stepped through the folding-doors into the broad, central passage in the conservatory, he removed a very elegant shaped hat of soft felt, and seeing Clara, bowed silently, with a simple, courtly air, seldom attained except by men of the Continent. Clara returned the salute, but remembering the European custom, did not offer him her hand.

"Madam," he said, "I have had several glimpses of your flowers from the outside, and I greatly desire to have a better view, if you will pardon my presumption."

"I am very glad to see you, sir," Clara replied "My father has often spoken of you, for he is one of your ardent admirers."

"He flatters me greatly. I am proud of his good opinion, for it is worth more than that of other men."

After passing, in a few minutes, those meaningless and unremembered preliminaries, inevitable between those meeting for the first time, and conscious of affecting each other and of being affected by a new and strange power, the count said: "To-night I hope to meet Dr. Forest at the Kendrick reception. You, madam, do not patronize the society here much, I think, or I should have had the pleasure of meeting you." Clara's perfect lips curled slightly, as she said, "No, I am nearly always at home since I returned to Oakdale."

The count had called for no other purpose than to delight his senses with the sight of flowers, of which he was excessively fond; but standing there among the magnificent array of colors, and breathing the delicious breath of jasmines and heliotropes, he saw nothing, was conscious of nothing, but the presence of a charming woman, whose every movement, every outline, was a study, from the poise of her regal head to the step of her beautiful feet. As the conversation continued, his wonder increased that there should be found in an out-of-the-way, unknown niche of the world like this Oakdale, a woman of such rare intelligence, such grace of bearing, and that clear and concise expression of thoughts, found very seldom among women, and not often among men, except a choice few. Then there was a modesty surrounding her like an atmosphere—not the modesty that is supposed to belong only to refined women, but the modesty of the philosopher, and which is as charming in men as in women, and equally rare in both. Yet she was self-poised, sure of herself, and when she raised her long, dark lashes, and flashed her splendid frank eyes upon him, he felt a diffidence in her presence, arising from his keen desire to please her, and which was as new to him as it was charming.

While they were talking, Min came to the door and stopped, watching the count. As soon as he saw her, she made him a curtsey—a thing she seldom did impromptu, though she practiced it often before Clara and with her, Clara considering it an art, like musical execution, not to be attained except by commencing early. Min somewhat overdid it on this occasion, but the count returned the salutation very gravely and impressively. Min laughed. This just suited her, for she was, as the doctor said, a born courtier. "This is your brother's child," said the count, addressing Clara. "Why, she is wonderfully beautiful!"

Minnie opened a conversation with the count, which soon developed so many purely family matters, that Clara suggested her going away.

"Oh, do let me stay, auntie dear. I won't talk so much any more." After a little silence on her part during which Min watched the count as a cat would a mouse, she asked, "Do you know what my name is?"

"I do. It is Minnie."

"What is your name? please."

"It is Paul."

"Oh, that is a nice name. Paul, are you going to stay to dinner?" she asked, insinuating her hand into his.

Both smiled at this outrageous freedom in the child; but Clara said, "Minnie, you must know——"

"Now, auntie dear, *please!*" and she pressed her dimpled fingers tightly over her lips, as much as to say, "Not one more word shall they utter."

"My child, auntie does not wish you to keep as silent as a statue, only you must not do all the talking; that is impolite." The count pressed the little hand still resting in his, and the little hand returned the pressure with interest, but fearing to be sent away, she maintained her silence, evidently by a most gigantic effort, and the conversation continued until Min, hearing the doctor's gig drive up, flew out of the conservatory like a streak. When she returned, it was in the doctor's arms. He set her down, and greeted the count with more deep heartiness than Clara had ever seen her father manifest to any man, and this cordiality was fully reciprocated by the count. "It does me good to see you again," said the doctor. "I was going to bring you to see my daughter. You must know it has been a long-cherished desire on my part that you two should meet. Knowing the opinions and tastes of both, I could predict that you would find much to like in each other."

"Permit me to say," said the count, "that you do me great honor. I have passed a more delightful hour than I ever expected to in Oakdale."

"That is good!" said the doctor, delighted to discover an unmistakable sincerity in the count's face, and he looked towards Clara.

"I see you expect me to be effusive, also," she said, blushing. "Well, then, I am too embarrassed to be original. I can only echo the sentiment of your friend, papa."

"My doctor," said Min, who could not keep silent any longer, "Paul won't stay to dinner; and we are going to have caper-sauce, and 'sparagus, and pudding."

"How can he resist such a *ménu?*" said the doctor, smiling, but are you not rather presumptive in calling the gentleman Paul?"

"No," said Min, decidedly. "He calls me Minnie."

"Indeed!" replied the doctor, amused at Min's justification.

"We shall be very glad to have you dine with us," said Clara, "if you will do us that honor; and papa can stay also, perhaps." But Von

Frauenstein, knowing his invitation was more or less due to Min's unofficial cordiality, declined, saying he was expected to dine with the Kendricks, which was the case, though he would willingly have forgotten that fact, had he felt perfectly free to obey his inclination. He added: "But if you will permit me, I will call again to see your flowers. You must know I have thus far given them no attention whatever." The look that accompanied these last words could not fail to flatter Clara. The count had the most charming voice imaginable, perfectly modulated, and in its low tones as indescribable as music itself.

Clara knew well, and every woman understands how, though it can no more be expressed by words than can the sensation experienced at the sound of delicious music, that this was not the last time she was to see the Count Paul Von Frauenstein, and the certainty was a deep satisfaction to her. As for him, as he walked away, breathing the delicate perfume of a little bouquet in his button-hole that he had begged from Clara, he wondered simply that there was such a woman in the world; but he, a man of the world, acquainted with men and women of the best rank in many countries—he knew well the secret of the charm that invested her: it was her freedom—a quality found very seldom in women, and for the best reasons. He met her as an equal on his own plane, and knew by instinct that no wealth, no social rank might win hand, much less her heart. There were no outposts raised by feminine coquetry, to be taken by storm, or by strategy. If she could love a man, she would turn to him as naturally as the flowers turn to the sun. During the rest of the day, the count's thoughts continually kept wandering back to that pleasant hour among the flowers; to the beautiful child, whose liking for him was so quick and frank in its expression; and especially to Clara, a worthy daughter, he thought, of one of the most admirable men he had ever met. And he thought of her, and saw her mentally, in other lights than simply a noble daughter of an honest and clear-thinking man; —but of that hereafter.

That evening the parlors of the Kendrick mansion were brilliantly lighted. A pleasant wood fire burned in the open grates, and everywhere there was a rich odor of flowers pervading the air. Mrs. Kendrick, still young in appearance, wearing a black velvet dress with a train, and her thin, white hands sparkling with jewels, received the guests in a rather solemn manner that said, "Man delights me not, nor woman either;" but the guests were in no way troubled, for they did not expect any manifestation of exuberant cordiality on the part of any of the Kendricks. There were but very few invited, all being "solid" men and their wives, with the exception of the Forests. It was a special gathering, having a special object—that of bringing Frauenstein and the solid men together for a special purpose: namely, the springing of a trap to catch the count's money for a grand life and fire company, of which he was to be president. The count had often talked as if he would some day settle in Oakdale, though the suave, impressible cosmopolitan had talked the same thing from the Atlantic to the Pacific coast, whenever be had been pleased with the enterprise, industrial advantages, or location of places; but Kendrick did not know this; and as the count's only relatives in America were the Kendricks, except the Delanos in Boston—and Boston the count hated—and as it was certain that Prussia was no *vaterland* [Ger.: fatherland] to him, the chances did look rather bright. But the idea of tempting Frauenstein with the presidency of a great joint-stock insurance company, showed that Kendrick knew as little of the man as Satan did of the One he took up "into an exceeding high mountain." Whoever is acquainted with the Mephistophelian penetration of Satan, must wonder at the shallow device. How could temporal power flatter One who said, "Blessed are the poor," and taught that we should take no heed of the morrow?

The count was apparently without any ordinary ambition. He had made his immense wealth by what proved to be shrewd investments during and before the war. He had bought and sold cotton, turned over gold in Wall Street, bought stock in many enterprises, and instead of commanding two millions, as Kendrick believed, he had actually at his control five times that amount and more. Society, especially fashionable society, was duller to him than a twice-told tale. He saw too well its miserable want of high purpose, its petty jealousies and rivalries, its instinctive worship of idols that to him were a vanity and vexation of spirit. One thing his wealth gave him, and that he enjoyed—the power to utter frankly his opinions on all subjects. No one criticised *his* radicalism; in him, it was only charming eccentricity, at the very worst. The only exception was Miss Charlotte, whom he had always highly esteemed. They had been fast friends for many years.

When Mrs. Forest entered the Kendrick drawing-rooms, the first thing she saw was Miss Charlotte Delano talking with Von Frauenstein. The latter she expected to see; but Miss Delano's presence was a surprise that gave her great uneasiness. This, however, was of short duration. Both came forward and greeted her; the count, with an easy courtesy, and Charlotte, much to Mrs. Forest's astonishment, rather more cordially than ever before. The three talked together for a few minutes, until Miss Louise Kendrick carried off the count to the piano. Then Mrs. Forest sought to relieve her overburdened spirit. Seeing that Charlotte was not likely to broach the subject, she said:

"I have not seen you, Miss Delano, since the unfortunate separation of Dr. Delano and my daughter. I can assure you it was as terrible a shock to my family as it must have been to yours."

"It is to be regretted, certainly," answered Charlotte; "but I trust it will prove for the best. I don't think Clara is to be blamed in the least."

Now Mrs. Forest had counted on a right dismal, mutual howl over the disgrace to the two families, and the sympathy she expected, from the moment she saw that Miss Charlotte was not disposed to avoid her, was totally wanting. Mrs. Forest began fear that the whole world was lapsing into loose and latitudinarian sentiments. Pretty soon the fact was revealed that Clara had visited Charlotte in Boston since the separation. By great effort Mrs. Forest concealed her annoyance. Clearly there was a secret kept from her by the doctor, for, of course, whatever Clara did he would know. To vex Mrs. Forest still more, Charlotte said that she had never really been acquainted with Clara until the separation, and that it was owing to the trial Clara had gone through that they had been drawn together. Here then was an anomaly; the very thing that had alienated her own mother from Clara had cemented the friendship between Clara and Dr. Delano's only sister! Mrs. Forest was at loggerheads with herself and the world generally.

While the count played an accompaniment for a duet by the twins, the solid men were talking in the further parlor, hidden from the piano by one of the folding-doors. The principal one, after Kendrick, was Mr. Burnham, one of the bank directors—a bald, clean-shaven, oldish gentleman, whose whole air suggested stocks, bonds, investments, and high rates of interest. He sat on an uncomfortable straight-backed chair, for lounging or ease was something he had never cultivated. Like Kendrick, making money was the only interest he had in life; not so much from any miserly feeling perhaps, as from long habit of thinking and scheming in that one narrow field. As many women grow by habit into household drudges, until they come to feel uneasy in pretty dresses and momentary release from the housekeeping treadmill, so these men felt uneasy, and almost out of place anywhere but in the counting-room. After a while the solid Burnham said: "I don't see, Kendrick, that we are to get a chance at the count to-night."

"Upon my word," said another, "he is as fond of woman's talk as a sophomore."

"A wise fool, eh?" said Kendrick. "Yes, these foreigners are funny dogs; but Frauenstein has a remarkably clear head, financially, though he's all wrong in politics—believes in female suffrage, for example. All the women like him, that's certain."

"H'm! Not difficult to find a main agreeable who is a count and a millionaire. Singular there should be so much attraction in a title in this democratic country."

"Frauenstein maintains that we are not a democratic country," said Kendrick; "that there never has been a democratic government in the world's history, because never one where all citizens have the ballot."

"Haven't they in this country? I should like to know," said Mr. Burnham.

"Why, women have not, and they constitute more than half of the adult citizens. I tell you, Burnham, you can't argue that question with the count. He's armed at all points."

"I've no desire to; but I don't feel like waiting much longer for him to get through his opera squalling and dawdling with the women."

Now it was a part of Kendrick's plan to broach the insurance scheme, not in a set business way, but to spring it suddenly upon the count in a general conversation when the ladies were present. He knew that many men, ladies' men especially, would be more vulnerable under such circumstances—less apt to manifest any closeness where money was concerned. The opportunity was soon found.

With the collation, or alter it, coffee was brought in—a thing never dreamed of at night, except when the count was present; then, indeed, it was available at almost any hour, for he was, like most Europeans, very fond of it. The solid men joined the group of three or four around a table, where the count was sipping his *café noir* [Fr: black coffee].

"Wouldn't you like some cognac in your coffee, Frauenstein?" asked Mr. Kendrick; and a glance at the waiter caused an elegant decanter to appear. The count measured out two tea-spoonfuls. Kendrick and the other gentlemen drank a tiny glass clear, and while Frauenstein was talking to Mrs. Burnham and Mrs. Kendrick about the beauties and merits generally of Oakdale, the solid men added valuable information about the increase in population and the enterprise of the town. This led up to the subject neatly, and Kendrick introduced the insurance scheme, and hoped the count would examine it. "We ought to start," he said, "with a capital of half a million—say a hundred shares, at five thousand dollars each. The truth is, everything is ripe for heavy insurance business and the capital can easily be doubled in a short time. The heaviest buyer would be the president, of course."

"That should be you, count," said Burnham, rolling the tiny stem of his glass, and looking boldly at a point between the count's eyes. The golden bait was not snapped at. On the contrary, Frauenstein threw cold water on the project. He said he did not believe in private insurance companies. The government should insure all its citizens. "Now this scheme," he said, "will benefit a few at the expense of the many. Make it a mutual affair between all the house-owners in your town, and I will 'go in,' as you say."

"How?" asked Kendrick, not liking to discourage any advance on the part of the count, whom he had just pronounced sound on questions of finance. "Give us your plan."

"Well, issue for a month, in your daily paper, a call to the citizens to prepare for taking steps to form a mutual banking and insurance company, and announce a meeting at the end of that time, when they will have discussed the matter very generally. Let the president and board of directors be chosen by the popular voice. Trust the majority for knowing who the honest men are. Let the shares be sold at one dollar, and limited to ten for each buyer, until a certain capital is raised. Above this amount, let any citizen deposit as much as he chooses, at the legal rate of interest, for the banking business. I will take all the stock of this part of the interest, if you like; for I am pretty nearly ready to set on foot a grand enterprise here in your midst—or just over the river, on the fifty acres of land I've bought there."

By this time all were eager to know what the count's proposition was; but he did not show his hand at once. He was, in fact, waiting for Dr. Forest, who, from the nature of his professional demands, was excused for coming at any hour. Mrs. Forest and her daughters had already retired.

Kendrick did not ask directly what the count's enterprise was. He only remarked upon the nature of the land, its soil and so forth, and while he was talking, Miss Delano, who was seated next the count, pulled back the little bouquet that was falling forward from his buttonhole, and said:

"How fragrant these are still! Where did you get them, Paul?"

"At your florists' here—the firm of Dykes & Delano. I was in their conservatory an hour or so, this morning, and had a very interesting conversation with Mrs. Delano. Why, she is a very cultivated, very charming woman. Why is it, Mrs. Kendrick," he asked, looking squarely at that lady, "that I have never met her at your receptions?"

Mercy! What a graveyard silence met this fatal question. Kendrick was fidgety; Burnham annoyed that the conversation had drifted away from business. Mrs. Kendrick, out of respect to Charlotte's presence, could not answer as she wished, so she looked into her coffee-cup, and the silence grew more and more oppressive. Charlotte did not consider herself called upon to speak. At length Mrs. Burnham said, smiling: "You ask, sir, for information, and I do not see why you should not be answered. Since Mrs. Delano came back to Oakdale, she has not been received in society."

"Indeed!" replied the count, sucking the coffee-drops from his long, silky moustache, and using his napkin. "Indeed! then all I can say is, so much the worse for your Oakdale society. Madame, that lady's presence would grace any society, however distinguished."

Mrs. Kendrick saw clearly, by the attitude and expression of her husband, that he was expecting her tact to guide the conversation into a smoother current; so she said quickly, and with some embarrassment, that it was not so much the fault of Oakdale society as of Mrs. Delano herself, who evidently wished for seclusion, and therefore her motives should be respected.

This did not satisfy the count. He saw clearly the same spirit that he hated and had fought all his life—the sacrifice of honest fraternal feeling to conventional forms. He knew, without a word of explanation, that this Mrs. Delano had offended society, and had been unforgiven; and further, that this offence could hardly be her separation from her husband alone, since such separations are of common occurrence. He knew Dr. Delano, and after meeting Clara, he was at no loss to understand the cause of the discord between them. He gave his opinions, therefore, very concisely and pointedly, upon the folly and short-sightedness of society, in refusing fellowship with any honest citizens whose education and refinement gave them a natural right to admiration and respect; and then he gave his opinion upon the special claim these women florists had upon the community, because of their brave effort towards gaining an independence through means which added much to the refinement and education of the people.

"You are a true friend of our sex, Paul," said Miss Delano; and addressing Louise Kendrick, she added, "You know Frauenstein means 'ladies' rock,' so he is rightly named."

"And on such rocks," said Kendrick, "I suppose they would build their church."

"There are not enough, unfortunately," replied Miss Delano, "for a grand cathedral, so we must build little altars here and there, wherever we can find a Frauenstein."

"You do me a very gracious honor," said the count, "but one I am far from deserving. I believe, though, I am always on the side of women as against men. I see very few really happy women; and they never can be happy, until they are pecuniarily independent. All fields should be freely opened to them. They are quite as capable of enterprise as men are, and of filling offices of trust. They should have the same education that men have. Men should give their daughters money, as they do their sons, and send them abroad to continue their education. Every man knows how culture and experience adds to the attractiveness of a woman."

"For my part," said Mrs. Burnham, petulantly, "I don't see the use of bringing up our daughters to be modest and home-loving, if just the opposite qualities are to be most admired."

"My dear madam," replied the count, "do you suppose a woman is less a true woman and a devoted wife because of her culture and experience?"

This led Mrs. Burnham to say that every one was aware that Clara Forest was well educated, and "considered" very superior, intellectually, but that she had not certainly been a model wife.

"You are wrong," said Miss Delano. "I find it very distasteful to me to discuss such a subject, but it is my duty to say that my brother, and not his wife, is at fault. The plain truth is, he did not show that he could appreciate her devotion."

"Why can't they make it up, then?" asked Burnham. "It looks bad to see wives cutting out in that way."

"If women were independent, as I desire to see them," said Von Frauenstein, "there would be much more 'cutting out,' as you call it, than you have any idea of. But, by the same token, it would make men more careful to carry the illusions of love into matrimony."

Here Dr. Forest was announced, and the conversation took a different turn.

Chapter 33
Legitimate, or Illegitimate

The doctor only stayed a short time, which was mostly employed in discussing the famous enterprise of the great French capitalist at Guise —the *Familistère,* or Social Palace. The count had been there on a visit, and he was eloquent in the praise of the work, which he called the most important and significant movement of the nineteenth century. "It points unmistakably," he said, "to the elevation and culture of the people, and to a just distribution of the products of labor." None present, except the doctor and Miss Delano, had ever heard of the great enterprise, and they listened eagerly, as if the count were telling an entrancing tale of some other, and more harmonious world.

"It won't work, though," said Burnham. "The equal distribution of wealth is a chimera."

"But, my dear sir, it *does* work," said the count. "It has been in splendid working operation several years, and pays six per cent on the invested capital. Do not lose sight of facts; and then, I did not say an equal, but a *just,* distribution of the products of labor, or wealth, for all wealth is that and nothing else. Depend upon it, we are living in an age corresponding to that of puberty in an individual. There are no very marked changes from childhood up to this period, except that of increase in size; and then, everything being ripe for it, there is a marvelous sudden transformation in six months or a year, and the child assumes all the characteristics of the man or woman. Ask yourself why the man who makes your plow, or tills your ground, should be inferior to you who muddle your lives away in counting-rooms or offices? You can't answer it, except to say the chances ought to be in favor of the one who has the most varied exercise of his muscles and mental faculties. I tell you, with the increased facilities for education among the people, and for travel and intercommunication, they are beginning to feel their power."

"Building palaces and living in hovels begins to strike the workers as something more than a joke," said the doctor; "but up to this time they have done it very composedly. They have woven the finest fabrics, and clothed themselves and their children in rags, or mean and cheap materials. Bettering their condition was next to impossible when they had to work from sunrise to sunset to gain a bare living; but shortening the hours of labor will work wonders. It will give men time to read and improve their mental condition."

"Yes, if it would only have that effect; but will it?" asked Kendrick.

"Of course it will not," said Mrs. Kendrick. "There are the three hundred workmen of Ely & Gerrish. They struck, you know, and got their hours reduced to ten; and I hear that most of them spend their extra time in bar-rooms and billiard-rooms."

"Well, madam," replied the count, "do you expect men who have been drudges, to suddenly turn out philosophers, and give their spare time to algebra and political economy? Why, many of them are no doubt so degraded by their lives of unceasing toil, that the bar-room is a culture to them, and getting drunk a luxury. But you must remember you have not collected the facts upon which to formulate a judgment. I do not believe the greater part of them, as you say, spend their time in bar-rooms and billiard-rooms."

"Oh, no doubt of it; no doubt of it," said Burnham.

"My dear Kendrick, you must have doubts," said the count.

"Not the slightest, upon my honor."

"Well, then, let us decide it in the English way. We have had a bet, you and I, before this. I'll lay you three to one, on any sum you like, that not one-third of these workmen spend more time in drinking-saloons or billiard-rooms than they did before their reduction of hours."

"Done!" said Kendrick, very sure of his money. "Let it be two hundred dollars."

"Oh, shocking!" said Mrs. Kendrick. "You are like two dissolute young men. I do not approve of betting."

"I don't approve of it either, madam," said the count, "but this is to establish the honor of the 'hodden grey;' and to make the transaction more respectable or excusable in your severe eyes, let us further decide, Kendrick, that whoever wins shall donate the money to your new hospital."

"Oh, that will be nice!" said Mrs. Kendrick, brightening. She was one of the board of managers, and had in vain tried to get her husband to subscribe anything further than the pitiful sum of fifty dollars at starting. The doctor also, highly approved of this disposition of the money. He had long agitated the subject of a hospital, and Mrs. Kendrick at last had come to be, he said, his "right-hand man." He was one of the committee to draw up the prospectus then under consideration. He wished especially to have the hospital so organized that not only the poor could avail themselves of it, but those in better circumstances—for the private family, he said, was no place for a sick person. He could not receive the necessary care without feeling himself a burden, which vexed and irritated him, and so retarded recovery.

After arguing upon the method of collecting the facts about the workingmen of Ely & Gerrish, and after calling out the count at some length on the particulars of the working of the *Familistère* at Guise, the doctor left, and Kendrick and Burnham returned to the charge of the insurance scheme. Burnham insisted that the growing enterprise of Oakdale, and its steady increase of population, made everything favorable for a "big thing" in the insurance line.

"I see," said the count, "that you are not disposed to take my suggestions about making your insurance a mutual thing among your citizens. Now, the longer I live, the more I am interested in the independence of the people. Your rates of insurance, in private joint-stock companies, are too high for the poor man, who needs insurance infinitely more than the rich do. Now, as for Oakdale enterprises, I see none so worthy of consideration as this well-managed flower business of Dykes & Delano. That is something worth taking stock in." Here Burnham turned away with ill-concealed impatience, not to say disgust; but Kendrick, anxious to keep on the right side of his rich guest and relative, said, smiling blandly.

"Well, count, one like you might invest in the Dykes-Delano paper, and still have a balance for our little insurance enterprise." The count did not at all like the covert sneer in this speech. "Kendrick," he said, "your heart is as dry and crisp as one of your banknotes. It is not touched at all by the struggle of these women, while to me it is inspiring. You never even told me of it, and I have had to learn the facts outside. They commenced with absolutely nothing but a few plants in a friend's bay-window. One of them sold her watch and jewels, I hear, to help build the second addition to the hot-house. I tell you, they ought to be encouraged and helped in every way."

"Pity they couldn't have kept respectability on their side. That would have been the best help," said Mrs. Burnham. Old Burnham could have choked her; not that he had more charity than his wife, but more policy.

"Respectability!" said the count, thoroughly aroused. "I wonder that women do not hate the very word. No woman ever becomes worthy of herself until she finds out what a sham it is—a very bugbear to frighten slaves. No woman knows her strength until she has had to battle with the cry of 'strong-minded,' 'out-of-her-sphere,' 'unfeminine,' and all the other weapons of weak and hypocritical antagonists. I tell you, a woman who has fought that fight, and conquered an independent position by her own industry, has attractions in the eyes of a true man, as much above the show of little graces, polite accomplishments, meretricious toilet arts, and the gabble of inanities, as heaven is above the earth. She is a woman whom no man can hold by wealth or social position, but only by the love his devotion and manliness can inspire."

No dissenting word followed this burst, which was Greek to the solid men. The count was a little daft anyway, on the subject of women, according to them. Mrs. Kendrick, after a moment, offered some safe, negative remark, and Burnham, anxious to neutralize the mischief his wife had done, said he thought a woman might, at last some women might, "work up" a business and yet remain feminine. Men were not so hard on women, it was their own sex. This roused Mrs. Burnham, for she knew well he talked very differently in the bosom of his family. She took up the thread of conversation. "I am sure," she said—and here occurred a little jerky interruption to her speech, the cause of which no one knew but her lord, who had kicked her foot under the table, which meant, in his delicate, marital sign language, "Hold your tongue!" But like many of the slaves, as the doctor called married women, she made up in perversity what she lacked in independence; so glancing spitefully at her "lord," she continued, "I am sure I think women have a right to all the money they can honestly gain, and if Miss Dykes had conducted herself properly, I should have much sympathy with her success."

"Was it her fault, Mrs. Burnham," asked the count, "that the man who won her affection did not marry her?-----"

"My dear Louise," said Mrs. Kendrick, begging the count's pardon for interrupting, "I think you had better retire. It is getting rather late for you."

"No; let her stay, my dear madam. I am not going to say anything that the Virgin Mary herself might not hear. Let her stay. I see she listens intently, and if to-night she gains a broader conception of the true position of her sex, you will hereafter rejoice in the fact. She is a pretty, a charming girl, just coming into the glare of the footlights on life's stage, with bandaged eyes. This is what you mothers all do; and then if they stumble for want of eyes to see the trap-doors of the stage, you blame them—not yourselves. Teach a girl to know herself—to consider all her functions as worthy of admiration and respect; teach her to be independent, proud of her womanhood, and she will turn as instinctively from the seductive words of selfish men, as from the touch of unholy hands. Now, this little woman, Miss Dykes, had no such teaching, no knowledge of the world whatever, no standard by which to measure the honor of men's motives; and, for believing and trusting, you, Mrs. Burnham, and other Christians, would stone her to death. But Nature is kinder than you are, madam, for it pardons her weakness, and compensates for her suffering by a most precious gift. Her child is one of the very brightest and loveliest I have ever met."

"It is certainly a very charming little thing," said Mrs. Kendrick, "and her mother's conduct is now, I believe, every way exemplary. I am truly sorry that her child is illegitimate."

"Illegitimate!" repeated Von Frauenstein, as if speaking in his sleep. "Why, all children must be legitimate. How *can* a child be otherwise? I must be a barbarian. I can see nothing in the same light that others do. Well, by heaven! I'll adopt that child, if her mother will consent. I'll take her abroad and educate her. I'll give her my name, and present her at a dozen royal courts. There'll be no question then, whether she is begotten by law or by the more primitive process of nature." The company were astounded.

"Good heavens, count!" exclaimed Mrs. Kendrick, breaking the silence that followed this speech. "Would you really do such a thing?"

"Yes, my dear friend. I'll do it—so help me God! and I'll bring her back to Oakdale, when her education is finished, a perfect queen of a woman. You call her illegitimate, madam, and yet the time may come when you'll be proud to kiss her hand!"

Mrs. Kendrick rose from the table, and the others followed. Miss Charlotte had retired some time before.

Kendrick, who could not imagine for a moment that the count was serious, was disposed to take the matter as a good joke. "If your knightly passion is the adoption of bastards, why have you never adopted any before? I think this is the first. Isn't it?"

"Yes; because I have never known a case where the mother, being poor and uneducated, rose out of her disgrace so nobly. The doctor tells me she is a great student—reads and studies regularly, while working like a martyr to get the flower business on a safe footing. I mean to go and see her to-morrow, and if she wants capital, I'm her man. It is just as safe an investment as your insurance business, though it won't pay so high a rate of interest." Kendrick could have strangled him. Burnham and his wife retired with sufficient discomfiture for any amount of conjugal infelicity. Burnham declared, as soon as the door closed behind the happy pair, that but for her "gabble about those women, Frauenstein would not have made such a fool of himself." Mrs. Burnham assumed the silent air of the martyred wife. So they went home to their grand house, second only in cost to the Kendrick mansion, and hid their heads to rest on two contiguous pillows, with as much justification for the proximity as the law allows. Meanwhile a very similar conjugal harmony expressed itself in the grander home of the Kendricks; but Mrs. Kendrick did not play the role of the silent victim as Mrs. Burnham did. As her husband was removing his cravat, she said, "Now here's a fine mess you've got into with the count."

"*I!* Well, that's cool. What do you mean?" asked Mr. Kendrick, not for information, as his wife knew; so she answered somewhat impatiently:

"You ought to know Frauenstein well enough to see that he would never sympathize with any narrow social distinctions. He's seen Clara Forest, thinks her unjustly treated, and so he has gone over to the enemy."

"Seen Clara? I should say he had seen the other, by the way he talked. Shouldn't wonder if he fell in love with that brat, and the mother too."

"That's as much as you know. Men never see any thing. I'm perfectly sure that he is smitten with Clara. That's the way it will end. You'll see," said Mrs. Kendrick, bitterly. She had long cherished the hope that Louise might win the count; but she spoke very despairingly about it now.

"Oh, I always told you that would never work. Men like that, know too well what a woman is. Louise has arms and led like spermacity[1] candles."

"Well, I must say, for a father to speak like that, is shameful," answered Mrs. Kendrick.

"It's all your own fault; you took her away from the high-school because she got hurt a little in the gymnasium, and sent her to that namby-pamby seminary of half idiots at Worcester. Didn't I always want her to work in the garden and in the hot-house, and develop her muscles? She'll always be sickly, just as she is now."

"I'm sure she has had a great deal of exercise, and her health is as good as mine was at her age, and she is not a bit thinner in flesh." Mr. Kendrick made no denial and his wife continued: "Working in the garden spreads out a girl's hands, and makes them red; and what man, I should like to know, ever likes hands and arms like a washer-woman's? You were always praising the smallness and whiteness of mine. I mean before we were married, of course." Still Kendrick was silent, but his thoughts were very busy. Someway the world was out of joint, and he was wondering if, after all, these radicals, with their talk about making women free and teaching them to depend on themselves, were not pretty near the truth. Here was Frauenstein, for example, rich enough to put a wife in a palace, and surround her with attendants, and he was always admiring women who worked. This he expressed to Mrs. Kendrick, and said that it certainly was commendable in Clara, since she would be a fool and throw away her rights as Delano's wife, to take care of herself, instead of coming home and living on her father.

"Of course," said his wife; "and we ought never to have cut her. You heard what the count said."

"Who's to blame for the cutting? Not I. Men don't cut women, my dear."

"Well, Elias, I think you can take the palm for sneaking out of a responsibility. Men don't cut women, indeed! I know they don't; but they insult them worse than we do. I know you bow as graciously to Clara as if she were a duchess; but would you let Louise visit her? You know you wouldn't. That's the way men take the part of women whom their wives and daughters avoid." Mr. Kendrick thought silence the best reply to this just reflection of his wife. He thought he could trust her to bring harmony out of the discord; for while he wanted to keep the count's money from straying away from the family, she, on her part, was equally anxious to secure his name and rank for Louise; and he knew she would hang on to that hope to the last.

The next morning, after breakfast, which had been a serene affair, showing no trace of the perturbation of the previous evening, the count drove over to the doctor's. The doctor was out, but would return very soon. Frauenstein waited, and spent the time mostly at the piano. The twins were both delighted, though timid, especially in the presence of such a lion. Linnie, after they had sung, asked him to say frankly what he thought of their voices. "Do you allow your sister to speak for you, Miss Leila?" he asked, turning his fine eyes upon hers.

"Yes—no," blushing and laughing just like nothing in the world but a young girl. "I mean yes, in this case," she finally managed to say.

"Well, then, yours has most power, but it is wiry. Miss Linnie's is more flexible, more emotional. She feels more than you do, or, rather, more than you *seem* to, when she sings. If you were both equally to cultivate your voices, and also continue your practice for the next five years, Linnie would win more applause for her singing, and you for your playing. That is my opinion; but I ought to add, as the French do, *maintenant je n'en sais rien."*[2] Then the count made them both speak French, he carefully constructing his sentences as much as possible after *Fasquelle's French Course,* which he knew was their text-book, they having no idea of the reason why they were able to get along so well with him. He understood their worst sentences like a Parisian. Any foreigner who has been in Paris will understand that. He will recall how, in his abominable murdering of the language, sentences which he could not for his life have understood himself, written or spoken, were instantly seized and graciously and gravely replied to, as if they had been models of elegance. When the count finished singing a charming aria in his best style, Linnie said, with enthusiasm,

"Oh, I wish my sister Clara could bear you sing!"

"She shall hear me sing," he said, looking up to Linnie, who stood on his left, with an expression in his face that she had never seen there. It affected her senses like a caress.

Pretty soon the doctor entered; and after greeting the count, he said, "What a fusillade of French! What a state of excitement these girls are in! I believe you are bewitching them both, Frauenstein."

"On the contrary, I am the victim of both, and I dare not stay another moment. I have come to take you over the river. I want you to see my fifty acres, on which I am going to build a social palace, if the gods are propitious."

It was a clear, balmy day in the first week of April that the count sought this interview with the doctor. So far in his life, he had never found a man who was so much "after his own heart." He believed in him fully from the first hour he conversed with him, since when they had corresponded, expressing their views fearlessly; and thus far had found them in perfect accord. To say they loved each other like brothers would by no means express the sentiment existing between these two men, so unlike in many respects, yet so closely in sympathy that thought answered to thought like the voice of one's own soul. During the drive, for they went past the fifty acres away into the country, neither asking for what reason, the count gave in detail his plans. "If I build this palace," he said, "I shall do it with this clear granite sand of the river. I know the secret of making stones of it—bricks, we call them—which, moulded in any shape, and tinted any hue, will last for centuries. I can have a man here in three days to conduct the work. He will guarantee that they shall be finished this summer. If I do it, it shall be a magnificent structure, beside which the palace of Versailles will seem the work of a 'prentice hand.' I can profit by the original palace at Guise, and make it much handsomer, though that is truly splendid. The apartments must be larger, and the whole should accommodate about two thousand people. Now, I have already one industry for its occupants. What is your idea for a second?"

"Making these very bricks," said the doctor, "if only you have got at the secret of their perfect durability, as you have, I know, or you would not speak so positively. But this industry would not suit all. You want one more."

"Of course. One that will employ women. What shall it be? I have thought of silk-weaving, for a certain reason of my own. It is proverbial, you know, that those who make the silks, laces, and velvets—pure luxuries, and the most costly—are the worst paid of any laborers in the world. Look at Spitalfields, England, and Lyons, the great velvet manufacturing centre of France. In India, those who make the fabulous-priced Cashmere shawls are the most pitiably paid of all. I am willing, if necessary, to lose a considerable fortune to prove that good wages can be paid to silk-makers, and yet have a fair profit on the product. I should go into that manufacture with some advantages. I have a first-class steamer already plying between San Francisco and China. I can get silk as cheap as anybody."

"Good!" said the doctor. "Let the third industry be silk-weaving." The count had not mentioned the first, but the doctor knew well he meant floriculture.

"There's only one thing lacking, doctor, and that is—the motive: the motive for the first step. That depends——" And suddenly checking himself and turning his horse in the road, he asked, abruptly, "Doctor, have you ever been in love?"

"With a woman—no; with a man, yes."

"I understand. You have met a man who responded to all the needs a man could respond to, but never a woman to respond to what you need there. That is my own case exactly, though I have loved, of course —few men more, I think."

"If men only knew," said the doctor, "how they cramp their own growth by making idols of women!"

"By idols, you mean slaves. Only free women are worthy of free men; and the time is not come, though it is near, when they will be emancipated. Then we shall see the dawn of the Golden Age. Men think they are free; but they are bound by many shackles, only they have thrown off some which they still compel women to wear."

From Chapter 43
The Inauguration of the Social Palace

. . . On either side of the court, half-way between the display of flags, were the words, in a mosaic of flowers, *"Liberty, Equality, Fraternity,"* the first word being on the lowest gallery, and *Fraternity* on the highest. Murmurs of admiration were heard everywhere among the immense audience. Suddenly the court rang with shouts of applause, and the band struck up *"See! the Conquering Hero Comes."* The count had entered the court ascending the platform, he advanced to the front and waited until the applause had somewhat subsided. He looked quite pale when he commenced:

"Friends, fellow-workers, and citizens:"—after a pause, which became even painful, he laid his hand on his breast, saying—"Can you bear with my weakness when I confess that my heart is too full for utterance? To say that this is the proudest hour of my life, seems to me but a lame and impotent phrase. No words that I am able to combine, are adequate to express the emotion that fills me to-night. But as I am expected to speak, I will not disappoint you and will do the best I can; and as there are many strangers present, I must endeavor specially to make myself intelligible to them. To you my fellow-workers, I need only say that the first Social Palace of America is finished, and I think it does honor to the hands that have built it." [Here the count was interrupted by cheers and protests against his modesty in giving all the credit to the workmen.]

"You do me personally too much honor. It is not much to advance capital for the building of an institution like this, following the example of one of the noblest lovers of humanity, who did *his* work without precedent, against opposition and discouragement of every kind. [Cheers for Godin.] This palace is built on the model of the first one ever founded —that at Guise, in France. That has been in successful operation now for several years, and I wish every capitalist within the sound of my voice to note well the fact, that it is a perfect financial success, paying six per cent. annually on the capital invested, which is as much as any commercially-honest capitalist in France expects to make." Here the count gave a detailed description of the organization and working of the Social Palace system, and then he continued:

"You have gone over the palace and the grounds today; you have seen the flourishing industries, you understand the provisions made for the children, the sick, the aged and infirm, and you can judge whether this institution furnishes the proper conditions for moral and intellectual growth [prolonged cheers]; but you may not yet be able to comprehend what the children of these industrious men and women will become, when they have grown up under the influence of the means for education and artistic culture which the grand institution supplies. They will despise drudgery by instinct, for it leaves the form bent and awkward, and the mind cramped and divested of beauty; and just as certainly will they honor labor as the great natural function of the human race, distinguishing it from the brutes. The reason why labor has not been honored heretofore, is because it has always been confounded with slavery or drudgery. With the abolition of slavery, we are just beginning to learn that man is not to be adapted to labor, but that labor, through machinery and scientific organization, is to be adapted to man.

"The primal object of society should be to make perfect men and women—perfect citizens. This cannot be accomplished without scientific training for the mind, and the free and harmonious development of the muscles through labor, with gymnastic exercises and games for the development of those muscles not brought into play by the ordinary industrial occupations. When a man continues many hours a day using only one set of muscles, as the blacksmith his arm, he must do it at the expense of grace, and strength, and beauty, which we should be taught to seek as a duty to ourselves and to our fellow-beings, since we have no moral right to transmit disease and ugliness to posterity. [Cheers.] No one should dream of finishing his education until he dies. Besides the exercise of the muscles by industry, every human being should have time during the twenty-four hours, for amusing games, for bathing, for dressing elegantly and becomingly, for social converse, for music or the drama, for regular study and drill in classes, and finally for sleep. All this may not be accomplished for the wronged and cheated adult generation of the present; all this and more will be the proud heritage of the children growing up under the blessings of a nobly organized social and industrial life. [Great applause.] Children growing up under such conditions, will be strong and beautiful, tender and wise. They will be strong through constant exercise, a varied and plentiful diet, and the natural stimulation of happiness. They will be beautiful, because to develop their bodies harmoniously will be the object of scientific study; and their faces will be beautiful because they will be moulded, not by anger, and cunning, and selfishness, but by generosity, candor, and love. They will be tender, because they will be taught to be proud of exemplifying the devotion of love, the grandest of all our passions, for it is the only one that exalts in us the dignity of the creative mood. Finally, they will be wise, for they will have acquired the sentiment of the brotherhood of man.

> 'Wisdom is humanity;
> And they who want it, wise as they may seem,
> And confident in their own sight and strength,
> Reach not the scope they aim at.' "

Such enthusiastic and long-continued applause followed the count's address, that he came forward again, and said:

"This time, my friends, I will forgive you for taking more notice of me than I deserve, since it reminds me of a duty I owe you. I wish to say to the thousands here present, and especially to the capitalists who may hereafter engage in the building of Social Palaces, that their task will be easier than they suppose; because men and women will work for their establishment with the same single-hearted devotion with which they have worked for this. I have been often pained to see the sacrifices that these noble workers have made. I doubt if one-half of them have taken the allotted hour at noon for their lunch; and I have seen carpenters, cabinetmakers, and decorators, seize a spade and dig in the trenches, rather than be a moment idle, when their own special work was interrupted by any accident; and be it said to the honor of labor, that the men who have done the most skilled labor on this palace, have never failed in equal respect toward these who have done the most mechanical and unskilled portions. A spirit of fraternal good-fellowship and unity of purpose has, so far as I know, characterized these men throughout every hour of the work from its commencement. This spirit is based on the sentiment of equality, the recognition of human rights everywhere, and is most significant, for it is full of promise for the future success of our great effort. And here I will mention one thing, not out of malice, but simply as a lesson. I am accused of advocating the 'leveling' principle. 'Frauenstein, you are a leveler,' said a friend to me to-day. Well, there is some truth in that; I would bring all the races and individuals on the globe up to the highest level; but I should be very sorry to do anything toward bringing my artisan friends down to the physical, intellectual, or moral level of certain aristocrats whom I know. [Laughter and applause.] It is undeniably the fact, that to-day the soundest views on education, on politics, on finance, on social organization, are supported, not by those who hold themselves above their kind—the drones of the community, who feed on the mechanic's labor—but by those who have an honest right to everything they own, and much more. The more I associate with laborers, even those who have had little advantage from schools, the more I am struck with the saving virtue that is in them. I confess I am almost disgusted with the very word aristocracy, for it has been vilely degraded, until it is applied only to those who would be ashamed to do an honest day's work of any kind. And what is this aristocracy? What are these *parvenus* of two hundred years, who would cry down the nobler aristocracy of labor, which is as old as civilization itself?''

4

"A Divided Republic:
An Allegory of the Future"
1885

LILLIE DEVEREUX [UMSTED] BLAKE
1833–1913

*T*hough born into an elite southern family, a latterday descendent of the Puritan *Jonathan Edwards, Blake was educated in New Haven after her father's death in 1837. Most unusual for a young woman of her era, she received private tutoring in Yale College's sophomore and junior year courses. Her first marriage to Philadelphia lawyer Frank Umsted in 1855 ended with his apparent suicide in 1859. She was left to support two daughters. She built upon the literary success of her novel* Southwold, *(1859), and turned her skill to profit. One of her most outspokenly feminist novels was* Fettered for Life; or, Lord and Master, *(1874) where she finds female friendship more supportive of women's well-being than the abuses and injustices that marriage often brings to women. She married again in 1866 to a Maine businessman living in New York, Grinfill Blake, who died in 1896, ending an apparently happy relationship.*

Her fiction-writing career lasted until 1882, her last fiction book containing the utopian feminist fantasy reprinted here. Thereafter, as this work suggests, she devoted herself to women's rights, especially suffrage. In 1883 she delivered a series of lectures refuting the antisuffrage sermons of the Reverend Morgan Dix, published as Woman's Place To-day. *From 1879 to 1890 she headed the New York State Woman Suffrage Association, and from 1886–1900, the New York City Woman Suffrage League. She was a contributor to Elizabeth Cady Stanton's controversial* Woman's Bible *(1895). Stanton urged her to run for head of the National American Woman Suffrage Association upon the retirement of Susan B. Anthony, but Anthony supported Carrie Chapman Catt. "For the sake of harmony," Blake withdrew her name: Catt was then successful in her bid (Blake and Wallace, 205). Unlike Anthony and like Gilman, whom she met in 1896, Blake refused to work only for suffrage and her social connections affronted Anthony's plain Quaker tastes. Illness plagued Blake's last eight years.*

In "A Divided Republic," Blake uses the device of sex separation to demonstrate a need for social change, like Mary E. Bradley Lane's single-sex utopia Mizora (1880–81), or Lois Nichols Waisbrooker's pacifist dream vision A Sex Revolution (1894). In the latter, the leader Lovella roundly condemns sexism, racism, and war as "immature destructiveness." Women must make their compassion felt in the world to erase war: love should be neither exclusive nor possessive.

References: Katherine Devereux Blake and Margaret Louise Wallace, *Champion of Women: The Life of Lillie Devereux Blake* (New York: Fleming H. Revell, 1943); Lillie Devereux Blake Papers, Missouri Historical Society, St. Louis; Denise D. Knight, ed., *The Diaries of Charlotte Perkins Gilman,* vol. 2 (Charlottesville: Univ. Press of Virginia, 1994); Elizabeth Cady Stanton et al, *History of Woman Suffrage,* vols. 3–4, (New York: Fowler and Wells, 1881, 1902; reprint, New York: Arno, 1969); William R. Taylor, "Lillie Devereux Blake," in *Notable American Women,* vol. 1 (Cambridge, Mass.: Harvard Univ. Press, 1971); Jean M. Ward, "Lillie Devereux Blake," in *American Women Writers,* vol. 1 (New York: Ungar, 1979); Pam McAllister, "Women in the Lead: Waisbrooker's Way to Peace," Introduction to Lois Waisbrooker, *A Sex Revolution* (1894; reprint, Philadelphia: New Society Publishers, 1985), 1–46.

Text: Lillie Devereux Blake, "A Divided Republic: An Allegory of the Future," in *A Daring Experiment and Other Stories* (New York: Lovell, Coryell, 1892).

This allegory was first read on Dec. 26, 1885, as one of a series of Saturday afternoon lectures. It was printed in the Phrenological Journal, February and March, 1887. It is reprinted just as it was originally given, without modernizing, as it contains many internal evidences of having been written at that time. For instance, the Forty-ninth Congress was then in Session, but we now have the Fifty-second. Washington and Wyoming were then territories, both of them having woman suffrage—they are now States, and only Wyoming is free. These and other statements that would not be appropriate to-day are left unchanged, as proving that it was written several years ago. "The Strike of a Sex," by Geo. N. Miller, was not published till 1890.[1]

The Forty-ninth Congress adjourned without enfranchising the women of the Republic, and many State legislatures, where pleas were made for justice, refused to listen to the suppliants. The women of the nation grew more and more indignant over the denial of equality. Great conventions were held and monster mass meetings took place all over the land. But although men had been declaring that so soon as women wanted to vote they would be allowed to, they still continued to assert in the face of all those efforts that only a few agitators were making the demand. An enormous petition was sent to the Fiftieth Congress containing the signatures of twenty millions of women praying for suffrage, and still Senator Edmunds and Senator Vest[2] insisted that the best women would not vote if they could.

Matters actually began to grow worse for women. The more honors they carried off at College the less were they allowed to hold places of public trust or given equal pay for equal work. Taxes of oppressive magnitude were imposed on them, for a new idea had seized the masculine brains of the country. They wanted to fortify our sea coast. The women protested in vain; they said they did not want war, that they never would permit war, and that all difficulties with foreign nations, if any arose, should lie settled by arbitration.

The men paid no attention whatever to their protests, but went right on levying heavy taxes and imposing a high tariff on foreign goods, and spending the money in monstrous forts and bristling cannon that looked out over the wide waters of the Atlantic in useless menace.

Drunkenness, too, increased in the land. It is true that sometimes women were able to procure the passage of some law to restrain the sale of liquors, but the enactments were always dead letters; the men would not enforce the laws they themselves had made, and mothers saw their sons led away and their families broken up, and still no man heeded their protests.

The murmurs of discontent among women grew louder and deeper, and a grand national council was called.

Now the great leader among women in this time was Volumnia, a matron of noble appearance, whose guidance the women gladly followed. When the great council met at Washington every State was represented by the foremost women of the day, and all were eager for some radical action that should force the men of the nation to give them a voice in the laws.

All were assembled, and the great hall filled to its utmost limit by eager delegates, when Volumnia arose to speak.

"Women of America," she said, "we have borne enough! We have appealed to the men to set us free. They have refused. We have protested against the imposition of taxes. They have increased them. We have implored them to protect our homes from the curse of intemperance. They have passed prohibition laws on one day, and permitted saloons to be opened the next. We are tired of argument, entreaty and persuasion. Patience is no longer becoming in the women of America. The time for action has come."

And this vast assemblage of women, stirred to the utmost, shouted, "ACTION!"

"I have a proposal to make to you," she continued, "the result of long study and consultation with the profoundest female minds of the country. It is this:—

"Within the limits of this so-called Republic there is one spot where the women are free. I mean in Washington Territory, that great State that has been refused admission to the Union, solely because women there are voters. I have communicated with the leading women of that region; some of them are here to speak for themselves, and others are here from the sister Territory of Wyoming. With their approval and aid I propose that all the women of the United States leave the East, where ancient customs oppress us and where old fogyism prevails, and emigrate in a body to the free West, the lofty heights of the mountains and the broad slopes on the coast of the majestic Pacific."

Wild and tumultuous applause followed this proposal, which was at once enthusiastically adopted by the assembled multitude, who after a few days of discussion as to the means to carry out these designs dispersed to their homes to make preparations for the greatest exodus of modern times.

In the early spring all arrangements were complete, and then was seen a wonderful sight. Women leaving their homes all over the land, and marching by night and by day in great armies, westward. All the means of conveyance were crowded. The railroads were loaded with women, the boats on the great lakes were thronged with them; the Northern and Central Pacific roads ran immense extra trains to convey the women to their new homes.

It must not be supposed that their departure took place without protest on the part of the men. Some of them were greatly dismayed when they heard that wife and daughters were going away, and essayed remonstrance, but the women had borne so much so long that they were inexorable—not always without a pang, however.

Volumnia had long been a widow, and therefore owed allegiance to no man; but she had a young daughter named Rose, who was as pretty as she was accomplished, and who cherished a fondness for a young man who admired her.

When she learned of the proposed exodus, this youth, whose name was Flavius, hurried to the railway station, reaching there a few moments before the departure of the train. The waitingroom was crowded with a great throng of women, but Rose was lingering near the door. Flavius seized her hand, drew her aside, and with eyes full of love and longing, said:

"You surely will not go, Rose; stay and let us be married at once."

Rose blushed, and for a moment trembled under his ardent gaze.

"Oh, Flavius, if it only could be!" she whispered.

There was a stir in the crowd as someone announced that the train was ready. Rose started as if to go.

"Stay, love, stay!" entreated Flavius.

She hesitated and raised her eyes; they were swimming with tears; "I cannot," she said, "honor before love,"—then she drew a little nearer—"but you can help to bring us back—obtain justice!"

She broke off abruptly as she heard her mother calling her name and hurried away.

Volumnia's great co-worker was a certain lady called Cecilia, and to her also there was a trial in parting. Her father was elderly and infirm, and although possessed of ample means, he depended much on the companionship of his daughter. For a brief moment she hesitated to leave him; then she said sternly: "The Roman father sacrificed his child; Jephtha[3] gave up his daughter at the call of his country; so will I leave my father for the demands of my sex and of humanity."

Then despite all entreaties and expostulations and even threats, which the men at some points vainly tried, the women everyone departed, and after a few days, in all the great Atlantic seaboard, from the pine forests of Maine to the wave-washed Florida Keys, there was not a woman to be seen.

At first most of the men pretended that they were glad.

"We can go to the club whenever we like," said a certain married man.

"And no one will find fault with us if we drop into a saloon," added the other.

"Or say that tobacco is nasty stuff," suggested a third.

Other individuals, too, were outspoken in regard to the relief they felt.

Dr. Hammond[4] declared that the neurological conditions which afflicted woman had always rendered them unfit for the companionship of intelligent men. Carl Schurz[5] said that the whole thing was a matter of indifference to him. No one took any interest in the women question anyway.

John Boyle O'Reilly[6] was relieved that no Irish woman would hereafter ask him hard questions as to what freedom really meant.

There was much rejoicing among the writers also.
Mr. Howells remarked that now he could describe New England girls just as he pleased and no one would find fault with him; and Mr. Henry James was certain that the men would all buy the "Bostonians," which proved so conclusively that no matter how much of a stick a man might be, it was far better for a woman to marry him than to follow even the most brilliant career.[7]

On some points the rejoicing was open. The men in Massachusetts declared that they were well-rid of the women; there were too many of them anyhow. The members of the New York Legislature held a caucus, irrespective of party, and passed resolutions of congratulation that they would not be plagued with a woman's suffrage bill.

And the Rev. Morgan Dix caused a solemn *Te Deum* of rejoicing to be sung in Trinity Church.[8]

Meantime Volumnia and her hosts had swept across the Rocky Mountains and taken possession of the Pacific slope. Not Wyoming and Washington alone, but Idaho and Montana, and all the region between the two enfranchised territories.

By an arrangement previously made with the women who dwelt in these lands the men were sent eastward, and in all that wide expanse of territory there were only women to be seen.

Under these circumstances they made such laws as suited them. The Territorial legislature, consisting wholly of women, speedily passed bills giving women the right to vote. There was no need to pass prohibition measures, as the saloon-keepers had gone East. Peace and tranquillity prevailed through all the borders of the feminine Republic. There were no policemen, for there was no disorder, but thrift, sobriety and decorum ruled, and the days passed in calm monotony.

Very different was the condition of affairs on the Eastern coast. The men for a while after the departure of the women went bravely about their vocations, many of them, as we have seen, pretending that they were glad that the women were gone. But presently signs of a change appeared. While the saloons did a roaring business the barber shops were deserted—men began to say there was no use in shaving as there were no women to see how they looked; the tailors also suffered, for the men grew careless in their dress; what was the use of fresh linen and gorgeous ties with never a pretty girl to smile at them? White shirts rapidly gave place to red and gray flannel ones; old hats were worn with calm indifference, even on Fifth Avenue, and after a time men went up and down to business unshaven, and slouchy.

Within the house there was also a marked change. One of the first sources of rejoicing among men had been that now they would be rid of the slavery of dusters and brooms, and after the women were gone the houses were allowed to fall into confusion. As no one objected that the curtains would be ruined, the men smoked in drawing-room and parlor as well as study, and knocked the ashes from cigar or pipe on the carpet without fearing a remonstrance. At the end of some months affairs grew worse. The amount of liquor consumed was enormous, the police force was doubled, and then was inefficient because it was impossible to find policemen who would not drink. Brawling was incessant; the men had become cross and sulky, and murderous rows were of constant occurrence. Burglaries and other violent crimes increased and the jails were over-crowded with inmates.

From the first the churches had been nearly empty, as there were no women to attend them, and after awhile they were all closed until the next Legislature ordered that they be turned over to the State; after which some of them were used for sparring exhibitions, and others were turned into gambling saloons, for draw poker had become the fashionable game, and men having no longer any homes gathered every night at some place of amusement.

The theatres were obliged to change their attractions, and instead of comedies or operas, feats of strength were exhibited. The laws against prize-fighting were repealed, and slugging matches took place nightly; dog-fights and cocking-mains also were popular and the Madison Square Garden, once the scene of a moral "Wild-West" was turned into an arena for bull-fights.

It was about this time that Henry Bergh,[9] who had vainly protested against some of these things, was defeated for Congress by a man who had won distinction by catching five hundred live rats and putting them into a barrel in fifty minutes. Matters went rapidly from bad to worse after this. John L. Sullivan[10] was elected President. The men were about to declare war against all the world, so as to have a chance to use their new fortifications, when Flavius, who had never ceased to long for Rose, called a secret council at the house of Cecilia's father and proposed that a deputation should be sent with a flag of truce to the women. To his astonishment and delight the idea was received with wild enthusiasm, and he and the host were appointed a committee to lay the question before Congress.

On their appearance at the Capitol, Senate and House of Representatives were hastily assembled in joint session to receive them, and as they entered the hall the air rang with cries and cheers. It was with great difficulty that General Blair,[11] who had been chosen to preside, could put the motion, which was carried with a wild hurrah of applause, and for many moments thereafter the noise and cheering continued; men hugged each other with delight; some tore off their coats to wave them in the air; many wept tears of joy—in short, the scene of enthusiasm exceeded that which is sometimes witnessed at a Presidential nominating convention when a favorite candidate has been selected.

In the fervor of delight which followed, all those who had ever opposed the women's wishes fell into the deepest disfavor. It was proposed to expel from the Senate Edmunds and Ingalls[12] and every other man who had voted against a woman suffrage bill. One member suggested that they be banished to the Dry Tortugas[13] with the Rev. Morgan Dix as attendant chaplain.

Calmer counsels ultimately prevailed, as it was discovered that the worst offenders were now thoroughly penitent, and discussion followed as to what terms should be offered to the women to induce them to return. Everything was conceded, everything accepted, and a deputation of the foremost men was appointed to convey their propositions to the feminine Republic.

But when these reverend seigneurs started, they found that a vast array of volunteers were ready to accompany them, a throng that constantly increased as the news spread, and the trains moved westward, for men left their farms, their counting-houses and their stores, at the joyful words, "We are going to bring back the women."

Reforms in dress took place as if by magic, no man not properly attired was permitted to join the train. The barbers, who had all disappeared, most of them having become butchers, were rediscovered, and although rather out of practice, succeeded in putting heads and beards in presentable trim. Tobacco was positively forbidden, any man detected with even an odor of smoke in his garments was instantly sent to the rear. Alcoholic stimulants of all sorts were also strictly prohibited, and draw poker went suddenly out of fashion.

Meantime, in the feminine Republic matters moved on serenely, but it must be confessed a little slowly. The most absolute order prevailed; the homes were scrupulously tidy; the streets of the cities were always clean. The public money, which was no longer needed for the support of police officers and jails, was spent in the construction of schoolhouses and other beautiful public buildings. Artificers of all sorts had been found among the women, whose natural talents had heretofore been suppressed. Female architects designed houses with innumerable closets. Female contractors built them without developing a female Buddenseck,[14] and female plumbers repaired pipes and presented only moderate bills.

But despite the calm and peaceful serenity that prevailed, it was not to be denied that life was rather dull. Women who would not admit it publicly, whispered to themselves that existence would be a little gayer if there were some men to talk to occasionally. Mothers longed in secret for news from their sons; wives dreamed of their husbands, and young girls sighed as they thought of lovers left at home.

Certain great advantages had undoubtedly flowed from the new order of things. Women thrown wholly on their own resources had grown self-reliant, their imposed outdoor lives had developed them physically. A complete revolution in dress had taken place; compressed waists had totally disappeared, and loose garments were invariably worn. For out-door labors blouse waists, short skirts and long boots were in fashion; for home life graceful and flowing robes of Grecian design were worn. Common-sense shoes were universal. The schools under the care of feminine Boards of Education were brought to great perfection; the buildings, large and well-ventilated, offered ample accommodation, as over-crowding was not permitted. Individual character was carefully studied, and each child was trained to develop a special gift. Ethical instruction was daily given and children were rewarded for good conduct even more than for proficiency in study.

Music was carefully taught, and, undismayed by men, women wrote operas and oratorios. Free lectures were given on all branches of knowledge by scientific women who were supported by the State, and debating societies met nightly for the discussion of questions of public policy.

Still, despite all this the women, as we have seen, sent many a thought across the rocky barrier that separated them from the East, and under the leadership of Rose some of the younger ones had formed a league having for its object the opening of communication with husbands and brothers in the masculine Republic.

Thus matters stood when on a soft June morning word came to the Capital from the sentinels on the watch-towers of the mountains, that a great horde of men was advancing up the South Pass. Now across this road, the most convenient to the outer world, there had been built a wall, in the center of which was a massive gate of silver, and at this point the masculine army had halted. The news of the arrival of the men occasioned great commotion, and a joyful host of women started forth to meet them, so that when Volumnia and the other dignitaries of the State reached the Pass, the heights above were filled with a great throng of women who, recognizing in the crowd below sons and brothers, husbands and fathers, were waving joyous greetings, which were answered by the men with every demonstration of delight.

By the order of Volumnia the great silver gate was opened, and the envoys were admitted. They were received in a tent of purple satin which had been quickly erected and their leader made haste to lay before the assembled women the terms they proposed.

If the women would only return to their homes the men promised that all wage-workers should have equal pay for equal work; that women should be equally eligible with men to all official positions; that the fortifications should be turned into school-houses; that the control of the sale of liquors should be in the hands of women, and that universal suffrage, without regard to sex, should be everywhere established.

When the women heard these words they raised a chorus that was caught up and re-echoed by the crowd outside. At this moment, Cecilia, who saw her father just behind the envoys, went forward to embrace him, and Flavius, taking advantage of the movement advanced to where Rose stood beside her mother. Clasping the blushing girl by the hand, he whispered:

"At last, love, at last."

Wives rushed into their husbands' arms; mothers kissed their sons; the men hurried up from the Pass, the women came down from the mountain; there were broken whispers and fervent prayers, sobs mingled with smiles, and bright eyes shone through tears, as loved ones separated by the stern call of duty were reunited.

After this there followed a mighty movement, in prairie and forest, by lakeside and river. Over all the land, homes were rebuilt, and society reconstructed. The divided States, now reunited, formed a Republic where all the people were in reality free.

5

"A Feminine Iconoclast"
1889

MARY H[ANAFORD] FORD
[n.d.]

Of Mary H. Ford we know that she published the novel Which Wins? A Story of Social Conditions *(1891) and the following critique of Edward Bellamy's* Looking Backward *(1888) in* The Nationalist, *a magazine promulgating his views. Through Nationalism Bellamy urged nationalization of industry and equitable distribution of wealth. Nationalist Clubs existed throughout the United States and attracted eminent members, including Charlotte Perkins Gilman. In* The Impress *(5 Jan. 1895, 4–5), Gilman wrote a stylistic imitation of Bellamy called "A Cabinet Meeting," its implicit critique being that the 1950 President of the United States is a woman, four of whose ten cabinet members are clearly identified as women, three as men, and three not indicated. Ford also calls Bellamy especially to task for his patronizing and paternalistic view of women. For instance, recall the character Doctor Leete in* Looking Backward *assuring the narrator that "under no circumstances is a woman permitted to follow any employment not perfectly adapted both as to kind and degree of labor, to her sex." In the industrial army, she is "under an entirely different discipline." Leete concludes, women are "wardens of the world to come," a duty they respect with "a sense of religious consecration. It is a cult in which they educate their daughters from childhood" (173, 180). Though as late as 1960 this sex-bias passed unrecognized, it is clear to 1990s readers.*

Ford's critique takes the form of a conversation between two women riding a streetcar (called "car" throughout most of the text), one of whom thrusts sharply satiric jibes at Bellamy. An eavesdropper reports.

Reference: Edward Bellamy, *Looking Backward, 2000–1887* (1888; reprint, New York: New American Library, 1960); Vicki Lynn Hill, " 'A Distinctly Curious Collection of Human Beings': American Women Writers in the Age of Reform," *PMLA* 98, no. 6 (1983): 1094.

Text: Mary H. Ford, *The Nationalist* (Nov. 1889): 252–57.

As I was sitting in the street-car the other day, the conductor rang the bell, and two ladies sat down beside me who were sufficiently beyond the ordinary in appearance to attract attention, and as the car was not full and they were animated, I became an involuntary listener. The younger one, of robust and beautifully developed figure, appeared rather fatigued, and, her companion alluding to the fact, she responded with considerable vivacity: "Yes, I should think I might look tired, considering the number of shocks I've received, and the extent to which my opinions have been altered since I left home this morning!"

"Why, what is the matter?" replied her friend, looking decidedly amused, "I should think you were sufficiently accustomed to have your opinions assailed and could resist all attack!"

"Assailed!" responded the other, "certainly, but assailed and shaken are two very different things. I went down town this morning an enthusiastic Nationalist, and now I don't know what I am!"

"Dear me! that is rather serious," answered the first speaker, for evidently Nationalism had been a strong enthusiasm with her young friend, "but what is the matter with Mr. Bellamy now?"

"Oh! Mr. Bellamy is not exactly accountable for my idiosyncrasies, of course," said the young lady with an amused little laugh, "but I'll tell you how it is. You know," she began playing with the tassel of her rather elegant umbrella, "I have been connected with a newspaper for the last two years, and my salary has been a very acceptable addition to the family income since father's death. My brothers have not been especially successful bread-winners," (there was a little sadness in her voice as she said this) "and my youngest brother would not be able to complete his college course without my assistance. Well, this morning at breakfast the young man commenced in that sophomoric tone which I never can endure, 'Frances, I have finished Looking Backward,' (his profound studies kept him from reading it before, you know,) 'and I must say I have been much struck with it, especially with its treatment of the woman question. You see it fixes that up very nicely. It's all right for you women to settle your own affairs, but it might be a trifle irritating, I'll confess, to have you interfering with ours. And then, of course, in Mr. Bellamy's adjustment of the case, the question of capacity is not touched upon. There's no doubt that women can arrange their own matters properly without the intervention of men,'—he had risen now, and stood before the fire-place curling the ends of his moustache—'and it's perfectly proper that they should do so.' 'How kind you are, Arthur,' (I replied), 'you don't happen to remember the name of that young woman, do you, who took a prize in the Harvard Annex[1] some time ago? The prize was for the best essay descriptive of Rome in the time of the Caesars, I believe.' No, Arthur didn't remember,—he has a very convenient forgetfulness about such things. 'Well,' I went on, 'the prize was open to the whole college for competition. The successful young lady from the Annex signed her name to the winning essay just with initials—E. T. Dawson, or something like that,—and they thought the winner was a man, but when the judges found that they had unintentionally bestowed the prize upon a woman, they refused to give her the full amount of the prize money, which was one hundred dollars, but offered her half, which she very properly declined. I think in that case women would, as you say, have settled their own affairs properly, and they would have given E. T. Dawson all of the prize money.' Arthur stopped curling his moustache at that, and I went out in a great hurry, fearful I might be ungenerously tempted to remind him to how great an extent I am managing his affairs just at present. Soon after, as I was walking downtown I met Mr. Eaton; you know what a delicate little creature he is; well, he walked beside me while he was waiting for his car and talked Nationalism, he can't talk anything else nowadays, and presently he said: 'Oh! we are going to provide for you ladies, Miss Frances, and we will be very careful of you, too; we shan't let you do anything beyond your strength, or exhaust yourselves with grinding arduous labors,' and he skipped beside me with his cane making circles in the air, for all the world like a benignant musquito [sic]. 'Mr. Eaton,' I said, 'are you going to take a car? Yes? well, your office is not so far down town as mine, but I walk every morning because I enjoy it, and I should think any woman who dressed sensibly and was not an invalid would do the same. I rather enjoy labor,' I added,—for I certainly do,—'and if I had to choose between being a blacksmith and doing nothing, I certainly should be a blacksmith!' He grew so pale over that remark, I was glad his car came along, and I left him and walked on. When I reached the office, there lay The Dawn[2] for this month. I opened it with a great deal of pleasure, for I had liked the preceding numbers exceedingly, and turning to the editorial page, the first thing I saw was an allusion to Nationalism and the woman question. Speaking of the same pet adjustment of woman's judicial functions which Arthur had alluded to, the editor says: 'This would be justice to all, without doing violence to the true distinctions between man and woman which some fear would be violated in the ordinary development of woman's suffrage.' Now that might have looked very innocent had I not already been exasperated by Arthur's much more frank statement of the same thing, but that had opened my eyes and I began to feel as if cords were tied around my ankles. Are the Nationalists afraid, I thought, that women will expect too much, that they already begin to draw the line so carefully beyond which we cannot go? I wonder if there are women angels," she added, fixing her eyes dreamily on the distant sky, "for if there is any sex in the other world, I don't want to go there, unless I can be a snail or a lizard or something so amorphous that my higher nature will never bother me."

"But surely," said her friend with a little sigh, "it is better to have some privileges and liberties than to have none at all, isn't it?"

"No!" replied Miss Frances decidedly, "I don't want to have any privileges doled out to me like slices of gingerbread cut thin! I want to feel that I can stand up under any star and shine just as independently and vigorously as I choose. The proper distinction between man and woman!" she added vindictively, "what would I not give to be a plain human being, instead of having been born an ornament to society!"

"I heard of a woman today who would suit you," replied her friend, "I think you might call her a plain human being almost, in spite of her sex."

"Who is that?" exclaimed Miss Frances eagerly.

"She is a delicate little woman not so stalwart as you are," continued her friend, "and was professor in a state university where the admirable law is in force that a married woman cannot hold the office of teacher. She fell in love with one of her pupils, and when he was fitted to take her place married him and let him be professor. After awhile as the proprieties were satisfied by the fact that the office was held by a male, the little wife let her husband go to Europe to complete his education, while she acted as substitute for him at home, did his work and supported him and their little girl during his absence. How she made the two ends meet out of her meagre salary I don't know, but she did all of that and smiles about it."

"That was noble indeed!" cried Miss Frances heartily. "And her husband, what does he think of woman's sphere and the proper distinction between the sexes?"

"What he?" asked the lady with a hearty laugh, "I think if his wife wanted to enter the lists against John Sullivan[3] he would consider it a perfectly legitimate activity for her, and he would have no hope whatever for Mr. Sullivan in the contest."

Miss Frances sighed a trifle enviously. "Ah! that is what I call love," she remarked admiringly, "Do you know," she asked on a sudden, "whether she darns his socks?"

"Very likely she does, if occasion demands it," replied her friend, laughing still more heartily, "but I happen to know likewise that he frequently mends his own socks and her stockings, while she reads Goethe to him."

"I wish I could meet that man," cried Miss Frances, "and introduce him to Mr. Bellamy. I didn't tell you my last experience," she added, seeing her friend's mystification. "There is a young man on our journal who" (Miss Frances blushed a little, while she looked indignant) "sometimes makes love to me—or at least says things which are very disagreeable."

"Surely," interpolated her friend mischievously, "the two terms are not synonymous!"

"At any rate," continued Miss Frances, "he was talking to me this morning about Nationalism and he took occasion to quote a remark Mr. Bellamy makes descriptive of the marital happiness that will accrue from his system in those pleasant days when it is established. He says that husbands will have more time for love. I never thought any thing about it until that young man spoke of it, but I wish now that Mr. Bellamy had dilated upon the subject more fully, for certainly," concluded Miss Frances with great decision, "if his idea of love is the same as this young man's, I should wish that my husband had very little time for it."

"Now, Frances!" exclaimed her friend smiling, "you know that you are extremely romantic."

"I know I am romantic," cried Miss Frances, "but you remember what Balzac says, there is nothing more ennobling than *l'Amour,* nothing so degrading as *la Passion,* and think of it!" she continued, "the French language makes *l'Amour* masculine, and *la Passion* feminine; could ever anything show more plainly what men have made of women? When our Elysium comes," she added, "there will be no such thing as *la Passion; l'Amour* will bind the hearts of men and women so that they will go through life hand in hand without bothering their heads about the 'proper distinction between the sexes.' Then husband and friend will be synonymous terms, and a wife will not have to be continually adding a new patch to her opinions to make them fit those of her husband."

"Do you think you will ever marry, Frances?" asked her friend, smiling as she paused for breath.

"Yes," replied the young lady quickly; "whenever I can find a Nationalist who I am sure will never want to go to the Club to talk over things!"

"But I thought you were not a Nationalist any longer, though I cannot see exactly why," said Miss Frances's friend, after a momentary pause.

"Well," replied Miss Frances slowly and thoughtfully, "you see women have never yet had a fair chance at any thing. They have always been put in the position of mendicants, and if they received anything, the world said, in effect, 'you are objects of charity and we will assist you.' Even in the days of the Troubadours when poets were singing the names of fair ladies all over the land, and when those ladies' hearts must have been full of poetry, they could not sing. Oh, no! convention required them simply to be well-schooled and well-dressed and manage their adorers adroitly!"

"But I don't see what that has to do with Nationalism," interjected her friend gently.

"You don't?" responded Miss Frances sharply, "then I suppose you fail to realize how selfish I am. I thought Nationalism was going to offer an equal chance to all mankind irrespective of sex, but it does nothing of the kind so far, it simply leaves us in the position of mendicants, saying, —very sweetly to be sure—'I'm going to take care of you, I'll let you do certain things which I am sure you are fitted for, and I'll see that you are fairly treated in doing them and that you have equal wages.' That is very good," admitted Miss Frances, "but it is not what I want, and I am considering whether it is worth while to pin my faith to something which for me will only be a make-shift—whether in fact I can be magnanimous," she added smiling.

"What would you have?" asked her friend thoughtfully.

"That is soon told," replied Miss Frances. "I prefer that the Nationalists should say to me, 'my dear young lady, we don't know what you are fitted for, but we want you to do whatever you are capable of doing best, and if you cannot tell what this is, we will give you an education which will enable you to find it out for yourself.' That is what I should call fair, and as long as they do not say this, they don't know what freedom is."

"You see," responded her friend, "they have no conception of what a woman's life is, and how convention hedges her about even in this nineteenth century."

"Yes, and do you know how I would teach them?" exclaimed Miss Frances warmly, "I should like to take every Nationalist, and bind him hand and foot for a day to one of those straight-backed gilded chairs one sees so often in old palaces. I should bind him with golden chains, fan him with perfumed fans, and feed him meanwhile with ice cream and French candy. Then he would realize what it is to be a *fortunate* woman, and why I want freedom and fresh air in such large, unlimited doses!"

The two ladies left the car at this point in the conversation, and as I observed the swinging graceful gait of Miss Frances, I could not avoid thinking to myself, "what dreadful things they said, and how true most of them are!" But surely, my thoughts ran on, Miss Frances will not give up her allegiance to the Nationalist cause. It can not afford to lose such staunch confederates.

6

Hilda's Home:
A Story of Woman's Emancipation
1897

ROSA GRAUL
[n.d.]

Of Rosa Graul, we again know little—only that she was a "poor, hardwork-ing, unlettered woman," according to the "Publisher's Preface" (ii). Hilda's Home *was originally serialized in* Lucifer, the Light Bearer *(1883–1907), a journal of sex radicalism, edited by Moses Harman (1830–1910). Sex radical-ism must be construed not as licentiousness, but as a means to attain a fuller humanity, to improve, not flout, laws. Consider several cases familiar to nine-teenth-century readers: novelist Mary Ann Evans (better known as George Eliot, 1819–80), and critic-philosopher George Henry Lewes (1817–78), or suffragist Lucy Stone (1818–93), and Henry Blackwell (1825–1909; editor and co-editor respectively of* The Woman's Journal*). As here, its believers often intended to conserve family and gender ideals through a freer expression of sexual love. As early as 1853, Elizabeth Cady Stanton (1815–1902) wrote Susan B. Anthony (1820–1906) that*

> A child conceived in the midst of hate, sin and discord, nurtured in abuse and injustice cannot do much to bless the world or himself [*sic*]. If we properly understood the science of life—it would be far easier to give to the world, harmonious, beautiful, noble, virtuous children, than it is to bring grown-up discord into harmony with the great divine soul of all. (Stanton/Anthony, 55)

Hilda's Home *depicts this "science of life" guiding the community's residents. This sentimental novel reveals women and men falling out of and into love—a love which when freely expressed was believed to extend beyond the beloved individual and to infuse a whole community with well-being. The last chapters of the novel depict an established community, dedicated to both free love and free labor relations. Contrary to Marie Howland's fiction of a Social Palace funded by Count Paul Von Frauenstein (Ger.: women's rock) and just ready to operate at the conclusion of* Papa's Own Girl *(also* The Familistère, *1874), this community exists for several years. And it is the brainchild of a woman, Hilda Wallace. Both experiments, however, are founded upon individual wealth.*

As Kansas anarchist-publisher Moses Harman attests in a Preface, Graul's *"central aim" in* Hilda's Home *is "the emancipation of womanhood and motherhood from the domination of man in the sex relation. 'Self-ownership of woman' may be called the all-pervading thought of the book" (ii). Harman further refutes criticism both of the novel's co-operative labor and its acceptance of capital, and disclaims the place of perfection in an ideal conceptualization. The book is rather a "suggester of thought upon some of the most important and most perplexing of the problems [of human life]" (iv). Readers of* Lucifer *wrote to suggest "Where to Practicalize Hilda's Home"—the Ozarks in southern Missouri or Corvallis, Oregon, both regions supporting twentieth-century communitarian societies (June 2, Oct. 6, 1900).*

These final chapters of the novel show family, community, and labor ideals.

Reference: William Leach, *True Love and Perfect Union: The Feminist Reform of Sex and Society* (New York: Basic Books, 1980); Hal D. Sears, *The Sex Radicals* (Lawrence: Regents Press of Kansas, 1977), esp. 273, 319; *Elizabeth Cady Stanton/Susan B. Anthony: Correspondence, Writing, Speeches,* ed. Ellen Carol DuBois (New York: Schocken, 1981); Taylor Stoehr, *Free Love in America: A Documentary History* (New York: AMS, 1979).

Text: Rosa Graul, *Hilda's Home: A Story of Woman's Emancipation,* Lucifer, the Light Bearer, nos. 613–87, June 1896–Dec. 1897 (reprint, Chicago: M. Harman, 1899, chaps. 42:377–80 [serial chaps. 56–57], 46:406–14 [serial chaps. 63–64], Conclusion: 420–26 [also serial Conclusion]). The book version is the source.

Chapter 42

. . . Hilda . . . , having been importuned, was trying to make plain that vague sweet dream of her future co-operative home, and none so attentive, or none more so than Owen. She spoke of the spacious halls where the ardent searchers after knowledge of any kind might find their teacher; of the library stocked with volumes from the ceiling to the floor; of the lecture hall and the theater; of the opportunities where every talent could be cultivated; of the liberty—the free life—where every fetter should be broken; of the dining hall where they would partake of their evening meal midst flowers and music; of the common parlor where every evening should be an entertainment for all wherein love and genuine sociability should always preside; of the sacred privacy of the rooms where each man or woman should reign a king or queen—the sanctum of each, closed to all intruders, consecrated to the holiest and divinest of emotions and self-enfoldment. She spoke of the grand conservatories filled with choicest flowers—the sweet-scented blossoms, the trailing vines, the exotic plants; of the spacious gardens, the sparkling, everplaying fountains; of the delicious, health-giving baths; of the life of unconventionality,—of the abandon; of the nursery rooms where baby lips were lisping their first words and little toddling feet taking their first uncertain steps; of the things of beauty surrounding the prospective mother; of the unutterably sweet welcome that awaited each coming child; of the full understanding that would be taught to woman of the responsibility of calling into life a new being; of how man would revere her, how he would wait and abide her invitation; of the sweet co-operation and planning how all should be worked to keep up the financial part.

"O," said she, "it should, it would be paradise!—this my dream. But ah me! it is only a dream."

As a being transfigured Hilda stood among them, her eyes shining, her cheeks glowing, her bosom heaving, looking far beyond them into space. A feeling came over Lawrence Westcot as with bated breath his eyes rested on her, of how utterly unworthy he was of the love of a creature so grand, so superior. A still, small voice whispered, "Make yourself worthy!"—and then and there a high resolve was formed in his mind that he would surely do so. A solemn vow rose as a silent prayer from the depths of his heart that some day he would realize that sweet invitation. With him every man in the room became conscious of a feeling of inferiority, but not an impulse to bow in humility. Rather each head was crested higher with a feeling of lofty aspiration.

Owen Hunter answered the closing remarks of Hilda's dream picture:

"Why, my dreaming maiden, should your dream be but a dream?"

A sad smile played about her lips,

"You forget that it is such an expensive one. It would take a fortune, an almost limitless fortune, to build us such a home. Of course we could be very, very happy in our little circle, as it is, in a much smaller and less expensive home, but I would have it large, so that we might welcome all who possess the same lofty thought to our circle, so that we should be able to give to the world an object lesson in the art of making life worth living, so grand and so glorious that the whole world would want to imitate our example."

Owen smiled.

"What an enthusiast! Take my advice, little one, and until this grand, this glorious home can be ours, help us with your lofty aspirations, and help us not to despise our more limited advantages and privileges. In the meantime we will try to become more worthy of so perfect a home—as some years must of necessity elapse ere it can be completed."

"Have I not said it is only a dream? How can I dare to hope it could ever be realized; and when I come to this home, day after day, and realize what privileges are ours the feeling sometimes comes to me, how wrong-headed I am to be constantly sighing for still more."

Owen shook his head.

"You are mistaken, Miss Hilda. Your sentiments and aspirations are not wrong. Harmonious and beautiful as is the life that has been granted you through the mutual understanding and sympathy of our kind host and hostess, it is by no means complete. So dream on, plan on, and if there is an architect in our circle he shall transfer these plans to paper, and, as soon as practicable, we will look about us for a suitable site, and when the spring sunshine calls all nature again to life, work shall begin, and what has so long been only a vague dream shall, all in good time, bloom into a living reality."

All eyes hung upon the lips of the speaker. All ears drank in his words. Could such a thing be possible? Only Cora seemed to understand. Pressing close to his side, she drew his hand with a caressing motion to her smiling lips. With a hasty movement he withdrew the hand to lay it on the head covered with the soft fluffy hair; he pressed it close to him. Hilda drew a step nearer and extending both hands,

"You mean—O, Mr. Hunter! do you really mean that it can be done? that the home can and shall be ours? But how? how?"

Cora slipped down upon her knees at Hilda's side and caught both those hands in hers.

"Did I not tell you long ago, when I told you that story of my heartaches and my noble lover, that he possessed almost limitless wealth? He could not be one of us did he not consecrate some of his millions to the happiness of others. It is in his power to lay the foundation stone for the future ideal society, by showing to the world an example of how people should live. Don't you see, my Hilda? Owen is wealthy, and he is going to build us our home."

Chapter 46

Five years have passed since the dedication of that beautiful home; years that have brought their changes, as time invariably does. The mystic rooms—the sanctum of the expectant mother—have been occupied, again and yet again. Our royal Margaret was the first to come under the spell of its sweet and wonderful influence. Giving herself up to the delightful occupations provided for in these secluded rooms, keeping ever in mind the grand result which was to come of it, one morning after a night of pain and suspense Wilbur kissed a fine, beautiful, healthy boy that was laid in his arms. Kneeling at her side with his head resting on the same pillow with the fair white face of his peerless Margaret the whisper greeted his ear:

"I am blessed today beyond the measure of woman."

Who shall say that his happiness did not equal her own.

Another had not been long in following her brave example. When Cora's baby girl was laid upon her breast Owen's measure of happiness was filled and tears blinded his eyes as he kissed the mother of his child.

The two sisters, Edith and Hilda, both brought joy and happiness to their lovers' hearts by presenting them with a miniature reflection of themselves, and Norman had held Imelda's boy to his heart.

By this time the babies that first came to the new home were making glad the hearts of their mothers by their childish prattle; some of the mothers were watching the first trembling footsteps, and Alice was waiting, watching for the coming hour. Milton watched with worshipful tenderness the little fairy whose love was life to him.

New faces also now greet us. New comers have helped to fill the precious home, who were just as good and worthy as those fortunes we have so long followed.

But to return to the young mothers. They did not devote all their time to their darling babies. O, no! Dearly as they loved them they found that they had other work to do while the little ones were left to the care of those who were perfectly trustworthy. Not to be petted, not to be pampered and spoiled, but left to those who understood how to get to the depths of each baby nature.

When it is remembered what preparation had been made for their advent it is not surprising that they were wonderfully good babies. When it is remembered with what joy they were welcomed—welcomed while still in the first stages of foetal growth; how carefully the prospective mothers had been kept under calm, sweet and pure influences; how their minds had been kept active without taxing their strength; how constantly their souls had been bathed in the luxury of sympathy and love; how every part of their natures had been kept teeming with life—overflowing life; how carefully undue excitement had been warded off; how they were given every opportunity for cultivating the higher human instincts,—the spiritual nature;—when all this is remembered we cannot help seeing that, on the principle of natural causation, the children of such mothers and of such influences could not be other than exceptionally well endowed and exceptionally well behaved.

But when the months had passed, during which the mother should give her personal care and attention to her cherished babe, it was transferred to the sole care of the experienced nurse, and she herself returned to her usual work, whatever that work might happen to be. There were so many fields open, and each made her choice. The head gardener was glad to get help in the tending and nursing of his plants and flowers. Nimble, dextrous fingers were needed to fashion the garments to be worn by the occupants of the home, and this large and beautiful home needed many willing hands to keep it beautiful. All this however was work which could be entrusted to and performed by stronger hands, if other work should prove more attractive, work in which more than ordinary intelligence and skill were required. Among our band were teachers of music and song, as might be expected of the artist soul seeking expression. Margaret had kissed her lover and baby good-bye and had given another season to her loved profession and had returned again with, O, such longing and love for the home and the circle of loved ones it contained.

But there was other work. The forty minutes required to reach the heart of the city were used by quite a number, morning and evening. In the heart of the city rose a grand emporium many stories high, where many hundreds of young women and men were employed, and which was the property of the home circle; an emporium which had been built by Norman and Lawrence and fitted up by Owen, and which was one of the largest business places in the great city; an emporium where people of all ages and sizes could purchase for themselves an outfit from the crown of their heads to the soles of their feet. There was the tailor's department and that of the dressmaker. There the milliner fashioned pretty headgear, and there are all the beautiful artificial flowers, of which countless numbers used from week to week were made. There the visitor would go from floor to floor, from department to department, and would find every place to have its own attraction, its own work.

But the most beautiful department of them all was that of the florist, where nature's handiwork was heaped up in wild and charming confusion, and where these floral beauties, by deft and cunning fingers, were arranged into designs without number, and in this department it was that you could see our own fair girls moving about, giving orders here, lending aid there, and again seeing that patrons were promptly served. All was life, all were busy, yet none were overworked as none worked longer than five hours here. At seven o'clock in the morning when the doors were opened, they admitted what was termed the morning "turn." And when twelve o'clock announced the noon hour the merry throng, laughing and singing arrayed themselves for the street and went trooping out like a merry flock of birds, for their day of work was over. It was a day's work, and thus they were paid. With the striking of the hour of one, the afternoon "turn" began, and others filled the places of the morning workers. So the faces of the saleswomen and salesmen were always fresh and smiling, with none of that tired, wornout appearance that is so often noticeable in the young faces you meet behind the counter.

Where were all these employees housed? Heretofore as these people generally are housed. Those who still had a father or mother or both living, live with them; in most cases large families crowded into two or three rooms. Others who were not so fortunate, had to submit to all the discomforts of cheap boarding houses, or lived in some stuffy back room or bleak attic. But a change was about to take place. Today the large business building is closed. No one moves about its wide halls and its many departments. It is a grand "fete" and gala day. Today is to be dedicated the grand new home which has been erected for them.

After two years of life in their co-operative home its inmates were convinced of its success and felt almost like thieves that they should enjoy so many privileges which were beyond the reach of those to whom they gave employment, and then the plans were made for a new home, and again Owen's millions did service and now a beautiful, grand structure had been erected. But not so far away from the place of work as their own. That would have been cruelty to the morning "turn" who were expected to be at their post at the hour of seven, and equally unpleasant for the afternoon "turn" as it would cause them to be late for their evening meal.

Right on the outskirts of the city, where fifteen minutes would be all that would be required to bring them back and forth, a site was bought upon the brink of the beautiful river, elevated just enough to be beyond the reach of any possible flood. A park had been laid out which in time would be one of the handsomest the city could boast of, with its miniature lakes, its splashing fountains, its dense shrubbery, its gleaming statuary and flowery banks. And right in the midst of these beautiful surroundings this monster home was built. For three long years the workmen toiled, until when finished it was the finest of its kind that fancy could depict. A place where home pleasures would be given the workers, such as they had never known; where every arrangement had been made to amuse, to instruct, to educate, to develop the inmates. It boasted of its school rooms, its college, its sculpture hall and artist's studio, its lecture hall and theater, where the best of traveling troupes were to be engaged, with perfect arrangements for the accommodation of those troupes. Here the players would not have to undergo the extra fatigue, after their tiresome work, to again dress for the street, catch the last cold car which was to take them to their place of lodging. No indeed! The theater of the workers' home was a marvel of its kind. Large, airy, comfortable and well furnished rooms were attached to it, a room to every player, so near and convenient to the stage that it was not required to dress in little boxes or holes for their work. Here they could dress in quiet and comfort and then rest until the signal to begin was given.

When through with their work, in the pleasant, comfortable dining room connected with the theater for the convenience of this hard-working class of people—how hard-working few, not of the profession, ever realize—a simple but refreshing repast was served, which repast was so restful and had so much real comfort in it that the traveling bands invariably forgot that intoxicants were absent from it.

Then there was a library with its thousands of volumes containing reading matter of every kind, but always choice, always select, always instructive. A large billiard room was also there. Then came the gymnasium for the development of physical strength and where both sexes were expected to participate. There was to be a singing class and dancing school.

The baths were not forgotten. Larger, more complete than at the first home—so many more were to make use of them here.

All arrangements were complete. A large, airy hall where breakfast and the mid-day meal were to be served. But here, as in that other home, the evening meal, which would be the chief meal of the day, was to be taken amidst nature's beauties in a large and beautiful conservatory. Owen had spent a fortune in furnishing it with the required plants which were of the rarest kinds. A miniature lake was formed in its center, wherein the little golden speckled beauties were dashing and splashing about in their merry chase. A fountain was reared in its center composed of a half dozen nude mermaids holding their hands aloft, their finger tips forming a circle from which the water was flung aloft in showering spray. Sweet voiced songsters filled the air with their thrilling music. Flowers bloomed in wild profusion; huge vases were filled with their brilliant treasures wherever they could be suitably placed.

At several places small artificial hills had been erected, ferns and grasses growing amidst the rocks. Through a small rocky ravine the water came tumbling into a basin below, forming a small lake. Palms, cactus and other plants were grouped at convenient places. Nooks and alcoves without number had been arranged wherein the tables had been placed and were now spread and awaiting the hungry guests, each table seating about a dozen and through it all rare, sweet music, coming from some hidden source lulled the tired senses to rest and quiet.

The last preparations had been made. The last garlands had been hung. To every room its inmate had been assigned, which promised them all the same sweet privacy when privacy was desired, as in the first and smaller home. Every room was furnished cozily and comfortably, and every inmate, if so they desired, could claim some musical instrument for their private use, besides which there was a music hall where first class musical instruments of all kinds abounded. A number of the best teachers had been engaged to supervise the different departments, to teach and bring to light the hidden talents that none might be lost, but all shine in their full glory.

The grounds were something wonderful, or in time would be so, when the years would have done their work. The drives were beautiful, so wide and clean. Ponds covered with waterlilies. Fountains everywhere. Lover's nooks and cozy retreats. Plants, shrubbery and flowers in glorious profusion, and artistic designs wherever the eye might rest.

Down the sloping banks of the river wide, spacious stairways of hewn stone had been made which led down beneath the laving waters. Skiffs, large and small were moored here, inviting and wooing lovers of the watery element to trust themselves to its glassy bosom, to be rocked on its silvery, rippling waves and be borne whither soever they might wish.

Owen had made a deep hole in his millions. Lack of funds should not prevent it from being a success. And now the new inmates of this wonderful home were waiting the summons of their first evening meal. All the "salons" of the lower floors were swarming with gayly dressed maidens and with young men attired in their best. Instinctively they knew that henceforth they must always put their best efforts to the front, and the blending of youthful voices in merry laughter made the listener glad.

But not all were young that were assembled here tonight. Many there were who had seen the darker side of life and who in all probability would prefer the solitude and quiet of their own rooms to the noisy merry-making of a careless and care-free youth.

And among all those who found a home within the walls of this magnificent structure those had not been forgotten whose labor had produced it, had made it the thing of beauty it now stood. As might be expected the builders had grown to love it as they worked, and the knowledge that they should enjoy its beauties and comforts when finished had stimulated them to work more eagerly and with extra skill until the day of its completion.

Conclusion

The evening meal is over. All have gathered on the broad veranda to watch the golden sunset as it dips its slanting rays in the river beyond. They are unusually quiet, even for this serious band. Last night's merry making has made them just a little tired, besides which their hearts are full of unuttered prayers for the future success of that new home.

Mrs. Leland is sitting in the comfortable depths of an easy chair. A sturdy little man of four summers perches upon her knee, patting grandma's cheek, tossing her hair in his efforts to smooth it, taking her face between both chubby hands and drawing her head forward so that he can kiss her happy, smiling lips and altogether making love in the most approved fashion.

Margaret is sitting at her feet, her arm thrown across her mother's knee, while her eyes with a happy, tender light follow the movements of her boy, and her heart swells with fond tenderness and pride at the knowledge that he is her very own.

At grandma's back stands Wilbur whose eyes also follow the antics of the boy when they for a few moments lose sight of the glorious sunset.

Mr. Roland is a visitor at the home tonight, and sits a little to the right of this group, quietly drinking in the scene before him in the pauses of the animated conversation he is carrying on with the brilliant little lecturer, Althea Wood, who also is a guest at the home tonight.

Farther to the left are various groups. The two pairs of sisters— Imelda and Cora, Edith and Hilda—have formed a circle, their babies forming the center of their attention. There are three little prattlers while one sweet little cooing innocent lies close to Imelda's breast.

O, the joys of young motherhood! And the group of men that were standing a little apart felt the influence of the spell and each thought his sweetheart had never looked more fair.

Alice in delicate health was reclining in an easy chair while Milton with adoring eyes stood over her chair ready to do her slightest bidding. O, if she were only safely tided over the coming hour of trial! And as the sigh escapes him his hand caressingly toys with the bright mass of shining hair.

Lawrence has his Norma perched upon his knee answering her many questions. She has grown to be quite a big girl now, but has never outgrown her early love for her papa, and ever with the old delight greets his coming. The two are so near to Alice that she can comfortably watch them, and while a smile of proud tenderness wreathes her lips, it is Milton's hand to which they are laid.

"My baby!" She whispers the tender words.

"A little longer patience," is Milton's whispered reply, "and your baby will be your own!"

Her hand went up to his face with a caressing touch.

"I know," she smiling said, "but it was Norma I meant this time."

He drew the hand to his lips as with a knowing smile he answered: "Ah, I see!"

Lawrence now and then let his eyes wander to the mother of his child, then they would turn to the group of fair young women where a pair of sweet gray eyes met his in a tender glance, then to rest on the little one reclining against his bosom. Which did he love most? His eyes lit up with a glad tenderness as they rested on the little one and then he drew the fair curly head so near him, close to his heart and hid his face in the fluffy masses; could he himself answer the question?

Many other faces we see which are all new to us, but they are all men and women worthy to be called by these names.

A group of the younger people have strayed down to the sweet-scented gardens gathering flowers as they go. Osmond and Homer are fast friends. Both are young men untouched by the rough hand of fate. Their young manhood, so perfect in its strength and beauty giving them the appearance of young kings, so proud, so lofty, was their bearing. Elmer, too, could scarcely be termed a boy any longer. His twenty years sat well on his broad shoulders and the eyes of the fifteen year old Meta shone bright as stars, her cheeks flushed as he chased her through the winding mazes of the park, and when he had caught her and kissed the rosy lips she submitted as a matter of course with the most natural grace.

Osmond had thrown himself at the feet of Hattie Wallace whose nineteen summers sat lightly on her shoulders. She was such a fairy and with rosy hued cheeks she listened to the soft, love-freighted words that fell in whispers from Osmond's lips.

Homer's companion was a dark, soft-eyed young girl, timid and shy who had been an inmate of the home for one year, where she had come with her mother who had fled in the dead of night from her husband and sought refuge in this haven of rest, and Homer was teaching the sweet Katie her first experience in the mysteries of love.

Aleda, the youngest of the Wallace girls was also there, and seventeen years had developed a truly pretty and healthy girl from the delicate querulous child. Another new comer had engaged her attention. Reading from a volume of Tennyson, a boy scarcely older than herself was reclining at her feet. He too had been brought there by a mother, not one who had fled the cruelties of an unappreciative husband, as she had never applied the title to any man. He had been a child of love.

His mother, in the wild sweet delirium of a first love, had abandoned herself to her artist lover without a thought of right or wrong. And he, pure and noble had no thought of wronging her. But disease had early marked him for its own, and ere the child of his Wilma had seen the light of day his own life had closed in that sleep that knows no waking, and she was left alone to buffet the storms of life as best she could, an orphan and without friends. With a babe in her arms of "illegal" origin, the path of her life had not been strewn with roses. But amidst all her privations and trials she had kept her love pure for her child and had fostered only instincts pure and holy in the young mind, and when she heard of the home she applied at its gates, telling her story in pure, unvarnished words, never dreaming of an effort to hide any of her past.

Only by the light of truth could the delicate fair woman thread her path through the world.

As might be expected, she had been received with open arms. Wilma, the mother of Horace, our young poet, and Honor, Katie's mother, could now be seen as they stand arm in arm watching the golden sunset and the children whose future promises to bring with it less of the pain that has so early drawn silver threads through their own brown locks.

The world at large knew not the full meaning of this home as yet. The world is yet too completely steeped in superstition and ignorance to have permitted its existence had the full meaning been known. The "Hunter Co-operative Home" it had been called, and thus it was known to the world. It was known that babes had made their advent therein, but none but the initiated knew that marriage as an institution was banished from its encircling walls.

Would you ask us if happiness was so unalloyed within those walls that no pangs of regret or of pain could enter there? Well, no! We are not so foolish as to make such claim. There are hours of temptation; there are moments of forgetfulness; there are sometimes swift, keen, torturing pangs that nothing earthly can completely shut out. Our heroes and heroines are not angels. They are—when the very best of them has been said—only intelligent, sensible and sensitive men and women—but men and women who are possessed of high ideals and who are striving hard to reach and practicalize them. They live in a world of thought. They do nothing blindly, inconsiderately; their every action is done with eyes wide open. In trying to gain the goal they have set themselves to reach, they strive not to think of self alone. The future of those who have been entrusted to their care, the young lives their love has called into existence, exacts from them much of self-denial. They are individualists, yet not so absolutely such that they do not realize that sometimes the ego must be held in check so as not to rob another of his, or her, birth right.

You ask again, "Does this home life, as you have pictured insure against the possibility of the affections changing?"

And again we answer, No! Certainly not. Such changes will and must come. Yet [is it] not to be expected that where there is liberty, in the fullest sense of the word, life will be a constant wooing? Is it not the lack of liberty that deals the death blow to many a happy, many a once happy home? to many a home that was founded in the sweetest of hopes, the brightest of prospects, only to be shattered and wrecked in a few short years? aye, even a few short months or weeks? And when such a change does come, in spite of all efforts to prevent, how great a thing it must be to know yourself free? free to embrace the new love without the horrible stigma of "shame!" as our modern society now brands it, and which stigma causes such unspeakable misery, such endless suffering.

And if a woman desires to repeat the experience of motherhood, why should it be wrong when she selects another to be the father of her [child], instead of the one who has once performed this office for her? Why should the act be less pure when she bestows a second love, when the object of this second love is just as true, just as noble, just as pure-minded as was the first one? Why should an act be considered a crime with one partner which had been fully justified with another?

Reader, judge me not hastily. Judge not my ideas, my ideals, without having first made a careful study of life as you find it around you. My words are backed by personal experience and observation, experience as bitter as any that has been herein recorded. Indeed I doubt if I should, or could, ever have given birth to the thoughts expressed in these pages had it not been for that experience—which is one of a thousand—and when you have carefully weighed my words, think of the good that must result to future generations when unions are purely spontaneous, saying nothing of the increase of happiness of those who are permitted thus to choose, and to live.

When, O, when will the great mass of humanity learn and realize that in enforced motherhood, unwelcome motherhood, is to be found the chief cause of the degradation that gives birth to human woe. When will they see that unwelcome motherhood is the curse resting upon and crushing out the life energies of woman; while on the other hand, the consciousness of being the mother of a desired babe, a child conceived in a happy, a loving embrace, needs no other blessing, no other sanction, no other license, than such act itself bestows.

7

"A Dream of the Twenty-first Century"
1902

WINNIFRED HARPER COOLEY
1876–after 1955

*A*lthough *the only daughter of a famous woman—Ida Husted Harper (1851–1931), social activist, author of* Life and Work of Susan B. Anthony *(3 vols., 1898, 1908), and an editor of* The History of Woman Suffrage *(vols. 4–6, 1902, 1922)—vital statistics of Winnifred Harper Cooley resist recovery. Her parents married in 1871; she must have been born in Indiana about 1876 since she was 20 upon receiving after three years' study an A.B. in Ethics from Stanford University in 1896. After a divorce in 1890, her mother had moved to Indianapolis, where Cooley was boarding. She became poet and class orator at the progressive Girls' Classical School, established in 1882 by May Wright Sewell (1844–1920). Her mother apparently moved with her to California for the college years. In 1899 she married the Reverend George Elliot Cooley, a Unitarian minister: they lived first in Vermont, but moved to Grand Rapids, Michigan, until his nervous breakdown, and eventually settled in New York City. She was noted for having founded there in 1923 a biweekly dinner-forum facetiously called "The Morons," drawing as many as 200 to 300 guests to hear the eminent lecture, debate, or entertain. By 1926, however, she was a widow. In 1939, she was still residing in New York City and passing summers traveling the world.*

A syndicated journalist, lecturer, and teacher, she expressed interest in a wide variety of subjects, among them women's issues, pure food, travel, literature, and current drama. She concluded a 1904 article on divorce with the claim

125

*that "thoughtless and immoral alliances" are the "canker at the[ir] root" (*The Arena *32 (Sept. 1904): 291–93). In 1904 Cooley published* The New Womanhood, *in which she surveys the historical roots of women's personal liberty—formerly confined to the occasional genius, now more generally possible to women as a class, she thinks. In addition the book covers such issues as single women, divorce, cooperative housekeeping, population control, and occupational access. Later she wrote articles defending suffragists, first against upstart "suffragettes" (*Hearst's Magazine *15 (Oct. 1908): 1066–71) and second against conservative, outdated suffragists (*Harper's Weekly *58 (27 Sept. 1913): 7–8). The dream vision that follows incorporates several of these concerns. Like Lois Waisbrooker in* A Sex Revolution, *(1894), one of Cooley's major concerns is pacifism.*

References: *Encyclopedia of American Biography* 7 (1937); *Notable American Women,* vols. 2 and 3 (Cambridge, Mass.: Harvard Univ. Press, 1971); Barbara Quissell, "The New World That Eve Made," in *America as Utopia,* ed. Kenneth M. Roemer (New York: Franklin, 1981), 166, 174; "Stanford [Univ.] Class of '96" (Stanford, Calif.: Stanford Alumni Assn., 1926), 127–29.

Text: Winnifred Harper Cooley, "A Dream of the Twenty-First Century," *Arena* 28 (Nov. 1902): 511–16.

It was New Year's night of the twentieth century. The new cycle of a hundred years had been ushered in by chimes and bugles, by jollity and revel, and I was wearied by all the excitement, and, sleeping, dreamed a dream. I dreamed that it was the first day of the *twenty-first* century, and that I, an old woman, somehow sojourning still upon the earth, was seeking knowledge as to the new conditions. My instructress was a radiant creature, in flowing, graceful robes—a healthful, glorious girl of the period: the product of a century of freedom.

"Tell me," I said, "what evolution has done for you, my fair Feminine Type." The maiden answered: "We have made such advances that I fear to seem egotistic if I tell you, for I have heard that at the beginning of the twentieth century the world actually considered itself civilized! I have tried to read the history of those early days, but ignorance, cruel injustices, and utter irrationality existing in a supposed free land affect me as unpleasantly in retrospect as the Spanish Inquisition affected you."

I felt somewhat insulted at this reflection upon my own times, and replied: "But we of the nineteenth and twentieth centuries made marvelous additions to the wealth and knowledge of nations. We invented the automobile, wireless telegraphy, and the Roentgen ray; we gave you a fine system of education, a democracy—"

"Not so," she interrupted. "You gave a republic; a corrupt, subsidized government, manipulated by greed, controlled by one set of selfish mercenaries after another, under partizan leaders; a one-sided affair at best, where only one sex voted, and an absurd electoral college registered the votes of States instead of counting the majority of the people. Now, we have unqualified equal suffrage—for all of the citizens are educated, and women are among the best voters; also the initiative and referendum, complete civil service, government control of public utilities—"

"Stop!" I cried; "I never could straighten out those technical names."

"You see," she explained, "in your day millionaires were made by getting control of that which the people were obliged to have, and charging what they wished, as if they were imitation gods, having a monopoly of Nature. They almost charged for the air you breathed! We have abolished oil trusts, private ownership of mines, railways, electric-light plants, and express and telegraph companies; and you would be amazed to see how the frightful discrepancies in individual wealth are done away with, without any artificial schemes of 'dividing up' personal property and giving the belongings of the industrious man to the shiftless. Ambition and individuality are still allowed; also private incomes. All these businesses are run as smoothly in the cooperative spirit as the Post Office ever was; and they pay for themselves, besides allowing the poorer people to use the necessities and comforts for a nominal sum. I wish I might tell you of the marvelous changes wrought along industrial lines, but the instances are too numerous to explain."

"You mean that sweat-shops are abolished?"

"All such, and a thousand other evils once considered almost a requisite of trade. The hours of labor in every department of work are greatly reduced. By using all the adults, permitting no dependent classes, either tramps, paupers, or idle rich, we have found that the world's work can be done by each healthy individual working five hours a day. You will readily understand how this benefits the indolent by compelling exercise, and the industrious by affording leisure, not to speak of the good that accrues to society by having all its members in a normal state, with time at their command for inventions, art, and letters."

"This accounts, also, doubtless, for the good health that seems to prevail?"

"There are many reasons—increased happiness, development of science, perfect sanitation everywhere existing. The abolition of slums was brought about chiefly by women."

"In my time, excepting the college settlement workers and the Salvation Army, there were few who seriously labored along such dirty lines."

"Some time ago women began to comprehend that, not alone for the safety of their own loved children but for that of all little ones, in the alleys as well as on the boulevards, there must be an eradication of disease, that the rising generation should not begin life hampered by unclean bodies and tainted morals. Hindered at first, by not having official power, the women did their best with the insidious, left-handed influence that always was recommended to them by men; but when given political freedom they went to work with enthusiasm, using the 'influence' *necessary* to effect transformations—the ballot. And so we have a fine sanitary condition and a healthful race."

"Marriage is as of old?" I timidly ventured.

"That depends upon what you consider was in vogue in your time. Monogamy was officially recognized but not universally practised, we have been told."

"I thought perhaps it is now abolished," I retorted.

"Oh, no; it is almost universal with us. The improvement in the average income has done away with the barrier of poverty, and a higher moral standard has abolished that nineteenth-century horror—the city bachelor. Every one marries, and the number of ideal unions is really very large. The age of marrying is a trifle higher, following the tendency of your time; but this is as it should be, for every one stays in college until at least twenty-two."

"Every one?"

"Yes, our compulsory education extends through college, and all, including universities, are free. As in your day, the happiest marriages were those formed by the products of co-educational colleges; so now, you see, all the unions are happy ones."

"I do not see many children?"

"No; they do not swarm the back streets like rats. But you will find, by our statistics, that the increase is sufficient to keep the race extant."

"Goodness! Are families regulated by law?"

"Hardly that; but the advance of civilization seems to go hand in hand with a decrease in population. The tendency toward having fewer children has been encouraged instead of censured by public opinion, which now, as ever, is the greatest ruler of mankind. Instead of bewailing the 'good old families of fifteen' or acting hypocritically, we frown upon people who bring more than two children into the world, unless they, by virtue of excessive wealth, health, morals, or talents, seem unusually well qualified to educate and nurture a family. Social Control suggests that men and women devote much thought to the minds and hearts of their youth; consequently, the character of children has increased marvelously as the number has decreased. Even their longevity is now prolonged, and the death-rate of infants is remarkably small."

"All this is strange and fascinating, though it would have shocked my contemporaries," I ventured.

"It is not unnatural. It is but the logical working out of civilization. Another cause for the finer type of childhood today is the tender love and congeniality existing between parents. The abolition of multi-millionaires prevents mercenary marriages, and a few simple laws discourage discrepancies in age between men and women; but unless physically and morally unfit, two persons strongly attracted to each other are expected to wed."

"All this is most remarkable; and, I doubt not, the inventions and all material matters have kept pace with these social and moral innovations. But how could such radical transformations be wrought—improvements, I grant, and desired by the prophets of my day—while human nature remained sordid, selfish, grasping, and sensual? Surely your last hundred years have not revolutionized the *heart of man?*"

"I think it is mainly due to our rational religion. It was a mighty struggle to overcome dogmatism, superstition, ritualism, emotionalism, and conservatism, especially as the leaders of our great Religion of Humanity had nothing exciting, dramatic, pompous, or mystical to offer in place of the old. But simplicity and sense at last conquered. The only weapon of the new church was Education; and at length all the old creeds crumbled away, and now are preserved in libraries, with the Icelandic myths and Vedic hymns, to record the development of the mind of man in its groping toward God."

"Is the new religion Christian?"

"Yes; its essentials are based upon the moral teachings of Jesus, but it does not fear to inculcate the best that has been worked out by every people that has struggled and suffered and aspired beneath the sun. It does not scorn the simplest death-song of an Indian if this expresses some noble conception of immortality more clearly than do the sages."

"And it is this world-religion that has wrought so many reforms in politics, economics, and morals?"

"Yes, and it has done more. By destroying the spite and fight over hair-splitting theological problems it has enabled men and women to turn their zeal and energy into practical ethics and philanthropy, and to believe that if all men are indeed children of God, and brother, they must act as such; and so we have attained Universal Peace!"

"Indeed? This must be something like heaven. The Bible proclaimed 'peace on earth,' but for two thousand years Christians seemed content with bloody war."

"We are not yet perfect, but we are no longer pessimists. The low rumble of insurrection heard in your day has died away, and all of us are bending every force toward the serious business of making life worth living and this world habitable, in a moral as well as in a material sense. Criminals, paupers, and tramps are practically unknown, and the strong public feeling toward one standard of purity—and that the highest—for men and women has elevated the social life of the whole world."

"I should think you would want never to die!" I cried.

"The rate of mortality is much lower than formerly; we know little of old age, in the sense of decrepitude, as of yore. We live better as well as longer lives, too," said the beautiful woman. "We do not profess any didactic knowledge of a future existence, but we hope and long for personal immortality, as people always have hoped and longed, and our scientists and psychologists believe they are about to prove it. We all try to live so that if our activities continue after death we may have somewhat approximated perfection upon this earth."

I awoke—to hear the ragged little newsboys (products of an imperfect social system) bellowing forth the financial crashes, murders, suicides, and scandals so glowingly regaled by the "yellow journals." I turned my face to the pillow, and prayed: "O God, may I live to do my small part of the world's work, and help to hasten the conditions that I dare dream will prevail in the twenty-first century!"

8

"A Woman's Utopia"
1907

CHARLOTTE PERKINS [STETSON] GILMAN
1860–1935

During the 1990s, Gilman is enjoying a veritable flood of critical interest. She remains one of the nation's most incisive thinkers about gender relations, although not about sexual, racial, or class issues. Her fiction and essays are cut from one cloth in their consistent concern to explicate or expose gender practices. Her awareness of the workings of gender in society began in her childhood home, from which her father Frederick Perkins departed when she was an infant and left her mother Mary A. Fitch to raise two children, the other being Charlotte's older brother Thomas. The family of three led a peripatetic existence, depending upon the good will of relatives.

Married at 24 to a young artist, Charles Walter Stetson, she fell into depression after the birth of her daughter in 1885. A trip to California to visit Grace Ellery Channing (1862–1937; Gilman's best friend and future wife of Stetson in 1894) restored her health, but only until she returned home. In 1888 Gilman moved with her daughter to Pasadena and in 1894 divorced Stetson. After his second marriage, she sent their daughter to join him. In 1900 she married a cousin George Houghton Gilman, who ably supported her venture into publishing, The Forerunner *(1910–16), where most of her utopian writing first appeared. After his 1934 death and terminally ill with cancer, she chloroformed herself in 1935.*

Financial support challenged Gilman throughout most of her life. During the 1890s, lectures to Nationalist Clubs were one means to earn a living; another

131

was editing and writing for The Nationalist *and* The Impress, *the organ for the Pacific Coast Woman's Press Association. A regular* Impress *feature written by then-Stetson, "Who Wrote It?" includes one of her earliest adult utopian titles—a stylistic imitation of Edward Bellamy, called "A Cabinet Meeting" (5 Jan. 1895, 4–5). In its emphasis upon political issues, it suggests the 1870* Man's Rights *by Cridge and the 1885 "A Divided Republic" by Blake.*

Gilman's 1907 "A Woman's Utopia" took a larger focus, one informed by her 1898 Women and Economics, *in which she insists upon the need for women's economic independence to meet the well-being of the whole society, women included. Central is the role of the mother, in anticipation of her 1915* Herland. *The 1900 dream vision* Reinstern *[pure star] by Eloise O. Randall Richberg features training for both sexes in childcare. While Gilman does not include this remedy, she does present shared parenting as well as gainfully employed and voting mothers and fathers. Like so much of Gilman's fiction, this too is marred by racism and elitism that readers must not ignore. It is important for its introductory statement of utopian purpose and as her first attempt at multi-installment fiction, even though never completed because the publisher of* The Times Magazine *"was punished for his rashness" in engaging Gilman "by the prompt failure of his venture" (*Living *303).*

References: Polly Wynn Allen, *Building Domestic Liberty: Charlotte Perkins Gilman's Architectural Feminism,* (Amherst: Univ. of Massachusetts Press, 1988); Larry Ceplair, ed., *Charlotte Perkins Gilman: A Nonfiction Reader* (New York: Columbia Univ. Press, 1991); Mary A[rmfield] Hill, *Charlotte Perkins Gilman: The Making of a Radical Feminist, 1860–1896* (Philadelphia: Temple Univ. Press, 1980); Mary A. Hill, ed., *Endure: The Diaries of Charles Walter Stetson* (Philadelphia: Temple Univ. Press, 1985); Joan Karpinski, ed., *Critical Essays on Charlotte Perkins Gilman* (Boston: G. K. Hall, 1992); Carol Farley Kessler, *Charlotte Perkins Gilman: Her Progress Toward Utopia,* (Syracuse: Syracuse Univ. Press, 1995); Ann J. Lane, *To "Herland" and Beyond: The Life and Works of Charlotte Perkins Gilman* (New York: Pantheon, 1990) and Introduction to *The Living of Charlotte Perkins Gilman: An Autobiography* (1935, reprint, Madison: Univ. of Wisconsin Press, 1990).

Text: Charlotte Perkins Gilman, "A Woman's Utopia," chaps. 1–4, *The Times Magazine* 1, Jan.-Mar. 1907; Chap. 5, page proofs, Arthur and Elizabeth Schlesinger Library on the History of Women in America, Radcliffe College, Charlotte Perkins Gilman Collection, box 21, folder 260, reprinted with permission.

Introductory

There is an instinctive demand for happiness in the human heart which has been so far most ignorantly misunderstood.

When it was plain animal happiness that we wanted; good and sufficient food, warmth, rest, the companionship of one's kind, with mate and young—all these natural impulses were at best attributed to "our lower nature," and at worst to "temptations of the devil."

So also in our steadily enlarging desire for human things, for the rich product of man's [sic] skill and social energy; all these wishes were called "worldly," "material," proofs of our mortal weakness.

Now, when we felt the still higher longing, that deep, strong instinct of a social creature for the love and peace and power of wide union, of manifold organization, and for the scarce imaginable delight of the multiplied sensation and expression of such full human relationship —all this was ascribed to "another world"—supposed impossible in this one.

Yet these are all natural instincts, the first kind natural to all animals, the last equally natural to social animals of our grade; and their presence in us is sure indication of their possible fulfilment.

Nature does not develop in fish a longing for foot-races; nor in pigs a passion for swimming. What a species is born desiring, is good for it.

We, being human, and having reached a high degree of socialization, are capable even now of methods of living which would guarantee in us a minimum of happiness far beyond our present average, and a maximum which we can scarce imagine.

But the longing is in us, the instinct, the demand for heaven, not after death, but here. This hope has found expression since we wrote books, in the numerous "Utopias" which earnest men have written; and it is to be noticed as time passes that the changes portrayed in these pictures of a better life are less and less distant from immediate conditions.

When Plato planned his "New Republic," the world was still mainly savage. When More's "Utopia" appeared, the world's average was higher; not to More's level, but nearer than in Plato's time. Our "Looking Backward" has scarce a feature beyond the grasp of the average citizen—as the traveling man remarked when he read it: "That's what we want!—and that's what we're going to have! The best of it is there's none of your damned socialism in it!"

The "Modern Utopia" of Mr. Wells is more subtle in analysis, and may not appeal so quickly to the general mind, but it is a very human world he makes, leaving a percentage of criminals and defectives to run their island communities to suit themselves.

We are beginning to see that Utopian dreams are to life what an architect's plans are to a house—we may build it—if we can. Of course if he has planned wrongly—if the thing won't stand, or does not suit our purpose, then we lay it aside and choose another.

But it is perfectly practical to make plans before you build; much more so than to build without a plan. So far society has grown like a coral island, each individual polyp contributing his [sic] calcareous mite, and the thing getting indisputably bigger. But society is not a mere aggregate of polyps—it is an organization of persons; and mere size is not enough. As the social organization becomes conscious it keenly appreciates its various discomforts and limitations, and seeks to remove them. In this work there is necessary clear and careful planning, lest our conscious steps lead us more astray than our unconscious ones.

Of one thing we may be certain—that the plan cannot be found behind us. It is not reversion which is needed—there is no going back to an earlier and "simpler" condition—we must go on to a later and better one.

Our previous Utopias have been of a large and glittering generality. They always assume extreme differences, another age, another country —another world. Even Mr. Wells, with his comet, must have another atmosphere, a complete and sudden change.

Now, if we are really coming to Utopia, there is a road to it. That road ends in a glorious future, but it begins here and now.

We need not only general Utopias, world schemes, necessarily laid far in the future, and involving so many preliminary stages undescribed; but we need particular Utopias, plans of betterment so plainly desirable that a majority will want them, and as workable and profitable as the other new inventions with which we are continually advancing our condition.

We have only to look back one century, before matches were invented, or steam locomotion introduced, to see how insanely visionary to the people of that time would have appeared the daily necessities of this. Also, we can see in the years behind us how our progress was needlessly impeded by the density, the inertia, the prejudice and cowardice and sodden ignorance of the multitude. A century of science has helped the common mind. Our socialized schools and libraries, our freedom of thought and speech, and our undeniable achievements, all make us better able to take further steps.

Now that a living man [*sic*] may mark the world's progress in his own lifetime, he can no longer deny it. We know we can move, we are willing enough, but we wish to be sure of the way.

Now is the time for practical Utopias. Heretofore all these visions of better living have been given us by men. Never a voice from a woman to say how she would like the world. The main stream of life, the Mother, has been silent. But she is vocal enough today. She speaks and writes, lectures and preaches, teaches in school and college, spreads steadily out into all human industries. And so far her voice is the voice of complaining.

Small wonder! She has caused enough, and centuries of dumb endurance to make up for. But even if one has cause for complaining, it is a poor business.

One feels like saying, "Well, well, admitting it is as you say—what do you want done about it?"

Suppose the Mother makes up her mind as to what she wants, and speaks.

Chapter 1
The Proposition

The proposition is not the same thing as the proposal—though both occurred that night. She refused one and accepted the other. A little about myself, to show how all this occurred.

My name is Morgan G. Street and I was twenty-five. My father, when I was born and my mother died, was a missionary in China; and ten years of childhood in China gives one quite a grip of the language and customs. Then he was transferred to an important post in India and I picked up Hindustani and general knowledge there, besides the schooling at home, of course.

When I was sixteen, father died, and I was adopted by a rich aunt in New York, sent to Harvard, taken abroad summers—most generously educated and provided for.

A year or two of law convinced me that I didn't care to practise it, and there was no need to—Aunt Henrietta was very rich. So I studied languages, for which I had a strong, natural taste, and traveled, and improved my mind. Uncle died and left his money to my aunt—she died and left it to me. At twenty-five I was the owner of as many millions as years; and proceeded to celebrate the coincidence by falling in love with Hope Cartwright.

She was a sort of cousin by marriage, or I never should have met her, probably, for she went to a coeducational college and was boiling over with ideas—kind of girl I never liked. But this one was irresistibly handsome, which I consider as a mean trick on the part of mother nature. That kind of girl has no right to be handsome—it's a delusion. Hope was, however, and a jolly nice girl, too; so though I had no use for any of her wild theories, I thought she would doubtless outgrow them—she was only eighteen—and I could give her a position that would take up her mind suitably.

Meanwhile I went with her to that preposterous R. G. U. Club she liked so much, because I could talk to her going and coming, and look at her during the evening. She wouldn't go to the theater with me—said she didn't need amusement at her age, and that our plays gave nothing else; said she needed the sleep, too—that late hours were bad for young people; said she had to study anyhow, she wouldn't go to anything I liked, and I had to go to this thing if I wanted her company to myself.

It was a sort of debating society—the "argue" club—some young and some middle-aged, all with the humanitarian bee in their bonnets, mad with the notion of helping the world.

I told them that if they really knew the world, even as much as I did, they wouldn't be so brash. "When you live in a nation that hasn't changed in four thousand years, you learn to take life as it is," I told them.

And then they all tried to convince me that some nations grow faster than others—that some were decadent and some on the upgrade—and that even China was moving now.

One of them was a competent business man, Mr. Hart, a big dealer in real estate, with plenty of money. He used to invest in these model tenements and talk about them. Model tenements! I told him to go and look at the houses in Benares—then he'd think all our tenements were model.

Then there was a young preacher—sort of Christian Socialist, I guess—and five or six girls, friends of Hope's, each with a fad, of course; one of them was daft about baby culture; one on cooking; one on dress-making; one on housekeeping; one was an artist; an illustrator, and so on. All nice girls enough. I used to smile at their enthusiasm, and think that pretty soon they'd all be married and could practise their fine theories where they belonged—at home.

On this particular evening they had finally succeeded in arranging for me to talk to them a little—a thing I hated, but Hope got me into it.

If it hadn't been for that I shouldn't have gone in at all, for Hope refused me on the door-step. But I am a man of my word. As you can imagine, I was not in a very amiable frame of mind. She wouldn't give a decent reason—wouldn't even say she didn't love me, but she said all our ideas were antagonistic, and we should be miserable together.

"Now see here," I said. "Admitting that we do differ—radically— we don't have to talk about our views all the time. You are very young, there is time to change, to grow together; won't you try?"

"You're not so old yourself, Morgan," she answered. "Maybe you'll do the changing. Your views are mostly from your circumstances and bringing-up—with that glassy Harvard veneer—but as you say, there is time to change. When we agree on the essentials of life will be time to talk of marrying."

Hope had a very firm chin. As I sat and watched her that evening, and heard the stuff they were talking, I realized how hopeless it was. She was right. If she didn't alter those vigorous and fluently expressed "views" of hers there was little hope for our happiness. And she was a very fine talker, too.

I made up my mind to leave for good and all. To leave those ridiculous people and their foolishness, to leave this noisy patchwork country that couldn't take life as it found it, to go and search the world for the place liked best, and stay in it. And there was that preacher blazing away about a new religion—and the writer talking about what literature could do when it was aroused to its responsibility;[1] and the baby-culture girl maintaining that what was needed most was a national system of child-rearing; and Hope—they all stopped to listen to her.

"Look at the miracles we have done in physical science," said she. "We have learned to understand something of material and physical forces, we work with them and have filled the world with wonders of speed and strength and convenience.

"Now, I maintain that when we study social materials and social forces we can combine them and do miracles in human growth and happiness. We need only to grasp the science—the principle—of it. We need the Social Inventor."

I was so thoroughly out of temper with the whole thing that I was not sorry to have to speak—though I hate it.

"You are all crazy," I said. "Perfectly crazy. Study your social materials, indeed! Go around the world and study them all—learn the stuff humanity is made of—the dull, blind, stupid, patient, immovable sedimentary deposit it is! See it live and die, swarming and helpless, for uncounted centuries, and never move a foot.

"We have our mechanical inventors, with their record of industrial war and physical slaughter; their accompaniments of vicious poverty, of disease and idiocy, of growing crime, of steadily increasing suicide. If Miss Cartright's social inventor can do no more for us than this he is no world savior.

"And you, with your new religion—or warmed-up old one—haven't we had religions enough and had them long enough to see that they do not alter human conditions at all?

"And you socialists—the bigoted party and the hybrid lot of outsiders—you think that you can clap a new system of living on society all at once, and make life turn and run to suit you! Why not teach clams to fly so as to escape their enemies?

"Can't science teach you anything? Can't you see from history that we all do approximately the same things in the same way, and the nations just die when their time comes, as men do?

"If you could leave the world for twenty centuries and come back, you'd find it at the same old game—no better and no worse."

Of course I don't remember all I said, but that was the gist of it. They all took it nicely enough, because they pitch into one another just as fiercely; but Hope looked rather white.

"If you go away and come back in twenty *years,* Mr. Street, I will show you such changes as will convince even you that humanity is improving at a tremendous rate of speed."

"Miss Cartwright is right," said the preacher. "As soon as humanity wakes up to its real nature—its real duty—its transcendent possibilities—it can remodel the world."

"I think she is right," said the baby-culturist. "There are thousands of children maturing every year with better brains than their fathers—in twenty years they will be a great power."

"I don't claim," said Hope, "that the whole world can be set right in twenty years; but that changes can be initiated and such results obtained as would convince even you that we were on the upgrade."

I rose to my feet again. "Now, look here," I said, "I'll make you a proposition. I'm sick of this country—sick of all this talk and fuss and fighting. I'm going off to travel the world over, and I shall be glad to stay my twenty years—or the rest of my life. And nothing would give me more satisfaction in a small way than to prove to this particular group of enthusiasts that you are all wrong. I want you to have a fair chance in every way, and I tell you what I'll do.

"I have $25,000,000. I can travel and live happily on the income of one million. I will invest four to accumulate till I come back—that will be enough for any man. And I will leave twenty for you people to play with. We'll have a little bunch of trustees; let's see—I have every confidence in Mr. Hart here—" (he was the business man, and an old friend of my aunt's)—"and in Mr. Jackson—" (he was the lawyer and an uncle of Hope's). "Miss Cartwright is the Social Inventor—she shall say what is to be done with the money.

"If I come back and find it all spent—all of you at swords' points—and the world no better—it will give me the satisfaction of saying, I told you so, at least.

"The money didn't cost me anything, and I've no use for it—there's enough left. Go ahead and see what you can do—in twenty years!"

Hope was looking at me with clear, level eyes, considering.

She spoke, as if to herself. "If I were inventing flying-machines—or storage-batteries—or anything I thought important to humanity—I'd take the money, and be thankful. Since I do believe I can start things up —make people a lot better and happier—what better use could you make of the money?" Then she sat up.

"I'll accept your proposition, Mr. Street," she said. In May, 1927, you can come back. I'll show you a happier country—and what's more, I'll return the twenty millions."

So I went away.

Chapter 2
The Return

I spent my twenty years in travel and research, learning most of the languages of the world, studying savage customs; gradually taking up ethnology and archeology, and working them out in the field; growing wiser as to human history as the years passed, and always refusing to read anything about America or listen to any talk of it. I never wrote a word to any of those foolish reformers—and never heard a word, either. I knew my banker's address—no one else knew mine. Now and then I caught boastful rumors of great things America was doing; but I was used to that old habit of national bragging, and paid no attention.

So when I docked at New York in 1927 I was unbiased and open to conviction; I had no prejudices—save those I started with. I came from South America.

The steamer was a great improvement to the old ones; but that was to be expected. I had never denied our rampant flood of mechanical "improvements." As to the passengers—I avoided them easily enough, yet could not help being struck by certain indefinable alterations in the women. But I was preparing a monograph on pre-Coptic dialects and kept mostly to my room.

As we swept up the harbor on a brilliant May morning I came on deck early, undeniably eager and curious, and conscious of a rising sense of gladness in being there, a foolish feeling of pride—as if these shores were any more beautiful than those of Norway or Ceylon, or as if I had any personal responsibility for them!

The first thing I noticed was the entire absence of smoke. Bayonne[2] lay bright and sparkling. Port Richmond was clean—the city itself rose pearly and clear-cut in the glittering sunshine—no black blanket hanging over anything. There was more color, too, in the buildings, and more greenness everywhere among them.

Next I saw that Liberty was standing higher, and had been gilded— a pillar of light by day as well as a torch-bearer in darkness. I smiled bitterly as I thought of all that went under that specious claim of world-enlightenment; but she certainly looked more attractive than she used to.

Then, watching the water with eyes long used to transparent tropic seas, I suddenly observed that it was clear—not perfectly so, but as light to darkness in contrast with the harbor broth I remembered.

"Probably they've learned to incinerate their garbage at last," I thought to myself, "and the use of electricity instead of steam must make an enormous difference." That was one of the things I couldn't help hearing of long since. Some one had invented a light, cheap storage-battery—and electricity was as common as coal used to be, or more so, and far cheaper.

The broken skyline of lower New York was there yet; but as I studied it I perceived first that there appeared to be no more of the towering monsters, and the old ones seemed somehow more harmonious than formerly.

Then, as we drew near shore, and later as I drove uptown, I noticed how little noise there was. It was not the silence of a mountain by any means, but stillness itself compared to the yelling and booming pandemonium I remembered on previous returnings.

When I sailed, the understanding was that I was to return and meet the Club on their annual closing meeting—the last Monday in May, but I had sent no word, meaning to walk in like that imperturbable Phineas Fogg after his trip "Around the World in Eighty Days."

Also I had taken pains to arrive a day or two beforehand, so as to get a general impression before I met them—or what was left of them. It wouldn't have surprised me to find them all vanished; but I knew Roger Hart would have at least a representative to tell me how the money went.

It seemed to me so colossal a piece of folly—my performance—that I had hated the thought of it ever since, and was many times determined not to come back at all. But at other times I felt differently about returning—there was no denying the size of my idiocy, and it would be a little consolation to measure theirs.

I had prepared myself for the usual mortification, irritation, and delay of our national customs office—but to my amazement there was none. That roused me. I turned to the man next at hand.

"What's become of the initiation ceremonies on landing?" I asked. "When did the customs system go?"

He was a young fellow, and looked a little dashed at first. Then he smiled brightly. "O, I remember," said he; "I was looking at some old 'Lifes' the other day, and there was such a lovely picture of Americans landing in their own country and being absolutely stripped, so to speak —standing around wrapped in blankets and things! Why, that was all stopped when I was a small kid—about 1912, I think. The women always hated it, you see—and when they got a good grip on politics they stopped it altogether."

"Free trade?" I asked.

"Free trade," he answered.

"How about objectionable goods—can they bring in anything and everything?"

"Why, yes, they can; but it doesn't pay. There are very stringent laws about the quality of goods sold, you see. And nobody has turned up bad enough to want to poison the whole country and willing to do it with no chance of a profit and a pretty certain penalty."

I didn't care to get my information from a mere lad, so I thanked him and turned away; but it sickened me none the less—women in politics! And apparently predominant, for our men would never have made this a free trade country.

Well, I could easily go away again. My views on women were pretty well defined before my departure, and I had seen no reason to change them from my study of existing people or ancient history.

The docks were clean and handsome. No coal-dust or smoke, no horse-litter; all was smooth and well finished, and the long line of electric cabs and other vehicles showed how it came to be so.

The steamer had offered a good supply of the latest city maps, with all manner of information and direction, but I was astonished none the less at the difference between this water-front and the one I remembered. The wide street was as smooth and clean as one in London; cleaner, for there were no horses.

The traffic was there, but the big rubber tires ran softly, and the chauffeurs used neither cracking whips nor hoarse shouts and curses.

The water was even thicker with craft than formerly, but they seemed to follow more regular rules of precedence, and moved freely and swiftly about; while the whistles which used to form so hideous a feature of all water travel around New York were far less frequent and actually musical in sound.

"There seems to be plenty of trade going on—free or not," I thought to myself.

As we rolled rapidly and quietly uptown I looked eagerly about me for further novelties. Most of the buildings looked the same—these rampant women could never have rebuilt New York in two decades. But I suddenly grasped the fact that below a certain grade there were none. There had evidently been a vast deal of pulling down of the worst rookeries; and where these had been were now new and fine-looking structures.

A comfortable room in a good hotel—even better than it used to be I found, a most admirable lunch, and I sat down luxuriously to a quiet smoke and a bunch of papers. I hadn't bothered with them on the boat —I was too busy looking. I rejoiced to note that the speckled sheet which represented our worst journalism was not among them—and I had ordered all.

That evening I went to see a play—in a new theater on Columbus Circle; a cool, quiet, comfortable place, lovely and simple in color and decoration, with a scale of prices quite European—excellent seats for half a dollar.

The play was realistic to the last degree, and so held the interest that I gave it no analysis till afterward; then finding that what had annoyed me so continually all through it was the insistence of two egotistic young people on planting their love affair—which after all wasn't final—in front of all the vital movement of the piece. It was a great consolation to have them quite ignored in the satisfying end.

By Monday evening I had read and heard and seen enough to go to the meeting with considerable information. It was clear that the world remained distinctly recognizable, that America was America still; but also that many changes had been initiated. Whether these were improvements and how far they were due to the idea of the R. G. U. Club—and my money—remained to be found out.

Let me see—just what was it those amiable idiots had undertaken to do? I had kept no record save a brief note in my diary: "Gave twenty million dollars to a pack of fools."

But I remembered that we were to meet in the same place on the same date after twenty years, and I entered the room with exact punctuality. There was a general uproar of greeting and congratulation; nearly all the members were there, including Mr. Hart, who was much the oldest; and all of them seemed unfeignedly glad to see me.

As for me, I confess I saw mostly one person, and that was Hope Cartwright. She had been such a handsome girl that I had dreaded—really dreaded—to see her after so long a time.

I myself had not changed—a man doesn't. My tailor's measurements were the same still, probably would be for twenty years more. But twenty years to a woman is a catastrophe. Wherefore I was more astonished than at anything I had yet seen when there arose to greet me the same girl I had left at eighteen, the same except that her expression had become sweeter and more restful, the fine lines of her active figure suggesting not only power but repose. A wiser face—an even finer face; the same rich color; the same vigor and joyous health; and she was—must be—thirty-eight.

Mr. Hart grasped me warmly by the hand.

"Welcome home, my dear boy," said he. "We have heard of you occasionally through your contribution to science and were always glad to do so. You never sent us word of your coming, but we expected you—we should have been bitterly disappointed if you had not appeared.

"This is a great moment. After your long absence, after your munificent endowment, after our twenty years of effort, we are proud and glad to see you again.

"And now, as President of this club, and in connection with Mr. Jackson, my fellow trustee, I take pleasure in returning to you the sum you left in our hands, twenty million dollars."

Mr. Jackson gave him the box of securities, and he handed it to me.

"You will find it all there, Mr. Street—shall I go over them with you?"

"No, indeed, Mr. Hart," I said. "This memorandum is quite enough. I am surprised and—er—grateful—to you; but, after all, the return of the money is the least vital part of the matter. I propose that it shall be postponed until these alleged improvements are established. They were to be such as to convince even me, you remember."

"Quite so," said Mr. Hart. "Quite so. But that will take some little time. We recognize that we must not only show the improvements, but show them to be due to our efforts; and then, furthermore, bring you to admit their value. This can hardly be done in one evening. Naturally we have prepared most carefully for this event. What we propose is this: That for the following week or so you will allow yourself to be 'personally conducted' over several of our more important achievements; and if, at our special meeting a fortnight hence, after seeing what we have to show and hearing what we have to say, if you do not consider America has improved by our efforts and ideas, plus your money,—why you get your money back just the same."

"You must excuse the English of one who has scarce spoken it since our last meeting," I said, rising to reply, "and the awkwardness of a man who knows all about languages, except how to use them. When I left you I was an ill-tempered boy; but I think my ideas were sound even then—and they have not changed. On the contrary, much travel, study, and contact with humanity in many lands has made me surer than ever that it is of one general quality, permanent in character, and that character pretty poor. In especial I am surer than ever of the natural position of woman in regard to society, and the evil consequences of interfering with it.

"What I have seen and read so far since my arrival is stimulating and confusing; but I find nothing which I recognize as better except in material comfort—and those advances I never denied. On the contrary, I hear of changes which seem to me most detrimental, and to indicate decadence rather than advance. Nevertheless there is an appearance of joyous triumph among you which seems to indicate an assured position, and I will cheerfully put myself in your hands for enlightenment."

There was a deal of eager talking and questioning about my travels, with congratulations on what little I had done in the scientific world, and we broke up, with an appointment for the day after next in which Miss Cartwright was to enlighten me on the woman question.

Chapter 3
The New Religion

Dale Edwards, the manager-in-chief of the Upgrade Publication Co., called next morning to show me the country he said. He was boastful of the smooth, shaded, dustless roads, the swift and cheap transportation, the amount of suburban living brought about by forcing the factories out of town; but I told him it was the effect on character that interested me.

"You sound like one of Wells's futurity books," I said. "Now sit down right here and tell me about people. What have you done to them? Start in from the time I went off." So he leaned back against a tree and began:

"Well, after you left, our next meeting was a stormy one, I can tell you. We didn't quarrel—your money was no apple of discord. We had confidence in the trustees, and in ourselves; but the enthusiasm was a whirlwind—the hope—the sense of power—the immediate prospect of big results.

"We all expected to live those twenty years, and be able to show you things. Finally we got it laid out like this: There was to be no haste. The work would be slow and hardly perceptible for the first few years —then grow faster and faster. We must begin with immediate demands —meet the people just where they were—give them things they would appreciate now. Some of our proposals could start at the same time— others must come later.

"But there was one of us who had not a moment's doubt about his share of the work, nor we either—that was Henry St. John. He started his church the next winter, here in New York. It made a tremendous impression. The next summer he preached at Chautauquas[3] all over the country—then began a round of the big cities—then the little ones. Not a state in the Union but knows him now—and loves him.

"The thing took hold at once, you see. He taught just what was wanted, common sense and comfort, boundless hope—with a handle you could take hold of; power and contentment; joy such as we never dared dream of before—on earth. The young people took it up all over the country, college boys and girls; it fitted the vigorous, clear young brains of to-day to a T. There were disciples by hundreds—young and old—to carry on the preaching. You see, it did not interfere with any other religion—that was worth anything; it did not contradict or oppose. It simply gave you such a satisfying mindful and handful that the others gradually faded.

"You know the churches were in a very wavering state when you left. All the growing minds were ready for the new presentation. It was like the rest of our plans—took the people where they were and gave them what they wanted, but on the upward lines.

"In a few years we had a new kind of theological school; homological, we call them. You must go and see one—they are great. We have them now as a part the college curriculum in many places; those who want to promote social progress on ethical lines by preaching and teaching take our course.

"This teaches the laws of the moral development of humanity and how to assist them. One has to be qualified in the natural sciences to enter; to understand biology in general, comparative zoology, some physiology and pathology, and sociology most of all. They study humanity, you see—what the thing is, how it works, how to help it. And there are ever so many big men—and women—at work now along these lines. As soon as they got ethics on a practical basis, clear and simple, it was introduced in the public schools. That was about six years ago. Now all our children learn common ethics as much as arithmetic.

"You would be amused to see them working away on the problems—and the reasons they give for their decisions! But they all get the conviction that there is a reason for this being right and that wrong; and they are quite as ready to condemn ignorance in ethics as they used to be in spelling. Then we have our courses of professional ethics. You see—well, the science altogether has developed so fast that I hardly know how to tell you.

"You'll have to study up—it's immensely interesting. But the point is, that while ethics is the science of conduct—all conduct, each branch of conduct has its ethics. We had the beginnings of that long ago—'medical ethics,' for example, and 'the artistic conscience.'

"But it is a regular science now, and every trade and profession has its growing body of ethical knowledge, and understands its relation to the general welfare. I don't mean, of course, that we have all become proficient and blameless; but the science is there, the young people study it, and the average of behavior rises faster every year."

"You're telling me a lot about ethics," I interrupted, "but very little about religion."

He looked at me, a little bewildered. "The fact is," he replied, "I'd forgotten that we used to differentiate them. Religion used to be something you believed, wasn't it? And ethics something you studied in college? And conduct—well, that came in anyhow. You studied this, believed that, and did what you pleased.

"Well—there's plenty of that left. You can't reform the world in twenty years. But you can begin. And there's so much of this new teaching now, and I've been in it so much, I forget that there are still several millions that haven't got to it. It spreads fast, though. You see, we have thousands of missionaries."

"Missionaries? Well, I am astonished. I know enough about missionaries—it amazes me that you have them yet."

"Oh, yes, we have them—it's a social instinct, you know. But they are hobbled." And he chuckled amusedly.

"Hobbled? What do you mean?"

"Why, we maintain that a religion ought to spread uninterruptedly, not to skip. We have to lift the standard of living where we are as high as is humanly possible before we go to work farther off.

"Of course, anyone can read and study and talk; but our church teaches that a religion is not alive until it *works*—that if ours is the best in the world we've got to prove it, that while any conspicuous immorality remains among us we've no right to go and brag to other people about our religion. So those ardent young souls who want to go to the ends of the earth to spread this wonderful new light are told that we've had quite enough of these varnish religions—ours wants to strike in. You see, it's no good if it doesn't work; and if it does work we can 'point with pride' to our results; and that will save a lot of preaching.

"You remember how it was—people ran around with a religion saying, 'Only believe this and you will be good and happy.' And the other people said, 'Are you good and happy—your people at home ?'—and we could only say, 'They would be if they would just accept our religion.'

"The answer to that was obvious, 'Go home and make them. If you can't convert your own people, how can you expect to convert us? If your religion doesn't work at home, how can you expect it to work here?' So we have a sort of intensive agriculture with ours.

"Instead of continually enunciating a set of first principles and leaving the public to work out the application as best they can, we make it the business of our religious teachers to trace and connect, to explain and apply—to make clear the full expression of the accepted truths.

"For instance, speaking of truths, take that plain question of ethics, the social danger of lying. In our theological course, instead of studying long-dead languages and the ideas and emotions of primitive races, we study this vast social organism of to-day, its health—which is virtue, its disease—which is sin. We study lying as we were studying cancer and consumption when you left.

"What is it? Where does it come from? What generates it—what encourages it? How can we exterminate it and prevent its reappearance? That was one of the earliest lines we started on—it was so common.

"Social life, you know, involves constant interaction between the parts; locally, between individuals, and generally between each individual and the whole. It is easy to see that if every one lied to every one else all the time there could be no society at all; and if, on the other hand, every one was perfectly honest all the time, society would be on the high road to heaven. Even the infant classes can be taught that much, with pictures and stories and dramatic representations.

"Yet this dangerous social evil was scarcely condemned by public opinion, and not recognized at all by the law. 'Perjury,' which is an extremely ancient offense, dating back to dense superstitious ages, when men were only expected to tell the truth under oath, was illegal; and so was libel; but plain lying, which does the mischief all the time, was not a legal offense at all. A blow with the hand was punishable—to 'trespass' on another's land—to sleep in the parks—but one could lie and lie and injure persons unmeasurably by it, without even a fine.

"We have made a special campaign against falsehood for all these years. In our school ethics it is made very clear, it is preached about intelligently, written about, lectured about. At last we have got the law to recognize it. A proven liar is fined, like a spitter; and if much evil has resulted, the fine is proportionate. But the judgment of the community is the factor behind the law; that was changed first. As soon as it was universally shown how injurious and contemptible lying is, it became easy to make laws against it. Of course, the great fountain head of lying was the position of women."

"What!" I cried in astonishment. "Lying—due to the position of women?"

"Why, yes. Haven't you read—Oh, no, you haven't read anything from America in twenty years! Well, you'll have occupation for twenty more to catch up. The idea is that women were maintained in a primitive relation to man, a subordinate, dependent position taking no part in our social growth. This kept them like a lower race among us, and preserved in them the vices and weaknesses of the lower races. And they were the teachers of little children!

"Children, as representing an earlier stage of race life; as weak and defenseless creatures; and as being absolutely dependent on personal management—to say nothing of their abounding young imaginations; are prone to deceit and evasion as well as straight falsehood; and their mothers made no head against it. There was no science of child-culture then, you know—any mother could do as she pleased with her own child.

"So the old race tendency to lying kept on and on—it was never educated out of the stock. So soon as women really became people—independent, self-supporting citizens—they took a new view of the child question. Almost all our babies share in the advantages of civilization now.

"They are taken care of with such wisdom and justice that there is scarcely any temptation to lie; and the whole thing is made despicable in their eyes. So soon as we get several generations brought up rightly, with better laws, and still stronger public opinion, we can outgrow it entirely."

"Is that the kind of thing your new religion teaches? That you can train humanity into perfection?"

"Perfection? No. Immense improvement—yes. As fast as we reach higher planes of conduct we see still farther heights to be descried; but we do teach ceaseless progress and how to make it. Our religion assumes that God is still busy in us, making society out of pre-social individuals; and that our business is to get into the game and help.

"It makes life tremendously happy and exciting. Here we all are, at various levels, on our way up from egoism to socioism.[4] For all the long, dark centuries we didn't know it—and life looked pretty black. No one expected much of this world except as a place to 'acquire merit' by a lot of arbitrary good conduct. What we looked forward to was the escape of some of us into a better life. The women were responsible for most of that, too."

"Of course—you blame women for everything. Women were the most moral sex, and the mainstay of the church aren't they now?"

"They never were more moral than men—except as a child tied in a go-cart is cleaner than a child playing in the gutter. They were the mainstay of the church, I admit-that's what I was saying. They kept the churches from growing. When you find a stagnant religion you find subject women. When women are free—and growing—you find a free, growing church.

"Our church to-day has as many men as women—especially young ones. A good many of the old folks naturally stick to the old teaching, where you simply had to believe, and so be saved. Our strong young people are far happier in learning what to do in order to help all humanity upward. Social service—just doing your own work well—is Christian duty now."

"Do you deny salvation?"

"We don't deny anything. We assert and prove. You can keep on believing and being saved all you want to, but if you join our church you have to do things."

"But have you no creed—no special doctrine—no worship? They used to say that religion had three parts—belief, worship, doctrine."

"Yes, I know they did. And it had three more—hope, fear, and selfishness. And plenty of others, too—you can't cut up religion that way. A religion is a general theory of life. It assumes such and such a God or gods, such a story of creation, such a scheme of conduct; and its emotions depended on its theory.

"Without a religion there is no large idea of how to live, how to place the mind in regard to life. The great attraction of ours is that it makes life clear and full of hope. We know which way to go and how to get on. Our social inventor is always coming forward with some new labor-saving device to promote social progress. And even in twenty

years you can see the results—everywhere. People not only behave better, but they, are happier—braver—more enthusiastic.

"I can't begin to make you feel the thing—I'm no preacher—go and
hear St. John. Or try young Fairchild, or Stevens, or Gould—there are
plenty of splendid preachers. And read—there are books enough. You'll
pick it up, you can't help it, it's in the air."

"But, look here," I said, "you keep telling me about certain views
of life, and certain improvements, but I get no clear idea of the central
doctrine of the thing, nor of any sort of worship. Have they no divine
service? Is there no prayer, no adoration, no communion with God?"

Edwards leaned back in the grass and looked at the sky.

"As we haven't any literature with us, and no church within ten
miles, I suppose I'll have to tell you the best I can. But you mustn't take
it as final: as I said before, I'm no preacher.

"The central doctrine is this: That the normal growth of man is
toward more perfect social relation; that all human duty, and duty to
God, lies one way—towards perfecting our social relation. Truth, love,
courage, cheerfulness, justice, courtesy—every virtue is called for by
social relation; every vice is a line of conduct which injures social relation.

"What we used to call selfishness and think so insuperable is now
recognized as only a 'mischievous rudiment'—a survival of the old individualistic period when it was right to be selfish.

"The change in the position of women has helped most in this, too.
They kept the world selfish."

"Women selfish?" I gasped. *"Women—selfish!"*

"Yes, of course," he went on easily. "Women very selfish and keeping the whole world so.

"I tell you they were kept in a position which maintained all manner
of primitive instincts; and that all selfishness is a primitive survival of an
outgrown status.

"They were devoted to their children, I grant you; but that is only
natural instinct, not selfishness. The devotion was often of no benefit to
the child—some times injurious. They were devoted to their husbands,
too—partly natural affection, partly selfishness. And if they were genu-
inely unselfish in regard to their families—why they made the family
selfish in proportion.

"There was no way out of it. Practically all women spent their lives
in the closest personal relationships and cared little for anything outside
them. Why, do you realize that our women used to justify child labor—
child labor, which is the real race suicide—on the ground that the poor
mothers needed the money?

"We haven't had a child at work in America since the women woke up, some eighteen years ago. We haven't had a child hungry, or cold, or abused—that anyone knows of—for ten years or more. Our women are people, now, I can tell you—and splendid ones. Wait till you see what they are doing in our schools, in city government, in business.

"But women as they were—Oh, they were selfish, even if they didn't know it. You see, with the doctrine of social relation—the scientific recognition of the working value of Christian love—it is vulgar and ignorant to be selfish, like bad table manners. Now women and men alike recognize that the one all-embracing duty is to love and serve humanity, and to *learn how*.

"We teach the children—the babies in the nurseries; it's in the kindergartens, schools, colleges—everywhere. That's our central doctrine, I guess,—Love in Action.

"As for worship and divine service—yes, I think there is more than there ever was. Have you been on the roof at sunrise yet?"

I certainly had not.

"Go and have a look. You'll see lots of young people praying."

"To the sun?"

"No—not to the sun. They are thanking God to be alive, that's all; and for the Light to see the way. Then we have splendid religious music, and dramatic services. You should see 'The March of Man,' every class in the schools is taken to see that."

"What is it? A labor procession?"

"No, you scoffer. You go to see it—you'll remain to pray. It's the real 'Pilgrim's Progress,'[5] a vivid representation, with all our wonderful scenic apparatus, of human evolution. It's in cycles, and so typical that you see in each stage what it was that pushed onward, and what it was that pulled back."

"Sort of mystery play?"

"Yes, if you like—the mystery of life, the real thing. No gods or devils—only natural forces. The villain of the piece is primitive man, always popping up and refusing to be civilized. And primitive woman —you should see her appear from out of a full modern costume! It's the philosophy of history in a nutshell. Then there's Tradition—stone blind and always interfering. We have some glorious work on the stage now; but I'm straying off from religion."

"What do you have to do to join?"

"You don't have to join. You just wake up and begin to live. If you see your way, all right. If not, you go to a specialist."

"A specialist in religion?"

"Yes, naturally. The trouble with our ministers used to be that they knew more about Hebrew legends than about modern business. Now, we don't live in Judea, nor yet in the Middle Ages. We are in America to-day, and hard at work. If our religion won't fit the Bureau of Agriculture and the Health Commission and the problems of transportation it doesn't belong to us, that's all. This one does. When some full-grown, able business man begins to see the sense of this religion, he naturally wants to apply it to his business. When he went to the old kind of minister he was told to follow the footsteps of Jesus[6]—but it is hard for a practical man to visualize those footsteps clearly enough to follow them. And as the minister knew nothing of manufacturing he couldn't advise him rationally.

"Now, our man takes a course in the ethics of production—written or oral as he likes—gets the best views going, with suggestion from others in the same work. He is given the history of this sort of work; what have been its special evils and why; what has been done to improve it and how; the present state of the business and what the best men are doing in it; plenty of discussion and open questions. He learns his place in social progress, and how to help things forward. Our young people learn all this now as they specialize—it saves time."

"Do you have Sunday services?"

"Yes—generally in the evenings. Sunday is a universal holiday, greatly loved and enjoyed, and most people prefer to spend the morning out of doors. But we have a short early morning service for those that like to start that way; and more in the evening, with preaching."

"And how about worshiping God?"

Edwards turned around and looked at me.

"Either I don't talk plain or you are uncommonly thick," he said. "What do you think of when you say God? An ancient Hebrew deity in the sky, with a lot of kowtowing and complimenting and swinging of censers, and sacrifices bleeding and roasting? Or some fierce Cotton Mather[7] kind of divinity, damning most people and enjoying it, with a few brands plucked from the burning to assail him with vocal music and fulsome adulation for all eternity? Nice Deity that!

"I tell you we worship God all the time—*by doing things*. And by enjoying the lovely world, appreciating it, learning the laws of life and fulfilling them. We get fairly drunk with enthusiasm sometimes, I can tell you. You see, happiness increases every year now; we understand things better, know more, enjoy more. And we grow to realize the immeasurable happiness of living, that it stretches out before us, without limit, that all our pains and troubles are unnecessary and can be overcome, outgrown; that we are all here together to help on the good work;

that we know how, and have begun, and can see it grow! I tell you there are times when we take one another by the hand and just cry—the gladness can not be borne.

"If I were God, I think I'd rather see people like that—happy and busy and full of enthusiasm, and loving each other in dollars and cents, as it were, than to have 'em praising me. But maybe it's not what you mean by worshiping God."

Chapter 4
Some Beginnings

So much had been said and indicated about the action of women in all these changes, that I had requested information on that subject to start with; and Hope Cartwright had undertaken to supply it. Her address was "Courland—100th street and Riverside drive."

Riverside drive was beautiful as of old—and far more so. Its skyline had become harmonious and impressive; the ribbon of green park was well kept, and no foul smoke from the opposite shore poisoned the air and defiled the trees and buildings. The western bank was thickly built by this time; but its climbing terraces and long lines of clustered houses among the trees were pleasing to the eye.

We drove through one of the four archways which showed bright glimpses of the inner court, and I descended in a place so lovely I had to stop and study it, eager though I was to keep my appointment. It was sheltered from the wind—for the great doors of the entrances were closed on the "storm side" and altogether in winter; full of sunlight, yet cooled by cross-draughts in summer from those same wide doorways; with tossing fountains, trees, and climbing vines, rich beds of flowers, shaded cloisters arched and pillared, room for games, for comfortable seats and tiny tables, for ferneries and singing birds and pleasant meeting-places; with the walls around it rich with mullioned windows, hanging balconies, and fine decoration.

It vaguely reminded me of Italy, of India, of Greece. It gave me that feeling of being "too good to be true"—of an almost theatrical beauty, as if regularly to live in such a lovely place were almost improper. Yet I found later that "The Courts of New York" were the subject of a poem recently published by one of the greatest of our modern poets; and that as I traversed the city and glimpsed them through the great gates, or was privileged to enter as a visitor, I found a never-ending charm in their rich variety. According to the taste of the architect and the residents they varied, here a bit of the Alhambra, there of Egypt, again of Rome; and some quiet Early English; some of Flanders or old Germany; some unique and strong, quite modern and American.

Then I remembered what used to be—the narrow checker-board of small, square, sordid "backyards," with their flaunting intimacy of laundry work, their vocal ecstasy of cats, and agony of dogs; the bleak "rears" of huddled houses, all turning their monotonous stone faces to the street and pretending to forget how conspicuous and unattractive was the mutual exposure of their backs. Now the sense of "rear" was all gone, for the whole wall-space was treated as one, and treated beautifully. Many of the blocks still consisted of separate houses, but even so the interior was made a walled garden of loveliness.

I found Miss Cartwright in a charming apartment, high up, with the wide Hudson spread before her, and the range of sunlit-glory from southeast to northwest. She seemed primed even to bursting with statements and explanations, and we wasted little time on openings.

"Sit in that big chair by the window," she said; "I know you like that kind—or used to. If you have to smoke, you may. Are you comfortable?"

I was, perfectly, and said so. The beauty of the view, the beauty of the room, the beauty of the calm, sweet vigorous woman with the wise eyes and tender mouth, were most satisfying.

"Now," said she, "I have to show you changes in human nature which you will admit to be improvements—is that right?"

"That is exactly right," I said. "Not merely changes in conditions— I admit, for instance, the beauty of this building and its inner garden, but the Hanging Gardens of Babylon[8] were doubtless as beautiful, at least—yet the Babylonians—!"

"Perhaps it would simplify matters if you would state what, to you, would be real improvements in human nature. Then if I can show you these as accomplished facts, you would grant us so much. I believe we set no limit to the amount of change to be shown?"

"No," said I. "Very little will satisfy me. If you can show me human nature to be in any degree wiser, kinder, truer, stronger, nobler, purer, braver, sweeter; if you can show me better health, better morals, better manners; more virtue and happiness, less dishonesty and greed, less vice, crime, disease, misery, and general cussedness—clear proof of change in any or all of these points—in twenty years—why, you win the argument, and I lose. But it will take a lot of proving." And I leaned back serenely in the big chair.

"All right," she began briskly, after jotting down my requisitions. "If you'll furnish the patience, I'll furnish the proof. First, I'll tell you what happened and show you things; afterward bring out the statistics. You shall be crushed by the facts and buried under the figures."

"Leave a hole," I begged, "a little hole for me to crawl out of!"

"No—you must dig out, or stay in! The best way, I think, is to begin by telling you what the women did. You remember what women were like when you left?"

"I remember what one woman was like—very clearly. As to the others, I have seen several since and they are still recognizable."

Hope used to profess annoyance and dislike for what she termed my frivolous gallantries; but now she only smiled—and her dimples were lovelier than ever. I found myself puzzling over the time passed—eighteen, twenty years—thirty-eight. What right has a woman of thirty-eight to such a complexion and such dimples? But she was talking:

"You will, I think, admit that in 1901 the average woman had few interests beyond her home and children, cared little for business, politics, or general progress, cared much for personal decoration, was a slavish observer of fashion and convention, had little physical strength and a rapidly waning beauty, and was a profound individualist and conservative."

"The average woman—yes, that is fair enough as far as it goes, though it hardly does her justice in some points."

"It is not exclusive, of course, but true so far?"

"Yes, I grant you that."

"Then if I can show you that the average woman to-day is interested in the improvement of the whole world, her own country, and especially her own city; that she takes a large part in business and politics, art and science, all industry and trade; that she has become stronger, more beautiful and dresses with wise good taste and personal distinction; that she is now organized and united in splendid co-ordination in every city, throughout the country and internationally as well; and is hand in hand with men in the highest progress, you will admit the change?"

"I will admit the change—a change of inconceivable dimensions—when you have proved it; but I will not admit the improvement, not in the slightest."

"No, I did not suppose you would—at first. When I have exhibited the changes and you have realized their vastness, will be time enough to let the improvement sink in. Now I'll tell you what happened.

"In 1907 there had already been tremendous progress among women, you know. All over the country—all over the world—their clubs and federations were drawing them together. They had made a place in industry and art and science, they had gained much in legal and political rights; they were even beginning to study their own business— for so long their only business—'Domestic Economy' and 'Child Culture.'

"The material was changing character very fast; but lacked co-ordination. And what kept them back most was a mistaken religious sense, a too limited idea of duty. Well, this new religious outburst swept across America like a prairie fire. It was both spiritual and practical, both individual and social. It illuminated all the confused problems of the time— correlated and explained them—cleared them away. It made life *clear*, bright, simple, full of hope. And in especial it took hold of this great mass of uneasy women, stirred their religious fervor to white heat, combined it with mother-love and the new pride of free womanhood—and turned it loose on the world.

"I know you don't like this, nor see the good of it—but I'm telling you the facts. Then, later, you shall meet the women—see them at work —see the results of the new methods on conditions and on people—see the kind of children we have now, and talk with men, see what our men think about it."

"I have talked with a few already," I ventured. "Some of them like it and some of them don't. But go ahead with your railroad millennium."

"An excellent name for it. Well—picture to yourself the country as you remember it: the large proportion of good, well-meaning people; the great amount of reformatory enthusiasm; the high average of intelligence; the vast capital—and this multitude of aroused women. Into this field came Henry St. John and preached *living*—not only in general exhortation, but with full, explicit direction. Each church was a center of social enthusiasm, of political activity. There was a new perception of the workable power of God; a new order of duties.

"The appeal to women was direct; it roused them to see that as mothers, *together,* they could do what they chose with the world; and that in duty there was but one choice—to improve that world as rapidly as possible.

"These preachers—men and women, too—unflinchingly exposed the selfishness, idleness, pettiness, and negative evil of so many women's lives; and the wasted devotion of others. They showed, so that no one could mistake, the way to change things—the immediate steps to be taken. In the old days we used to have sermons that aroused this same glow of enthusiasm to do right—but they never gave any directions as to what to do—and the glow died unavailing.

"This church had its organizers—men and women of splendid talent. They planned, slowly and practically, a program of advancement; they formed a party—The New World Party, and the women joined it almost *en masse*. Plenty of men did, too. I can't begin to tell you the exact steps—it is so long a story; but I can summarize."

"Now, see here, Miss Cartwright, you are abusing the women just as Edwards did—has this new religion nothing to say about men? Weren't men selfish and —"

"Yes, selfish, but not idle and not petty. Men practised the sins of commission—plenty of them; but meanwhile they kept the world going. Women practised the sins of omission, nearly all of them. The poor housewives did nothing but wait on their own families—a grade of duty belonging to the stone age; and the rich ones didn't even do that. Men did all the social service—nearly; and the women sat back and blamed them for the way they did it. I doubt if a civilization run solely by women would have been much better.

"Well—they got municipal suffrage for women, everywhere, within five years—the demand was irresistible. Better civic management was so clear and practical an issue that majorities agreed on that almost at once.

"To this great body of women the city problem was a simple one— they could see clearly, under the leadership of their great teachers, that a great number of persons living close together required certain conditions for health and comfort; and that as they made the city—*were* the city— they had a right to these conditions. Being women, and new to the business, they were unhampered by traditions either of economics or politics.

"They rose and rose, a vast, swift, peaceful revolution; town after town was captured by these enthusiastic 'city mothers,' and things began to be done. Honesty, efficiency, cleanness, health, beauty, order, peace, economy—these were their purposes; and they accomplished them.

"You must have been struck by the improvement in buildings?"

"Yes, indeed—even before landing. And I am still wondering how so much was done in so little time."

"These new city governments established a minimum of comfort and convenience in living accommodations and gave the owners five years to come up to it. After that, if not properly improved, they took possession of the property, paid the owners just what it was worth and no more, destroyed and rebuilt. We have had thirteen years since then, less or more, and that is a long time nowadays. In the meantime we ourselves—the Upgrade Co.—had built models which worked so well that they were rapidly adopted by city governments everywhere. By this time you will not find a city in the land without some municipal dwelling-houses; and in many, here, for instance, there are acres of them."

We talked for some time, for I had made notes of my line of questions and intended to prick as many bubbles as possible. Finally, Hope arose. "You have seen bird's-eye views of New York as it used to be," she said.

"Yes—to my sorrow."

"I'm going to give you another now. You don't mind air-cars, do you?"

"On the contrary. I have tried them in Paris; but I understand you have carried them much farther here."

"Yes, they are fairly general now, and the little ones extremely popular."

We stepped into the car and soared up softly to where the air was like that of a mountain-top, and hung, balancing like a buzzard, in slow, smooth inclines.

The city lay long and bright beneath us, clear as a map in the smokeless air.

"Do you use no coal at all now?" I asked.

"Not in the cities. It is burned on the spot where it can be mined cheaply enough and the power transmitted. In all the great cities we use electricity altogether. That's one reason the flowers and trees grow so well, and the roofs are such fair child-gardens."

She stayed first at quite a low altitude, that I might gaze down into those rosy nests of beauty and fragrance, the central courtyards.

"How do you get so much room? The 'extensions' used to choke up the backyards in my time—and the apartment-houses fill them."

"We have not cleared all the apartment-house blocks yet, as you can see; but in most of them—and in the private-house blocks that have adopted the new system the space is gained simply enough, by eliminating the workshops."

"Workshops? I suppose you mean the kitchens."

"Yes, the kitchens and all their adjuncts. The private house of New York to-day stops at the parlor floor. The family has all the room it ever had, to live in, but the space below is otherwise occupied. We build deep; heating, lighting, and ventilating by electricity. The work-rooms are wonders of convenience and beauty—but I'll show you over a block later. Look now at our North Park."

I gasped with delight. Some genius, some great artist, had had his way with that wide bay of green between Fort George and King's Bridge. A huge amphitheater, with hills all about, and the placid Harlem, wider than of old, flowing clean and bright across it. There were houses in plenty, but so grouped and arranged as rather to add to the effect than injure it; roads that curved, footpaths and shaded avenues, wide meadows for amusement, speckled with playing children, and flowers in great sheets and patches.

"I'll make my first admission," said I. "Knicker-bocker nature at least must have moved an inch to admit of this rescue of so much loveliness from the jaws of business."

She smiled serenely. "Yes, we are very proud of that park. It was a big fight. The City Mothers finally took possession of the whole upper end of the island—all that was left of the original beauty of what must once have been a world wonder. It is more thickly settled than you think —the rents pay well for it, and the *living* there is worth while. But I want you to look at the south end." We swung softly southward; and again I gasped, in amazement, this time. The East Side—the Lower East Side—that ghastly blot on our civilization, that hotbed of consumption and worse evil still—now lay open beneath us, with broad, tree-shaded avenues, parks and parklets everywhere, and the same flowery, sunlit, open courts in the great blocks of houses.

"This is all a municipal quarter just here," she pointed out—"the rest private undertakings. That group of blocks there where you see so many flowers is where we began—the Upgrade, you know. You can't judge the beauty of the piers from here—there are recreation piers and baths almost every other block. The water is clean now, you know; but you can see the Water Road."

I could indeed. The whole island city was rimmed with a wide driveway, alive with traffic mostly, but double-lined with trees for all that, and spreading to quieter beauty toward the upper end. Broad avenues crossed the narrow island frequently, and I could see where tunnel and bridge connected it with both its neighbors so freely that it seemed an island no more.

"What have you done with the people?" I inquired. "It was thick enough before, and there should have been some increase in twenty years. Unless the New World Party has eliminated children?"

Again that motherly smile of hers instead of annoyance. She handed me a binocular, saying: "Look and see." And a very little scrutiny showed me that not only the parks and squares, but—yes—the roofs, everywhere, were alive with children.

"I should say, from this casual glance, that you had eliminated the grown people instead," I admitted.

"I remember those roof gardens—or the talk about them—they seem to be universal now." I swept the glass up and down over the city. No smoke, no steam, no chimneys, and miles upon miles of flowery, sunny, breezy roofs, with babies and children as thick as daisies.

"Yes, we have made a city fit for children at last. But if you want to see where the people are we'll go a bit higher and show you."

We soared to the height of a mile or more, and I could see a radius of forty miles on either side of the city. It reminded me of a book I read once, "A Cityless and Countryless World."⁹ Like a vast spider-web the white roads ran—green roads, I might almost say, for the trees that lined them, farms, gardens houses—more houses, houses everywhere; some dotted singly, but most in groups of varying sizes around small parks with larger buildings in the center; it was as if the hard, dark, close-packed kernel of New York had burst like popcorn, and become a far more beautiful and wholesome thing, ten times its former size.

"There have been wonderful things accomplished in twenty years," said I. "I can see that much, easily. But so were there in the previous twenty years—without altering my old friend, Human Nature. I can see better roads, better homes, better transportation"—for the electric cars flew like shuttles through the wide web of light and shade; the whole great fabric below me pulsed and throbbed in the swift circulation of social life. "But you might have 'the beauty that was Greece and the glory that was Rome'—and people no better than the Greeks and Romans."

"You are right there, of course; but you can hardly think that a people such as you knew, and left in scorn, could accomplish so much improvement in living, in twenty years, without having become both wiser and more harmonious.

"New York is only a sample, you must remember. Every city on our map is changed like this. Think what it means—in twenty years of aroused motherhood we have 'cleaned house' for our children; cleaned the streets, cleaned the water, cleaned the air; we have room enough to breathe in our houses—the new building laws see to that—and in our courts; the streets are wide and shady; the traffic is comparatively noiseless, and greatly reduced in volume, as you can see."

"I was just going to ask about that," I said, swinging my glass slowly over the city as we slid to lower levels again. "I see a fine stream of activity around the south end, naturally, and a lot of movement in the parks and boulevards; but very little you could call traffic up-town. I've noticed it before—now that I think of it. How have you fixed that?"

"By eliminating the kitchen," she answered. "You see, in a residence quarter there was practically no traffic at all except for kitchen service. Each block had as many kitchens as there were houses—or more for the flats. In the crowded apartment-house streets there would be as many as five to ten hundred kitchens to a block—sometimes more. Even if they had all patronized the same shops this would have meant at least five hundred deposits of ice or milk, of bread, of meat, of groceries, every day; with confectioners, florists, and dealers in kitchen furniture beside. In our dreadful coal age there was also the rasping clatter of the coal-chute and shovel, the smoke and dust above, ashes and cinders below—and the wagons of the refuse men to remove the remains of what the wagons of the supply men had brought—a nice, quiet, clean system of living! Nice for the children particularly—who had only those streets to play in—streets of dirt and noise and disease. Now our residence streets are as clean as—as a piazza. One thing our City Mothers did was to put an end forever to the snow problem."

"That certainly indicates an improved intelligence," said I. "I'm no social inventor, but it always seemed to me a little discreditable to see a big, modern city fumbling with a two-foot snowfall as if they had never seen one before. What did these enlightened women folks do to that?"

"In the first place, they reconstructed the streets. Our old pavements were made for horses, you know—when the horse was sent back to the country, where he belongs, we could change our plans.

"The streets of New York—and of most of our other cities as well —have been wholly reconstructed. Each street is a tunnel now—the main connecting ones, I mean; a clean, large, finished tunnel. Having no horses, the pavement is differently made, and with our cheap electricity we simply heat the street when it snows—just enough to run it off; and the roofs, too.

"All the pipes and wires are in the tunnels, easy to get at; and all the freight business. A little passenger business remains, but not much, and only for long-distance expresses. You see the open street being free of freight traffic allows of safe and speedy surface travel, and cheap power does the rest."

"I should think the decentralization of business would help too," I suggested.

"Yes, I forgot that. Now that the women are at work everywhere they have brought small business nearer home for their own convenience, and scattered the big ones out of town."

"I shouldn't think it was sanitary to have business places near the homes."

"Why not?"

"Because of the noise, dirt, smells and other incidentals—"

"Those were only incidentals, you see, not essentials. Women don't like to work in such conditions and changed them very fast. When they couldn't be changed, the hopelessly offensive industry was promptly banished to wider grounds. But take an enormous business like the clothing trade. Hundreds of thousands of our women are working in that; and in such clean, quiet, pretty shops as are by no means bad neighbors. We'll go down presently and see some of these. But I wanted you to see with your own eyes what twenty years of aroused common sense has done for city life. Remember, this is only a sample. We have, in twenty years, abolished the slum."

"Have you abolished the slumites?"

"Of course—they didn't make the slum—the slum made them. You never heard of a body of poor people building a 'lime block' for themselves, did you?"

"Why, no—but if they went into a once-decent neighborhood they soon reduced it to a slum."

"Did they cut down the big, comfortable rooms into little ones? Did they raise the rents so that nothing was left for decent living?"

"Oh, well, if you are going to talk that way, I withdraw. But where did this body of female philanthropists get the labor to do this incredible amount of work in such a short time?"

"The labor was on the spot—and coming in at the rate of a million a year."

"And where did they get the money to pay for the labor?"

"Just where it was always got—out of the labor itself."

"Now, look here, Miss Cartwright, I was never much of an economist—even of the old kind—and your sort is quite beyond me. You show me improvements costing billions; and say the country is covered with them. I should like to know how you did it. Where do you get your capital?"

"It is a little difficult to tell you all I want to as quickly as I want to," said she, "but it was like this: We began with your capital—the twenty million dollars. This was carefully invested in models of various sorts; model houses, blocks, villages, summer resorts, businesses, and they all paid, giving us an enormous income. Then came the flood—religious enthusiasm and people contributing—Dowie's funds[10] were nothing to it. We had more offered than we could wisely use—it just banked up, so that we had to refuse it, and recommend them to our special advisory Bureau of Investment.

"Thirdly—and this is the main thing—as we rapidly proved that a rightly managed business was social service—and that social service was an admirable investment—bringing sure returns in money, public honor, and an easy conscience—why, the capital of the country began to flow our way. It is not all our work—this tremendous change; we showed them how, that's all. People weren't bad—they were just ignorant. Nowadays people invest their money in these magnificent schemes of public service, just as a plain business venture. So the capital for progress is practically unlimited."

"And what did you do with your millions of poor people while you were rebuilding your cities?"

"Provided employment outside, of course. The removal of so many mills and shops made a great difference; but the immediate undertaking was our great Road-building Association. You remember how people were beginning to stir on that subject? We started by wholesale, the Upgrade began it and city after city fell in line.

"We went at it as an army does; we had construction trains, supply trains, and house trains, too—accommodation for pleasant living—summer schools —comfortable living for families. There are several miles of roads in our country. We paid excellent wages, emptied the city in summer quite a bit, and employed the remaining workers to destroy and rebuild.

"When cold weather came and the people flocked back, there were miles of new homes to work on. We got the whole country interested. You see these storage-batteries multiplied the motor-cars a thousand-fold—everybody wanted good roads. We got city laws—county laws—State laws—and national laws to help us, with a well-balanced general and local taxation. It has raised the value of the whole country, and added to its wealth, and employed 'surplus labor' in a way most beneficial to those otherwise employed. It took up the overplus of immigration in a most convenient way; and it settled the negro problem."[11]

I sat up at this and looked to see if my old friend was joking; but she seemed serious enough.

Chapter 5
City Living

Our big bird dropped us softly down to a perch on Grand street. Well did I remember that sordid, dirty, and over-populous thoroughfare. It was populous still; but save for the clear and frequent signs I should never have known it, so great was the difference to eye, ear, and nose.

"I'm going to let you see poor women at work," said Hope; "and how they live. There are very few women now who are not at work—

and such are very properly pitied as incapable or despised as unwilling, or both."

"Do you mean married women?"

"Of course I do. Women in general are married, and ought to be; their industrial position is not affected by that. Marriage is a personal relation, but industry is a social relation. Maid, wife, or widow—bachelor, husband, or widower—these conditions do not alter one's social duty. Why should they?"

"Why should they?" I echoed. "Because wifehood and motherhood are more primal and sacred duties than typewriting and millinery."

"Do you mean wifehood and motherhood—really?" asked Hope with a quizzical smile, "or cook-hood and housekeeper-hood?"

"I know those arguments," I replied with some heat; "and ignore them. If the wife and mother goes out to work, the home and children are neglected—that is sure. They may all board in the same place—but that is not a home."

"All right," she said, "we won't argue—we never did accomplish much that way."

She took me to a block of six stories, yet not too high, for the ground-floor was level with the street and mostly occupied by shops, and a projecting, deeply corniced roof gave an Italian effect and reduced the height, apparently.

The concrete walls were pleasantly colored and decorated—(again I saw how the absence of coal enabled us to have painted cities gay as flowers)—and the inner court was a rose-garden. On the second story women were at work in wide, bright, many-windowed, rose-fragrant shops.

"This is a typical place," she said to me as we entered one; "you will find such in all big cities; but this will do as well as any; it is one we built ourselves and is our pet example. It is occupied by what used to be 'poor people'—there are none so poor now except the wrecks in the asylums. Their trades are mostly such as can be followed where they live; and in this populous community that is a great attraction. These women you see at work are mostly married women."

I surveyed the scene with interest. Several of the workers knew my guide and smiled cordially to her. Just then one of the girls rose, went to the forewoman's desk, and had her card marked; and then began to play on the piano. It was the last half-hour of the morning shift; and they all rose now, reported their time as they passed out and scattered. The younger ones betook themselves to the court, where they walked and chatted; some others I saw go into a doorway from whence proceeded the sounds of gay music and of dancing feet.

"They are the better for a bit of exercise before lunch, you know; but here is Mrs. Whiteberg[12] waiting for us." I was introduced to this lady, who greeted me with cordial interest.

"We are to have the pleasure of your company at lunch—and you are to study our housekeeping a little, I believe," she answered. "First, I must go up and get the baby—will you come?"

I was most willing—it was just this getting the baby that I wanted to know about. The lift took us swiftly to the roof where Mrs. Whiteberg soon found her youngest, happy in the sunshine, watching a number of other roly-poly infants tumbling about on a wide, soft mat, in the care of a sweet-faced woman of forty or thereabouts. On seeing his mother he promptly remembered that he was hungry and stretched his arms to her, leaping with eagerness. It was a pretty sight to see her catch him up and cuddle him, and presently Mr. Whiteberg appeared from the playgrounds just beyond carrying one toddler and leading a strenuous five-year-old.

"We'll be back presently," Hope told her. "I want to show Mr. Street around a little."

What amazed me most was the space. Except for the young people and some old ones in the court below, the whole block seemed to empty itself on the roof; and yet the mothers sat apart, nursing their babies; families grouped together, and children were still playing merrily.

"How do you get so much room?" I asked Hope.

"The roof space of a regular New York block, with the promenade extension, is 130,000 square feet," she answered; "and we do not have more than three thousand persons in our most crowded blocks now. In 1907 there was one with 6,173!—more persons to the acre than anywhere on earth—to our shame. If all our residents were on the roof at once they would still have standing room of more that 7 ft. × 6—which is giving to each family the space of nearly 15 × 15. Let us walk around. There is a band-stand on each side, as you see, plenty of seats; this outer promenade—the inner one is slanted at the corners for running;—then here are the playgrounds for babies—here for the next older children— here the wired-in places for ball games—here the water sports."

I stopped in delight. A shallow pool some fifty feet long and thirty feet wide was alive with bobbing, splashing, hilarious youngsters, carefully watched by numbers of teachers.

"These," said Hope, "are the children of the lower East Side—in twenty years!"

I said nothing.

We now joined the Whitebergs, and went down to their rooms. She was a pretty woman and prettily, though simply gowned; he a keen, intelligent young fellow, an electrician, he told me, and stationed in that very building.

"It's a good deal of a job," he said, "keeping up the service in these blocks. There is the warming system—the whole place is kept at a good temperature in winter, with a little heater in each apartment besides, where you can warm your hands or feet, or heat water, or dry things. We heat the roof when it snows, too. Then there's the lighting system and the cooking—it keeps us pretty busy."

"I'm glad to see that men are working still." I said. "I had rather expected to see women doing it all."

"No," he answered seriously. "About sixty percent of the women are at work now. Some are too old, some won't, and ever so many are too stupid and clumsy."

"You see, the 'clinging vine' is not in much demand nowadays," said cheery Mrs. Whiteberg, hugging her baby, already asleep, before she left it in the nursery on our way down. "But come—it is time to eat."

Their apartment was a little one, four rooms only; but as there was no kitchen it seemed ample for the family of five. It was exquisitely neat, beautiful in color and proportion, and cozy and homelike as well.

"What a charming little home!" I said. "How do you find time to keep it so dainty, Mrs. Whiteberg?"

"I don't," she said. "The cleaning goes with the rent. I lock up my closets and drawers if I wish, but the rest of the place is dusted daily and washed weekly. We leave our beds to air when we go to work. When we come back it is as you see. Will you sit here, Mr. Street—you here, Miss Cartwright." She rung a bell beside the dumbwaiter and presently there appeared certain covered dishes, hot and steaming, with service for five.

"Do you enjoy having strangers come into your home like that?" I inquired, and she and her husband placed the things on the table.

"Had you a close personal acquaintance with your chambermaid in the old days?" she replied. "I'd rather have two brisk competent 'strangers' in my home for twenty minutes a day than to have incompetent ones in it all the time—or to do all the work myself. I'd rather make shirtwaists than beds—that's all."

"The little ones are all taken care of upstairs," the father said. "They have meals oftener, special milk, and are most carefully watched—it is better for their health."

"Then you don't see your babies except—"

"Except morning and night, like any other working man; and an extra glimpse at noon, as you observed. Did the men twenty years ago have more?"

"Why, no—but their mothers did."

"Now, Mr. Street," began Mrs. Whiteberg, somewhat ruffled, "I see just as much of my children as the average woman used to except for the first two or three years. And it was in that first few years that our babies used to die so fast—if you'll remember. Now they do not die. They are well, happy, beautifully cared for; and we mothers are not wholly fools." She blushed a little and looked at Miss Cartwright, who smiled amicably.

"The fact is," Mrs. Whiteberg went on, "I did try for a year or two to be with the children when Morris here was little; but—it was very wearing, and they did not like me. I was cross, I guess—too tired. Now I am always well and cheerful and they love me. Do you not, Morris?"

Master Morris embraced her with an ardor that well-nigh upset the cocoa-pot, and as I had seen on the roof, all three had shown eager affection to both parents.

"May I ask questions?" I was promptly assured I might.

"What are working hours in these days?"

"They vary in different trades and in different places; but in none is it more than eight now, and most only six."

"And your present class of laborers, for instance —what do they get, and how do they live?"

My host and hostess looked at one another consciously.

"We were the poorest class of laborers when we began," said she briskly. "I came from Russia and Morris from Germany.[13] Our parents were peasants—we were dirty, ignorant children. But this heavenly country!"—she caught Hope's hand and kissed it devotedly.

"We have very different arrangements for receiving our immigrants now," said Hope; "and these friends came along just as we began to do things properly. New York had recognized her position as 'reception committee' in our great national enterprise."

"Do you mean the Government has made itself an employment agency for foreign labor?"

"I mean much more than that. Ours is the first country where human beings of all sorts could meet and mingle freely—so giving room for the free selection of type and unlimited improvement of the race. The nations vary. America selects and combines. But it was all done clumsily, under protest, and with great loss and waste. Now we allow a certain number each year, from each country—and take care of them."

"I should think you do!" burst forth the man. "I shall never forget it—never! To come sailing up that splendid harbor in the glitter of sunlight—the great golden Liberty shining on us—the kindness and courtesy and encouragement with which we were received—and then the Education! Love this country? I worship it!"

"You see, we recognize the economy of special training for strangers" said Hope; "and stations are placed for that purpose all over the country. There is work provided, easy enough to leave strength for learning; and all hands are given a special course in our language, institutions, ethics, economics and purposes. Mr. Whiteberg chose his profession early. But when he and Nina were married they only earned the 'minimum wage' between them."

"And that is?"

"That is now two dollars a day for both men and women. As prices are more reasonable than they were, they can live better for the same money."

"Let me show him," said Mrs. Whiteberg eagerly. "My sister—my older sister and her husband are still on this pay—they came too soon! But look—they live in this house here—they have five children—and this is how they live on their twenty-four dollars: The rent is five dollars—they have five rooms, you see; the food is seven dollars; the clothing is five dollars—and the education three dollars, so there is three dollars a week over for assessments, or to save or what you please, car-fares and such. And they have saved already—in the fifteen years since houses like this were built, and these wages paid—almost a thousand dollars! It would be more but for some sickness.

"We get more than that," she continued, "because of the Education. Morris earns four dollars a day—and I work only six hours and get two dollars. So we have thirty-six dollars a week; and we save—lots!"

It was work-time again, and they bade me good-by, with warm invitations to come again. They escorted Master Morris back to his kindergarten playground and went to their several tasks—I saw him give her a surreptitious hug as they parted—and Hope proceeded to show me over the building.

"The ground-floor is all stores, halls and such places," she explained, "and the second in this block is workshops. There are many trades, but mostly some kind of clothing work. You noticed those big chimney-like things on the roof? Those are the ventilating pipes. There is a perfect system now—the air of all the rooms changes constantly, but keeps its temperature. There were fifty women in that work-room we were in—but it was fresh, you remember?"

"Yes—that is another reason why it seemed so unreal—all the workshops I was ever in have smelled abominably."

"No wonder—bad air, dirty clothes and dirty bodies, too. Now we bring up all the children—all, mind you!—to a thorough water education."

"What on earth is that?"

"Why, they have it to play in as babies, they swim before they walk, they have a bath every morning of their lives—and form the habit."

We descended to the basement-floor and entered a large, clean room, glistening with tiles and glass, pleasant in color. Electric stoves were grouped in the center under a graceful bell of aluminum that hung like a big flower over them and took all the odors of cooking to the tall pipes above.

"There are about 3,000 persons to feed in this block; about 500 are babies and have only milk and what is prepared in the nurseries; but there are some extras—we allow for 3,000. That makes only 750 to a kitchen, you see. And our big hotels used to cook for far more than that. Twenty-five cooks, dishwashers and servers to a kitchen—with system we can manage on that basis. Here is the freight entrance."

A wide door opened upon the subway; and as we were looking a bell rang, it slid back, and a freight-car stopped level with the threshold. The storerooms under the sidewalk opened from this landing; traveling cranes ran overhead, and a load of supplies was put away in an incredibly short time. The ice plant was located by the storeroom, which opened also into the kitchen; space, labor, and time were conserved to the utmost.

"There is one buyer for the block—with a tremendous patronage," went on my proud guide. "He gets good food at wholesale prices. The city food laws insure excellence—the women saw to that very promptly. We get good milk now, the year round, for four cents a quart. But that is one hundred and twenty dollars a day for milk—to a block. They deliver it from tank cars right into the kitchen tanks, and both are cleaned and sterilized daily. Come and see the diningrooms."

Large, airy, beautiful, light, opening on the rose-bordered court and the street also—with separate tables for families or parties, and long ones as well—these were as attractive as the kitchen. There were no costly or elaborate decorations, but the proportions and color were satisfying and it was quite evident that the standard of design had risen appreciably.

"A good proportion of our families take their meals in their rooms," Hope told me. "It costs no more to send it upstairs than to serve it on tables, but there are numbers of young parents and others unattached who prefer the dining rooms. Then here is where the dinner-pails are filled or food bought any time."

Where a wide-arched passage pierced the middle of the block, the main entrance and exit for that side, was a long lunch-counter arrangement, with pigeon-holes for pails, all numbered. These were left at night with the order; cleaned perfectly and filled for the morning exodus.

"Food is ridiculously cheap now," she told me. "You see our meals by the week are less than five cents apiece per capita; for two or three cents a first-rate lunch is given; and for ten cents you can have a banquet."

Next we saw the Amusement Halls. There was no cellar to the block, except for the engine-rooms and such places, but the basement floor was nearly two stories in height, giving proper proportion to these larger rooms.

I had never realized before how much space was wasted in cellars and kitchens. Here were these ample accommodations for cooking and eating, with dancing and leisure halls, gymnasia, reading-rooms, and, under the sidewalk, a space altogether of 61,000 square feet—were swimming-tanks, bowling-alleys and billiard-rooms. Everywhere good ventilation and good light, cleanliness and beauty; it was quite evident to me that whatever the people were, the conditions of living had improved enormously.

"These amusement places they pay for," she explained to me; "but the charge is small, and wages good enough to allow it. If they don't like their own, they go to other blocks, or to larger and more public ones—there is no restriction. Often they club together and hire these halls for themselves."

"How on earth do you manage the prices? You tell me these building absolutely pay."

"There are two big lines of saving involved, the main leaks in our old system of 'domestic economy.' Economy! In no part of that foolish, wasteful, wicked way of living did we squander more than in what was called 'housekeeping.' We wasted—to put it briefly—over a third of our labor and two-thirds of our living expenses. Domestic economy!—the worst waste in the world!

"Now we have stopped both leaks. We can feed people well, at a dollar a week each: because we buy and cook for great numbers together, and we can pay for our beautiful buildings with all their advantages and for first-class care and training of the children, because the mothers earn as well as the fathers."

"They don't earn as much, do they?"

"Not generally, when they have young babies—nursing mothers do not work over six hours a day, in two shifts. But they get two dollars for that—enough to pay half of the feeding, clothing, and education of three children, and support themselves, too. The father does his half and a little more—in view of her larger service as mother."

"You still recognize motherhood, then?"

She laughed outright.

"You would-be irritating man! Why do you take such pains to be disagreeable? We recognize motherhood now—for the first time. People used to talk about it a good bit—write about it—paint pictures of it—but they never knew what they were talking about! Now we have begun to see what civilized motherhood is—and we find it the mainstay of our whole system of living. It is the voting mother who has made these brilliant, happy cities—this new world of education—you'll hear about that later—these homes that are really built for children."

"But why should the mother work at all, beyond her duties to her children?"

"It is by working that she fulfills her duty to her children—that is the whole secret of it. Mother-hood specializes now—all bear children —unless they are unfit; but only some rear children—those who are naturally able and who love the work.

"It is one of our greatest professions. We have whole colleges to study it in—an imposing body of literature—years of special training—and a constant succession of under-studies and assistants. No child to-day is left to the bungling experiments of an unaided mother. Consequently, we do not have the wholesale infanticide of older times. Our babies live —and are happy."

"What is the rate of increase?" I asked, maliciously.

"Are you hinting at Malthus or Roosevelt?"[14] she replied with a twinkle. "Both are out of date. The first effect of our improved treatment was a rise in the rate of increase—simply because we saved lives. But as the years passed this declined gradually, because we do not have as many children born now. If this curve continues, in another twenty years we shall have a well-nigh stationary population.

"Now, don't say 'race suicide,' I beg of you. I do not save a man's life by not killing him—and I do not take a child's life by not bearing him! Child-labor was race suicide, absolutely; and we have stopped that long ago. The reason for this gradual change is that as women grow into a richer, broader, stronger personal life they do not, like poor crowded plants, just 'run to seed.' "

"Then you cut off the supply at the top and leave it in excess below, do you?"

"It always was in excess below—and always will be. The mass of the population is less specialized than the more highly organized racial servants—naturally. But we have no longer as low a grade of people as we used to have. When all the world learns wisdom we shall have no more such anywhere. We are constantly improving the quality of the stock as a whole; and replenishing the higher grades by the best education for all.[15]

"You remember how great men occasionally popped up from very ordinary ranks of life? We don't lose any such now. Every child has a chance to be his very best—or hers.

"That's the mother idea nowadays—how best to care for all the children born—and how to produce better ones. We take a conscious interest at last in our great function—the improvement of species."

"It used to be maintained that the female transmitted established types and the male introduced variations."

"Yes—that's all right. But the female introduces variation, too, and selects among males. That's another idea of the new motherhood. We will not marry the inferior men."

"What becomes of them, pray?"

"Nothing—they enjoy life as human beings and become—extinct. We make better ones."

This last exposition of Miss Cartwright's had taken place as we darted uptown again in the express.

"How do you keep it so quiet?" I suddenly asked her. "As I remember the subway one could not talk without a raucous screaming."

"I don't know the mechanics of it," said she, "or the acoustics, perhaps, I should say; but it is a very strong point with us now. We have found noise as disagreeable as dirt and almost as dangerous, and we won't have it. With clean and quiet cities the death-rate had dropped to a minimum—with the good food, too, and all the other things. And that is one reason we can do with a smaller birthrate. It is much better politics to have three children and keep them all than to have six and lose three. Here we are—we're to call on my friend Mrs. Gordon."

"Is she a working woman, too?"

"Of course; but not a poor one. This one makes dresses—a beautiful trade, and one that gives employment to great numbers. About ten per cent of us are dress and cloak makers and ten more for underwear, shirt-waists and the like. There is a fifth of the women accounted for, in a clean, quiet, easy, suitable trade, which does not take them away from their children. Millinery, furs, jewelry—take it altogether, it is nearer a third I think—you can find the figures in our labor reports."

We ring the bell at a door in a New York residence block, just as I remembered them except for two things. The "stoop line" now enclosed a border of green, irregularly massed, here a clump of bushes, here a tree, often a spreading vine and always grass; the steps were less massive and projecting; and the area doors, the darksome, descending steps, with their decorations of garbage and ash carts, had entirely disappeared. In their place were wide lunettes, evidently giving light to rooms below. Mrs. Gordon greeted Hope with affection, and me with undisguised interest.

"I'm very glad you have come, Mr. Street," said she. "It is a wonderful pleasure to meet such a—such an—"

"Such an antiquity, you might say," I ventured; "such a left-over; such an anachronism."

"By no means—such a novel point of view, is the phrase I was groping for. We are all used to these things and do not notice them; and it is a joy and pride to show our progress to one who is not a foreigner after all, but an American. Let me show you the shop—and then we'll have tea."

The room at the back was a perfectly appointed sewing-room, splendidly lighted, the entire north wall being glass and opening onto a glass-enclosed balcony.

"In summer we sit out here, you see," said our hostess. "Let me introduce you to Miss Eldon and Mrs. Howard—Mr. Street." Two beautifully dressed women greeted me as gracefully as if they had not been working in a dressmaker's shop, and pointed out to me the advantages of their view, which was indeed most charming. These courts were a constant surprise to me, they were so dissimilar—and all so beautiful.

"It is really after hours," said Mrs. Gordon, as we examined the fittings inside. "They are usually all gone by five; but that bit of work those two are on was so interesting they wanted to finish it today."

They departed presently, and we sat on the balcony enjoying the delicious tea which Mrs. Gordon made on an electric heater, while a remarkable transformation went on in the room inside. Two soft-footed maids appeared from somewhere, all the loose stuffs in the room were laid on shelves which ran like bookcases around the room and rich curtains were drawn before them; the sewing machines and pressing apparatus were placed in the corners behind tall decorative screens, and the great work-table, cleared and uncovered in a jiffy, became a handsome dining-table. Then the doors were closed on us for the moment, and the room sucked clean of dust and lint by an exhaust set permanently in the wall. "One has but to open the slide, press the button, and take care not to be blown out with the dust!" explained our hostess. Ten minutes— the doors were opened, the maids gone—and a cool, softly tinted dining-room replaced the equally attractive, but so different workshop.

Then the children came in.

9

Five Generations Hence
1916

LILLIAN B. JONES
[n.d.]

After earning an A.B., Lillian B. Jones resided in Fort Worth, Texas, where she taught English at Terrell High School, located in an African-American neighborhood. A yearbook photograph shows her to be light-skinned. She is among the earlier African-American women to combine public-school teaching and writing careers: a later notable example is Jessie Redmon Fauset, 1882–1961. In 1916, Jones boarded at 1200 East Tenth Street and shared with James I. Dotson a job-printing business, named Dotson-Jones Printing Company, located in the Dunbar Building at 911½ Jones. Eventually, she owned her own home at 1109 Humbolt Street East. In 1929 she became a telephone operator. The Fort Worth City Directory, 1916–1930, provides this information, as well as verification of race identity by (c) beside persons or businesses that were "colored," that is, African-American. We know no more about Jones's life.

So far as is now known, Jones is the first African-American woman to have written a utopia. In it, Grace Noble, "high brown" daughter of an ex-slave, teaches and writes while her close friend Violet Gray becomes an African missionary. Grace later marries a physician and raises children. Each achieves her "dream of life" and the improvement of her race.

Before Jones's generation, few African-Americans wrote: the prerequisite education, rooms-of-one's-own, and incomes became available to most women of color only within the last century. In 1853, Anglo Sarah Josepha Hale, 1788–1879, editor of the influential Godey's Lady's Book, *wrote* Liberia; or, Mr.

Peyton's Experiments, *a novel locating a black utopia in African Liberia, a nation of black American emigrants. Like Hale, Jones also idealizes life in Africa for African-Americans, but her thinking occurs within the context of the African-American Niagara and Marcus Garvey movements. The Niagara movement, following a 1905 meeting of black intellectuals in Canadian Niagara (to escape discrimination in Buffalo, New York), was the first protest against post-Reconstruction white-racist backlash and led to the foundation in 1909–10 of the National Association for the Advancement of Colored People (NAACP). By the close of World War I in 1918, Jamaican Marcus Garvey (1887–1940) had begun his shorter-lived movement, reaching its peak in 1920–21. It capitalized upon communal unrest and urged flight to Africa.*

Near-contemporary African-American writers Frances Ellen Watkins Harper (1825–1911) famed for Iola Leroy *(1895) and Pauline E. Hopkins (1859–1930) for* Contending Forces *(1900) provided important contemporary models. Jones antedates the epistolary voice, the missionary example, and the moral import of Alice Walker's* The Color Purple *(1982).*

References: *Fort Worth City Directory,* 1916–1930; Carol A. Kolmerten, "Texts & Contexts: American Women Envision Utopia, 1890–1919," in *Utopian and Science Fiction by Women: Worlds of Difference,* ed. Jane Donawerth and Carol A. Kolmerten (Syracuse: Syracuse Univ. Press, 1994); Arnold Rose, *The Negro in America: The Condensed Version of Gunnar Myrdal's "An American Dilemma"* (New York: Harper, 1964); Ann Allen Schockley, *Afro-American Women Writers 1746–1933: An Anthology and Critical Guide,* Boston: G. K. Hall, 1988.

Text: Lillian B. Jones, *Five Generations Hence* (Fort Worth, Tex.: Dotson-Jones, 1916), chaps. 6, 10, 16. The original text was edited to approximate current usage in punctuation and syntax, and thereby clarify the author's meaning for readers. Otherwise the author's style and diction remains untouched.

Chapter 6

A friend of Miss Gray's was soon hurrying home in a carriage with her and Miss Noble.

It was a quiet little home on the outskirts of the city. In the front yard were various kinds of flowers growing promiscuously about. Principally among them was a bed of sweet peas of many colors. The front window was nearly hidden by honeysuckle and a large bucket of wandering Jew hung suspended between the ceiling and floor of the front porch. The back yard ended in an abrupt hill, broken by numerous grassy terraces, till far below spread pastures of bright green where grazed numbers of cattle, and in the distance partially hidden by the trees meandered the river—a beautiful pastoral scene possessing just the drowsy sweetness of a Sabbath afternoon, fitted to bring out of one only that which was best.

Miss Gray's friend knew of her engagement with Miss Noble and, like the wise woman that she was, had an excuse to go away with her husband and bade Miss Gray to rest. Consequently, the two friends had the afternoon to themselves.

Miss Gray lay upon a lawn bench, a pillow beneath her head; Miss Noble sat near stroking the hair from her friend's brow.

"My dear Violet," began Miss Noble in those soft tremulous tones that always gave force to her words when she was deeply in earnest. "I hardly feel worthy to address you. I have always had such great desires to do something really worth the while, but as I reflect now, and as I sit in your presence, I feel that my life has been utterly worthless. With all my lofty desires, in comparison with the service you have rendered our people, what have I done? Even now, I must be true to you as to myself: when I ask myself whether I could make the sacrifice you make, my heart selfishly replies 'no.' There then must be something that I hold dearer than service to my people, and Oh, Violet, I feel so hypocritical, so insignificant in my own estimation. Talk with me, encourage me; you always know just what to say." Her eyes pleadingly sought those of her companion who met the parted lips with a kiss.

"'Tis not given us all to serve in the same capacity," Miss Gray quoted in a soft chant as she sat up. "Are all apostles? Are all prophets? Are all teachers? No, our gifts differ; we are only exhorted to covet earnestly the best gifts. Who, saving God himself has the right to compare our gifts? No, Grace, I know your life has not been spent worthlessly. You are, I feel, destined to accomplish a great work. You possess wonderful ability. Do you remember how Miss Saunders used to commend your compositions? She thought then she taught an embryo author." Miss Gray smiled at this reminiscence of college days. "Have you never thought to write, Grace—such a field for service and such a vast audience?"

Miss Noble's head had fallen into the lap of her friend: her slight frame shook with convulsive gasps, the tears fell thick and fast.

"My dear, look up! What is it? Have I wounded you?"

"No, no," replied Miss Noble, trying to smile through her tears, "you have touched upon the secret of my life even to you, my tenderest and best though it is for this very purpose I come to talk to you: I scarcely have the temerity to admit that I have dared hope to produce anything worthy the perusal of my fellow-man [sic]. The inspiration with the theme came six months ago; then I felt equal to the task but I'm not so sure now. Other incidents have occurred in my life, and though I am as eager now as then, I fear I lack some of the enthusiasm. When you mentioned what you did, I could but weep for pure joy that you had not forgotten these early desires of mine—and to fancy that it might be possible for me to succeed."

"Most certainly," replied Miss Gray, "but tell me, dear. Of what will you write, or would you like to tell?"

"To you I would tell anything, especially this because I know you will believe me. You know I would not lie to you after all that has passed today, and the high esteem in which I hold you.

"It all came about that autumn afternoon of which I have told you. I had spent a week of distressing reflections. It seemed a week of horrors to our people throughout the land, of which I read in the daily papers: there had been a lynching not far away and it seemed that the end of my endurance was reached when numbers of my race, men and women and even children, were attacked upon the streets of one of our leading cities, brutally assaulted, and forced to flee like hunted beasts. Out of the anguish of my despairing heart I cried to God that day, prayed for strength and endurance. I walked through the woods, I saw God in each tree and flower, in each gentle breeze that scattered the autumn leaves at my feet. I felt so close to Him, I felt His presence in my soul. After a few hours of sore travail in the valley I ascended the hillside. Reaching the summit, I stood gazing at the landscape spread before, but I saw not the fields of ripened corn, nor those where swayed the cotton blossoms, not even the homes of my friends in the region below. I saw the Negro for more than fourteen generations of oppression, attended by theft from their native shores and crack of the whip about their heads. I saw the land deluged in blood until this unnatural state was abrogated. I saw legislative disenfranchisements and all manner of discriminations; I saw prejudice above, below and around us. There arose a cry for peace, but the voice of mighty statesmen proclaimed that there could be no peace till the Negro recognized his position as vastly inferior to his Caucasian[1] neighbor; and when I thought of the numbers of bright girls and boys whom I knew, and of generations to follow—each evol[ving] into a higher degree of enlightenment, and remembered that these could never be free men and women, never feel that they might sip the very essence of life be they so inclined, my heart was sore and I would have turned away and continued my journey in sorrow." Here her voice sank almost to a whisper. Her eyes shone like stars, the slightest tremor stray[ing] about her lips. [With] Miss Gray hold[ing] tightly the little hand, she continued, "I seemed suddenly to be transported to another land and clime. The topography of the country had changed and I seemed to feel a sense of growing warm—though you remember I told you there was a norther. The season also seemed to have changed, for it was a time of sowing rather than harvesting. I fancied I stood upon an immense plateau: below me flowed a river but recently returned to its channel; above me were sunny skies and floating clouds. I looked long and steady at the scene, pondering the singular coincidence. I saw a people, a black people, tilling the soil with a song of real joy upon their lips. I saw a civilization like to the white man's about us today, but in his place stood another of a different hue. I beheld beautifully paved streets, handsome homes beautified and adorned, and before the doors sported dusky boys and girls. I seemed to be able to penetrate the very walls of business establishments and see that men and women of color were commercially engaged one with the other.

"I was as if thunder struck when a voice, a still small voice, yet seeming to penetrate my inmost soul, cried in thunderous accents 'Five Generations Hence'! I was stunned as the truth began to dawn upon my soul: the land was Africa, the people were my own returned to possess the heritage of their ancestors. I descended the hillside, hope kindl[ing] anew in my heaving bosom.

" 'Tis no idle tale I tell you, Violet. I beheld it all as plain as the noonday sun. I have deliberated upon the matter and, do you know, I have become convinced that there will be a final exodus of the Negro to Africa, not a wholesale exodus like the moving of an Indian reservation, but an individual departing, an acquiring of property in that unexplored land, and the building of a new nation upon the ruins of the old."

"Think you," quietly interposed Miss Gray, "that, with the present low birthrate and the great mortality with us, five generations hence there will be enough to form that great nation in Africa you so aptly picture? You know it has been averred that since the Negro has developed no marked civilization of his own, could not evolve one in rivalry with that of the white man, and could never become amalgamated with him, he is doomed to extinction."

"It is not true," replied Miss Noble; "the very laws and the amalgamation so abhorred are our safeguards that the perpetuation of our race is assured. If we were originally a part of the white race and have by some physical evolution produced these racial characteristics, then it is possible that [with] other and adverse forces being brought to bear, we might finally be lost in that family whence we sprang, but not become extinct. As a separate and distinct people we have a destiny to weave, and no force, oppression, or amalgamation can deter that edict of God.

"But it has been discovered before now by thinking people that the two races can never live in harmony, one with the other, side by side, until one concedes the mastery, or both concede the spirit of equality. And there can exist no equality between peoples so unlike in physical characteristics, temperament, wealth, and education.

"The Negro as a race is yet a child, and like most natives of warm, southern climates he is pleasure loving, impetuous, superstitious, and fond of gray dress, very unlike the hardy practical races of the North.

"Side by side the contrast is too great; the Negro ejects little originality in his dress, manner, or custom because his training has ever been, that all that is lovely and desiring belong to the white man, and being an easy going people he chooses to mimic rather than originate. This brings him into the contempt of his white neighbor and with it [their] feeling of superiority and monopoly.

"But away from these influences, where the little Negro maiden need not compare her little blue-eyed blonde doll baby with her 'nigger boy'; divorced from the theory that our correct temperature must be taken by a physician of the opposite race; few[er] bosses to advance us money for food and bury[ing] our dead—yes, away from these conditions, Negroes can see each other's virtues, gain self-respect, and learn the great lesson of self-reliance as a race.

"All saving the old Negro seeks to forget slavery, saving the spirit of gratitude that it is no more. The young Negro wishes to blot out of his memory that dark period of his history. But this the average white man keeps constantly before him, and few can rise to the dignity of a man or woman when constantly reminded by those in authority that their position of master and slave is not far removed.

"God in his wonderful providence permitted us to be stolen from our native shores and used to build up a powerful civilization: what have we profited thereby? We have learned the art that is the backbone of power and dominion—that of labor; we have learned forbearance and certainly [have] not been permitted to become guilty of the awful sin of pride. We have learned much of the white man's boasted civilization, and by his help the Negro is educating himself to return, I fancy, to his natal soil and begin anew his destiny, which is taking such time in weaving.

"Have you considered that of all the continents it is of Africa that least is known, that no one nation has gained permanent control of that vast land? Our geographies tell us that owing to the excessive warmth and moisture, and the prevalence of swamps, it is not yet known whether or not Africa is likely to be permanently occupied by the white race. Can one not read between the lines when he remembers that the Negroes' home is in the hot belt?"

"Yes," replied Miss Gray, who possessed the wonderful trait of being a good listener, "though I confess I hadn't connected the incidents."

"Yes," resumed Miss Noble, "it is only a question of time: even now the Negro has entered upon the new era. It is only through oppression, though, that the end is hastened—not permitting him to imagine himself secure, and the greatest advantage is that the persecution is general. If a difference were made because of color, education, or wealth, the class above would soon set in judgment upon the other and instead of lending a helping hand to his brother beneath, would draw about himself a wall of non-intercourse as strict as the castes of India. But we are united by a common bond: we rise or fall with the blackest son of Ham[2] or the fairest daughter who admits one drop of Ethiopian blood in her veins. The chain is no stronger than its weakest link; the race cannot ignore its most depraved villain.

"Oh, Violet, tell me! You are so wise! You know I am passionate and apt to possess a superabundance of enthusiasm. Do you think it possible that I may give to the world this inspiration with power to compel them to appreciate its solemnity? Dare I hope to admonish a race to begin the weaving of so strange a destiny?

"There are times when it seems mere folly that a Negro woman of moderate education dares to address the public in a literary way, but 'tis not literary fame I seek: 'tis a message I bring, and ah!" she said waving her arm gracefully toward the exquisite scene below, "when I can feel, upon witnessing such scenes, the throbbing of my heart as I do now, I feel that I am so close to God I would aspire to anything that is noble and worthy. I would have my people behold the beauties of nature while I whisper the message."

"I think it is possible," said Miss Gray without removing her glance from the scene below, "that with God to help, you may trust the story of your inspiration to find an audience. Forget yourself; tell it to the public with the same fervor you have told it to me. Think only of those whom you wish to serve, and leave the remainder to God.

"My work now will have for me a new meaning; I shall consider myself the advance guard of a mighty nation. Who knows but Grace's children may read of the work of Violet Gray, the early missionary, in their African histories some day? Success to you, ardent girl; swerve not from your purpose, and perhaps some of your own posterity may in that sunny land compose the national hymn."

Miss Gray smiled as she said this, but some how her words impressed Miss Noble that she was terribly in earnest. "I shall write you often," Miss Gray continued, "and God grant, my young friend, that you may sow here the seed that will bring universal light to the African jungles."

"I shall attempt it," said Miss Noble.

Chapter 10

It is possible, that nothing could have so completely and quickly brought Miss Noble to a deep realization of her mission and responsibilities as to find upon going to the post office the next morning a letter from Miss Gray.

She, somehow, regarded Miss Gray as a kind of superior being. She had ever regarded her since the far away days at Bishop as possessed of a more than ordinary character, but since that sabbath at the First Church, when Miss Gray had spoken from the sincerity of her soul, she had seemed to her a being of another world: her ideal of gentle, self-sacrificing womanhood, a character worthy of emulation.

Miss Noble felt many times that Miss Gray's association with her, and her opinion of her actions, had caused her to develop her finest and noblest instincts, as she budded into womanhood, and now, even now, when she is so close to thirty, there was no earthly power that spurred her on quite so forcefully as the thought of Miss Gray's approval.

Miss Gray's letter ran thus:

My Dear Grace:—
Of my stormy voyage across the Atlantic, and the many things that interested me, I have kept a correct diary, and I am sending it for your perusal as in this letter I wish to speak of other things.
My mind reverts to our last afternoon together. I see you—your

hands clasped in mine, lips slightly parted, the light of conviction flashing from your eyes, delivering to me the message that seems more real each day.

Many years ago, when I was but a little girl in pinafores, we lived on a farm. My evening work was to go for the cows, and I remember how I was wont to let down my hair and with bared feet go bounding down the lane. At the house where my mother was a servant, I was ever restrained, but in those delicious moments—my hair flying in the breeze, with no person in view, nothing but the grandeur of the setting sun above me, and on either side fields of living green, breathing deeply of the generous air about me—I then fancied that I knew absolute freedom. But oh! Grace, I shall never be able to impress you, dear, you, who understand so well, with the spirit of freedom that permeated my very soul, when my feet were placed for the first time upon African soil.

I lost sight of the strange faces and objects around me. Thoughts filled my mind of other times, when a few curious natives were lured from these shores and taken to distant lands to endure a servitude worse than death, and then I saw my own feet placed once more upon the beloved soil returning to tell the story of the Cross.

I forgot that I was not alone. Almost unconsciously I took a handful of the delicate soil and lifted it reverently to my lips. It seemed that the pungent earth gave forth the delightful odor, as of the quintessence of love and welcome.

Since I have been here, I go down to the shore each day and watch the tide come in. I like to listen to the waves; they sing a song that I alone can understand. I some times sit for hours—often, till the rising tide bathes my feet and each ripple of the shining waves seems to bear upon its foamy crest slowly, but surely, from the ocean's dark bosom, a mighty nation.

Another time, I see them recede and it seems so long a time till they shall bring to me those whom I love; but they ever sing their weird melody and when l listen closely, I can discover the burden of their song to be, "they shall come, yet a little while and they shall come."

Hasten the story, dearest Grace: 'twill take years, but they shall know at last. I believe it is the unalterable decree of God.

As I passed through a crowd of foreigners on my way to the shore yesterday, I witnessed the meeting of two Americans, a woman and a man, strangers I knew as no sign of recognition lighted the other's eye, but I heard him say softly as he lifted his hat, "My country 'tis of thee"; instantly the lady replied graciously, "Sweet land of liberty."

'Tis indeed, a grand and glorious union under the stars and stripes, a government, whose constitution stands for equal rights to all and special privileges to none, but notwithstanding the absence of prejudice in that law, I think of the many who execute the law and their natural repugnance to those who are descendants of former slaves, and I fear that Old Glory's ample folds are a trifle too narrow to enwrap the black man.

I think of hundreds, yes thousands, in that bonny land, who have for us some feeling of brotherhood, who take time from their lofty pedestal to let fall the rope to the man farthest down, but millions of others come before me whose antipathy for our race knows no bounds.

I have met an old native woman who tells me of strange traditions possessed by her tribe.

It was only a few nights ago, during one of their weird dances, as she and I sat apart, that she told me the story of a far away chief whose cheeks were never dry but wept day and night because of a people who would come—with faces like milk, hair like cow's tail —and bring woe to his people. Thus this old man, whose eyes had never beheld a white man, foretold his coming to bring desolation to our unfortunate ancestors.

But what surprised me most and took my thoughts so quickly to you, my dearest Grace, is that this poor old heathen woman believes, with a firmness born of despair, that some day the sisters and brethren will come gathering from over the mighty waters to make their homes with them.

Yes, Grace 'tis a prophecy common to them that the Negroes will return to Africa.

I dare say, even now, you are far on your book. Work diligently and trust the Lord. We have lost so much in failure to do this.

Give all that is best in you for "The harvest will surely come."

Your loving friend,
Violet Gray.

Chapter 16

When Miss Noble returned to Hammond, she told Mrs. Westley of her intention to accept Dr. Warner, and that was the one drop needed to fill her friend's cup of joy.

When Dr. Warner came two days later for his answer, Mrs. Westley contrived to be away with the children, and the lovers were alone.

They met in the little sitting room. Miss Noble thought he never looked so handsome. He had walked from the station and, having wiped the perspiration from his face, the short thick curls clung damp and disorderly upon his brow and high upon his neck. His hat he left in the hall, and he stood before her questioning, one brief moment—the flash of his eye and the nervous biting of [his] mustache tell[ing her] the high tension of his feeling. He started to approach her, took several quick steps, then stopped short and extended his arms. He said no word but admiration, pleading, love: all cried out eloquently in [his] look as he waited.

Instantly, all the world was forgotten, all the pent up tenderness of a life time was set free, and Miss Noble was nestling in her lover's arms.

"Oh! Grace, my darling, my own, my precious love," he cried rapturously as he gazed into the liquid depths of her loving eyes. "I did not know such happiness could come to men."

She did not reply. In supreme moments she could never talk, but she lay her head limply against his breast like a tired child, while her whole body quivered with delight.

Pearlia, coming upon them unexpectedly a few minutes later, heard Miss Noble exclaim in a sort of foolish school girl tone, "Oh! Carl, I am so happy."

Seeing Pearlia, she clasped the wondering little miss in her arms and cried out gleefully, "Dear Pearlia, I am to be married; you shall wear a pretty white dress and white slippers to the wedding and carry white bride's roses."

It was a merry party at the Westleys that night, and Dr. Warner returned to tell that dear old mother over in Galveston that [within] a few weeks he should bring home the sweetest woman in the world.

To add to Miss Noble's joy the very next morning there came the following letter from Miss Gray:

My Own Dear Faithful Friend:—

I daresay you have mourned me as dead, a prisoner, or sick of some dreadful disease, but I am glad to say I am alive, well, and among friends.

I have passed through many strange vicissitudes since I last wrote you, and I shall write of them at another time, but now, I wish to talk about your book. It was a long time in reaching me. As you will observe from this letter, I have left the coast and moved far into the interior, where I feel I am so much needed, but finally it did come, and though get[ting] mail here requires no end of trouble, I feel amply rewarded.

I have read the book carefully line for line, and I know now it was an inspiration. You have handled the subject well. The argument is clear and reasonably convincing, and what pleases me very much is that you have told [it] with the same quiet simplicity with which you told me so long ago.

As I read your book, I wondered that so few of our people write, when the world knows so little about us really—so little of our hopes and aspirations, so little of the sting we feel at insult and injury. Ah! yes, Grace, so little the [world] knows of what some of us really suffer, while our race is classed as certain species of animals with instincts peculiar to its kind or tribe, having little reasoning ability and incapable of great suffering. [Other] people, who ever go with laughter and song upon their lips, and realize not the perilous times through which we are passing.

Good people they are who [nonetheless] take us not seriously, who know little from personal contact, read only that which is written by opposite and more often prejudiced races, and thus form their impressions.

If these people are to know that we possess the higher sensibilities, that there are those of us who possess the higher sense of honor, the keenest appreciation of the good and beautiful in everything, that we really suffer like other peoples, then there is no pen but the Negro's that must lead [them] to see. No life save one that has been torn by the anguish of despair can vividly picture the suffering of [our] people.

There are those who write of the Negro from a theoretical point of view, even from an experimental as pertaining to the few, but when the Negro himself, who knows the life of his people, pours forth the passions of his soul, it is as the startled cry of [a] wounded animal lost in utter darkness.

I caught the wail of your stricken heart as I pored over your book, Grace. I heard the cry of millions in that sunny land for a panacea. I lived over the impossible conditions between the races, the stubbornness of the American people in their desire to restrain white supremacy, and the persistent encroachment of the black man. I knew that after a while the most conservative must see the wisdom of your argument.

Various nations have settled here principally because of commercial interests: few there be, who consider this home; they look with fond hearts to the time when they shall be financially able to return to their native land—whether England, France, Holland, or elsewhere—and build homes for themselves upon their natal soil.

The American colonist never succeeded as long as he looked back to old England as home. The very name [of Africa] bears the stigma of the black race, which is in itself a bar to the white man's calling it home.

'Tis the fires of patriotism, of undying love of home, swelling in the heart of man that enable him to push a country to its highest development. This I repeat, the present inhabitants have not, but to the Negro 'tis home, sweet home; as a flower transplanted in other soil will thrive best when returned to indigenous soil, so the Negro once here will feel a spirit of manliness and patriotism that he has never known before.

Those are beautiful pictures your imagination leads one to see of this dark land, but I am glad that you are wise enough to caution against forming fantastic notions of a modern Canaan,[3] for 'tis sure no land flowing with milk and money. No indeed, he who succeeds here as elsewhere must do so by the sweat of his own brow, the exercise of his own brain or muscle tissue, or he is doomed to greater want than in bustling, hustling America. But here with the spirit of hope and faith permeating his breast, every field he reclaims from the jungle, every mine he helps develop is to him as so much personal wealth stored away to comfort the lives of future generations of his race.

I am glad also, my dearest Grace, that you warn against premature and wholesale departures, for of course this Israelitish exodus is out of the question—first, because the Negro is so identified with America's progress that the business interest would not stand for it, and sections where [Negro] labor forms the back bone of success would hesitate at no rashness to pervert such a blow to public interest; second, it would take wealth, at least fair means that the Negro as a race does not possess; and third—saying nothing of transportation, admittance, etc.—the race is too young yet to stand alone: as much as the white man needs [Negro] labor, we need his culture, his business and executive ability. We must know more of their wonderful civilization. Nigh two centuries and a half of bondage and a half century of servitude is too great a price to pay and go away without it.

I am reminded of the colonists, who soothed their consciences into permitting our importation and enslavement, by seeing missionary work in bringing us from a heathen state into the light of the gospel, later by educating us and permitting contact, however humble, with so superior a race. Though we may impugn the motive of many, all this we admit is true, and I see in your book that, spurning any attempt at persuasion or foretelling possible coercion, you simply prophecy that they will return home with the spoils.

And I do believe it all so firmly, though never in my day. I have not conjured up any false hopes to sustain me in my work. I do not look for them to come, rich and powerful by thousands to establish a mighty government that shall startle Christendom. Oh! no. I can fancy their coming as those weary pilgrims on bleak New England's shores, but the desire for freedom will grow as [they] become more educated. It will be less easy after awhile to choke down the feeling of resentment at repeated injustices, less easy to conform to the white man's idea of the Negro's place, and being a naturally peaceful people and so weak, comparatively, his only resort will be to make more room that both may expand.

In closing, I want to remind you that we forget not to pray, lest some be mistaken in the prophecy, and like those early disciples watching for our Savior's speedy return, forget all else, for they must certainly beware or the whole plan be thwarted, or at least delayed by over zealousness.

They must get along with their neighbors; their relations are so woven one with the other that a disregard of relations by either side proves detrimental, and of course the greater harm is wrought upon the weaker people.

The white man needs the Negro only to the extent that his service contributes to his welfare; the Negro needs his wealth to supply his physical and mental wants. The relations are and should be purely business ones, and when the Negro fails to realize this and improve his opportunities to become a greater necessity, he shows a lack of tact and good common sense.

Write me soon. Your letters are so long reaching me, I can imagine that many things have occurred that will interest me much.

I wanted to know about yourself. Write me a long newsy letter.

I have yet much to say.

Always your loving,
VIOLET.

10

Seth Way:
A Romance of the
New Harmony Community
1917

CAROLINE DALE [PARKE] SNEDEKER
1871–1956

Born in New Harmony, Indiana, a great-granddaughter of the communitarian experimenter Robert Owen (1771–1858), Caroline Dale Parke heard stories of early Harmony from her grandmother Caro Neef Owen. Caroline went to school in Cincinnati. There she studied piano at the College of Music. In 1903 she married Charles H. Snedeker, Dean of the Cathedral of Cincinnati. The couple moved to Hempstead, New York. Until his death in 1927, her husband encouraged her career as an author of children's books—several set in ancient Greece or Rome, several depicting New Harmony. For example, Downright Dencey *(1927) and* The Beckoning Road *(1929) concern a Quaker family of Nantucket, Massachusetts, who decide to move to New Harmony. For adults, she wrote* The Town of the Fearless *(1931), a fictionalized version of her own family history as connected to New Harmony. She also edited* The Diaries of Donald MacDonald *(1942), an Irish resident of the New Harmony experiment.* Seth Way *(1917), from which this excerpt comes, is a fictionalized biography of another community resident, Thomas Say (1787–1834), who was a professor of natural history at the University of Pennsylvania. Frances Wright (1795–1852)—feminist founder of an unsuccessful communitarian experiment at Nashoba, Tennessee (1826–30), which had as one goal to provide a free existence for African-American members—may have been a prototype for the*

189

heroine, Jessonda Macleod. For this book the author used the pseudonym Caroline Dale Owen. As in earlier writing by Phelps, Howland, and Graul, the position of women in marriage receives prominent concern.

References: Alethea K. Helbig, "Caroline Dale Parke Snedeker," in *American Women Writers* (New York: Ungar, 1982), 4:122–124; *Junior Book of Authors,* 2d ed. rev., ed. Stanley J. Kunitz and Howard Haycraft (New York: Wilson, 1951); Carol A. Kolmerten, *Women in Utopia: The Ideology of Gender in the American Owenite Communities,* esp. chap. 4 (Bloomington: Indiana Univ. Press), 1990.

Text: From *Seth Way: A Romance of the New Harmony Community* (Boston: Houghton, Mifflin, 1917), 398–401.

But what is this?" she exclaimed,—"this legal paper addressed to me?"

"Suppose you open it," I suggested.

Like a Christmas child she unfolded it.

"But I don't understand," she said, glancing at the paper and stopping to question my face; "is this a letter you have written me?"

"No," I said; "it is my marriage promise. I don't know how I had the courage to write it—for I wrote it months ago."

She still seemed to question, so I went on:

"One day Robert-Dale and I talked together about you and how you had a right to your own perilous daring. And then I got him to show me those laws which even out here in this new Indiana give a woman no rights to her own property or her own sacred person. As I came home picturing you with your character subject to such laws, I grew very indignant. I tried to meditate what I ought to do to make you free of them if"—I smiled into her face—"if I should ever have the chance. That night, very late, I came up here, lighted my candle, and wrote out this."

"You good, generous man," she called me with tears; for she had seen what the paper contained. "Read it for me, Seth. You see I cannot."

So I read it to her in a low voice, not disturbing Mr. Maclure at his work:

MARRIAGE LINES

This day I enter into a matrimonial engagement with Jessonda Lucrezia Maria Giovanni Battista Macleod, a young woman whose opinions in all important subjects, and whose mode of thinking and feeling, coincide more intimately with my own than do those of any other individual with whom I am acquainted.

We contract a legal marriage, for we desire a tranquil life, in so far as it can be obtained without a sacrifice of principle.

We have selected the simplest ceremony which custom and the laws of the State recognize and which in consequence of the liberality of these laws involves not the necessity of calling in the aid of a member of the clerical profession—

"But we *are* calling a preacher," she interrupted.

"I thought that, perhaps you would wish one, though when I wrote I had in mind the Quaker way."

"Yes," she answered, "that is better, we will have it the Quaker way. Your father was a Quaker, Seth. Your own father and mother must have been married in that way."

"Yes, they were," I said. And taking her hand in mine I pursued my reading:

—a profession, the authority of which we do not recognize, and the influence of which we are led to consider often injurious to society. The Quaker ceremony, too, involves not the repeating of those forms which we deem offensive, inasmuch as they outrage the principles of human Liberty and Equality, by conferring rights and imposing duties unequally on the sexes.

The ceremony which we have chosen consists simply in the signature by each of us of a written contract in which we agree to take each other as husband and wife according to the laws of the State of Indiana, our signatures being attested by those of all our friends who may be present.

Of the *unjust rights* which, in virtue of this ceremony, a[n] iniquitous law tacitly gives me over the person and property of another, I cannot legally, but I *can morally,* divest myself. And I hereby earnestly desire to be considered by others as utterly divested, now and during the rest of my life, of any such rights—the barbarous relics of a feudal and despotic system, soon destined in the onward course of improvement to be wholly swept away, and the existence of which is a tacit insult to the good sense and good feeling of the present comparatively civilized age.

I now set down these sentiments on paper as a simple record of the views and feelings with which I enter into an engagement, important in whatever light we consider it—views and feelings which I believe to be shared by her who is to become my wife.

SETH WAY.

"Jessonda," I said, as I unfolded the paper with unsteady hands, "whatever you may receive from priest or magistrate, these will be your true marriage lines."[1]

"Yes, oh, yes," she whispered. Then suddenly she took the paper from my hand and ran with it to Mr. Maclure.

"Look!" she cried, her eyes yet bright with their tears. "See what your dear, good son wrote for me long ago when I did not deserve it."

Maclure adjusted his glasses and read it smiling—puzzled, of course. He stopped midway.

"But this date," he declared, "is six months back. Seth Way, this is the most audacious piece of presumption I ever heard of!"

"It is not, it is not!" cried Jessonda. "They are the most honest, beautiful words a lover ever penned!"

Then she stopped in confusion.

Maclure ceased smiling, and I saw his face soften as he looked at my darling's flushed cheeks and glad eyes.

"Jessie Macleod," he said, "I am going to take back something that I have said about you. Seth can tell you what it is. You are worthy of your happiness, though you have won the heart of the most honorable young man I know."

"Now you shall be our witness," said Jessonda, and taking the pen from Maclure's desk, she wrote, in her fine bold hand,—

> I gratefully concur in these sentiments.
> *Jessonda Lucrezia Maria Giovanni Battista Macleod.*

And handed it over for him to sign.

11

Mildred Carver, U.S.A.
1919

MARTHA [S.] BENSLEY BRUÈRE
1879–1953

*A*ttending *Vassar College (class of 1893), the University of Chicago, and the Art Institute of Chicago, Martha S. Bensley painted portraits in Chicago from 1895 to 1903. From 1899 to 1901 she taught at the Steven School in Chicago. In 1907 she married Robert W. Bruère, an author and specialist in industrial relations. In a 1910* Outlook *article, "The New Home-Making," she explained she "kept no maid" but would "never hesitate to spend money for any labor-saving device." They collaborated on her first book* Increasing Home Efficiency *(1912), a work recommending domestic training for both sexes. The Bruères believed that both men and women should know how to manage a household and that women should not be solely responsible for domestic duties. From 1919 to 1947, both were associate editors for the* Survey, *a magazine of social issues: as well as articles, she contributed amusing scissors-cut illustrations. In a 1923–24 six-installment* Survey *series called "What Has She Done With It?" she discussed the effect of suffrage. In 1927 Bruère wrote another* Survey *series on prohibition, which appeared as* Does Prohibition Work? *She collaborated with Mary Ritter Beard (1876–1958), a friend of long standing, on an anthology of women's humor called* Laughing Their Way *(1934), to which she contributed several cartoons. Letters of Charlotte Perkins Gilman document frequent weekend visits between the couples beginning at least by 1920. In 1935, Bruère, as a "dear friend" of Gilman, reviewed her just-published autobiography,* The Living of Charlotte Perkins Gilman. *From 1934 to 1936 Bruère's*

194 / Martha S. Bruère

service as an administrative assistant in the U.S. Forest Service led to her writing
Your Forests *(1945). In addition she was an active clubwoman. In 1953 she
died of a heart attack. Robert survived her. A correspondent writing her on July
1, 1937, had observed, "You have a way of wedging in eager young people
and throwing open windows for them in making their choices in life" (Survey
Associates).*

Her utopian bildungsroman Mildred Carver, U.S.A. *(1919) revises Edward Bellamy's industrial army of* Looking Backward *(1888): women and
men enlist for one year in a Universal Service of public works where job assign-
ments depend upon individual preference rather than upon sex or class. Serialized
in* The Ladies' Home Journal *from June 1918 to February 1919, before
appearing as a book,* Mildred Carver *depicts an upper class young woman
developing a social conscience from her year of Service:*

> And as Mildred went on with the unaccustomed occupation of
> trying to think it through, there came to her a sort of picture, very faint
> and blurred as though it hadn't been fully developed on the film of her
> mind, of a whole people working together for the things that they all
> needed to have. And just by virtue of this vision, dim and misty as it
> was, the aversion with which she had entered the Service vanished and
> she was filled with a tremulous delight in the new adventure in which
> she—Mildred Carver, an independent, free swimming human being—
> was embarked; and she knew way down in the bottom of her soul that
> she was just beginning to be conscious of, that she wouldn't give up
> the chance of it,—no, not for anything that the world had yet seen fit
> to offer her, beloved daughter of the rich and great as she was (59).

*Her resolution of her dual need for work and love constitutes the novel's plot. Of
this particular issue activist Crystal Eastman (1881–1928) wrote at about this
time, "How to reconcile those two desires in real life, that is the question."
(Quoted, Sochen, 51).*

*Excerpts stressing the complexities of marital choice and commitment to
meaningful work follow. The immediate paragraphs show the relationship between marriage and the Universal Service obligation as well as the democratizing
effect of participation in this Service. The book's conclusion, reprinted here,
differs from the serial in that neither expresses the sentiment that in order "to
devote her life to the great work of feeding the world," they must "let go of the
kind of life where you can have everything you want at once!" (Feb. 1919, 93)*

References: Martha S. Bensley Bruère, Social Welfare History Ar-
chives, Univ. of Minnesota, Records of Survey Associates, folder 982;

Record Room, Alumnae House, Vassar College; Charlotte Perkins Gilman Papers, Arthur and Elizabeth Schlesinger Library on the History of Women in America, Radcliffe College, folders 117, 270; Carol Farley Kessler, "The Grand Marital Revolution: Two Feminist Utopias (1874, 1919)," in *Feminism, Utopia, and Narrative*, ed. Sarah Webster Goodwin and Libby Jones (Knoxville: Univ. of Tennessee, 1990); Carol A. Kolmerten, "Texts & Contexts: American Women Envision Utopia, 1890–1919," in *Utopian and Science Fiction: Worlds of Difference*, ed. Jane Donawerth and Carol A. Kolmerten (Syracuse: Syracuse Univ. Press, 1994); Ann J. Lane, personal communication, February 16, 1983; *The New York Times*, Aug. 11, 1953, 27. For background, see June Sochen, *Movers and Shakers: American Women Thinkers and Activists, 1900–1970* (New York: Quadrangle, 1973); Harvey Green, *The Light of the Home: An Intimate View of the Lives of Women in Victorian America* (New York: Pantheon, 1983).

Text: Martha S. Bensley Bruère, *Mildred Carver, U.S.A.*, *The Ladies' Home Journal* 35–36 (June 1918–Feb. 1919); reprint, New York: Macmillan, 1919, chapter 3: 15–18; chapter 4: 22–25; chapter 26: 253–63, 273–76; chapter 28: 286–89. The book is the text source.

From Chapter 3

What do you mean by nearly breaking my neck like this?"

"Mildred and I are going to be married!"

"Well, what of it? Everybody always supposed you would be."

"But I can't go into the Service then."

The older man looked his son over speculatively.

"It looks to me as though you've forgotten that you've got to go into the Service whether you want to or not. They don't ask you whether you're going to be married, or vaccinated or graduated or anything else—they ask you if you're eighteen years old and if you are you have to go. In your normal frame of mind you know this as well as I do. Mildred has got to go into the Service too. And you ought to know, if you don't, that the law doesn't recognize any marriage between people who haven't served their year."

Nick drummed impatiently on the steering wheel.

"But I'm going to marry Mildred."

"I haven't the slightest objection to your marrying Mildred. She's a fine girl with a good little brain of her own, and she wouldn't be marrying you for the money. I imagine everybody would be pleased about it. But the Universal Service isn't a thing you can dodge, my son. Every excuse that can possibly be thought of has been tried already and unless you are physically disabled or mentally deficient—and I'm proud to say you're neither—you've the choice of going into the Service or going into jail, and incidentally losing your citizenship, and so has Mildred. Don't be a fool, Nick."

"But, dad—Mildred—I asked her to marry me this evening!"

"That's all right—the most natural thing in the world! But after all, Nick, though I believe in early marriages, eighteen is a bit too young even from my standpoint, and I think Frank and Mary Carver will agree with me. I'm glad Mildred is willing to marry you. It greatly diminishes the chance of your making a fool of yourself over some one you couldn't marry—but I'll not aid or abet any son of mine in being a slacker. If I remember the date, both you and my future daughter-in-law—bless the dear child!—will be drafted in about six weeks."

Nick started his car again and drove home in absolute silence. His mind was oscillating between thoughts of Mildred—so wonderful as he found her under this new emotion—and thoughts of the Service which he had so passionately desired back there at the fire.

Chapter 4

Mildred would have been glad to oversleep the next morning but that was not a thing countenanced by her mother. Mrs. Carver was busily engaged in training her daughter in the virtues of princesses which seem to be much the same whether these fortunate young persons have titles and live in Europe or merely have breeding, birth and fortune and live in America. So in spite of her new consciousness of importance as a girl who had given her promise of marriage and so settled her life in its preordained channel, Mildred came to the family table at the usual time, ate just as hearty a breakfast as usual, put just as much cream on her dish of late peaches and showed just as fundamental an objection to oatmeal as she usually did.

Mildred watched her mother, serene and trim as one who is about to attack competently the country routine of consulting her housekeeper, surveying her gardens and instructing her secretary. Mrs. Carver was physically no great contrast to her eldest daughter, a little darker, a little less tall and slender, just a trifle less differentiated from the dead level of the race, as being one joint further back on the parent stem. Mildred wondered if her mother would be surprised to know she was going to marry Nick. What would her father think? He was a silent man, tall, blonde and, to the eye, English. A shade finer than his wife in the details of culture, but very like her in type. Mildred looked like both her parents without any conflict of features.

Mr. Carver was just finishing his eggs in the imperturbability born of the conscious ability to follow the command of taking no thought of what he should eat or what he should put on when Wicks came in with the morning letters on a tray, a function which he performed in the country, Waddell the butler being left in charge of the New York house. There was a pile of letters for her mother, a few for her father, two for her mother's secretary, Miss Price, a Wellesley girl, one for Junior's tutor, Mr. Harmine. After all these had been laid beside the plates, Wicks came back around the table, stopped for an appreciable moment behind her chair, and then with a hand that was not as steady as the hand of the perfect footman should be, put beside her a large square envelope, redirected from New York, and marked in the upper left-hand corner:

Department of Universal Service
Washington, D. C.

Mildred took the envelope uncomprehendingly and opened it. A stiff printed announcement,—large, formidable,—summoning her, Mildred Carver, by the authority of the President and Congress of the United States, as she was eighteen years old to enter the National Service on the first day of October and to remain in it for twelve months thereafter. She was to indicate on the enclosed blanks the division of the Service she preferred, and be ready for departure when she was notified. It was signed by the Secretary of Universal Service. . . .

. . . There were no gaps of knowledge or experience or circumstance for their talk to bridge; even in years they were too equal to strike fire. They thought alike, they had done the same things, they knew the same people, and now they had concerned themselves in the same love affair! Why, they might have been married twenty years! But of course even if their engagement did need considerable prodding to come up to expectations, their marriage would make up for it. Their only new interest was to go over the lists labeled: "Open to recruits from cities of 500,000 inhabitants and over," and decide which should be their first, second and third choice. It was something which lent substance to the rather attenuated unrealities of their love affair.

"You see, Mildred," said Nick rather dolefully, "the work that is open to us is mostly in the country or at least in the very small towns. There's work in the post offices in all the cross roads; and there's road making and transportation—I suppose that would be fixing tracks and sweeping cars and entrancing things like that—and forestry and agriculture and mines and all this column of queer things like geodetics and hydrostatics, that I don't know about,—and of course there's the army and navy and nursing—but none of it smiles much to me. Arthur Wintermute told me he registered for aviation. I don't see how he could run an aeroplane—he's never done a thing in his life. He never goes anywhere without that valet, Mapes, tagging along. I guess he thinks Mapes can run the plane for him."

"I wonder," said Mildred slowly, "what it would be like to really work—to have to do something whether you wanted to or not."

"Like nothing we know anything of," commented Nick shrewdly, looking speculatively about.

They were sitting on the south veranda—a long plane sweeping past rows of windows and around the bulging circle of the billiard room. Each chair had been set in its proper place, each cushion plumped, each rug straightened that day—but not by them. Before either of them was awake the steps had been washed—by some one else. Some one else was rolling the tennis court over by the road for them to play on; some one else was bringing vegetables up from the garden for them to eat. Nick's car, cleaned and polished by some one else, stood in the drive. Beside Mildred stood a tea table set with a service of silver, and it was not necessary for them even to pour their own tea for Wicks hovered in the offing to do it if required. Certainly work was not one of the things they knew anything about.

"Even if we chose the same thing we wouldn't be together," said Mildred rather wistfully; "they always send the boys and girls on different trains. Why, Alice West never saw any one she knew the whole year!"

"What did Alice choose?"

"She couldn't decide so they put her into one of those botanical experiment stations and she spent most of her time taking care of new sorts of beans and peas, measuring the water she gave them and keeping the temperature just right and feeding them a lot of different stuff to see what would happen. She told me she was a sort of plant nurse. She liked it a lot though, and Tommy West told me she was going to some college to learn about plant chemistry only her mother doesn't want her to."

Nick's finger was traveling down the column speculatively.

"I'd hate to work on a railroad or sort letters in a post office. I suppose in the Forestry you'd nurse the trees the way Alice West did the beans and peas. No—now that I think of it, Wicks told me what you do in that—say, Wicks," he called, "come and tell us about the Forestry Service."

The footman was much embarrassed. It is one thing to talk to a young gentleman, man to man, when you are going to a fire with him in the middle of the night, and quite another to stand in your distinguishing but not honorable uniform and tell a lovely young girl whom you serve, and her quite obviously accepted lover about the greatest year in your life—and that so small a thing compared with what they may expect for themselves! But after a moment Wicks forgot himself in telling what it meant for him to be living with boys who had come from every other part of the country—to have been given the sort of academic training he could have got in no other way—training in the structure of trees, in the cell theory of growth, in the lives of insects and their habits.

"Why, I just got to see how it was the world was goin' on—trees and insecs and the way the rocks happened, too. You can't never feel the same about anything again."

And the thing that the footman didn't say in words, but which was implied in every syllable—and he became very much less of a footman as he did it—was the great difference it made for him not to be working for any one individual but for everybody together.

"Uncle Sam's a great old boss," he said.

When Wicks had become the footman again and carried away their tea, Nick went on studying the blanks discontentedly.

"If they'd let me run an automobile I'd like it well enough—if the roads were decent." Then he stopped suddenly. "I *might* do that!"

"Do what?"

"Road making—it's got something to do with automobiles anyway."

"Oh, Nick!"

"Well, I would like to know about them—why they wear out and everything, and from what Wicks says I guess they'd teach me that."

"But road making, Nick!"

"Well, Mildred, I've got to choose something, you know."

They argued the matter for days and got more fun being together because they had something new to talk about. They could set their teeth into the fact that they *had* to go into the Service whether they wanted to or not. And just at the last moment when the blanks had to be returned to the government, Nick did make road making his first choice and Mildred registered for agriculture.

From Chapter 26

Two days later as John Barton came down the Carvers' stone steps whose costly whiteness he was blind to, a young man stepped up to him.

"Is this Mr. Barton?" he asked; "I'm Nicholas Van Arsdale. If you are going to your hotel, may I walk with you?"

John Barton had never heard of Nicholas Van Arsdale, but he expected surprises in New York and the lad did not look formidable.

Nick had to call on every bit of that Dutch determination which had held him building roads in the desert because he thought it was his duty to his country, in order to get started on his talk with John Barton. Out of the corner of his eye the boy studied the man of whom he had heard so much; whom he hated with a fierce, young jealousy; whom he wanted to persuade. Nick appreciated the tall, thin figure, the strong, clean features, and most particularly the charm which his age and experience might have for Mildred, as he plunged desperately into his talk. As they swung up Fifth Avenue through the alternate patches of bright light and deep shadow, the city was tidying up for the night and putting itself to bed. The last rumbling buses went by with their young Service conductors whistling on the back step; Universal Service postmen were making their last collections from the boxes; burly night policemen had begun their rounds. New York was settling slowly upon its pillows.

"Do you want to marry her yourself?" John Barton asked bluntly when Nick had blurted out the case between them as he saw it—the case which determined Mildred's career by her marriage and hung her happiness on the man she accepted as a husband.

Nick was silent while their heels beat out the time for half a block.

"No," he said slowly, "I don't! If it were a question of marrying Mildred—just that all by itself, it,—well, you know how I feel about that I guess. But I couldn't take her out to wherever I might be making roads; she'd be miserable! And I couldn't come back to New York and just live the way her people do."

"They seem pretty comfortable to me."

"They are—they're deadly comfortable—I couldn't *stand* it."

"Couldn't stand being comfortable!"

"Not that way—not giving up the work I know I ought to do—not stopping helping making roads that the government needs to move the crops and the ore and the lumber on! I can't go back on my duty to my country because I want to marry Mildred! I'm not such a poor sort as that!"

"But you'll be moving about and perhaps you'll get into something better than road making. If you waited a few years don't you think you'd be able to support her comfortably?"

"It isn't that," said Nick, "it isn't being able to support her, it is being able to make her happy! That's why I am talking to you, Mr. Barton. What I want is to make you see the reasons why Mildred ought not to marry me, are just exactly the reasons why she ought not to marry you. If you care anything like as much as I do, you have no right to marry her at all."

John Barton stopped abruptly and turned on Nick. He was obviously angry with the slow white anger of New England that turns men speechless. His hands clenched themselves in his pockets, his teeth set hard. How dared this young whippersnapper try to dictate what he should or should not do!

Nick faced him bravely. Like two primitive warriors they stood opposite each other fixing the destiny of the woman they both desired. To them she was a lovely and desirable appendage—the flower of some man's life—only they differed widely from their prehistoric ancestors in that it mattered desperately to both of them that she should be happy. Was not the life they took for granted for her the natural life of the fortunate woman? Wasn't the choice they conceded to her the choice between possible husbands? Weren't they torn now with the intention of saving her from the contingency of a foolish choice? If she was not literally the prize of some man's bow and spear she was at least the prize of his powers of persuasion. That she might be expected to have plans for herself not bounded by marriage had not occurred to either of them. At last John Barton turned and walked on up the avenue.

"You don't seem to remember that she has promised to be my wife," he said finally.

"Yes, I'm considering that and also the fact that she once promised to be mine."

"What!" cried the man, turning on him.

"Oh it was when we were both kids—before we went into the Service. Nobody would let us be engaged then and when our Service year was over I couldn't stop working for the U.S. just because I didn't have to any more. So I didn't come back."

"I see. You thought you couldn't give up your work and she

wouldn't be happy the way you had to live. Well, it's different in Minneapolis. I can give her a good home there. I guess we'd be able to hire help if she needed to. I can get a brick house through one of those building and loan associations and furnish it up right. I'm saving money every year. They tell me the schools are first class when we get around to need them. The city is pretty and the climate good. I'm not going to say how much I care for her, because that is a question between her and me, but I will make it quite plain to you, young man, that I care enough."

"You don't care enough if you marry her—you wouldn't marry her if you did. You don't care as much as I do, if you don't just let her alone!"

The older man kept himself in hand.

"I look at it this way; the girl is grown up and she has the right to choose what man she'll marry. If she wants you, all right. You are young and good looking, and I suppose you're well educated. Road making isn't the job I would pick out for myself, because you can't settle down and have a home of your own—and a woman likes a home of her own, and ought to have it; but you look smart and I guess you could get into something else easily enough. You knew her pretty well before she went into the Service, and I have known her pretty well since, and I don't see any reason why she wouldn't be happy enough if she married me. It all comes back to what she wants to do."

"No," Nick broke in, "she might want to do something that would make her miserable. I want to save her from the chance of making mistakes."

"And still you don't intend to ask her yourself?"

"No, I don't. Because I think she oughtn't to marry either of us—the kind of a girl she is, and the life she's had!"

"She was a good little worker in the mill," said John Barton.

"I know," said Nick desperately, "it isn't that! Mildred would work or do anything else she had to do. It's the things outside of your work or mine that would make the difference. It's the whole life that matters—she ought to be quite a different kind of a girl."

"Well," said John Barton slowly, "you haven't convinced me and you haven't persuaded me. I care for her and I am going to marry her. You have got the right to cut me out, if you can—but she's engaged to me now and I'll keep her if I can. There is just one thing I think that we ought to agree about. That is, not to tell her that we talked it over. I should think it would make a girl mad to be talked over like this."

"Yes," said Nick, "I think it would, and if you told her that I have been trying to persuade you not to marry her, I know just what she would think of me."

The older man held out his hand and Nick with his lips trembling and his brown eyes filling, put his slowly into it.

"I don't think," said John Barton slowly, "she would make a mistake in taking either of us."

"And I think," said Nick unhappily, "that it would be just like death for her to marry either you or me."

To neither of them did it occur that Mildred Carver might be anything but the natural "second" in the game of some man's career. She had spent her required term in the government service, but what of that? Wasn't she the same feminine complement she had been before?

Nick knew that having had a year of work, it was his patriotic duty to go on with it. John Barton's work was his personal, inseparable religion. But both of them took it for granted that the duties of Mildred's citizenship had all been paid.

Nick flung round and started south again and John Barton stood watching him.

"Poor kid—he's in love with her all right, but I don't see what I can do about it. Besides he probably wouldn't be able to support her for a good while."

John Barton walked on to his hotel, thinking contentedly of the little home in Minneapolis—out in one of those new suburbs where he could buy through a building and loan association. He'd get her an upright piano—perhaps a Victrola,[1] if Mildred would rather have it—and they'd keep a girl. His mind pictured transiently a golden oak dining table with a highly varnished top and machine carved chairs and a sideboard to match. He seemed to get a flash of bright color from the rug and see lace curtains hanging primly at the windows. All these dreams of the future were plain to John Barton, but the realities of the present were heavily obscured. He could see the straight road from the mill where he earned his modest salary to the little red brick cottage where he meant to spend it, but he never even suspected the devious network that led from mines and mills and factories, from railroads and public utilities, from government bonds and steamship securities, from foreign investments and domestic holdings, to the house on Washington Square.[2] The signs of great wealth were not visible to him because they manifested themselves in forms he did not know. Had Mrs. Carver been bedecked with diamonds instead of wearing around her neck a modest string of what looked to him like white beads,—had she rustled in silk—had Mildred's arms clinked bracelets and her clothes dripped lace he might have understood.

But what was a simple red brick house facing an imperfectly groomed park that it should enlighten him. He intended to have a red brick house himself shortly and there were plenty of parks in Minneapolis. Of the cash equivalents of pictures and draperies, rugs and china he knew nothing. He had never bought a chair or a table or a dish in his life. There did seem to be a good deal of "help" about, but that was probably a New York custom—and they did have a motor. Well, didn't he hope to buy a Ford when they got the house paid for? The Carvers were well off —he could see that—but he was not conscious of any overwhelming financial disparity between him and Mildred. And then his mind settled on something very small and soft and warm, being rocked by the fireside, and something very fat and blond learning to walk, and something very active and vigorous, and perhaps a little unruly swinging his books by a strap on his way to school. And John Barton's eyes crinkled up at the corners and his teeth gleamed between his lips and he entered the lobby of his modest hotel.

The next day Nick, entering the Carver house just as luncheon was over, saw John Barton catch at Mildred's hand as they left the dining room.

"Nick," cried Mildred when she saw him. "Oh, Nick!" and then recovering herself, she held out her hand quite formally. Mrs. Carver greeted him with a little anxious catch of the breath and Ruthie and Junior fell upon him in glee.

Mildred turned to introduce the two men but John Barton said gravely:

"I met Mr. Van Arsdale last night."

There was something of the condemnatory preacher in his tone.

Mildred looked from one to the other in surprise.

"We took a walk together—and had a talk."

"Yes," said Nick with a quaver in his voice, "we had a talk and I want to have another now—and Mildred with us."

"I don't think that would be necessary—and I don't see that we have anything to talk over anyway. I thought we settled it last night."

Mildred, the last vestige of color gone from her face, turned into the library.

"Come in here, please," she said in a high little voice.

Her mother hesitated on the threshold and then let the three go in without her. She realized that her work on that situation was done. She had written for Nick and he was here. The immemorial triangle of two men wanting the same woman had been created and they must solve it

between them. As she went up the long curving stairs she was trembling
—so much hung in the balance of the next half hour!

Out by the great fireplace Mildred faced the two men, though her
cheeks were white and her lips trembling.

"Well?" she questioned in a clear, light voice, as sober as a bell and
as insistent.

They were dumb before her—she seemed to them both quite suddenly, to be another person from the young girl whose happiness they
were so concerned in safeguarding—an individual, an independent
human being quite able to determine her own life and with plenty of
characteristics in addition to charm and lovableness. They had both
thought of her as looking at life through eyes only half opened to the
things they saw in it. What could the obligation to serve the state mean
to her now that her Service year was done? But she stood as a new thing,
—a judge set over them.

"Well?" she questioned insistently.

John Barton turned to Nick as if to offer him the first chance to
speak and Nick regarded him resentfully.

"Mildred, I heard that you were going to marry Mr. Barton and I
came back to ask you not to!"

John Barton interrupted him:

"He waited for me when I left you last night and tried to persuade
me not to marry you—I thought we agreed not to mention the matter
to you—but Mr. Van Arsdale seems not to have understood it that
way."

"I know that was what we said, but I've been thinking of it ever
since and I know we were wrong and that I hadn't any right to keep my
agreement about it. It's so awful anyway that just breaking my word
doesn't seem to matter. I care so much more about not having you
miserable than looking like a cad," Nick plunged ahead.

"I did ask him,—Mr. Barton, not to marry you. I told him he's no
right to ask you to live in such a different way and among such different
people. And the things girls like to do just aren't in Minneapolis to be
done. You'd hate it! You wouldn't be happy and I couldn't stand it not
to have you happy—Mildred!"

Nick, growing incoherent, put the weakest side of his case foremost.
As Mildred looked at him her color came back and her eyes began to
flash with a light that was not at all gentle.

"I don't see, Nick, how it can matter to you."

The boy crimsoned.

"I know Mildred—I should think you'd feel just that way—only—
you know, don't you—that's the reason I stayed away? I knew you'd
hate the kind of life out there in the desert or anywhere else where there
weren't any roads and had to be some built. It wouldn't be right to take
you way out there—even if—you—"

"Even if I wanted to go?"

Nick looked at her unhappily.

"What do you think I want to do, Nick?"

"Why, what every other girl does, I suppose,—have a good time
and get married."

"Well, I don't—or at least that's only part of it. I want to work! I'm
a citizen just as much as anybody else and I've got to give my share of
patriotic service just like any man or any ten men. I've got to do something that needs to be done!"

A light began to grow in Nick's eyes and he stepped hastily towards
her; this was a new Mildred he had never dreamed of—but she drew
near to John Barton's side and slipped her hand in his—

"And so I'm going to marry the most splendid and noble man there
could be, Nick. It doesn't matter whether I live in Kamchatka [Siberia]
or the middle of the Sahara Desert—it's all the same. I'm going to help
him to see that the flour's made right and packed right, and shipped on
time; and I couldn't help being happy doing that, could I? I can get along
without the concerts and the dances and the dinners and the shows—we
didn't have any of these things in the Service and I didn't miss them half
as much as I miss the Service now. And as for the *people*—Why, Nick, I
met every kind of people there are while I was out there, and now I just
meet all the same kind. It's so *dull*. I can't *stand* it, being so uninterested
all the time! And so I'm going to be married, Nick, and work and do a
lot for the country just as though I were in the Service all my life. You
needn't bother about my being happy—I couldn't be anything else!"

Nick stood looking at her, his mouth a little open—he tried to
interrupt her several times and failed. He was younger than John Barton
and the implications of what she said struck him more quickly—the real
Mildred of the new day was more visible to him. He felt that he must
define his own changing attitude, but John Barton drew Mildred's hand
through his arm and stood beside her.

"You said, last night, Mr. Van Arsdale, that if I cared for Mildred,
I wouldn't marry her because the life she'd lead would make her unhappy. I guess you can see that that wouldn't be so. Of course she won't
have to work the way she's thinking of. I earn enough to take care of
her."

"Not work? Why, of *course* I'll work. It isn't a question of having to! It's what I want to do!"

It was evident that John Barton didn't take her seriously. He had got just so far in democracy as the idea that it was the patriotic duty of all men to serve their country all the time, but he hadn't extended his idea to include all women,—certainly not to include his prospective wife.

Nick felt he must try to make her see.

"But just marrying and going to live in Minneapolis isn't all there is to it, Mildred;—and just working in Minneapolis doesn't make the people or the place any different. If you don't mind the way it is away from New York—why, you know, it isn't much worse in Arizona or Kansas or anywhere else where they're making *roads*. And they're as important —roads are—as anything! Why, you can't even get the wheat up to the flour mill without them! So, if you'd go to Minneapolis to live—why wouldn't you—"

Nick was stopped because he couldn't understand why Mildred was looking at him from some remote glacial epoch. He had no idea what he had done, but he stopped abruptly in his certainty that he had done something.

"Nick," said Mildred at last, very slowly and with a dangerous iced intensity, "Nick, suppose you don't go on with that. You don't seem to understand that I *love* John Barton."

John Barton had waited his whole life for this splendid young mate. His heart sang and the blood sped to his cheeks as he tramped up the beach beside her. It was love of her little hands and trim feet—of her blue eyes and her gold hair—her swift gleaming smile and the quick upscale laugh that followed it—the soft red that flooded to her low, well set little ears when he kissed her suddenly. In between these moments of joy he tried to make love to her in words.

But here he met with difficulty. Mildred wanted him, when it came to talking, not to tell her how beautiful she was, or how he thought of her night and day, or how happy they were going to be in Minneapolis, but of the wonderful work of feeding the people and how she was going to help him do it. She wanted him to paint her future as an assistant priest at the altar. It was a sort of religious exaltation she craved from him, a thing that neither the church nor any social effort had ever been able to give her—nothing but John Barton himself speaking as the Priest of the Service. She wanted from him the same things that earlier generations had got from the perfume of ascending incense, from the Perpetual

Adoration and the chanting and the rolling organ; what, earlier still had come through the witch dances and the dervishes; and way, way back in the dim, almost prehuman stage, from the shaking of the war gourds, the sight of the war feathers and the swift rush of the tribe on the common foe,—this, and a chance to put her developing creative instinct into work,—a chance to serve her country.

With John Barton it was the mating instinct, strong, clean and direct. With Mildred it was something quite different, more complex, and far more difficult to satisfy. She got much more joy out of the sound of his voice telling how the farmers of the north-west organized the Nonpartisan League, than out of the touch of his lips on hers. She didn't analyze her own sensations, was quite unconscious what they meant; but again and again she turned the love talk into talk of the things he was doing and that she would do with him; and again and again he turned it back. At last he seemed to understand and fell silent. They were climbing up Tode Hill Road[3] when they came to a little leafless wood with a carpet of fallen oak leaves and the blue bay spread out before them. Mildred stopped to catch her breath. Her cheeks were flushed with the crisp air, her eyes were shining, her lips were smiling with happiness. Never had she looked more beautiful.

"Will you be too cold if we sit here on this little wall for a moment?" he asked very gravely.

He took her left hand out of her muff—pulled off the glove finger by finger, and put it gravely to his lips.

Mildred, I love you with all the love there is in me—but I'm afraid that you don't love me."

The girl protested in frightened haste.

"I know you think you love me, dear—it isn't that. It's that you don't know."

It was a very sober hour for both of them when John Barton put the case against himself. Honestly and deliberately he did it, as an upright man who would not take what was not his merely because he could get it. The case was two-fold,—the first and lesser part, that the things she must give up as his wife would make life a hardship for her. The second and great part, that she didn't care for him as she thought she did. John Barton said in everything but words that the role of prophet wasn't the one he cared to fill. He was a lover and he wanted to be loved, not as a leader, but as a man.

There was one moment when Mildred turned to him, holding out her, hands.

"But I can't give it up—I can't! Don't leave me with nothing in the world to *do!* Why, it's like being dead!"

Then he caught her to him again, but only for a moment. He sprang to his feet and tramped resolutely up the road and resolutely back. Out of his pocket he took a little case and out of it a ring, perfectly conventional and set with a little diamond. Catching up her bare left hand, he slipped it on the third finger.

"Mildred, this is a sign that I'm not going to marry the woman I love more than my own soul—will you wear it for me?"

When they got back to the house in Washington Square she was white and drawn as she had never been before.

"I must see your father and mother before I go."

John Barton stood bravely before them, his arm around Mildred.

"I want to tell you that we are not going to be married. I have found that I love your daughter too much to take her, even with her own consent, unless I am sure that she loves me more than she loves the work I am doing. She has told me that she hasn't anything to do—any real work—that she cares about. I wish that you would let her go on working. She made a good record in the mill, and in the field, too. I don't suppose you knew that what she was really going to marry me for, was a job—and that's almost as bad as marrying for a home. I'd just like to say, now that I'm at it, that I appreciate the way you've acted toward me —you've been white.[4] I know how you must have felt about Mildred's marrying me—brought up as she's been and living the way you do. You didn't think I cared about the money, I know, because I guess it must have been pretty plain I didn't know about it. You knew I wasn't a fortune hunter, anyway. It's a bad thing when anything has got to come between a man and a woman except not loving each other—when we get the world fixed right, there won't. Well, good-bye."

From Chapter 28

. . . They stood apart from each other—these two young citizens of the democracy in embarrassed silence, frightened at their own emotion. This was not what they had intended. It had done itself.

Mildred, looking at Nick, thought that he had never seemed so definitely an aristocrat, so far removed from any possible understanding of the new kind of things she had grown to care for—of work, and what it ought to mean to everybody to be a citizen. And yet never had he seemed so attractive, so personally dear and desirable. But she knew she was going to stand by her resolve!

"Mildred," said Nick, and there was a new tone of assurance in his voice, "Mildred, I've come back to ask you to marry me. I've tried to make myself believe that I could get on without you and I find I can't.

I'm not going to wait while you try and decide whether you love me more than anybody else or even if you love me at all. I'm just going to make you marry me because I love you so much."

The girl colored with resentment.

"I know I acted like a fool when I was here before,—when I talked to Mr. Barton. I guess I didn't know how sore I was till afterward, and I know I hadn't an idea how much I loved you. But you've just got to forgive me because I know better now—you've got to."

Mildred looked down at her fluttering fingers—they were a little stained with ink with which she signed the firm letters—Henriette couldn't get it all off. When he paused for breath she began.

"Nick!" her voice was very low, "Nick, I've got to tell you something right away. It's—it's very important. I—I don't think you'd like to marry me now—even if you think you would—I'm quite different from what you think I am—from what I used to be—I'm not the kind of a girl you'd like any more at all."

"Not the kind of a girl? Oh, Mildred, there couldn't be anybody else in the world I'd care for. I know you're trying to let me down easy. And I can't bear to think of it—but—but."

"Nick!"

"But I've got to make you understand."

Mildred's face was changing,—the boy plunged on.

"You see, Mildred, I just can't go on with the kind of thing you're used to—not after my Service year, I can't. Why, when I think of Torexo[5] and seats under every tree and the cut grass; and then of the way it looks in Arizona when you're up on a rock at sunrise and the valley below gets blue and purple and pink—and then you plan out where a road ought to go and *help to put it there*—Oh, Lord! I got to thinking of that house in Fifty-sixth Street father's keeping for me to live in—just the same sort of a house I've always seen—and even when I thought of your being there, I couldn't seem to stand it at all. It's beastly to say this to you only it would be worse for me not to."

Nick caught his breath but he didn't look up and forced himself to go on.

"And so, Mildred, that was why I stayed away. I didn't think I had any right to ask you to go away from everybody you knew and everything you cared for. And I knew I hadn't any right to give up my work. I couldn't be a slacker, Mildred, even if there wasn't any war. I never thought you'd feel the same way about it till you said how you were going to work with John Barton—and even then I thought you didn't understand it yourself. And I was too jealous of him to try and think it out anyway. But I met him in North Dakota and he told me that you weren't going to be married after all, and how you were working on super-steel that I'd never heard of before. And after that I thought I'd *never* get leave to come here, and then that the train would *never* get in!''

Nick stopped literally for lack of breath. Mildred still stood fluttering her ink stained fingers.

"I—I was going to tell you too, Nick, that you'd be disappointed in the way I felt about things—you see I couldn't tell myself last year what I know now! But it's so dull here! I like to ride and dance and everything —only there's nothing else at all! And when I was driving a tractor in Minnesota and sometimes not seeing anything but a rabbit for half a day —why I was part of everything myself! I was part of the government and I was almost as important as the crops themselves. Why, it mattered to everybody in the country how I did my work! But it doesn't matter to anybody how I dance or dress and that's all I had to do here. I couldn't stand it so I'm working every day in father's steel mill. They're making super-steel for reaper blades because I broke so many in Dakota. And I'm finding other things that ought to be made of steel that won't break, and trying to get people to make them of it and then to use the things after they're made. Oh, Nick, it's *wonderful!* And that's what I wanted to tell you about—I've got to do my work as a citizen too. I can't give it up!''

Mildred tried to look at him dispassionately in the light of her weakening resolution. She repeated to herself that in spite of what he said about his work he hadn't cared enough about her to come back all winter—and was surprised to find that this had become a matter of no importance! She called up the intention to devote her life to the great work of feeding the world,—and found that it didn't stand in her way! How was it that the Chinese lilies in the corner smelled so much like the late tuberoses at Torexo? What was this sea of riotous disquieting perfume that invaded the staid drawing room in Washington Square? Mildred trying to lift her chin above it, looked straight into the eyes of Nick Van Arsdale. Was he coming toward her or was it her own footsteps that were bringing them together? She tried to pull herself together and decide what she was to do. Then in answer to her own question she heard her voice say:

"Nick, if you think we could do it together—''

12

A Visitor from Venus
1949

GERTRUDE SHORT
1902–1968

Gertrude Short was born on April 6, 1902, in Cincinnati, Ohio, to professional actors Stella and Lewis Short. He died in 1958. Short herself was a stage, screen, and vaudeville comedienne, with a career spanning over thirty years, from 1913 until 1945. She was once wife of screen director Scott Pembroke. At eleven years old, her first screen role was Little Eva in a silent version of Harriet Beecher Stowe's Uncle Tom's Cabin. At 22, she starred as a "funny, cute little fat girl" in RKO's "The Telephone Girl" series of twelve shorts, 1924 silent comedies including such titles as Bee's Knees, King Leary, Sherlock's Home, When Knighthood Was in Power, and William Tells. In 1927 she played the heroine's Pal Bubbles in Tillie the Toiler (continuing as a comic strip during the 1940s).

During the 1920s and 1930s, she filled many small roles, made the transition from silent to talking films, but rarely received mention in film reviews. She appeared in some forty-six silent movie features and, after sound films emerged in 1928, twenty-eight feature films and five shorts. The 1925 Beggar on Horseback cast includes Short as the sole, wealthy pupil of a struggling composer, who is duped into proposing to her: he is saved by her belief that he was joking. This role gained the clearest praise for her acting that she received: she was "efficient" (New York Times, 6 June 1925, 9) and "ideally cast" (Variety, 10 June 1925, 37). In 1930, she played the sister of the lead actress in The Last Dance. One of the more interesting films in which Short played a minor

212

figure was the 1937 remake of the popular melodramatic novel, Stella Dallas *by Olive Higgins Prouty (one-time patron of Sylvia Plath), starring Barbara Stanwyck, who received an Oscar nomination.*

During World War II, Gertrude Short left the screen to work for Lockheed Corporation, an aircraft manufacturer, where she remained until retiring in 1967. She died after a brief illness in Hollywood on 31 July 1968, survived by a niece and nephew, her death occurring nearly two decades after publishing A Visitor from Venus. *Her years at Lockheed clearly gave her an insider's view regarding women and aviation.*

Not surprising given her long career as an actress, A Visitor from Venus *demonstrates Short's facility with dialogue, which seems close to that of a radio script. It joins a feminist utopian tradition including the all-female utopia of Mary E. Bradley Lane's* Mizora *(1880–81) and Charlotte Perkins Gilman's 1915* Herland, *the sex-separation of Blake's 1885 "A Divided Republic" (selection 4) and Lois Waisbrooker's 1894* A Sex Revolution *(reprint, Philadelphia: New Society, 1985); the feminist political critiques of Gilman's "A Cabinet Meeting" (The* Impress, *5 Jan. 1895, 4–5), in which a woman is "President of the United States" in 1950 and women fill some four out of nine cabinet positions, as well as the 1916* With Her in Ourland, *where a woman from Herland reacts with revulsion to our world at war; and the satire about women of Claire Myers Spotswood's 1935* The Unpredictable Adventure: A Comedy of Women's Independence *(reprint, Syracuse Univ. Press, 1993).* A Visitor from Venus *anticipates by some two decades the 1970s outpouring of feminist utopian science fiction.*

References: John T. Weaver, *Forty Years of Screen Credits, 1929–1969,* vol. 2 (Metuchen, N.J.: Scarecrow, 1970), and *Twenty Years of Silents, 1908–1928* (Metuchen, N.J.: Scarecrow, 1971); David Ragan, *Who's Who in Hollywood, 1900–1976* (New Rochelle, N.Y.: Arlington House, c. 1976) John Stewart, *Filmarama,* vol. 1: *The Formidable Years, 1893–1919,* and vol. 2: *The Flaming Years* (Metuchen, N.J.: Scarecrow, 1975–77); Jeb H. Perry, *Variety Obituaries 1964–1968* (Metuchen, N.J.: Scarecrow, 1980); Evelyn Mack Truitt, *Who Was Who on Screen* (New York: Bowker, 1983); *Magill's Survey of Cinema,* Dialog file 299 (Pasadena, Calif.: Salem Press, 1990).

Text: Gertrude Short, *A Visitor from Venus* (New York: William Frederick, 1949).

Rain . . . .Rain freezing on my wings. Don't know whether I'm still over the States or across Canada. Ought to be a law that mountains have different colors for different countries, like maps; then I'd know when I crossed the border. Now my radio's out, the gas is about gone, and I'm 'way off the beam . . . lost!"

Her strong fingers grasped the stick more determinedly. Determination was reflected in her wide gray eyes. But the young, fair face was taut and tired from the long strain. The high altitude and vista that had given her buoyancy and a sense of domination only a short while ago, now carried a threat. San Francisco and safety seemed far away.

"If I hadn't been so determined to have a fifth freedom, I could now be safe in a cottage . . . or at least a kitchenette. I could be warm, well-fed, even in luxury. No! I, Roberta Renfrow, one-time successful secretary to an exacting executive, engaged to a handsome hombre, had to have another freedom: just to be myself. And now . . . ugh! phew!"

Now the plane had dropped into an air pocket like a tank into a shell hole. She pulled out of the dive. The fuel indicator dived down too . . . and it did not climb. " 'Bout empty." The steady, husky voice she had used to nerve her in many an ordeal in the air, struck a new note of uncertainty now. "Have to hit the silk soon . . . and I don't know where I am! No place to land in this!" "This" meant snow fields, steep slopes, grimly dark wooded valleys. Towering, windswept, glaciered peaks glittered with the coldness of revenge in the wet, gray light.

Hope ebbed, and so did the gas in the tank. Tired, stiffened fingers fumbled with her parachute, made sure it was in order. She felt in her jacket to be sure she had matches, revolver, and flares to attract a rescue plane or other aid. Now she had done all she knew to prepare for the leap. She thought a prayer without words.

"What's that?" It was a sharp cry: she did not recognize her own voice. Her plane swept over a small plateau, while her alert eyes took in details. "Looks like someone sliced a mountaintop off flat across!"

Warily, she circled it. "Why, it's been used to land a plane on. Plane landing gear tracks in that ice, nothing else! Took off again, too . . . no wrecks about!"

Hope reversed its dive, as she flew around a second time, banking, dipping. Suddenly the sun burst the cloud bank with a barrage of gold that gilded the icy field and spilled over the edges.

"There's a house in that valley below!" She was down now with scarcely a jolt. "All of a piece, my plane whole, too. If that uncivil instructor could see me now, would he admit a woman could manage a plane in an emergency landing? Not Flynt. He'd only bellow 'what you doin' 'way off here? Think you're discovering a new country? Women fliers, bah!'

"Well, that's what I get for being patriotic, taking a man's place delivering planes, so the man can deliver a knockout punch with bombers from an assembly line in the North. That's how they described it, caught my girlish fancy and I signed up for the duration and six months. And here I am, griping like a GI!"[1] Laughing, she emerged from her cockpit and stalked across the field.

"I'm tired, hungry, got to have shelter for the night. Got to get to that house I saw before dark. Path should be about here, near this. Why, this is a plane shed! That's what I could not make out above. But what for? It's too small for planes that fly this route. Got to hurry!"

She quickened her steps as her anxious eyes saw the cold evening air was pushing the last sunlight over the horizon of peaks. She rounded a boulder, and there a few feet away, was a cabin built of unhewn flat stones. No other building was near, but lower down the slope a few weathered timbers and denuded foundations seemed to bear a relation to the shed on the ice field above. She glanced at the wide chimney and her heart reversed its climb. "No fire. Maybe there's nobody home and the house will be locked!"

Determinedly, she knocked on the door. No answer. She pounded louder. No answer. Then, frantically, she used both fists. Still no answer.

"Well, I'll stop being polite and go primitive!" Mounting the single stone step she braced her shoulder against the door, drew down the wooden latch, pushed hard, and sprawled on a fur rug inside. Then, relieved that there was no one to see her, she drew herself up by the door.

"Wonder who could live 'way up here !" she exclaimed as she looked about. "All these furnishings!"

She closed the door on the wind and cold. Expert eyes checked the layout. Apparently one room. A huge fireplace in the center wall was opposite the door, flanked by great panelled cabinets reaching from the floor to a low-beamed ceiling, roughly-hewn and smoke-cured. The room doubled its width in length. Four windows paired off and faced each other at the room ends, with striped drapes drawn back. One end held a low couchbed, the other a long table heaped with books around a kerosene lamp. Two chairs of evident use and comfort stood, one before the table, the other near the couch. By the fireplace was a hassock. Queer, lovely prints were on the walls; deep-piled vari-colored rugs on the floor. All this she took in hastily as she crossed to the fireplace.

"No fire here for days!" Even in her warm clothing she felt the room's chill. "Well, they left me wood cut just right, and they knew their kindling, too." She gathered some handfuls of chips, leaves and pine splinters from a box; then, squatting down, she began to lay a fire. After that, she pulled her match folder from her jacket pocket, thinking aloud, "Wasn't a Girl Scout all those years for nothing!" Soon the warmth of burning wood perfumed the air, and she sat down on the hassock.

"Thank you, Father, for bringing me this far. I'm safe now," she breathed gratefully.

Then she wondered. "They may return any minute, and I simply have to stay here until I can find a way out with that plane. At least I didn't wreck it. But that won't win me any glory. I should not have lost my way, and they may not like to find me here."

"They?" She frowned in puzzlement for she suddenly decided on intangible evidence that this place had been lived in by a woman, alone. The deftness of furniture arrangement, the tidy hearth, the whole atmosphere, she felt, emphasized this.

She removed her flying jacket and boots, and then her helmet. She basked in the ruddy, roaring fire's warmth, until her eyes rested on a small pearl box on the mantel, with iridescent rays from its rounded surface shining softly in the firelight. "Wonder what that could be? But her interest was not sufficient to offset the terrible inertia that was upon her now. "So sleepy I'll just rest a minute and then look at that funny box, shaped like an oval bar of soap. Got to find something to eat soon."

Automatically, she started to fasten the door. One always did that in hotels in cities. But she thought better of it. "Owner might return and want to come in." Half asleep, she reached the couch and was conscious of the rich softness of the heavy blankets she pulled about her. Then the last half of sleep, a dense curtain, blacked out even dreams.

"How long have I slept, I wonder?" She glanced at her wristwatch. "Oh dear! I forgot to wind it. After all these months that I have lived in this split-second world with my watch as my governor, to forget to wind it! And no radio to get the time!"

She looked out of the sunny window down the slope where unbroken snow sparkled as far as she could see. "The last light shone in that other window on my feet. Now the sun wakes me, shining in my face. It's another day!" She saw the log in the fireplace was now a mass of embers. The room was warm. Helmet and jacket on a chair, parachute on the floor, boots before the fire, recalled the previous day's hazard and deliverance, and recalled her present precarious situation.

"Wonder where the owner is?" Going to the door she looked out. No signs of life about. No footprints. Even her own had been obliterated by the drifting snow.

"Well, whoever lived here must have eaten sometimes. Wonder what's in those cabinets?" She approached the one at the left of the fireplace. It opened at the turn of a knob revealing shelves, smaller cabinets with doors extending to the ceiling. "Looks like a kitchenette where a woman lives alone and likes it, or pretends to, even as I do."

She opened a smaller cabinet and found an alcohol stove. She mused: "Now, if I can find some coffee," she began opening cans, more cabinets, sniffed all about. There were cases of various kinds of soups, fruits, vegetables, but no familiar breakfast foods, no canned milk and no coffee. "Well, it will be a funny breakfast, but uninvited guests are not choosers." She settled on a can of tomato soup, recalling "Some of these things have high ration points. Must be some hoarder's paradise where she comes just to eat!"

A drawer yielded a can opener and some silver. A cabinet contained some strange, but beautiful china. She recalled a tripod by the fire when she found a smoked pan. Simple addition brought the embers, tripod, pan with soup in it, together. She filled the can with snow outside the door, and added it, stirring thoughtfully, "If only I had something to eat with this soup." A further search yielded some crackers in an unbroken package. She sniffed them appraisingly. "Nice dry mountain air keeps 'em fresh." She felt almost contented. There was somehow an air of contentment in this room.

"Whoever lived up here was in no hurry! Everything shows leisure. Furnishings spaced just so, prints hung exactly. That box on the mantel . . . must examine it after I get my breakfast." She sighed: "Nice not to be rushed, to know no time. I've been so pushed around these last months, what with everybody in a hurry. I've not had a breather since Dick went away. She brought herself up with a mental period.

"Got to stop thinking of him right now. No news for months. Just must not think of him at all. That's the safe thing to do. Women have work in this war. No time to splurge in tears and lonely longings, and I'm glad for that!" All this, while the soup heated, now it bubbled, boiled. Briskly, militarily, she emptied the pan into the bowl. With unmilitary haste she ran to the table with it, lest she drop the hot dish.

Pushing aside some books to make room, she was amazed to find one was in German. She picked up another. "Italian! Oh! And these are French. But most are English. These are Chinese, or maybe Japanese. And I don't know what these are . . . Greek, or maybe Russian. Languages were not on my study course."

Back of the table across the entire end of the room was a bookcase, and a strange assortment filled it. Puzzled, she commented, "I don't see any of the best sellers recently howled, no 'choice-of-the-month' selections." She found poets from many lands, with histories, philosophies and geographies. "Well, there is an assortment on religions and governments, but this old Bible has seen the most use. Looks like grandfather Renfrow's." Her soup cooled as she studied this unusual assortment. Then hunger again demanded attention, and she ate thoughtfully frowning in what Dick termed her "stifling study" manner.

But Roberta was not thinking of Dick just now. Her breakfast finished, she pushed the bowl and cracker box aside. She opened a huge atlas with colored maps of the world. "Why, look at all those airfields in every country marked in red ink and listed on this margin. Can this be a hideout for spies?" A tremor ran through her at the thought.

"And what if they return and find me here?" Again she looked out of the window down the slope. "Anyone would have to come that way, unless from the airfield above." She listened, but there was no sound except the soft slur of winter winds around and down the wide chimney. "I can't take off without some gas. Wonder if some is cached here?" She was excited at the thought, and studied the room for clues. "Too bad they did not give us a course in FBI sleuthing. Maybe if I had read more detective thrillers I would now know my way about up here."

She turned again to the table, thoughtfully. "These books and magazines on aviation. All are fairly new. I can see that. These on stratosphere flying cover things discovered since the war's start. And these late dates on radio transmission and transcription, yes, and here are some on television, all used as textbooks from the way they are marked and pages turned down. The whole setup gets more puzzling, everywhere I look! These beautiful furnishings, now that I can see them better. They are different in color and design from any I ever saw, or even saw pictured! And they are so little used."

"Spies could fly in here" she mused. "This is a wilderness, little known to our foresters, or to the Canadians, if I am in Canada. Japs in the Aleutians. They had planes there. They could have found this place too. Some of their planes or balloons are small enough to use that field and shed up there. Hide it, so it could not be seen from above. Many of them were educated in this country the better to serve Japan and they knew this war was on the way. They could have explored this region before the war, maybe blasted this field, and prepared this hideout. Those airfields, all marked! They could have used those hooks and magazines. But that Bible? That looks strange. Somehow, it doesn't add up!"

Suddenly, she heard voices. Dimly. But no plane had been heard overhead. No sound of footsteps came from outside. The voices were growing louder. They were not outside. They were in this house! For a moment she hesitated. Visions of a secret room with an outside door behind the closed cabinet pushed at her.

"That's it!" No words came to her lips. "They are Japs watching this route and the planes we fly across to Russia and China. They don't want them to get to China. We've lost planes in this wilderness." She listened intently. "They don't seem to have found I'm here. Must be a way around the hill. Fire's low. No smoke to be seen. Haven't found my plane. Better beat them to the draw, keep them locked in that cabinet. Make them think many of us are on the way here to take them. Got to bluff!"

She pulled the revolver from its holster, unable to bear the suspense any longer with those voices murmuring. She ran to the cabinet, noiselessly opened it. There was a huge closet large enough for a bed, but no bed was there, nor was there any outside door. Quantities of women's clothing lined the walls, colorful, beautiful, foreign. But no living thing was in this place.

"But the voices?" Then suddenly a thought flashed: "The pearl box on the mantel . . . a radio!" She whirled back to the mantel. A panel across the front of the box was lighted. "It *is* a radio . . . and it's television, too!" Awed, she slipped soundlessly down on the hassock facing it. "A picture-play in color," she breathed.

Two figures moved against a weirdly beautiful landscape, across a shining airfield, as though made of glass. Behind them was the bare outline of a plane. "It can't be so, because I see houses and trees right through it." Then, awed, she whispered, "It's a transparent plane!"

Now the radio had attained more volume. It had been slow coming into sound focus, as though from far away. The figures were very near now and moved ever closer towards her. "Such lovely, soft voices. I can't tell whether they are women or men. Can't catch any words yet."

The figures on the screen entered a building. Then they appeared in a living room. Roberta saw the furnishings were strange, yet somehow familiar. "Why those furnishings are just like these, here in this room!" The figures sat down on a couch facing her. The one who seemed the younger carried a small wand-like instrument. Now she dropped it into a socket.

"She has on flying clothes, too," Roberta observed. "But the other one . . . I can't make out what she's wearing, but she is so beautifully dressed." She studied them carefully. "I would say they are both women, but I am not sure. They look alike. I've seen old people, like grandfather Renfrow and grandmother. They looked alike because they had lived and thought together a lifetime," Roberta mused. "They seem to have reached that age when sex is not a division between them, and yet they are so young!"

Roberta's thoughts were suddenly interrupted by the words over the radio, spoken by the apparently younger of the two on the screen.

"Oh, it is so good to be back where there is quiet living! What they term peace on Earth. I have seen such terrible things on that planet!" Roberta saw the pilot shudder.

"You were away a long time, Zua." There was a hint of gentle reproach in the voice of the other person, that enhanced its affectionate note.

"Yes, I was away longer than I intended, Veh," the first speaker continued. *"There was so much to see, so many things to learn, because they still have so many languages. I use Earth's terms, you see, and use one of the most common of their languages that we both are familiar with from their radios. English, they call it. I found at this time it is almost impossible to get from one of their divisions to another. And their divisions! They are without number. Another difficulty is that they are suspicious of strangers. They ask so many unnecessary questions: 'Who are you? What's your name? Are your papers in order? Where are you from? Why do you wish to go to such a place?' For that reason, I found it was easier to disappear at times, and live in a tiny house in the mountains of a little-known country."*

"You found a safe place, then, to land and hide your precious plane. Oh, that was my dread for you! How to get onto Earth, and how to leave safely! Tell me!"

"I found, Veh, they are trying to build ships to take them into the stratosphere. They have had some success, but they have not learned to build invisible ships like mine, that need no large load of fuel. Even their rocket ships have to have that. The atomic forces of the universe are still an almost unknown realm to them, so they can't make use of those forces as we do here, and as power for interplanetary ships. They have sky-ships, and I found so many of these above earth's surface, that one more did not matter. They could not shoot at what they

could not see above them, except by technical finders, and I knew how to escape them!"

"Shoot at your plane, Zua?" the other gasped. *"What do you mean, why would they want to?"*

"Because there is a war searing that planet, and for that reason it's going to be hard to explain a lot of things to you. Wars are without intelligence, so no reason may be found for many things that happen when they are carried on. You know we have studied Earth's voices for years. Deciphered the meanings of some languages, especially the one most heard, that we are using now. For this reason, I did not find it difficult to learn to speak. I made use of my power as a Venusite to appear among them as one of themselves. Being able to make myself invisible, I could get the drift of their words and ways before appearing. Because of our higher development, I could grasp what I needed to know to get about."

"I can't understand why they would be hostile to you! You went on a mission of good will and planetary neighborliness!"

"War warps everything. I learned to adjust myself. I would appear as a refugee from another country in the one I visited. That explained differences in speech, and a lack of knowledge of the country's customs. They have a saying, " 'You do get around a bit, don't you?' " She laughed joyously. "Well, I did! Someday ask me to tell you about a surly sergeant when I impersonated a WAC!"[2]

"What's a WAC?"

"Women acting competently," Zua mimicked a radio commentator. *"That's not their official title, but it explains their role. Once, to get where I wanted to go, I dressed as they did, ate what they ate, sometimes with difficulty. I even worked among them! There are cities named Venice on Earth. I could say I was from Venus and they never suspected I was from another planet. I sold some of my jewelry. I needed to do these things to get money. That's the means they use for getting anything done or just getting anywhere, on Earth."*

"You did not bring back what you took with you. I suppose you found use for it on Earth?"

"Yes, the rugs, blankets and other personal things I used to furnish the little stone house I lived in. It was bare and vacant when I found it. An old mountaineer made some furniture for me from old lumber," Zua continued. *"I brought back some unusual things. I will show them to you later."*

"But you are back, and safe! That's what matters."

"It was a difficult ordeal. Sometimes I just had to fade from the clutches of the Gestapo in that division where people have become baser than you can imagine. Strange too, only a few years ago they had appeared to be highly cultured. It was only in material, scientific development. Now Earth has learned

that their standard of moral values was debased in inverse proportion to their material achievements. Hope the lesson will not be lost on them. Their wickedness is even beyond the rest of Earth's peoples' comprehension. I will speak but little of that lost division."

"You puzzle me, Zua," Veh was startled. "You make Earth sound so difficult. It's confusing."

"I could not make you understand by any means I know, the degradation of some of Earth's elements."

"That would be Germany and Japan," Roberta nodded solemnly from the hassock.

"Everywhere I found strange things, strange beings, and stranger divisions among them. We wondered at the radio voices reaching Venus, remember? Most of them were of heavy quality. Only rarely did we hear the finer tones. Here, where voices are balanced, it is hard to understand the difference. But not on Earth! They have the queerest concepts. Earth's inhabitants are called peoples. When warring as now, they call each other the lowest animal names. I had to study their histories and religions to find what this war was all about."

"Well, could you find any explanation? I have listened over the air while you were away, and it seemed to be a struggle between democracies, whatever they are, and some sort of totalitarian government."

"What they term democracy is a governmental idea we would understand, although it is obsolete here. It is vested in the people who control with laws, enforced by its chosen officers. It has its basis in the conception that man wants to do right and live with others so inclined. But it is still necessary to have guardians enforce it, because it is not yet generally acknowledged that man is rightfully governed from within his consciousness. As understood by us, it is man including the state."

"And what is opposed to this idea?" Veh asked, puzzled.

"The lowest idea is enslavement, physical, mental and religious, of the many by the few, for the exploitation of the many by a few for selfish purposes. The people who came under this idea were mesmerized to accept a false theory of government; that the state is supreme and includes the individual."

"I see, Zua. They have not grown to where they are governed individually from within, as we are on Venus. Did you see any hope of their eventual freedom?"

"Yes. I believe there are millions who do what is right because it is right. To them the laws on their books are just so much copy-paper. Their government is from within in obedience to what they term their God. They are spoken of as 'law abiding.' In reality, their consciousness is the law which has been made into statutes and rules of government."

"I would judge from what you report that Earthites are on the right path. But why are they so long in abolishing wars?"

"*That is largely due to another division that seems never to have been thought of by Earthites. That lordly, domineering voice on the radio is man. In all languages it means the same, and that is 'the boss.' On earth it is 'he' the boss, and 'she' the bossed!*"

"Boss? Zua, what is a boss?"

"*Another name is 'man-ag-her.' And believe me he does!*" Zua laughed, ruefully. "*This boss is the creature of primary importance. He is what they call 'man.' The secondary creature is 'woe-man.'*"

"What does she mean by secondary creature?" Roberta's expression became more puzzled.

"*They have a word on Earth for sorrow. They prefix that word to man, and that gives them woman!*"

"What a silly thing to say!" Roberta stiffened with scorn and indignation.

"Well," Veh sighed "*we had a desire to help that little Planet. She seemed to be suffering so much lately, judging from the tumult she makes on the airwaves. Now since you have visited her, you think we can't do it?*"

"*I don't see how we can help them much just now, Veh,*" Zua said unhappily.

"*It's because they are backward, living in the period corresponding to our most calamitous past, isn't it?*"

"Yes," Zua answered, "*but there is a dawn of progress. Their best form of government is a reaching out for individual dignity and freedom. True, they have not advanced to where they have entire government from within, as when each is governed as here, by the Only One, so they still have their struggles.*[3] *But they are learning.*"

"Well, I never . . ." Roberta was more puzzled. "Am I an Alice in Wonderland without a guiding rabbit? Where is this Utopia, anyway?"

"*It was all so confusing, Veh,*" Zua continued. "*I tried to get some idea of their present mental stages, to compare life there with life on Venus. I found them so immature.*"

"Life on Venus? Whatever can she mean? And Earth immature? Well, that's just plain silly." Roberta was tempted to switch off the radio in disgust. But the next words caught her attention anew.

"*You see, Veh, they prophesy evil from other divisions on Earth, and expect it. That's why they have spies.*"

"What are spies?"

"*They are people who pry into the secrets of foreign governments. They work on the sly and try to keep informed on all new developments that a possible enemy might make in offensive means. They rush to beat each other to some new knowledge of destructive power. It's amazing. To that end they use spies.*"

"Well," Roberta observed thoughtfully, "I never sized it up so, but the way she puts it: a spy is to pry and to try on the sly to get the best of another country . . . huh!"

Unconscious of Roberta listening and commenting, Zua continued, *"So I did not dare risk finding out what they would think of someone from another planet. Once, while I was there, they had a radio play, an invasion from Mars. This drama was widely broadcast.*[4] *They were so in the habit of depicting evil that the play caused a tumult. Many tried to learn where the Martians landed. They wanted to fight them to defend Earth! All because they think of Martians as warlike. Yet they have never seen an inhabitant from that planet! In the dim past they happened to call that planet 'Mars,' which means 'wargod,' and then they judged the inhabitants must be that way. It could just as well have been our planet they called Mars, and then we would have been thought of as warlike. Such funny logic."* Zua shook her head sadly.

"Then, there was no invasion?" Veh asked.

"Oh, no!" Zua seemed to be living the incident over, for at the recollection she laughed gaily, and so infectiously that Veh joined her.

"At least the trip to Earth did not destroy your happy balance and sense of humor." Veh was satisfied.

Roberta puckered her brow in an effort to remember.

"Why, there was such a radio play, before the war, before Dick and brother Bob went into service. I remember. They called a telephone operator to get directions. They wanted to fight for Earth. How sheepish they were when they learned of the hoax!"

"They really think their planet is the most important in the entire universe," Zua added. *"So they think there could be beings who want to take Earth away from them."*

"What would inhabitants of other planets do with Earth, if they had it?" Veh's question was in wonder. *"Don't they know that planets meet the legitimate needs of their inhabitants, and correspond to their development . . . that as they unfold in intelligence, their planets unfold correspondingly? Or, rather, they awaken to find all they need is on their own globe? The Only One has willed it so. Our planet, now, is surpassingly lovely, but we outlawed destructive forces many centuries ago."*

"Yes, Veh. One has only to visit such desolation as Earth now shows to realize the beauty of Venus. Earthites do not know that other planets are more wonderful than theirs because of advancement through the ages since war was abandoned as a planetary policy and all have turned to arts of peace, of helpfulness, and the beauty of living in harmony. Since that time, plenty and leisure is had for all without strife."

"It seems now it could never have been otherwise on Venus. But it was so dark here, once, according to our history," Veh conceded.

"*I had to be satisfied with learning of Earth's present development to see how far we have progressed beyond their era. Upheavals they are now experiencing, with terrible new forces unleashed, will not let them continue to drift and dream aimlessly as so many of their nations have done through thousands of years, while evil men schemed their enslavement and destruction. They will have plenty of work to do when this conflict is over. More important than the winning of wars is the education for peace. Our concept of government from within, only a change in their cultures can give them. They're so immature.*"

"Well, maybe we are just coming of age," Roberta commented hopefully.

"*I remember,*" Veh reminisced, "*we were so excited when we learned their use of the air-waves for sound and vision. We learned we had much in common, and wanted to communicate with Earth. But evidently, they had no receiving apparatus to catch our beamings. We never heard them acknowledge these. We long have received messages from them, but these were not beamed to us but to other Earthites.*"

"Yes," Zua picked up the thread of remembrance. "*That was before the present conflict. They were talking of brotherhood among nations . . . always brotherhood, never sisterhood. . . . We have had these relationships so long we are now one nation, so we could understand their aspirations. We wanted to help them make this desire a reality.*"

"*We found,*" Veh continued, "*so many things we could not understand from words. We would need to see them closely. Their television is still imperfect. It could not help us much. Then too, they have so many uses for the same words, that their radio speech was sometimes misunderstood. But we were thrilled to find intelligence was universal, not just planetary and confined to Venus. Remember?*"

Zua nodded affirmatively. "*That's true. Then I began to plan the building of my space ship, such a plane as we had never attempted before, and what they still dream of on Earth . . . an inter-planetary plane.*"

"Yes," Veh picked up, "*and how concerned I was when you began trial flights to nearby planets until I was convinced it was safe. Then you said you were ready to go to Earth!*"

"*You really were disturbed then. I was afraid you would not let me go.*"

"*Yes, I was apprehensive. And after you left, and no word came from you, I wondered if you reached Earth, how you landed, how they received you. Oh, I went over it again and again! But I knew you were trying to serve Earth, and therein your safety lay. The Only One willed it so. But would you be able to leave Earth and return to me? That was another question. While you were away, everything seemed to get worse there. And I could hear nothing from you, and no radio mention from Earthites of your having reached there!*"

"One time I doubted," Zua confided. *"Places I wanted to see were under attack from planes of opposing forces. I landed on what I thought was a deserted field. But I was heard flying in. Fortunately, materials in my plane eluded detectors, so they could not hit me with their bombs. For a moment I was concerned. If they destroyed my plane, having no materials, I could not build another. It would have been terrible to have had to stay on Earth always!"*

"Well, nobody asked you to!" Roberta snapped. "As though any other planet could equal our beautiful Earth! But how ridiculous to get all 'het up' over a silly radio play."

"So you think we can't help Earth." Veh was plainly disappointed.

"Not now." Zua shook her head in sad negation. *"It would arouse their suspicions to try. When they have returned to sobriety, and this war drunkenness is over, it might be possible. They are in no mood now to have an outsider interfere. Earth's family quarrel may leave nothing but ruin, but it cannot be stopped by us. Such violence is not recorded on Venus. Their very destructiveness will sicken and sober them. Then they will strive to find the means for settling disputes, and learn, as we did long ago, that there is no need for strife. Their planet has sufficient for all good for them. They have advanced in material knowledge, but are lagging in human relations. They have failed to keep these two developments in step. Had they done so, their findings for the promotion of peace would be in the ascendancy rather than their efforts to wipe each other out. They are paying a high price for their failure to keep pace morally and spiritually with their material knowledge and science."*

"Well, I'll agree with that," Roberta admitted.

"When they stop fighting, we may make contacts with them that they will understand," Zua continued. *"Perhaps then we can aid them, if we can convince them we want no part of Earth."*

"Of course not. Such nonsense!" Veh was impatient. *"Why should we want any of Earth?"*

"We don't, of course, but it is so hard to explain. There's so much we don't understand. No wonder, when they don't understand themselves! As I said, they are like children, so immature!"

"I don't understand what you mean by immature," Roberta bristled. "Why that's just plain nonsense! People have been on Earth and developing, too, for centuries!"

"Let's consider their mental processes," Zua went on, unaware of Roberta's outburst. *"These are of the first consideration with us. Many other things matter with them: color [race], cultures. Think of me still among them. I was there so long by their standards, not by ours. One lives so much faster there. So, consider me as still among them as I tell you these things."*

"I hope you can explain so I can understand, Zua. So far, it's just confusion."

"Well, that's what Earth is now, a mass of confusion. Races they call themselves. It is a kind of people, yet it is a game, a running against, a contest. And they seem to be pushing each other about as races, and have done so for centuries."

"Races of peoples, races of games," Roberta puckered her brow. "I'll admit it sounds confusing."

"Somehow, we never think about color on Venus, just about character. Earth has black, brown, red, yellow, peoples and mixtures. They vary greatly in their treatment of each other. The ones called 'white' are supposed to be most intelligent. But much of their activity bears no relation to intelligence as we know it. It's just immature destructiveness."

"Well, it does sometimes resemble little boys experimenting with fireworks, determined to make them as noisy as possible," Roberta agreed.

"Other races are stirring," Zua continued. *"They show a quickening of intelligence. What the future for all of Earth holds, it is too difficult to determine. For one thing, the white race seems to feel it is superior generally."*

"The white race has always been superior!" Roberta stoutly challenged.

"But," Zua added, *"they are unable to fathom mysteries of centuries' old monuments built by other races while the white race was still an infant in culture. There is the one test we would make: the whites are more advanced in their theories of government, in their acknowledgment of spiritual and moral values, in their humanness for unfortunates, and in their subscribing to higher standards of living, and in some degree of equality between sexes, recognized as necessary, but not often practiced. Sounds like a riddle, doesn't it?"*

"Guess I'll have to admit we are in a mess, all right," Roberta sighed ruefully.

"To begin with," Zua picked up the narrative, *"they have the two sexes. We would call them Fatherforms and Motherforms for it is only in form, and not in mind, that we recognize a difference. They call Fatherforms 'Adam' and Motherforms 'Eve.' That seems the original names given them in their greatest book, the Bible, but more about that later. This Adam is considered superior. He is the man, the boss, the man-ag-her, as I told you before. He makes and administers the rules for living on Earth!"*

"Huh, that's what you think!" Roberta chuckled. "If you had caught on you'd know that Eve makes the rules. She only lets Adam think he does!"

"*Governments are set up and administered by Adam,*" Zua continued, "*and Eve is under his domination. She is rarely created as an intelligent equal of Adam in any way!*"

"That's not true!" Roberta's voice rang out so loudly in protest that she startled herself.

"*Eve is not considered of much value after she has lost her physical youth,*" Zua went on. "*She is thought not to have enough intelligence to carry on work requiring mental astuteness. Each has its exceptions, but I see nothing to cancel the rule in that. When Eve reaches the age of forty, by their measurement, she is on the way out, as they say on Earth.*"

"*How old is forty?*" Veh's placid brow was puckered in puzzlement.

"*Well, let's see.*" Zua cast about for a comparison. "*I was about that when I began building my space ship to go to Earth.*"

"*But Zua, you are not old.*" Veh was astonished.

"*By Adam's standards,*" Zua smiled, "*I have long since ceased to be of any value. All I had to learn about using atomic action for propulsion, about insulation through changing temperatures and densities, all about atmospheric pressure, these things took time and experimentation, too much time for an Earthite to live out, even an Adam!*"

"*But it did not seem long, Zua,*" Veh protested.

"*It was so long that even if I had accomplished all that on Earth, I would have been too old to come to Venus.*"

"*Why, you don't seem old, even now! I wonder if you ever will,*" Veh insisted.

"*Veh, Earthites live lives of such scattered energies that conflict with each other, and also within each individual, that they appear much older in the same period than we who live on Venus. Life's currents are so much smoother here.*"

"*What's the reason for Eve's low standing on Earth?*" Veh returned to this as an item of interest.

"*It's her own fault, I'd say. Long ago she found that glamour and flattery won favors with Adam, requiring little exercise of effort, and less intelligence.*"

"*What's glamour? I have never heard some of the words you use on the radio, Zua.*"

"*You don't hear so much about it, except in their fancy clothing and perfume ads. But you see it. Eve is treated as a bit of prettiness, served up fancily, frocked and frilled in frippery, spiced with perfume. She's considered a delectable concoction, often quite dangerous to take on!*" Zua chuckled.

"*Dangerous? For whom? You're so unclear, Zua.*" Veh frowned.

"Dangerous for Adam, but he likes her that way." Zua indulged a bit of malicious laughter.

"I don't understand that at all." Veh still frowned.

"You wouldn't. Nor 'sex appeal,' nor 'it' nor any other terms for glamour."

"Wish I had some of those clothes and perfume now." Roberta looked down at her flying suit with distaste. "Dick wanted me to stay home and wear them. We quarreled, too, our last evening together. I can't forget his words, 'I want you like you were before this idea of flying entered your head. I want to come home to find you in flowered dresses, flowers in your hair, flowery perfume that caresses me when I come near. That's the way you were when we met, remember? I don't like you in that unholy outfit. And I want you to marry me before I go over.'

" 'Dick, I just can't. There was mother, left with Robert and me, twin babies. My father never got back from France.'

" 'Well, I'm coming back,' he said. He really believed it when he went away. 'I want to come home to a wife, and I want to hear my son's voice, even if he cries!' I wouldn't marry him then. Now he may never get back to me." Tears hung on her long lashes.

But the radio voice cut in again:

"In a recent century, Eve has been given more freedom. She'll have a real purpose in the future, find more important things to interest her than merely being glamorous. Since she has had a part in winning the war, she stretched her mental muscles, as well as her physical ones. Her moral and spiritual fibres have stood up to the test of this struggle. Never again will she fit into the groove."

"What do you mean, 'groove?' " Veh asked.

"It's a narrow cut-out channel. Eve's groove has been as home-maker, as child-bearer whose sons grow up to fight in their generation. Eve is supposed to accept this status without question, as her proper sphere of influence."

"A groove! Yes, that describes it," Roberta thoughtfully considered, "that's what I rebelled against with Dick, only I didn't name it. I wanted to think things through for myself. When he was around, he was so masculine and domineering that I was not sure of things being right that he did not agree with. I wanted to serve my country, too. That's why I am flying these planes now. I've had time to think on these long, lonely trips. Now this radio star is putting it into a pattern."

"The trouble has always been," Zua continued, *"that Eve has pretended she knew very little, had little intelligence compared with Adam. She learned Adam liked her to be decorative and amusing, and she did not want to offend him by a display of wisdom; Eves who have stood out in some ways in history were*

usually ridiculed and shunned by Adam. So, even intelligent and well-trained Eves of strong character play dumb to catch an Adam, afraid they won't win a husband if Adams learn how clever they are!"

"What do you mean, 'play dumb?' " Veh prodded impatiently.

"Oh, that's another of Earth's queer words. It means 'unwilling to speak.' " Zua chuckled.

"Why, women are accused of doing all the talking!" Roberta was quick to protest. "And you're wrong about us wanting to rule, that is, openly. I don't know that we even want equality acknowledged. We might lose more than we would gain. We do rather well with our glamour, I'd say!"

"Do you think Eve will ever be free from these handicaps?" Veh sounded a doubt.

"It must be so. There is no other way out of their problems. Once they are stirred to see the need for their intelligent contribution to Earth's advancement, they'll find the way to make the effort count. Eve is not so dumb!"

"But you say they want to gain their ends without effort. From what you report they will not do much to help themselves, let alone help Earth solve her problems!"

"They will be forced to, Veh. There is no difference in intelligence. One Earth country has discovered that. Eve is an equal with Adam in war and at home. They are not used as pin-up girls in some places."

"What's a pin-up?"

"A beautiful girl, composed of beautiful limbs, topped by pretty face. There are no old Eves used as pin-ups, you may be sure. Their idea of Eve is still a demand for physical attraction. Pin-ups can go to camp while the originals stay home."

"Why cannot Eve put a stop to war, if she makes the effort?" Veh pressed.

"She has never used much organized influence in that direction. War is Adam's institution. He starts and stops them. Eve is expected only to bring forth Adam's sons. She may pour a lifetime of devotion into training these children for peaceful pursuits, only to be pushed aside, and made to see all her work undone, in a war."

"Why has she not rebelled against such monstrous practices that demand such a sacrifice?" Veh was vehement and indignant.

"It's a peculiar glorying, Veh, in this war sacrifice. It's as old as time with Earthites. Centuries ago they offered their children to another fiery god, Moloch. Eve's sacrifices were supposed to be so sacred that she dared not weep for her loss, lest tears offend. Today, Eves offer them to another fiery god, Mars, and still sacrifices are too honorable for tears. They must be proud of sons who die on a field of glory!"

"Then, only if Eve refuses to bear Adam's sons can she stop wars," Veh was thoughtful. *"Doesn't Adam consider his son, nor his Eve when he plans a conflict? What do the sons think of it?"*

"Adams who have survived other conflicts plot and plan the wars from a safe distance. Young Adams have no voice in the matter. All they have to do is take orders and fight to try to rectify blunders made in settlement of previous conflicts. It is always those who have no part in causing the wars who must fight them. They must pay for the older Adams' bungling with their lives. So the play goes on, one generation after another."

"Well, what is the solution, Zua?" Veh was not hopeful.

"Yes, you tell us what we can do to stop war, if you know so much." Roberta was grimly challenging.

"Do you think Eve can be freed from these bonds, Zua, mostly of her own building? Do you think she can win freedom for herself and bring peace on Earth?"

"She'll have to do it. But her concept of Eve must be exalted. She must see to it that no Eve is held in slavery as a sex-creature. They would not think of treating Adam so."

"Can Eve be freed from such handicaps?"

"If Eve will work at this as hard as she does in other directions. Governments will improve when Eve shares in policies, helping to shape them to protect her sons. Some Eves have made wise rulers through their inherited powers. None has been elected to fill a chief executive office."

"Will Adam grant Eve such opportunity to assume responsibility?"

"No, Adam will not. Eve will just awaken to her right and take these things in charge. Once Earthites believed in the divine right of kings to rule. They still believe in the divine right of Adam. They have yet to acknowledge the divine right of Eve. Their philosophy 'It's a man's world' is obsolete."

"Wonder who ever thought up such a play, anyway!" Roberta found it difficult to turn off the radio, in spite of her disturbed thought.

"Eve is an individual. Adam is a gang animal. When growing up, he plays in gangs. He is found in clubs and other organizations, all of the gang order, and never seems to get over it. His love for buddies in his gang in war is nearly sublime. War was once considered a gallant sport for such a gang. How they loved the glory of fighting and winning victories . . . those that survived! Only one who was outside, and seeing these things with objective view, could see in war Adam's love of prowess and display."

"But what does war get them, Zua, that they could not better secure otherwise? And what do they do when a war is over?"

"When war is over, and death and destruction are found the real winners, Adams gang up again, and write treaties. Few ever read them, much less understand them. In a few years they are forgotten. It is easier to fight another war than to interpret aright their pledges. Indeed, Adam has wound these about him like a cocoon. Someday Eve will just cut through the red tape and get a job done. Peace insurance should be her contribution."

"What's tape?" Veh questioned. "What does it mean to be wound up in it?"

"I would say it meant to be tangled up in the conflicting and often meaningless phraseology of treaties."

"But why red?"

"I don't know . . . red has many meanings. It's a term of reproach for some peoples with ideas of government differing radically from democracy. Earthites say they 'see red' when they mean they are angry. When not financially solvent, they say they are 'in the red.' Once an Earthite told me of an embarrassing incident, and asked 'is my face red?' I assured her it was not. I never knew what I was supposed to answer. Anyway, it was something different!"

"If their ideas of government, religion and other matters are as mixed up as their use of words, how can they ever get any clear idea of world betterment? Why, we would not dare give them the scientific knowledge we have! They might explode Earth out of the universe!" Veh was aghast at the prospect.

"Between wars, they take time out to dream, plan and talk international friendship, world peace organization. They even spend a trifle toward such ends. But when there is a war on, then they can spend, and the sky is the limit. Strange, isn't it, that they are so niggardly in spending, working and sacrificing for peaceful ends, to live in friendship, but set no limit on spending to destroy each other!"

"Why, with their intelligence, Zua, is their idea of world order so monstrous and antiquated?" Veh's tone was more of anger than sorrow.

"Alas, there is no glint, no glory, no brave color, no bands playing, in the quiet heart-searching arts around a conference table. They must have a brave show. Still so immature!"

"It looks worse, the more you say, Zua. What's your idea of help? What's to be done about it?"

"Earth needs mothering, Veh," Zua's voice was compassionate. "Adam is like a little boy, ever wanting to play with larger, noisier engines and explosives, just to see what happens. He has gone about discovering and building such destructive things that they are getting beyond the control of their originators. They are really frightened now. Eve must come to their rescue to stop all this on Earth. The time is past when she will be expected only to bind up wounds made by the fire-crackers. She must stop their making the crackers!"

"Well, I think it is about time Eve busied herself." Veh was positive.

"We know some things they don't, Veh, about explosives. You recall how I experimented with lots of force ideas before I found that exploded atoms could be used as a drive for planes. They are just beginning to use this universal force on Earth, and so far, only for the destruction of lives and property in war. You recall how we have seen several planets disappear from their orbits in times past, and heard of others? Just one great explosion, then they were gone."

"Yes, Zua." Veh was excited with the new idea. *"There was that one we studied so long, much like Earth. We were never able to get a response from it, but much of its sounds seemed to be like ours, and like those we hear on Earth. That was long ago, before we had developed radiation as speech, wasn't it? Then it just blew out of existence."*

"Exactly. And since we can use radio transmission, and Earth can too, we find we could communicate some of our knowledge of forces. But we dare not do so until Earth has become more peaceful in her activities. I believe that in that lost planet where there seemed to be sounds of strife, as on Earth now, they just developed forces and instead of using them for peaceful pursuits, used them to destroy the whole planet, perhaps in the endeavor to destroy something else, maybe group against group."

"Veh," Zua's earnest voice roused Roberta to renewed alertness, for she had been apprehensive about the last weapon used in Japan, *"how can we get a message to Earth that they must stop their self-destroying activities, and turn to arts of unselfishness and sisterly affection, or else disappear? How can we tell them of things we have witnessed with other planets?"*

"I don't know, Zua. You were on Earth, can't you see a way out for them?"

"Yes, you tell us what we can do to save Earth!" Roberta's voice was demanding.

Zua sat quietly thinking. Then, as much to convince herself as her hearers, she resumed:

"Eve is not naturally an organizing creature. She is individual. Her thinking is closer to the welfare of the child and home, the smallest unit of government, and the most intimate in all lands. As the mother, it has been her child and her home. Now she is beginning to think in terms of the world-wide homes, and the children in them."

"Just thinking about them?" Veh prodded.

"She is beginning to organize to do some things. Not on a grandiose scale. She is not much impressed with insignia, banners and bands. But she has won some freedoms and is using them to win others. She will be required to win many more, to be a completely free agent in many divisions, if Earth is ever to be a safe place. In some nations she has dared to go further and call the Only One

'Mother.' Earthites recognize what they term their Heavenly Father as a Supreme Being. When they recognize this Being as Mother, too, it will bring complete peace on Earth, such as Venus has known for ages."

"Doesn't it seem strange, Zua, that the Only One could ever be thought of as less than complete parentage?" Veh was contemplative. "I can see that calling the Only One 'Father' gave Adam prestige as a son, that perhaps Eve, as a daughter, would not share."

"Yes, it has done that. Their Book of Books was written entirely by sons, not daughters of the Only One. In one place it states: 'the sons of God saw the daughters of men, that they were fair, and they took them wives of all that they chose.' However, much of that book is Divinely inspired, and the Only One has been given a mother's attributes in its most inspired pages. But that concept is not generally accepted on Earth yet. When the Earthites recognize the Only One as both Father and Mother, they will have the basis for a complete solution of the war evil."

"Do you think Eve visualizes such a dawn of peace on Earth?"

"No, Veh, I do not believe she has so analyzed that tendency and its ultimate goal. When allowed, she has been the loving and gentle minister of binding up the wounds of suffering Earthites. Now she is serving on all the battlefields in missions of mercy. Until a century ago she was not allowed to do even that. Eve overcame ridicule and legal obstacles to do as much as she has done in that way. That proves that once she is awakened to her rightful role, she will win new freedoms through her loving service. Strange, that she should have to fight even for the right to express kindness. In the end, she'll win."

"Fight for that? I thought fight was Adam's prerogative!"

"Words have so many meanings in Earth's languages. Fight can be anything from an interplay of legal wits to the sinking of a battleship, or the destruction of a city. It's used in games and in politics as well!"

"Well, if you are a visitor from Venus, you've learned a lot, thought of things I never thought of," Roberta was pondering.

"But Zua, how does that fit into Eve's present activities, when she is helping to win wars, not stop them? From what you said, she is fighting and making war goods, isn't she? Wherein does she differ from Adam, then, about fighting?"

"I know it sounds contradictory to say that besides serving in merciful ways she is working in factories, building sky ships, land ships, sea ships, gigantic bombs, such an array of destructive forces impossible to compute."

Roberta sighed dejectedly, "It does seem that these two lines of effort cancel each other out."

"Tell me no more of their evils and wars, their confusions and contradic-

tions! If you have a hopeful view, I would hear that, but let's have done with it!" Veh was stern.

"Among mothers of men," Zua continued, *"love is leaping boundaries, and the thought is spreading among fathers, too. They are skipping color lines, creeds. Mothers are mothers the earth over. To them I look for the regeneration of Earth. Some have lost both husbands and sons in this, or in the first war of Earth. Millions of Eves lost one or the other. Their hearts' desolation may well be transmuted into organization for world-wide education of their children to prevent future conflicts. Surely, none would deny them this solace, nor their right at the peace tables of Earth."*

"Yes, we Eves have worked together to help win this war." Roberta was in agreement. "Why should we not continue to work together in these same organizations to win peace? Most important, to insist on world-wide education to prevent such things from happening again. Many of us will have no other reason for living. Husbands, sons and lovers will not be coming home. I know if Dick does not return, I will be empty of hand and heart. I'll have to find something worthwhile to do to take the place of my love for him, to fill my life."

"Adam might have avoided the awful cost of many wars had he done two things: let Eve have a voice in Earth's affairs, and paid more heed to the Earth's greatest teacher of love and brotherhood. Strangely, they say naught of sisterhood." Zua's tone was gentle as she continued. *"Yet this Jesus was rather more like a daughter than a son of the Only One, even by Earth's standards. He expressed more compassion and love than anyone on Earth. He was beyond their understanding then, and even today, to a large degree. Only a few understood Him, so they did away with Him. Adam's war thinking could not abide His teachings."*

"Have Earthites no personal lives? What about the home ties you mention?"

"They have as confused and varied ideas about human loves as about the Only One. Even this planet we live on is likened in their eyes to a pagan goddess of love. Strange concepts they have of love! Eve is supposed to be better than Adam but must appear a little doubtful to be most attractive! On Earth, love is exclusive and possessive. They would not understand our relations on Venus. Some day they, too, will climb higher, look over the rim of sex and see how another war-god, named Cupid, has played tricks on them, making them think they are so different, and then watching them blunder in needless misunderstanding. When once they see through this deception, and learn not of their differences but of their likenesses and equality, they will work together in harmony. They will understand love as we know it: no desire to possess selfishly,

only a wish to share mutual joys and helpfulness to each other. Then they will not need a bit of wildness, love-madness, to determine their degree of affection. Why, they even have a saying that they are 'crazy about' each other!"

"I thought crazy meant being mentally off balance." Veh was puzzled again.

"That's just it," Zua explained. *"Much that passes for love is just that. And of course it does not wear well. Even Earthites cannot stay crazy all the time, even through their short life span."*

"Eve must have a hard time." Veh sighed sympathetically.

"She has a harder time than she knows," Zua added. *"She has so much to learn growing up. When she has learned it, she is often too old to use it. Her knowledge leads to frustration and weariness, instead of everlasting joy. Earth's culture, art, music, literature, all reflect these conflicting love views. Just now, in their stress, their cultural ideas have become trivial and evanescent, so as to distract their attention from their Earthwide problems needing solutions. I found no staying qualities in much that appeared. A new book, another song, a fresh play . . . and have no remembrance of what they read, sang or saw yesterday, or at best, last week."*

"Well, and just where do we go from here?" Roberta unhappily wondered.

"I saw these diversions as a kind of opiate," Zua went on. *"That's something they take to deaden pain. When the effect wears off, the pain is still there; it isn't healed that way. So, like Earth's problems, Eve will awaken from this deadening inertia to find something must be done to bring an end to strife, and that she must do it."*

"Well, you surely know something of our problems. Suppose you tell us some of the answers!" Roberta demanded.

"In all of this confusion," Zua continued, *"many recognize the need for more love on Earth. They spend much time, effort and money in preaching love to one another."*

"You mean Adam's love for Eve?"

"Oh, never that! They sing that, write it, play it up in all kinds of fancy ways. It would seem to take all their time, if you judge from those sources. Strangely, they do get many worthwhile things done. No, the love they preach about is that unselfish love we know as children of a Common Parent, the Only One, and have for each other here, expressed in unselfish service without expectation of reward."

"Who preaches about that kind of love, Zua? Does Eve?" Veh questioned.

"Who do you suppose would do all the preaching or teaching, from what I have told you of Earthites? Preaching places are filled with Adams, although Eves are most often in attendance. Their greatest Teacher, remember, came through a woman's understanding of the Only One. So it is but natural that Eve feels a closer kinship with His teachings. She is mostly in attendance, although she must listen to His teachings strained through Adam's interpretation. But they seem to see nothing strange in that! However, this concept is slowly changing, as is also their concept of heaven."

"What's heaven? I don't understand." A puckered brow displayed Veh's puzzlement.

"Oh, that is not to be understood on Earth, either. It's their great unfathomed mystery. It seems to be a place where they intend to retire when they leave Earth and where they expect to be as good as they want to be without the usual hindrances."

"Why cannot they be as good as they want to be on Earth?"

"Too busy doing other things. However, they seem to find time to do the things they really like to do. They have time for play, games and fights."

"Why do you mention fight again? I thought fight was war, and you make it so many other things, Zua, you will make me more confused than ever!" Veh was a bit belligerent.

"Yes, once more I will mention it. Fight is a popular sport, too. A game of bitter, bloody fighting of two Adams in a center spot with other thousands looking on. Once I watched the faces of these spectators. They were fighting, too. They gave and felt every punch. They enjoyed it all. I think wars must have started as a sport, and see what they have grown up to! It is Adam's latent love of fight expanded to its limit. It's still a game with them. Once it was a gentleman's test of skill."

"Much of their teachings about valor and glory must be done against this backdrop of some evil in others against which they must contend, an evil outside themselves," continued Zua. *"Such teaching given to youth implies that war is needed to develop heroic character, that evils may be corrected by wars, that when things come to the worst they will have to fight it out, and a sort of secret hope that things may come to the worst, with many, so they may fight it out!"*

"Of all the weird concepts, Zua!"

"Worse than weird. It's tragic!" There was no levity in Zua's voice. *"Someday they will start with themselves as their great Teacher showed them. His method was the overcoming of evil within consciousness, and taught that what goeth out of a man (his evil intents) is what defileth the man. They are beginning to see that evil intent towards others is the only defilement."*

"Well, that's rather a raw explanation, but it just about adds up that way!" Roberta soberly agreed.

"So, their heaven will improve," Zua continued *"with their improved concepts. I think many now realize that a static heaven has little to offer active beings, and these people feel that an unselfish desire to serve each other on earth will unfold a better heaven to grow up to."*

"Well, that sounds sensible and tangible," Roberta nodded approvingly. "A heaven of doing good here on Earth as a sort of practice field."

"Then they will bring heaven down to Earth," Zua continued, *"and stay there always."*

"It all sounds so confusing and inconclusive to me. I don't see how you can have any hope of betterment on Earth, unless there is something more to lend hope tha[n] what you have revealed," Veh expressed doubt.

"You will recall I mentioned their Bible." Zua leaned forward earnestly.

"How truly beautiful she is!" Roberta observed, wonderingly, "not so much outside as within, like light behind a beautifully colored screen. If the light were not there the screen would be just another screen."

"All their highest concepts of life and of a hereafter are to be found in that Book. Their highest aspirations cluster around it. Much of its gathered wisdom is merely history, but its inspired word contains teachings in accordance with what we know and have proved of the Only One. They are such teachings as brought us out of chaos into our present enlightened era. That's the bond between us and the highest hope on Earth."

"That accounts for our understanding as much as we do of Earthites," Veh conceded.

"There is another prophesy in that Book, one most often overlooked."

"Yes?" Roberta bent forward to catch every word.

"That prophesy was made on Earth shortly after their Jesus left it. It is attributed to Him in converse with a loyal student. It is that once again a messenger of comfort, a woman, would bring forth a man child and he would rule all nations with a rod of iron. I puzzled over that. Most of Earth's affairs show the Bible's teachings have had some fulfilment, but I wanted to understand this, for it seems yet in the future. Jesus had been gentle, but He never swerved from righteousness. He could not he bent to do evil's bidding, nor could his true followers. They might be martyred, but they could not bend, yield their sense of right. So I saw it was a rule of right that was an iron rod, unbreakable and unbending. Yet, because Jesus was loving, compassionate and forgiving, and his martyred followers were so, this new rule of government would be loving government, stable and dependable and would last forever. It would not be of one over others, but each from within, governed by love for all without.[5] Something like the rule we have on Venus."

"That is a promise, in Revelation!"[6] Roberta was amazed at Zua's knowledge.

"And this messenger will be identified with her message. It will not be taken from her, as the first one was from the gentle Virgin's Son, and made into something over which to wage wars, or what they called crusades. So, through this will come Eve's full liberation. She will then take her rightful place as an equal in Earth's advancing ages."

Zua leaned back, as though she had finished her story.

"Oh, I hope all this may be so!" Roberta was lost in thought. "If I should have any sons, then they will not need to grow up to follow brother Bob and my darling Dick, even as they followed their fathers, out into another world war in another generation. Neither I, nor any mother, will need to worry that all we do to prepare our sons to live for good, will only make them better targets for some more destructive force than any yet known. Even worse than this horrible atom bomb! These are some of the things I felt and could not say to Dick. I did not want to carry such a load through life as my mother did, and her mother before her.

"I have felt, with women helping to win this war, that we will have the right to demand our share in making the peace, and the world-wide rule to keep it. Somehow, men have never been able to do that. They have not the patience to solve problems. We have learned patience through helping children settle quarrels down the ages. But what are our men but our children grown tall?

"We must face this problem. We must use our hard-won place to help make and keep the peace. We've been thinking about a lot besides glamour these past years. Ours is the capacity for keeping peace, and we must do it now. It was bad enough with old weapons, but with this unspeakable atomic horror hovering over all the world, we must make a lasting peace. There won't be enough left to salvage in another war. Men won't do this, without our aid, or they would have done it long ago. I see now what she means by our being immature. She is terribly, terribly right!"

"Do you really see hope, then, that Eve will take up her burden, so that this promised messenger will gain a hearing?" Veh was again interested.

"Yes, there are signs. Earth has long been expecting this messenger. On Earth, as here, messengers come when there is thought receptive enough to receive a new light. They expect it will be blazoned in glory, be ushered in with pomp, visible to Earthly eyes. That's a mistake Earthites always make about a great truth appearing among them. Quietly it will come, like water under sand."

"What do you mean, 'water under sand?'" Veh was again puzzled.

"Because it is deep-flowing in consciousness. No one knows where it will flow to the surface. Many have speculated about its appearing. One saw it in

this way: 'in the twentieth century (that's the present time on Earth) war will be dead, frontier boundaries will be dead, dogmas will be dead. Man [sic] will live. He will possess something more than all these: a great country, the whole earth, and a great hope, the whole heaven.' "

"Why, Victor Hugo wrote that!"[7] Roberta was again amazed at Zua's knowledge.

"Perhaps, even now," Zua continued, *"while Adam is making war as he was when Jesus was on Earth, somewhere least expected, as before, the messenger has appeared, or will appear. That deep-flowing stream of heaven consciousness will rise to the surface, with a new revelation, as water flows up through sand. A book in the hand of an angel will be in evidence. That's the promise!"*

Brooding, Roberta recalled her childhood. "Grandpa used to read the Bible to me. He often spoke of the Promised Comforter.[8] When father did not return from the first World War, he turned more and more to his Bible. He said the world was still too divided in its selfish interests to have learned its lesson. But mother and grandmother were not comforted. 'What does a promise of a Comforter yet to come, and trinkets such as medals mean to me? I have lost my heart's treasures.' Now they too are gone. Twin Robert and I remain, and here we are in another war. I'm glad they are not here to see it."

"On earth there is a deep, unmistakable reaching out for surer, safer knowledge of the Only One," Zua was confidently summing up. *"The Good One of the whole universe. Prayers of men in battle terrors on land, adrift on frail rafts in measureless oceans, in disintegrating sky ships over enemy lands, are answered, they know not how, and they wish to know. There is an unceasing and abiding realization that a beneficent Being in the universe is somehow above their strife, that they can lean on and touch His love and are lifted from despair and danger. We know they will find true knowledge. It may take a long time, with so many conflicting thought-currents, but only thus can they resolve their differences, and keep peace on Earth. It is still a strange place, Earth!"*

"As you say," Veh agreed, *"a strange and confused planet!"*

"Yes, and now so very sad. Sadder than they know, when we contrast it with our peace, because the solution of their problems is within reach. But there is hope. Light is breaking, old concepts are fading. All the viciousness now coming to the surface will be conquered by love in the hearts of the Eves. They will come into their own in mothering the Earth. With this service, their capacities for compelling and keeping peace will multiply. Places in government and education will be theirs. They must help keep the peace they make, or Adam will explode Earth out of the universe!"

"She is so sure of what she says," Roberta wonderingly conceded, "like one who has tested much."

As though further to assure, Zua confidently continued: *"Then there is the Promised Comforter, the one to come. A woman! Greater than Eve! Some believe she is already on Earth. Possibly. I saw some signs. Could I have remained among them longer perhaps I would have known."*

So she finished on an unfinished hope.

Silence filled the room where they sat in companionable silence. Silence in the stone cabin. Roberta was lost in wonder and in hope. "Oh, if there could be some sure remedy for the solving of this everlasting war problem! There never was so great a need for love, as Grandfather saw it. Just goodness and mercy. Maybe, if we Eves make an effort, a way will be prepared for the Prince of Peace. He said he would abide always, to the end of the world!"

Now Veh noticed for the first time the wand dropped into the socket. She cried out, startled, *"Oh, Zua, how could you have turned on that universe broadcaster? Why, this conversation has gone out over the whole universe!"*

Zua smiled, satisfied. *"There is just one place where it will be heard. Only one radio receiver set capable of catching its beam, the one I took with me to Earth to keep in touch with you at home. I left it on Earth, tuned to receive television and record a message from us here. This conversation, as I planned it, has taken place. That is why I used an Earth language. It seemed unfair for me to have been there, and nobody there to know of it.*

"Some day, someone will find his way up that mountain far to the north on the trail of their skyships. Often I heard them when I was at home in that cabin, which a recluse, a miner, built long ago. I found it from the air with a snowfield landing place. I commissioned an old mountaineer to build me a shed where I could shelter the plane from snow. There I would come to rest from Earth's confusions, study their lore, and tune in on you here at home. Sometimes you forgot I was listening for news, and I could not reach you with my voice. But my heart was at home.

"Down the valley a few miles was a river, and although it was dangerous, this old mountaineer could navigate it to bring in his supplies. He had a small stock, and would sell me some at times. He acted as a forest aid on lookout for fires. But he had great disdain for 'airyplanes,' was superstitious about them, didn't dare to come close to one. He said they were devil-birds. Well, many of them on Earth are that now, dealing death and destruction. He thought there was something wrong with a 'furrin woeman' who wanted to fly. And, anyway, there was nothing in his Bible about planes, so that just closed the subject as far as he was concerned."

"Did he know you were from Venus?" asked Veh.

"Once when he questioned me, I told him I was. He said, 'I thought ye

was a furriner. So ye're from Venice! That old city on the water in Italy. I read about it once!' " Zua laughed at the memory.

"Someday someone will find my radio with a transcription, and will be able to reproduce it. I studied their methods and adjusted my radio to them. And they will find my message in a language of their own!"

Pleased and relaxed, Zua looked about her. *"This, dear heart,"* she sighed contentedly, *"is what I wanted to return to. This dear, familiar room. So good to be home again, with you, where love is not an unstable emotion, but a dependable habit, restful and gracious. If only Earthites could learn that! They really have a beautiful statement of love in their Great Book: 'Love suffereth long, and is kind . . . seeketh not her own . . . is not easily provoked . . . thinketh no evil.'⁹ Someday they will take it out of the Book and use it in daily lives. Then their differences will fade away."*

She was alerted by the radio: *"There! Some one has moved the dial. Our connection with Earth is being broken! Once that is done, someone on Earth will need to remake the connection before there can be further communication to that planet!"*

Roberta had been touching the dial, entranced still by this unearthly story.

"What a strange play! Wonder what station it is? There seems to be no signing off. No sponsors' announcement. No pause for station identification, either. No products have been mentioned. And they speak of being on Venus! That's the love goddess. Yes, but it's a planet, too! Now it is finished and I want to know what station it is!"

She twirled the dial, but no sound came, and the panel had become dark. She twirled it back excitedly, just in time to catch the words *"someone on Earth will need to remake that connection before there can be a further communication from us to that planet."* Then . . . only a dead silence, turn it as she would.

"Am I dreaming?" she looked about her in wonder. "But there is a radio on the mantel. There are all those books, these furnishings, and the clothes in the closet!" Carefully she examined the radio. "Yes, there is a transcription. This must be my secret. Someday, I'll give it to the world!"

Then she recalled her present situation, alone here in the snowy wilderness with no gas to get out. A sense of desolation struggled with courage, as she firmly reassured herself. "There must be a way out, down the mountain. She spoke of a . . ."

Just then she heard the sound of feet, crunching on the hard crust of the snow. She looked out the window, down the slope, and saw a mountaineer bundled against the cold, now very near the door.

"The radio!" She rushed back to the mantel. "I don't want anyone to have this but me." She won in the race to reach it, tore loose the fastenings, and thrust it inside her flying jacket, just in time. The unlocked door was opened without a knock by an elderly mountaineer, ruddy-faced, blue-eyed, with frosty eyebrows.

A gruff voice called: "Thought I heer'ed an airyplane stop up thar on the hill last night. So, ye're back, be ye?"

He looked at her closely and was startled. "Why, ye're not the woman who has been up there betimes the past year, be ye? Ye're 'Merican, ye're now, same's me. Funny she was, furrin-like. Never saw her plane. Heard her fly it out and back sometimes. Never can understand why women want to be cavortin' round above the clouds in men's clothes. Seems as how ye're place is at home with children. Don't hold with flyin'! Nothin' in the Bible about airyplanes."

He still stood inside the door, but now he stepped outside, and called over his shoulder. Roberta was seated on the hassock, hastily donning her boots.

"Come on now, I'll take ye down the mountain to my place. Get in touch with a furrester there. He's got a phone. He'll notify your folks. Not hurt, be ye?" Even in his solicitude he was gruff, and added, "Darnation, these modern flyin' women anyhow!" He started grumbling and moving down the broken path over which he came.

Roberta glanced with longing at the room, now sunlit and colorful, adjusted her parachute, and stepped outside, closing the door behind her. Meekly, and in silence, she followed the old man down the trail.

Appendix
Notes
References

Appendix:
Annotated Bibliography of U.S. Women's Utopian Fiction, 1836–1988

Scholars know too well that the work of historical recovery is slow. The following bibliography is a guide to the number of utopian works by United States women known to have been published since 1836 when the first appeared: "Three Hundred Years Hence" by Mary Griffith. I include nearly 300 titles, one as early as 1824 containing a very brief dystopia. While my work was made easier because of the previous compilations of Daphne Patai, Kenneth M. Roemer, and Lyman Tower Sargent, I am sure that the work of recovery is still not complete. This bibliography includes nonfiction as well as fiction, juvenile as well as adult, short as well as book-length works, and several individual chapters, the more fully to recover women's visions of utopia. The bibliography is more inclusive

For the compilation of this Bibliography, I am grateful for support from NEH Grant FB-25581-88, as well as from the Pennsylvania State University for granting me a sabbatical leave, a Research Development Grant, and a grant from the Institute for Art and Humanistic Studies. In addition, I would like to thank the following library staff: Jean Sphar, Susan Ware, and Sara Whildin at the Delaware County Campus, and Charles Mann and Sandra Stelts at the Rare Book Room of Pattee Lirary. Without their dedicated work, I could not have completed mine. Colleagues, many from the Society for Utopian Studies, have also contributed substantially and I thank them. They include Nan Bowman Albinski, Marleen S. Barr, Jane Donawerth, Libby Jones, Lee Cullen Khanna, Carol Kolmerten, Arthur O. Lewis, Janice A. Radway, Kenneth M. Roemer, Lyman Tower Sargent, and Lynn F. Williams. This Bibliography is reprinted directly from the version published in *Utopian Studies* 1, no. 1 (1990): 1–58, with no annotations or updated listings beyond 1988, but with corrections and additions through 1960, the time period that is the focus of this anthology.

Readers must not assume that the lack of updating derives from any lack of new utopias by women: simply examine such recent important titles as Marge Piercy's *He, She and It* (1991), Suzette Haden Elgin's *Earthsong: Native Tongue 3* (1994), or Octavia Butler's *Parable of the Sower* (1994). Time and the focus of this particular anthology dictated otherwise.

before than it is after 1920. No juvenile works or short stories appear after 1930, time having prevented comparable inclusiveness. I have tried especially to include utopian content from notable authors, even when this is meagre. With borderline cases, I have chosen to include rather than exclude.

Taken as a whole, these works provide us with the imaginative roots of feminism: they frequently mirror what women lacked and what women wanted at the time when the books were published. Such fictions are best read not as blueprints for perfect worlds, but rather as guides suggestive of improved possibilities. The definitions of utopia governing the content of this list are those already established: *utopia* is the general term meaning "no-place," or sometimes "good place"; *eutopia* specifies the dream or "good place," while *dystopia* indicates the nightmare or "bad place" (see Sargent for discussions of and references on definition). Besides eutopia and dystopia, there exists a third subtype, the satiric utopia or antiutopia, wherein a society is turned upside down as a means of discrediting it. Utopian fiction in the twentieth century includes yet a fourth subtype, the ambiguous or critical utopia, which is neither good nor bad but unfinished, still in the process of becoming (see Moylan).

These utopias exist as one (or a blend) of several possible forms: a description of an ideal society; a dream from which a dreamer wakes to reveal the wonders of another world; a voyage to an exotic land or distant planet, which the visitor observes for a later report; a pioneering expedition to a frontier where an ideal society can be created, untainted by established practices; a long sleep, from which a reporter wakes in an ideal future society and which may later be dissolved into a dream; the future of one's own society explained by a future resident; an outsider's view of one's own society; a visitor's description of a utopian homeland markedly superior to the author's country. Typically, utopias in the nineteenth century are set somewhere in the contemporary United States, a fact revealing the effect of literary realism upon even so romantic a genre as the utopia (see Kessler 1985).

A major concern in nineteenth-century utopias by women is women's awareness of the constraints that domestic responsibilities place upon their social equality. In fact, several of the items on the list are here by virtue of their utopian feminist reforms, especially in domestic cooperation. Owenite utopian socialists located such reform at the center of their concerns. This is a utopian reform more central than critics have previously realized (and more central than suffrage to utopists); consequently, we need to stress it more than we have done in the past (see Hayden 1981; Kolmerten 1990; Leach). Typically it finds expression in utopias closer to literary realism than to romanticism. The more realistic utopias do not require human or social perfection, but rather show societies superior in some way to what was known at the time. One of the areas receiving marked reform attention was women's role in society. Women's alternative vision has slipped out of our historical record: this bibliography places particular emphasis upon women's utopian arrangements for women's lives. Jane Tompkins reminds us, in *Sensational Designs: The Cultural Work of American Fiction, 1790–1860,* that women fully expected their fiction to effect social evolution, if not revolution:

utopian writing carries up to the present "sensational designs" for cultural adjustments—not as blueprints, but as alternatives for readers' thoughtful consideration.

From 1920 to 1960 (a decade which saw a marked change in utopian content), interest in women's issues became less militant but did not cease. Historian Nancy F. Cott, in *The Grounding of Modern Feminism,* focuses upon re-constructing our understanding of the United States "woman's movement" of the 1910s–1930s from which emerged the feminisms of the later twentieth century. Nineteenth-century volunteerism continued as public action congruent with women's sphere, and men continued to resist women's achievement of suffrage, accomplished (as Cott shows) in an age when the power of the ballot sank in the face of the rising power of market corporations. Utopian content reflects these conditions. Authors imagine far more limited possibilities for women than previously. Wifehood and motherhood become the norm once again; authors little question their centrality. While the Depression pushed women out of the work force to make way for men, the assumed heads of households, World War II pulled women back again to replace men leaving for the battlefronts. Save for a brief fling with "togetherness" in the 1950s, women did not again return home, but instead have marched steadily forward toward paid labor beside men.

From 1960 to the present, the various feminisms share a utopian vision not limited to the needs of women alone, but extending to children and other powerless or marginalized social groups. A new world view emerges, which is congruent with the social movements for civil rights, women's rights, gay and lesbian rights, rights of the handicapped and elderly, and ethnic validation, and which is informed by the movements to preserve the world's ecology and environment, control waste, stop nuclear proliferation, promote world peace, and enhance professional ethics. The list continues to increase. Three general areas emerge— community, environment, and spirituality (see Barr 1981 and 1987; Freibert; Khanna 1984; Kessler 1984). The continuing flow of utopian writing by women encompasses all of these concerns. Given the magnitude of the problems confronting humanity at the turn of the twentieth-first century, authors look outward into space, forward or backward in time, or inward into psychic depths, to locate clear space for alternatives to present conditions. With the exception of communitarian experiments, eutopias are often not set in the contemporary United States, or even on Earth. Space exploration and colonization replace a closed western frontier, though "new wave" science fiction as practiced by women may construe the frontier to be internal or psychological, spiritual not material. In fact, fantasy, magic, and the supernatural hover on the borders of some recent feminist utopias, which can overlap with "sword and sorcery," a subcategory of science fiction featuring sword fights and the supernatural. In the twentieth century, fantasy and science fiction replace romance and literary realism as the genres having the greatest impact upon utopias by women.

Concern for a wide range of women's issues replaces marriage as a regular plot component. All utopias by women are not, however, feminist. By *feminist* I mean "favoring women's rights and valuing that which is female," a narrow definition. *Antifeminist* will thus mean "antifemale." And *sexist,* by analogy to *racist,* will mean "sex-biased or accepting gender-role stereotyping." People of either sex may be sexist toward their own or the other sex. (For an overview of feminisms in the United States, see Hester Eisenstein's *Contemporary Feminist Thought.*)

The bibliography is arranged chronologically by year and alphabetically within each year. Titles are listed by year of first publication, as well as I can determine, with additional editions, reprints, or microfilm collections so noted. Three microfilm sources occur. I provide the full citation for each here and abbreviations henceforth:

1. *American Periodicals, 1741–1900.* Ann Arbor, Michigan: University Microfilms, 1963. Citations appear as Coll. American Periodicals, Series 2.675.

2. *History of Women: A Comprehensive Microfilm Publication.* New Haven: Research Publications, 1976. Citations appear as Coll. History of Women 4896.1.

3. Wright, Lyle H., ed. *American Fiction 1774–1900.* Vols. 1, 2, 3. New Haven: Research Publications, 1968, 1971, 1971. These volumes are based upon Wright's bibliography of the same title.) Citations appear as Coll. Wright 1.1073.

A list of selected references (Bibliography, Definition, Tradition and Selected Critical References) supporting the foregoing introduction and the annotated bibliography appears at the end of the book. Finally, to facilitate the use of the following bibliography, alphabetical indexes to authors and to short titles appear at its end.

1836–1919

[1824]

Sedgwick, Catharine Maria (1789–1867). *Redwood: A Tale.* New York: E. Bliss and E. White. Reprint, New York: Garrett, 1969.

  Embedded in a novel of manners are three chapters (Book 2, chaps. 14–16) depicting a Shaker community as a dystopia, particularly because of the community's repression of sexuality.

1836

Griffith, Mary (–1877). "Three Hundred Years Hence." In *Camperdown; or News from Our Neighborhood.* Philadelphia: Carey, Lea and Blanchard. Coll. Wright 1.1073. Reprint, Philadelphia: Prime Press, 1950. Also in *American Utopias: Selected Short Fiction,* edited by Arthur O. Lewis, New York: Arno, 1971. Excerpted in *Daring to Dream: Utopian Stories by United States Women, 1836–1919,* compiled by Carol Farley Kessler, Boston: Pandora/Routledge and Kegan Paul, 1984.

  In a dream vision of the United States placed three hundred years into the future, the central place and accomplishments of women amaze the male narrator. Dream novelette.

1841

[Chamberlain, Betsey (–   )], Tabitha (pseud.). "A New Society." *The Lowell Offering* 1:191–92. Coll. American Periodicals, Series 2.675. Reprinted in *The Lowell Offering: Writings by New England Women 1840–1845*, edited by Benita Eisler, New York: Harper and Row, 1977.

A Lowell mill worker's dream vision of the resolutions to reform her world stresses family responsibility, fair labor practices, mental and physical work for all, and education specific to each sex. Sketch.

1848

[Appleton, Jane Sophia (–1884)]. "Sequel to the 'Vision of Bangor in the Twentieth Century.' " In *Voices from the Kenduskeag*. Bangor, Maine: D. Bugbee. Coll. Wright 1.39. Reprinted in *American Utopias: Selected Short Fiction* [includes "Vision of Bangor in the Twentieth Century"], edited by Arthur O. Lewis, New York: Arno, 1971. Excerpted in *Daring to Dream: Utopian Stories by United States Women, 1836–1919,* compiled by Carol Farley Kessler, Boston: Pandora/Routledge and Kegan Paul, 1984.

An unenlightened United States man receives guidance from a twentieth-century gentleman, who corrects the former's mistaken underestimation of women in all areas of life. Sex differences are recognized and accepted. Dream dialogue; novelette.

1853

Hale, Sarah Josepha [Buell] (1788–1879). *Liberia; or Mr. Peyton's Experiments.* New York: Harper and Brothers. Coll. Wright 2.1064. Reprint, New Jersey: Gregg, 1968.

Virginia planter Mr. Charles Peyton experiments with ameliorating Black lives—first a collective Virginia farm, second a Canadian community, and finally the Liberia Colonization Society. This final utopia is less patronizing of Blacks than typical of the era and demonstrates the energy and ability of a people freed. Communitarian polemic.

1866

Davis, Rebecca Harding (1831–1910). "The Harmonists." *The Atlantic Monthly* 17:529–38.

A man recalls having visited Economy, Pennsylvania, with a physician and his son. The father decides not to join the Rappites because their narrow patriarchal viewpoint has twisted their lives, the hoped-for eutopia does not exist, but is rather an ironic caricature of soured ideals. Short story.

1868

Phelps [Ward], Elizabeth Stuart (1844–1911). *The Gates Ajar.* Boston: Fields, Osgood. Reprint, Cambridge, Mass.: Belknap/Harvard Univ. Press, 1964.

Not a utopia, this best seller provides a rationale for Phelps's 1883 and 1887 "Gates" books in projecting the heaven in which women's needs would at last be met as compensation for life's losses.

1869

Corbett, Elisabeth T. (–   ). "My Visit to Utopia." *Harper's New Monthly Magazine* 38:200–204. Reprinted in *Daring to Dream: Utopian Stories by United States Women, 1836–1919,* compiled by Carol Farley Kessler, Boston: Pandora/Routledge and Kegan Paul, 1984.

In post-Civil War United States, eutopia for woman is marriage made to her order. Short story of present alternative.

1870

Alcott, Louisa May (1832–1888). "The Sunny Side." Chap. 13 of *An Old-fashioned Girl.* Boston: Roberts.

Four young women—a sculptor, an engraver, an author, and an art student—share rooms and cooperate in thus making a home for each other. This independent and self-fulfilling foursome share a "religion"—to help one another. This chapter from the novel provides an early example of cooperative living, such as depicted in Charlotte Perkins Gilman's fiction (1908, 1910).

Cridge, Annie Denton (–by 1884). *Man's Rights; or, How Would You Like It?* Serialized in *Woodhull and Claflin's Weekly* 1, nos. 17–25, 27 (3 Sept.–19 Nov.). Dreams 1–5 published separately (under same title), Boston: William Denton. Coll. Wright 2. 658. Dreams 1–3 reprinted in *Daring to Dream: Utopian Stories by United States Women, 1836–1919,* compiled by Carol Farley Kessler, Boston: Pandora/Routledge and Kegan Paul, 1984.

A woman dreams of satiric role reversals that make ludicrous the "cult of true womanhood" when it is practiced by men. Nine such dream visions in original serialization.

Kirby, Georgiana Bruce (1818–1850). "My First Visit to Brook Farm." *Overland Monthly* 5, no. 1 (1870): 9–19.

A narrative, autobiographical essay, relating a one-week stay at the "Community" of Brook Farm. Nonfiction.

Woodhull [Martin], Victoria Claflin (1838–1927). "A Page of American History: Constitution of the United States of the World. An Address. Delivered in Lincoln Hall, Washington." N.p.: Norman Sawyer. Reprinted in *The Victoria Woodhull Reader,* edited by Madeleine Stern, Weston, Mass.: M. and S. Press, 1974.

A world government modeled after the Constitution of the United States. An interesting feature is the extension of the franchise to all adult citizens—those eighteen and over—with the exception of idiots and the insane.

1871

Alcott, Louisa May (1832–1888). *Little Men: Life at Plumfield with Jo's Boys*. Boston: Roberts.

Jo March of *Little Women,* now the wife of Professor Bhaer, with him runs Plumfield, a farm school for girls and boys. The educational community constitutes an experimental microcosm for demonstrating communal living which, unlike Bronson Alcott's Fruitlands, does exhibit gender equality for all ages. Romantic novel, USA.

Harbert, Lizzie Boynton (–   ). *Out of her Sphere*. Des Moines, Iowa: Mills.

This feminist novel embodies the heroine Marjorie's right both to work and to marry, to leave the prescribed and limited "sphere" of depending solely upon a man for home, money, and position, and instead to work in equality beside him in the world, yet with no desire to become a man. Social critical novel, USA.

1873

Alcott, Louisa May (1832–1888). "At Forty." Chap. 20 of *Work: A Story of Experience*. Boston: Roberts. Reprint, New York: Schocken, 1977.

The novel concludes with the prospect of women of all ages, races, and classes constituting an inclusive sororal community in which they work to improve each other's conditions. Conclusion of novel as utopian vision.

Alcott, Louisa May (1832–1888). "Transcendental Wild Oats: A Chapter from an Unwritten Romance." *Independent* 25, (1873) nos. 1569–71. Reprint, *Transcendental Wild Oats,* edited by William Henry Harrison, Harvard, Mass.: Harvard Common Press, 1981. Also found in *Woman's Journal* 5 (21 Feb. 1874); *Silver Pitchers,* Boston: Roberts, 1876; *Bronson Alcott's Fruitlands,* compiled by Clara Endicott Sears, Philadelphia: Porcupine, 1975; *Alternative Alcott,* edited by Elaine Showalter, New Brunswick, N.J.: Rutgers Univ. Press, 1988.

A short autobiographical romance set in 184- New England derives from her experience of living at her father Bronson Alcott's "Fruitlands," a communitarian experiment where women's labor made men's rumination possible. The community might have been called "Apple Slump," Mrs. Abel Lamb suggests in conclusion. Narrative essay.

1874

Howland, Marie [Stevens Case] (1836–1921). *Papa's Own Girl; A Novel*. New York: Jewett. Coll. Wright 2.1290. Reprinted as *The Familistere; A Novel,*

Boston: Christopher, 1918; Philadelphia: Porcupine, 1975. Excerpted in *Daring to Dream: Utopian Stories by United States Women, 1836–1919,* compiled by Carol Farley Kessler, Boston: Pandora/Routledge and Kegan Paul, 1984.

Engagingly readable, the novel makes equitable relations between women and men basic to the improved conduct of society in L—, Massachusetts, where a European count finances a Social Palace. Feminist. Communitarian romance.

Phelps [Ward], Elizabeth Stuart (1844–1911). "A Dream within a Dream." *The Independent* 26, no. 1316 (19 Feb.): 1. Reprinted in *Daring to Dream: Utopian Stories by United States Women, 1836–1919,* compiled by Carol Farley Kessler, Boston: Pandora/Routledge and Kegan Paul, 1984.

A dream vision reveals marriage to be a potential earthly utopia.

1879

Douglas, Amanda M[innie] (1837–1916). *Hope Mills; or, Between Friend and Sweetheart.* Boston: Lee and Shepard. Coll. Wright 3.1611.

Though the romance concludes typically with marriages, they are interclass. The mill-class hero implements his vision of industrial community, modeled after English and French Utopias; mill women establish a cooking school. The experiments prosper. Idealistic; not feminist. Communitarian romance.

Phelps [Ward], Elizabeth Stuart (1844–1911). *Old Maid's Paradise.* Boston: Houghton, Osgood. [Sequel: *Burglars in Paradise.* Boston: Houghton, Mifflin, 1886. Detective fiction. Reprinted together as *Old Maids and Burglars in Paradise.* Boston: Houghton Mifflin, 1898.]

Paradise exists on Boston's North Shore, where two women sharing a summer cottage, demonstrate not only that they have no need for male protection, but that males naturally provide not protection as widely touted, but peril for unsuspecting women. Tongue-in-cheek, satiric paradise; role reversal.

1881

[Lane, Mary E. Bradley (–)]. *Mizora: A Prophecy.* Serialized in *The Cincinnati Commercial,* Nov. 1880–Feb. 1881. Published in book form, New York: G. W. Dillingham, 1889. Coll. Wright 3.3203. Reprint, edited by Kristine Anderson and Stuart Teitler, New York: Gregg, 1975. Excerpted in *Daring to Dream: Utopian Stories by United States Women, 1836–1919,* compiled by Carol Farley Kessler, Boston: Pandora/Routledge and Kegan Paul, 1984.

Reached through an entrance at the North Pole, Mizora is an all-female society where education is the highest concern. Society, though nonviolent, is hierarchical and white-racist. All-female society.

1882

[Wood, Mrs. J. (–   )]. *Pantaletta: A Romance of Sheheland.* New York: American News Company. Coll. Wright 3.6064.

General Gullible voyages by balloon to Sheheland, where Capt. Pantaletta in the Republic Petticotia demonstrates the negative outcome of gender role reversal in a satire on female power and governance. Conservative politically; antifeminist. Space travel.

1883

Phelps [Ward], Elizabeth Stuart (1844–1911). *Beyond the Gates.* Boston: Houghton, Mifflin. Coll. Wright 3.5755. Excerpted in *Daring to Dream: Utopian Stories by United States Women, 1836–1919,* compiled by Carol Farley Kessler, Boston: Pandora/Routledge and Kegan Paul, 1984.

The domestication of heavenly "mansions" shows a father houskeeping while awaiting the arrival of the rest of his family, and a daughter at last finding her destined heart-mate. Alternative vision.

1884

Shelhamer, M[ary] T[heresa] (–   ). *Life and Labors in the Spirit-World. Being a Description of the Localities, Employments, Surroundings, and Conditions of the Spheres.* Boston: Colby and Rich.

The spirit of a woman deceased in 1877 permits us glimpses of a future afterworld more conducive to the development of human potential—whether belonging in an earlier life to someone common or uncommon; female or male; black, Indian, or serf. Instructional methods and cooperative societies provide strategies for improving the lives of all. Spiritual fantasy.

1885

Blake, Lillie Devereux [Umsted] (1833–1913). "A Divided Republic: An Allegory of the Future." *Phrenological Journal* (Feb.–Mar. 1887). Reprinted in *A Daring Experiment and Other Stories,* New York: Lovell, Coryell, 1892.

A short story depicting in fantasy how gender inequality might be rectified by first creating a "divided republic": all women emigrate from the eastern states to the Territory of Washington, where women are voters. Reunion occurs only when true freedom extends to women as well as men. USA, feminist near-future.

Campbell, Helen Stuart (1839–1918). *Mrs. Herndon's Income. Christian Union.* Published in book form, Boston: Roberts. Coll. Wright 3.890.

Social reform accomplished by individual initiative: Margaret Herndon, recipient of her husband's substantial income, uses it to overcome individual distress wherever she finds it. She believes in the Ultimates, a society whose members practice the utopian principles of helping others and avoiding strife. Social critical novel, then-current USA.

1886

Alcott, Louisa May (1832–1888). *Jo's Boys, and How They Turned Out*. Boston: Roberts.

The students at Plumfield (1871) mature and graduate. Most of them successfully take into the world beyond the Plumfield farmstead values inculcated by Professor Bhaer and Jo, by now a much lionized author. Utopian romance.

Campbell, Helen Stuart (1839–1918). *Miss Melinda's Opportunity*. Boston: Roberts. Coll. Wright 3.889.

A group of working women join in a one-year experiment in cooperative housekeeping: they expect to live cheaply and well in a duplex house bought by Miss Melinda and thereby avoid the restrictiveness of "homes" for "working girls." Exemplifies the Owenite communitarian, experimental tradition of domestic cooperation. Social reform romance, then-current USA.

1887

Dieudonné, Florence [Lucinda] Carpenter (1850–   ). *Rondah; or Thirty-Three Years in a Star*. Philadelphia: Peterson. Coll. Wright 3.1539.

A borderline eutopia of Sun Island on Parzelia becomes possible at the conclusion of this multiple-viewpoint "history" of a space adventure, which includes finding a winged fairy people.

Dodd, Anna Bowman [Blake] (1855–1929). *The Republic of the Future; or Socialism a Reality*. New York: Cassell. Coll. Wright 3.1557.

A Swedish nobleman writes in dismay to his friend in Christiania about the New York Socialistic City he finds in December 2050. Though women now perform only two hours of domestic work, still foreign courts so dislike contact with female arbitrators that the latter concede rather than negotiate! The narrator bemoans a loss of individuality. Alternative future.

Phelps [Ward], Elizabeth Stuart (1844–1911). *The Gates Between*. Boston: Houghton, Mifflin. Coll. Wright 3.5762.

Heaven provides the society within which a male physician learns to be a sensitive parent and spouse. Alternative vision.

1888

Cruger, Mary (1834–1908). *How She Did It or Comfort on $150 a Year*. New York: Appleton. Coll. Wright 3.1326.

Unmarried and from a recently impoverished family, Faith Arden builds her own house, takes in a widowed mother with daughter and son, and sets up a self-sufficient "very Eden of beauty," a cooperative household. Owenite tradition of cooperative domesticity, with the corrective twist that a son participates as much as a daughter. Social reform romance set in then-current USA.

1889

Ford, Mary H. (–   ). "A Feminine Iconoclast." *The Nationalist* (Nov.): 252–57. Reprinted in *Daring to Dream: Utopian Stories by United States Women, 1836–1919,* compiled by Carol Farley Kessler, Boston: Pandora/ Routledge and Kegan Paul, 1984.

A streetcar eavesdropper reports a conversation in which one woman reveals to another the patronizing and paternalistic view of woman inherent in Edward Bellamy's nationalism. Short story.

Mason, Eveleen Laura [Knaggs] (1838–1914). *Hiero-Salem: The Vision of Peace.* Boston: J. G. Cupples. Coll. Wright 3.3633. Excerpted in *Daring to Dream: Utopian Stories by United States Women, 1836–1919,* compiled by Carol Farley Kessler, Boston: Pandora/Routledge and Kegan Paul, 1984.

Set in northern Wisconsin in the near-past, the Eloiheem Commonwealth established by one founding couple seeks to remove religious, racial, class, and sex inequities. Spiritual community.

Mead, Lucia True Ames (1856–1936). *Memoirs of a Millionaire.* Boston: Houghton, Mifflin. Coll. Wright 3.3675.

Set in then-contemporary United States, the novel presents a scheme for ameliorating lives of the earth's helpless and degraded peoples—especially women—through a Christian Missionary Fund, established by benefactress Mildred Brewster when she inherits millions from a former lover. Economic utopia.

[Woods, Katharine Pearson (1853–1932)]. *Metzerott, Shoemaker.* New York: Crowell. Coll. Wright 3.6058.

In a troubled world realistically presented, Metzerott participates in an urban commune whose members espouse a eutopian socialism. They encounter upper-class resistance, but although membership changes, the group continues. One of its activities is a boarding facility. Communitarian romance.

1890

[Knox], Adeline Trafton (1845–1889). *Dorothy's Experience.* Boston: Lee and Shepard.

Dorothy "Dolly" Drake, whose education in a denominational seminary included the expectation of promoting "human betterment," establishes a society to fund a utopian mission expressly to aid homeless women by providing rooms, meals, meeting rooms, and an employment bureau. This duty to the world does not preclude a happy marriage for her. Utopian romance.

Pittock, Mrs. M. A. Weeks (–   ). *The God of Civilization: A Romance*.Chicago: Eureka.

A Pacific shipwreck leaves a California woman and friends stranded upon a tropical island suggestive of Hawaii. The bronze-skinned natives with their relaxed appreciation of natural and human sensuality win her allegiance: she marries, refusing to leave when chance permits. Romantic fantasy.

Stone, Mrs. C[harles] H. [Margaret Barber Stone] (–   ). *One of "Berrian's" Novels*. New York: Welch, Fracker. Coll. Wright 3.5264.

Couched as fiction by Bellamy's future novelist Berrian from *Looking Backward* (1888), this work accepts Bellamy's traditional gender roles, even though women as well as men head institutions in St. Louis of 1997. Not feminist. Futuristic romance.

1891

[Bartlett, Alice Elinor Bowen (1848–1920)], Birch Arnold (pseud.). *A New Aristocracy*. New York: Bartlett. Coll. Wright 3.359.

In the suburbs of a western United States metropolis, a Christian community Idlewild demonstrates a "new aristocracy of head and heart" where strong women may marry on their own terms. Communitarian romance.

Brodhead, Eva Wilder McGlasson (1870–1915). *Diana's Livery*. New York: Harper. Coll. Wright 3.677.

Kentucky Shaker community appears to be less than eutopia as individual members resort to alcohol or suicide. Instead marriage promises greater possibility for satisfied living, as a young woman Naamah chooses to leave the community to live with the man she loves, an artist and landowner. Communitarian romance.

Freeman, Ruth Ellis (–   ). "Tales of a Great-Grandmother." *New Nation* 1:458–60, 505–7, 569–77.

In the summer of 1980, author Alpennar Peck interviews his 102-year-old great-grandmother Marshall Peck in the northern United States. Sections 1 and 2 reveal her memories of 1891 conditions—since ameliorated—for writers, mothers, and workers. Section 3 projects 1980 technological innovations and social changes for women and employees.

Livermore, Mary A[shton Rice] (1820–1905). "Cooperative Womanhood in the State." *North American Review* 153:284–95.

An expository essay describing women's cooperative organizations, from the Civil War Sanitary Commission (a volunteer nursing force which she headed) to the WCTU. Nonfiction.

Yourell, Agnes Bons (–   ). *A Manless World*. New York: Dillingham. Coll. Wright 3.6170.

An old man tells his newly affianced nephew of a dystopian prophecy
—a theory of a manless world where noxious gases make procreation impossible, where anarchy increases after Gentiles annihilate Jews, and the last
woman takes her own life. The nephew discounts the theory by assuming
his uncle suffered early loss of love. Alternative future.

1892

Harbert, Lizzie Boynton (–   ). *"Amore"*. New York: Lovell, Gestefeld.
     The novel demonstrates that a true home is headed by two people, not
one. The heroine Theodora Dwight starts the Triangle Club, whose goal is
discovering truth. She believes that love casts out fear and diminishes evil
so that love may rule society. Thus a peaceable commonwealth results, in
which a "new woman" enjoys the right to love and the opportunity to
serve. Feminist, reform romance, then-current USA.
[Moore, M. Louise (–   )]. *Al-Modad; or Life Scenes beyond the Polar Cir-
cumflex. A Religio-Scientific Solution of the Problems of Present and Future Life.*
Shell Bank, La.: Moore and Beauchamp. Coll. Wright 3.3817.
     An 1879 diary of travels to the Arctic records visitor Al-Modad's obser-
vations of a cooperative industrialized society where women and men are
equals, their sexuality freely expressed, and kinship with all people practiced. Interesting. Communitarian utopia.
Tincker, Mary Agnes (1831–1907). *San Salvador*. Boston: Houghton, Mifflin.
Coll. Wright 3.5500.
     Set in a remote and mountainous area, the Christian community of
San Salvador exists to protect the needy and defenseless. Gender roles are
conservative. The birth of a son concludes the novel. Communitarian romance.

1893

[Jones, Alice Ilgenfritz (1846–1906) and Ella Merchant (1857–1916)], Two
Women of the West (pseud.). *Unveiling a Parallel: A Romance.* Boston:
Arena. Coll. Wright 3.5627. Reprint, New York: Gregg, 1975; edited by
Carol A. Kolmerten, Syracuse, N.Y.: Syracuse Univ. Press, 1991. Excerpted in *Daring to Dream: Utopian Stories by United States Women, 1836–
1919,* compiled by Carol Farley Kessler, Boston: Pandora/Routledge and
Kegan Paul, 1984.
     A male traveler to Mars visits two societies where ideal women are the
equals of ideal men, though one society values the material and the other,
the spiritual. The parallel unveiled is the common human nature of women
and men. Space travel spiced by satiric repartee.
Winslow, Helen Maria (1851–1938). *Salome Shepard, Reformer.* Boston: Arena.
Coll. Wright 3.6027.
     In nineteenth-century New England, heiress and millowner Salome

Shepard instigates labor-management reform. She creates a model mill community replete with union-requested working conditions, as well as a residence hall with rooms for cultural activities. Marriage to her mill superintendent concludes the novel. Utopian romance.

1894

Knapp, Adeline (1860–1909). "One Thousand Dollars a Day: A Financial Experiment." In *One Thousand Dollars a Day: Studies in Economics*. Boston: Arena. Coll. Wright 3.3178.

Distributing income from the Golconda mines daily to those 18 years and over—"every man and every woman"—solves wealth inequity. But for the strategy to succeed, a San Francisco man innovates a labor exchange to provide needed services. Economic fantasy.

Waisbrooker, Lois Nichols (1826–1909). *A Sex Revolution*. Topeka, Kans.: Independent. Coll. History of Women, 4896.1. Reprint, edited by Pam McAllister, Philadelphia: New Society Publishers, 1985. Excerpted in *Daring to Dream: Utopian Stories by United States Women, 1836–1919*, compiled by Carol Farley Kessler, Boston: Pandora/Routledge and Kegan Paul, 1984.

Pacifist as well as feminist, the "sex" revolution occurs when women refuse to follow men's lead to war: Mother Love is the force empowering social amelioration. All occurs in one woman's dream vision.

1895

Stetson [Gilman], Charlotte Perkins (1860–1935). "A Cabinet Meeting." Studies in Style series. *Impress* (5 Jan.): 4–5.

A woman as President chairs a cabinet meeting of the Board of Administration of the United States of America as its member secretaries deliberate upon a plan stressing education as a central component of social progress. Imitation of Edward Bellamy. Reformist future politics.

Lease, Mrs. Mary Elizabeth (1853–1933). *The Problem of Civilization Solved*. Chicago: Laird and Lee.

Nonfiction exposition setting forth a government that observes Christian ethics. No mention of women's issues; racist and imperialist attitudes.

[Sherwood, Margaret Pollack (1864–1955)], Elizabeth Hastings (pseud.). *An Experiment in Altruism*. New York: Macmillan. Coll. Wright 3.4914.

A woman narrates an abstract tale of a group pursuing altruistic goals with slow progress yet perseverence. Spiritual alternative.

Von Swartwout, Janet (–   ). *Heads or the City of Gods: A Narrative of Olumbia in the Wilderness*. New York: Olumbia.

A group travels through the Adirondacks to enjoy the wilderness and to search for truth in their discussions of a "new order of builders" for the general good. Eutopia more discussed than established, though the group of four men and four women observe their own principles, insofar as eight people can constitute a society. Communitarian alternative.

1896

[Ames, Eleanor Maria Easterbrook (1830?–1908)], Eleanor Kirk (pseud.). *Libra: An Astrological Romance*. Brooklyn: E. Kirk.

The heroine Elizabeth "Libra" Eastman finds that her utopia is freedom, which for herself lies in refusing marriage. She believes marriage changes women into "whipped dogs," although a good friend still prefers marriage. Then-present USA sex-egalitarian romance.

Burnham, Elcy. *Modern Fairyland*. Boston: Arena.

The alleged reform of Fairyland merely duplicates nineteenth-century practices and technology: the author's present occurs as utopia. Though a woman is the instrument of change, she yields government to her spouse. Not feminist; juvenile.

1897

Graul, Rosa (–   ). *Hilda's Home: A Story of Woman's Emancipation*. Serialized in *Lucifer, The Light Bearer*, nos. 613–87 (June 1896–Dec. 1897). Published in book form, Chicago: M. Harman, 1899. Excerpted in *Daring to Dream: Utopian Stories by United States Women, 1836–1919*, compiled by Carol Farley Kessler, Boston: Pandora/Routledge and Kegan Paul, 1984.

In the United States of the 1890s, a woman's ideal and a man's fortune permit a group committed to "free love" to establish a cooperative home in the "west." The venture then expands to include the establishment of a cooperative business emporium in which all are partners, as well as the construction of a home for emporium partners. Communitarian romance.

Orpen, [Adela Elizabeth Rogers] (1855–   ). *Perfection City*. New York: Appleton.

Eastern settlers arrive in the commune of Perfection City, Kansas, a mere village founded by Mme. Morozoff-Smith and viewed by its residents as an "earthly paradise." The city disbands as villagers realize that not the ways of the world, but "the human heart needed reforming first of all." Communitarian romance.

1898

[Clarke, Frances H. (–   )], Zebina Forbush (pseud.). *The Co-opolitan; A Story of the Co-operative Commonwealth of Idaho*. Chicago: Kerr.

Between 1897 and 1917, a group solidly establishes Co-opolis in Idaho, an economic and political cooperative for women as well as men. An important figure is novelist Caroline Woodberry Braden, also wife and mother, whose success receives ample recognition. Communitarian romance.

Mason, Eveleen Laura [Knaggs] (1838–1914). *An Episode in the Doings of the Dualized*. Brookline, Mass.: E. L. Mason. Coll. Wright 3.3632.

This brief work, peopled by many *Hiero-Salem* characters, demonstrates the human potential of dualized (androgynous) people. Spiritual community.

1899

[Adolph, Mrs. Anna (–   )]. *Arqtiq: A Study of Marvels at the North Pole*. Hanford, Calif.: Author. Coll. Wright 3.30.

Narrator Anna, in a dream, travels to the North Pole where she experiences a society without birth, marriage, or death, where women rule equally with men, and education continues for life. Dream vision of exotic journey.

Morgan, Harriet (–   ). *The Island Impossible*. Boston: Little, Brown.

In a children's dream world, closer to a Robinsoniade than to eutopia proper, one remains a child, can travel great distances in little time, escape all evil, enjoy equality of the sexes—even superiority if one is female. Coming adulthood requires departure from the island. Juvenile fantasy.

1900

Mason, Caroline A[twater] (1853–1939). *A Woman of Yesterday*. New York: Doubleday. Coll. Wright 3.3631.

To escape a loveless marriage, heroine Anna Benigna Mallison joins a North Carolina egalitarian community Fraternia, where she resumes training interrupted by marriage and regains the direction of her own life. Finally she departs for India as a teacher. Communitarian romance.

Richberg, Eloise O. Randall (–   ). *Reinstern*. Cincinnati: Editor Publishing.

A woman's dream vision of train travel to an unknown planet reveals a society of loving, broadly educated individuals, where both sexes train for and participate in parenting, and where adult working responsibilities occur in conjunction with those for child rearing. Extraterrestrial vision.

1901

Corbin, Mrs. Caroline Elizabeth Fairfield (1835–   ). *The Position of Women in the Socialistic Utopia*. Chicago: American Association Opposed to Socialism.

Nonfiction essay. Wide-ranging denunciation of historical communitarianism and socialism in Europe and the United States as constituting a foe to Christianity, the purity of womanhood, and the authority of parents. Feminism seen to be allied to socialism.

Henley, Carra Dupuy (–   ). *A Man from Mars*. Los Angeles: B. R. Baumgardt.

Asylum resident Professor Darlington, interviewed by a stenographer, relates his visit to Mars after a head injury. Martians are highly developed cerebrally and enjoy apparent sex equality. Alternative vision.

1902

Cooley, Winnifred Harper (c.1876–after 1955). "A Dream of the Twenty-first Century." *Arena* 28 (Nov.): 511–16. Reprinted in *Daring to Dream: Utopian Stories by United States Women, 1836–1919,* compiled by Carol Farley Kessler, Boston: Pandora/Routledge and Kegan Paul, 1984.

By New Year's Day 2000, women will have obtained a just place in United States society, according to a woman's dream on New Year's Day 1900. Short story.

Hawkins, Mrs. May Anderson (–   ). *A Wee Lassie; or, A Unique Republic.* Richmond, Va: Presbyterian Committee of Publication.

In then-contemporary Alabama, inspired by the deathbed vision of an orphaned "Wee Lassie," hero Glenn Hildegarde establishes "a unique republic"—a home-school to provide poor boys with the opportunity to learn skills for self-support and thereby remove conditions that lead convicts to commit crimes. Two marriages between people successful in ameliorating social injustices conclude the plot. Social reform romance.

1903

Kinkaid, Mary Holland [McNeish] (1861–1948). *Walda; A Novel.* New York: Harper.

Prophetess Walda, beloved of the school master in Zanah—a religious colony located in a secluded United States valley—defies colony rules repressing sensuous and sensual expression by leaving for the love of a visiting stranger. Communitarian romance.

1904

Gilman, Charlotte Perkins [Stetson] (1860–1935). "The Beauty of a Block." *Independent* 57 (14 July): 67–72.

The last half of the essay explains "what we might do" to improve city blocks, namely plan apartment houses or hotels around courtyards providing recreation spaces, arrange roof playgrounds for children, and furnish common spaces to equal clubhouses in attractiveness. Nonfiction; New York City setting.

1905

Crow, Martha [Foote] (1854–1924). *The World Above, A Duologue.* Chicago: Blue Sky Press.

Traditional lovers search for a way out of their dank dystopian underground world via a pathway toward "the world above," presumably eutopian. Borderline, minor example, dramatic dialogue between two speakers.

Evans, Anna D. (–   ). *It Beats the Shakers, or a New Tune.* New York: Anglo American.

The novelette stresses the relation between the sexes as crucial to social improvement: marriages require shared rights and responsibilities between partners to realize the human possibility of "pure Eden on Earth." Lacks specifics. Dream vision.

Fry, Lena Jane (–   ). *Other Worlds: A Story Concerning the Wealth Earned by American Citizens and Showing How It Can Be Secured to Them Instead of to the Trusts.* Chicago: Author.

On the planet Herschel, the family Vivian provides a model for controlling the trusts so that industrious people may enjoy their own wealth. Both women and men participate in economic management. Families are central social units, but women enjoy greater independence than was true for 1905. Economic romance.

Rogers, Bessie Story (–   ). *As It May Be: A Story of the Future.* Boston: Gorham.

Mary Tillman, deceased in 1905, regains consciousness in 2905, a future society resembling the "perfect harmony" believed in 1905 to exist in heaven. The brief eutopia sketches a society where violence no longer occurs, and social supports permit women to live without excess housekeeping or home-caring burdens. Alternative vision.

1906

Gale, Zona (1874–1938). *Romance Island.* Indianapolis: Bobbs-Merrill.

A fanciful tale of dystopian intrigue and eutopian romance, its plot moves from New York City to an island southwest of the Azores, "a heavenly place." There, a submarine-wrecked father is recovered, and his daughter and her lover betrothed. Borderline eutopian romance.

Wheeler, Mary Sparkes (1835–1919). *As It Is in Heaven.* Philadelphia: Universal Book and Bible House.

Set against the turn-of-the-century USA, a woman writes an account of her arrival in heaven, experienced as a family utopia. Racist, ethnocentric.

1907

Gilman, Charlotte Perkins [Stetson] (1860–1935). "A Woman's Utopia" [chaps. 1–4]. *The Times Magazine* 1 (Jan.–Mar.): 215–20, 369–76, 498–504. Page proofs for April are located in the Arthur and Elizabeth Schlesinger Library on the History of Women in America, Radcliffe College, Collection 177, Charlotte Perkins Gilman Papers (1860–1935): box 21, folder 260—chap.

4 "Some Beginnings" [published tearsheets] and chap. 5 "City Living" [proofs].

This partially published fragment anticipates Gilman's later eutopia (1911) in its vision of changed lives for women—better education, "voting mothers," specialized housekeeping, remunerative work, integration of children into adult living. It also reveals her racism and elitism. Near-future (20 years hence) eutopia, USA.

1908

Gilman, Charlotte Perkins [Stetson] (1860–1935). "Aunt Mary's Pie Plant." *The Woman's Home Companion* 6 (June): 14, 48–49. Reprinted in *Charlotte Perkins Gilman: Her Progress Toward Utopia,* Carol Farley Kessler, Syracuse: Syracuse Univ. Press, 1995.

The women of New Newton have all established businesses offering various household services; thus are they individually richer and their town collectively more prosperous—"this prancing young Utopia." Then-contemporary USA; social reform, eutopian realism.

Martin, Nettie Parrish (–   ). *A Pilgrim's Progress in Other Worlds; Recounting the Wonderful Adventures of Ulysum Storries and His Discovery of the Lost Star "Eden."* Boston: Mayhew.

Balloonist/sky cyclist Ulysum Storries progresses from one perfect planetary world to another, each exhibiting a different arrangement between the sexes, blends of innovation and conservatism. As Ulysum never admits to having a wife on Earth, he attracts women as guides, each querying him about Earth so as to reveal their own more equitable condition for women. Space travel.

1909

Gilman, Charlotte Perkins [Stetson] (1860–1935). "A Garden of Babies." *Success* 12 (June): 370–71, 410–11. Reprinted in *Charlotte Perkins Gilman: Her Progress Toward Utopia,* Carol Farley Kessler, Syracuse: Syracuse Univ. Press, 1995.

Adults work together to establish a baby garden for the health and welfare of mothers and children. The story demonstrates men participating in the changed behavior necessary for women's lives to expand. Then-contemporary USA; social reform, eutopian realism.

Wiggin, Kate Douglas [Smith] (1856–1923). *Susanna and Sue.* Boston: Houghton, Mifflin.

A mother Susanna, with her daughter Sue, escapes a drunken, philandering husband by entering the Shaker community of Albion, Maine, where she finds temporary relief as she defines her personal needs. A change in her husband convinces Susanna to leave and reunite her family. Wiggin stresses people's needs for differing living alternatives. Juvenile communitarian romance.

1910

Gilman, Charlotte Perkins [Stetson] (1860–1935). "Her Housekeeper." *The Forerunner* 1, no. 4 (Jan.): 2–8. Reprinted in *Charlotte Perkins Gilman: Her Progress Toward Utopia,* Carol Farley Kessler, Syracuse: Syracuse Univ. Press, 1995.

Mrs. Leland—actress, "widow," mother of a five-year-old son—lives on the top floor of a boarding house, her meals brought up in a dumbwaiter. The house is kept by Arthur Olmstead, who loves her and refutes each of her objections to marriage—"previous" unhappy marriage, a son, a profession, a desire for her freedom and her lovers, her dislike of housekeeping. Olmstead notes that she never had married and that her experience has, in fact, taught her what she does want in a husband. Marital utopia.

Gilman, Charlotte Perkins [Stetson] (1860–1935). "Martha's Mother." *The Forerunner* 1, no. 6 (April): 1–6.

Martha's mother comes to New York City to run a boarding house for young women. Her daughter Martha Joyce is stenographer and typist in a real estate office. The boarding house thus provides good lodging and food, plus a mother to keep off men she doesn't want to see as well as a place to have fun with those she enjoys. Only women board, but men, too, are "mealers." Domestic cooperation.

Gilman, Charlotte Perkins [Stetson] (1860–1935). *What Diantha Did.* Serialized in *The Forerunner* 1 (Nov. 1909–Oct. 1910). Published in book form, New York: Charlton, 1910. Excerpted in *Charlotte Perkins Gilman Reader,* edited by Ann J. Lane, New York: Pantheon, 1980; *Charlotte Perkins Gilman: Her Progress Toward Utopia,* Carol Farley Kessler, Syracuse: Syracuse Univ. Press, 1995.

Diantha Bell demonstrates how a cooked food delivery service and cafeteria can through cooperative effort relieve women of individual domestic drudgery. The novel belongs in the tradition of early nineteenth-century Owenite socialism—part of a "grand domestic revolution" of late nineteenth-century United States "material feminists." Social reform, eutopian romance.

1911

Gilman, Charlotte Perkins [Stetson] (1860–1935). *Moving the Mountain.* Serialized in *The Forerunner* 2. Published in book form, New York: Charlton, 1911. Reprint, Westport, Conn.: Greenwood, 1968. Excerpted in *Charlotte Perkins Gilman Reader,* edited by Ann J. Lane, New York: Pantheon, 1980; *Charlotte Perkins Gilman: Her Progress Toward Utopia,* Carol Farley Kessler, Syracuse: Syracuse Univ. Press, 1995.

A male narrator lost for thirty years returns to the United States of

1940 to find women filling positions formerly allotted only to men. Futuristic romance.

1912

Gilman, Charlotte Perkins [Stetson] (1860–1935). "Her Memories." *The Forerunner* 3, no. 8 (Aug.): 197–201. Reprinted in *Charlotte Perkins Gilman: Her Progress Toward Utopia,* Carol Farley Kessler, Syracuse: Syracuse Univ. Press, 1995.

A nameless male narrator recounts his female companion's memories of Home Court as they drift down the Hudson River. This utopian community included child-care and baby culture in rooftop playgrounds; amenities for other age groups also exist.

Gilman, Charlotte Perkins [Stetson] (1860–1935). "Maidstone Comfort." *The Forerunner* 3, no. 9 (Sept.): 225–29. Reprinted in *Charlotte Perkins Gilman: Her Progress Toward Utopia,* Carol Farley Kessler, Syracuse: Syracuse Univ. Press, 1995.

Maidstone Comfort is utopia as a summer resort community, featuring kitchenless cottages. The female narrator is a friend of Sarah Maidstone Pellett, manager-owner, and Mrs. Benigna McAvelly, the funding-finder who connected Molly Bellow's inheritance with Sarah of Maidstone Comfort.

Gilman, Charlotte Perkins [Stetson] (1860–1935). "A Strange Land." *The Forerunner* 3, no. 8 (Aug.): 207–8. Reprinted in *Charlotte Perkins Gilman: Her Progress Toward Utopia,* Carol Farley Kessler, Syracuse: Syracuse Univ. Press, 1995.

This briefly sketches a land "strange" for having as its social goal the desire to make people more perfect.

1913

Gilman, Charlotte Perkins [Stetson] (1860–1935). "Bee Wise." *The Forerunner* 4, no. 7 (July): 169–73. Reprinted in *Charlotte Perkins Gilman: Her Progress Toward Utopia,* Carol Farley Kessler, Syracuse: Syracuse Univ. Press, 1995.

Beewise and Herways are established in California by a group of college women, who decide to show what can be done to improve society. One of them has inherited $10 million: the group forms a combination to make a little Eden.

Gilman, Charlotte Perkins [Stetson] (1860–1935). "A Council of War." *The Forerunner* 4, no. 8 (Aug.): 197–201. Reprinted in *Charlotte Perkins Gilman: Her Progress Toward Utopia,* Carol Farley Kessler, Syracuse: Syracuse Univ. Press, 1995.

London women plan "to establish a free and conscious womanhood for the right service of the world." They plan a government within a government, an organization of women, an Extension Committee, a Co-operative

Society. They will employ "women only" or the "right sort" of man. They give each other new hope.

Gilman, Charlotte Perkins [Stetson] (1860–1935). "Forsythe and Forsythe." *The Forerunner* 4, no. 1 (Jan.): 1–5. Reprinted in *Charlotte Perkins Gilman: Her Progress Toward Utopia,* Carol Farley Kessler, Syracuse: Syracuse Univ. Press, 1995.

Husband-wife law partners, George and cousin Georgiana, are found in northern Washington by Jimmy-Jack [Mr. James R.] Jackson, George's former best friend. Jimmy-Jack's wife Susie, a self-centered pleasure-seeker, divorces him. He's then free to ally himself with George's sister Clare Forsythe, his first love, now a sanitary engineer. All live in the same residence hotel. Marital utopia.

Gilman, Charlotte Perkins [Stetson] (1860–1935). "Mrs. Hines' Money." *The Forerunner* 4, no. 4 (Apr.): 85–89. Reprinted in *Charlotte Perkins Gilman: Her Progress Toward Utopia,* Carol Farley Kessler, Syracuse: Syracuse Univ. Press, 1995.

Eva Hines, widowed as result of an accident, retains her own counsel (not her brother) for advice and gains information from travel. She uses her husband Jason's money to build in his memory The Hines Building, but according to her own notions of social service—a utopian scheme to raise the consciousness and knowledge of her town by housing therein a library, auditorium/theatre, men's and women's lounges, swimming pool and gym, roof tea-garden, and club meeting rooms. Social critical story, then-current USA.

1914

Gillmore [Irwin], Inez [Leonore] Haynes (1873–1970). *Angel Islan.!.* New York: Phillips. Reprint, New York: H. Holt; New York: New American Library, 1988.

Set on a remote Pacific island, five shipwrecked men representing an array of male types find themselves without women until five winged women approach. Eventually they pair off and children are born. Men want to forbid women to fly, but women threaten to desert. Prefigures *Herland* but is conceptually simpler, though gender issues are likewise central. Eutopian fantasy.

1915

Gilman, Charlotte Perkins [Stetson] (1860–1935). *Herland. The Forerunner* 6. Reprint, New York: Pantheon, 1979. Excerpted in *Charlotte Perkins Gilman Reader,* edited by Ann J. Lane, New York: Pantheon, 1980. Reprint, *Herland and Selected Stories by Charlotte Perkins Gilman,* edited by Barbara H. Solomon, New York: New American Library, 1992. Excerpts [chap. 5] in *Charlotte Perkins Gilman: Her Progress Toward Utopia,* Carol Farley Kessler, Syracuse: Syracuse Univ. Press, 1995.

Discovered by three adventurous United States men, remote Herland, an all-female society, makes Motherhood its highest office. Many invidious —as well as humorous—comparisons emerge as the adventurers receive education about Herland. Amazonian society.

1916

Albertson, Augusta (–   ). *Through Gates of Pearl: A Vision of the Heaven-Life*. New York: Fleming H. Revell.

An earthly pilgrim recounts her dream-vision of a heavenly eutopia of jewelled streets and gates, where angelic guides conduct pilgrims on tours. Influenced by Augustine's dream of a City of God.

Fisher, Mary Ann (1839–   ). *Among the Immortals: In the Land of Desire*. New York: Shakespeare Press.

A gossipy, ethnocentric, spirit afterworld set about 1916. Women less inferior, but class hierarchy remains. Marriage differently defined. Ambivalent view of women. Spiritual fantasy.

Gilman, Charlotte Perkins [Stetson] (1860–1935). *With Her in Ourland. The Forerunner* 7. Reprint, Westport, Conn.: Greenwood, 1968. Excerpted in *Charlotte Perkins Gilman Reader,* Ann J. Lane, New York: Pantheon, 1980; chap. 11 in *Charlotte Perkins Gilman: Her Progress Toward Utopia,* Carol Farley Kessler, Syracuse: Syracuse Univ. Press, 1995.

A Herlander woman tours our world just after World War I erupts. The contrasts between our ways and hers astonish her into satiric commentary. Blend of satiric dialogue-travelogue from viewpoint of visitor from eutopia.

Jones, Lillian B. (–   ). *Five Generations Hence*. Fort Worth, Tex.: Dotson-Jones.

Grace Noble, "high brown" daughter of an ex-slave, teaches and writes while her close friend Violet Gray becomes an African missionary. Grace later marries a physician and raises children. Each achieves her "dream of life" and the improvement of her race. Alternative future.

Shapiro, Anna Ratner (–   ). *The Birth of Universal Brotherhood*. Kansas City: Burton.

Just after World War I, a new political party—the Assembly of Peace —develops. Relationships between women and men become egalitarian with four marriages occurring. Worldwide service to humanity is life's goal. Then-immediate future United States, eutopian romance.

1917

[Snedeker, Caroline Dale Parke (1871–1956)], Caroline Dale Owen (pseud.). *Seth Way: A Romance of the New Harmony Community*. Boston: Houghton, Mifflin. Excerpted in *Daring to Dream: Utopian Stories by United States Women, 1836–1919,* edited by Carol Farley Kessler, Boston: Pandora/ Routledge and Kegan Paul, 1984.

An historical romance of Robert Owen's New Harmony, the novel shows the community faltering, but relations between man and woman are established by an egalitarian contract. Historical romance.

1918

[Bennett, Gertrude Barrows (1884–?1939)], Francis Stevens (pseud.). "Friend Island." *All-Story Weekly,* September 7. Reprint, *Under the Moons of Mars,* edited by Sam Moskowitz, New York: Holt Rinehart Winston, 1970.

Retired sea-captain, questioned by young man, recounts her shipwreck on Friend Island, a sentient, hospitable Pacific Island with a heart and a name, Anita. Feminist sex-role reversal. Short story.

1919

[Bennett, Gertrude Barrows (1884–?1939)], Francis Stevens (pseud.). *The Heads of Cerberus.* N.p.: Street and Smith, 1919. Reprint, Philadelphia: Polaris Press, 1952.

Dystopian future of international scope, with overtones of espionage. Traditional gender roles. Time/space travel. Borderline.

Bruère, Martha [S.] Bensley (1879–1953). *Mildred Carver, U.S.A.* Serialized in *The Ladies' Home Journal,* 35–36 (June 1918–Feb. 1919). Reprint, New York: Macmillan. Excerpted in *Daring to Dream: Utopian Stories by United States Women, 1836–1919,* edited by Carol Farley Kessler, Boston: Pandora/ Routledge and Kegan Paul, 1984.

In post–World War I United States, a Universal Service in public-works enlists women and men for one year with regard not to gender, but to interest and aptitude. Work becomes as crucial for a woman as marriage for a man: each needs both. Alternative future.

1920–1959

1920

Gilman, Charlotte Perkins [Stetson] (1860–1935). "Applepieville." *Independent* 103:365, 393–95 (25 Sep.).

Applepieville depicts an improved rural town, congenial to social activities, with farms radiating from a community center like the wedges of a pie. Essay.

Johnston, Mary Ann (1870–1936). *Sweet Rocket.* New York: Harper.

The Sweet Rocket Road leads school teacher Anna Darcy into Virginia woods hundreds of thousands of miles away: her mind becomes the vehicle for space/time travel. Her visit with former student Marget Land refreshes by showing new selves being born as consciousness widens in an encouraging environment. Alternative vision.

1922

Kayser, Martha Cabanné (–   ). *The Aerial Flight to the Realm of Peace*. St. Louis: Lincoln Press.

An unidentified narrator records a balloon flight to a dream world where all are healthy, happy, and loving. Education is central. Abstract, not feminist. Dream vision.

Scrymsour, Ella M. (1888–   ). *The Perfect World; A Romance of Strange People and Strange Places*. New York: Stokes.

A strange, underground, Earth-dystopia: an earthquake destroys the dystopia just after characters launch a trip to Jupiter, a Utopia where only men work and women must wait to be asked in marriage. Sexist. Postcatastrophe romance.

1923

[Thompson, Harriet Alfarata Chapman (–1922)]. *Idealia; A Utopia Dream; or Resthaven*. Albany, N.Y.: Lyon.

A woman visits a community—for the elderly, the orphaned, the invalid—modeled after a resort. Its male director explains special features—wheeltables, parlorettes, and social activities. Communitarian alternative present.

1924

Cleghorn, Sarah N[orcliffe] (1876–1959). "Utopia Interpreted." *The Atlantic Monthly* 134:56–67, 216–24.

Four varied interpretations explain the evolutionary causes for the existence by 1995 of a eutopian Family Order of society and of the Discipline of Happiness: control of natural energy; social ills shared by concerned women; unequal ownership abolished; nomadry as "open pasture for human spirit." Brief alternative future.

Pettersen, Rena Oldfield (–   ). *Venus*. Philadelphia: Dorrance.

Two women from Utopian Venus land near Chicago to educate a young woman in phases of past existences. Love is the universal utopian condition and mating between women and men, its highest expression, is initiated by women. Spiritual romance.

1925

Dell, Berenice V.(–   ). *The Silent Voice*. Boston: Four Seas.

After an unnatural postcatastrophe interim of women's rule, women return to their natural place at home and fulfill their duty to bear Aryan children. Women have greater control in marital relationships, but the state represses the individual. Paradise is ideal sexual union. The "silent voice" in each is an understanding of real liberty, of the true America. Futuristic romance.

1928

Gazella, Edith Virginia (–   ). *The Blessing of Azar, A Tale of Dreams and Truth*. Boston: Christopher.

Azar, a commercial magnate, establishes and finances a community called The Friends, founded upon equitable commerce. Azar sees the sexes as two halves of a perfect whole, in which each sex enjoys liberty comparable to the other: a male, or head of the state, oversees legislative functions; a female, or body of the state, guides the masses. Communitarian romance.

Gilman, Charlotte Perkins [Stetson] (1860–1935). "A Proclamation of Interdependence," one-page typescript [September 1928]. The Arthur and Elizabeth Schlesinger Library on the History of Women in America, Radcliffe College, collection 177, Charlotte Perkins Gilman Papers (1860–1935): box 9, folder 184.

Five reasons are enumerated to justify a call for a conference of all the nations of the earth to draw up a Federated Union of the World.

1929

Irving, Minna. "The Moon Woman: A Tale of the Future." *Amazing Stories* 4, no. 8: 746–54.

Professor J. H. Hicks believes he has discovered a serum causing "suspended animation," or apparent temporary death. Finding no human experimental subjects, he arranges a test upon himself. What results is a dream vision of 3014, an only vaguely-delineated future USA in which marital love triumphs. Eutopian sketch.

Snedeker, Caroline Dale Parke (1871–1956). *The Beckoning Road*. New York: Junior Literary Guild.

An historical romance of the Harmonists and the failure of their community, this juvenile work stresses Pestalozzi pedagogy and the triumph of young love. Juvenile utopia.

[Wright, Mary Maude Dunn (1894–1967)] Lilith Lorraine (pseud.). *The Brain of the Planet*. "Science Fiction Series No. 5. New York: Stellar.

A male scientist's 1935 experiments on thought transference lead through global communication to the advent of a Marxist socialist world by 1970. Androcentric future fantasy; authoritarian, centrist. Short story.

1930

[Wright, Mary Maude Dunn (1894–1967)] Lilith Lorraine (pseud.). "Into the 28th Century." *Science Wonder Quarterly* 1, no. 2: 250–67, 276.

On a May 1932 visit to his home in Corpus Christi, Texas, Antony finds himself lurched into the 28th century. From four rainbow-haired young people (with one of whom he falls in love), he learns about the history of Nirvania, the new one-government world, health practices, education for human potential, and sex egalitarianism. But he has had a dream caused by a "time powder." Eutopian future USA.

Vassos, Ruth (–). *Ultimo: An Imaginative Narration of Life Under the Earth*. New York: Dutton.

Brief, abstract utopia, reported by male narrator as he is about to depart the stiflingly perfect society existing inside the earth after temperatures on the surface fell too low to sustain life. Little on women (the word never occurs), save indication of "birth-permission cards," but otherwise free cohabitation. Space travel.

1931

[Kirk, Mrs. Ellen Warner Olney (1842–1928)] A Daughter of Eve (pseud.). *A Woman's Utopia*. London: Ernest Benn.

Given from a first-person viewpoint, this satiric utopia directly corrects aspects of contemporary England: for instance, Parliament retains two Houses—"the moribund Lords" now replaced by women, the Commons continuing to be men only. Nonfictional, tongue-in-cheek expository description.

1932

Martin, Prestonia Mann (1861–1945). *Prohibiting Poverty: Suggestions for a Method of Obtaining Economic Security*. New York: Farrar and Rinehart.

Assuming that making a living is society's goal, then a national livelihood plan to organize youth of both sexes between ages 18 and 26 to industrial production could provide to the population all needed goods without buying or selling. Satiric critique of masculine finance. Economic reform tract.

1935

Spotswood [Owens/Wanders], Claire Myers (1896–1983). *The Unpredictable Adventure: A Comedy of Women's Independence*. New York: Doubleday. Reprint, edited by Miriam Kalman Harris, Syracuse: Syracuse Univ. Press, 1993.

Set in the land of Err, a satire about woman's independence includes a eutopia of the New Chimera, where love rules freely. Women's independence is satirized, yet demonstrated in this comic adventure. Picaresque satire.

1937

Sterne, Emma Gelders (1894–). *Some Plant Olive Trees*. New York: Dodd, Mead.

An historical romance of Napoleonic refugees' Vine and Olive colony in Demopolis, Alabama, the novel depicts failed ideals. The focus upon the relation between a colony founder and his wife includes her critique of his treatment of her and hence attention to women's position in utopia.

1938

DeForest, Eleanor (–   ). *Armageddon; A Tale of the Antichrist*. Grand Rapids, Mich.: Eerdmans.

In an anti-Semitic and antifeminist dystopia set in California and Palestine, twin sisters compete for love and survival during the years of intrigue preceding the arrival of a Christian millennium after a bloody "armageddon." Future fantasy.

Morris, Martha Marlowe (1867–   ) and Laura B. Speer (–   ). *No Borderland*. Dallas: Mathis, Van Nort.

The borders exist between lives, times, and states in this exotic adventure, where past prefigures future as two male archeologists explore. Spiritual alternative.

Rand, Ayn (1905–1982). *Anthem*. London: Cassell. Rev. ed., Los Angeles: Pamphleteers, 1946.

A male narrator envisions an extreme individualism as a positive alternative to a state-controlled community. Anti-feminist. Anti-socialist eutopia.

1943

Dardanelle, Louise (–   ). *World Without Raiment, A Fantasy*. New York: Valiant.

After all man-made goods have disintegrated from a climactic increase in temperature, a nudist colony spreads from California throughout the United States. People appreciate a natural world without the products of technology and become healthy, loving individuals. Both sexes enjoy freely given, nonexclusive love. Futuristic romance.

1945

McElhiney, Gaile Churchill (–   ). *Into the Dawn*. Los Angeles: Del Vorse.

Jeanne Wallace, aviator, is downed on the Pacific Island of Heaven. She acquires "astral" powers enabling her to communicate with parents and the man she loves. A goal of loving contribution to the world's welfare, reunited with her lover, will guide Jeanne's future. Spiritual fantasy.

1949

McCarthy, Mary [Therese] (1912–1989). *The Oasis*. New York: Random House.

A vacation colony as ideal community disintegrates. Satiric treatment explodes utopian hopes and particularly bares marital discord. Communitarian satire.

Short, Gertrude (1902–1968). *A Visitor from Venus*. New York: William Frederick.

   Accustomed to all-female Venusian society, a visitor reports her dismay at Earth's sex-unfair arrangements. Satiric. Extraterrestrial all-female alternative.

Sutton, Paralee Sweeten (–   ). *White City: A Novel*. Palo Alto, Calif.: Palopress.

   Aviators lost over Antarctica find a eutopian White City where the white light of understanding has raised all to greater levels of teamwork, equality, and achievement. Gender roles unclear, though male visitor predominates; father and daughter reunited. Futuristic romance.

1950

Barber, Elsie Marion Oakes (1914–   ). *Hunt for Heaven*. New York: Macmillan.

   Pastor John Bliss begins his "hunt for heaven" after the 1886 Haymarket riot and trains his daughter Rebecca to carry on the principles establishing his Christian Colony. It fails because the kingdom of heaven can be founded only within a given individual. Rebecca abandoned such principle for passion. Historical romance.

1952

Barnhouse, Perl T. (–   ). *My Journeys with Astargo; a Tale of Past, Present, and Future*. Denver: Bell.

   Young men from Colorado in the spaceship Astargo travel among planets and discover a utopia on Perfecto (described in three of 57 chapters), where conditions improve through each passing year. Vague; not feminist. Space travel.

1955

Brackett, Leigh [Douglass] (1915–1978). *The Long Tomorrow*. Garden City, N.Y.: Doubleday.

   An ambivalent consideration of technology with its power to destroy or ameliorate. A technological social remnant exists within a twenty-first century agrarian society akin to New Mennonites of the "past." Two adolescent youths find the technological past of the twentieth-century mainstream. Futuristic romance.

1956

[Meek, Doris (1912–   ) and Adrienne Jones (1915–   )]. Gregory Mason (pseud.). *The Golden Archer. A Satirical Novel of 1975*. New York: Twayne.

A satiric anarchy within a rule-bound theocracy, set on a Connecticut island in Long Island Sound in 1975, the "Sane Asylum"—the octagonal Archer family residence—exhibits some anarchic values shared by recent feminist utopias. Family utopia.

1957

Maddux, Rachel (1912–   ). *The Green Kingdom*. New York: Simon and Schuster.

The Green Kingdom is a condition of realizing potential, whether creative or affective. Men fare better than women. But the dream contains its antithesis as well—isolation, violence, death. Spiritual romance.

Moore [Kuttner], C[atherine] L[ucile] (1911–   ). *Doomsday Morning*. Garden City, N.Y.: Doubleday.

About 2000, an antigovernment network based in California succeeds in toppling a dictatorship, whose strategy was to use theater-in-the-round as a cover for gathering information about the rebels. Future dystopia based upon absolute control of communication; eutopian grassroots network overpowers control.

Norris, Kathleen [Thompson] (1880–1966). *Through a Glass Darkly*. Garden City, N.Y.: Doubleday.

Characters move from one world to another, from eutopian afterworld back to present dystopian world to alleviate ills. Heroine works to help children; concludes with her marriage. Spiritual romance.

Rand, Ayn (1905–1982). *Atlas Shrugged*. New York: Random House.

Against a panorama of United States business and industrial corruption, a small group of the best minds—predominantly male—gathers to await a future moment when they can return from their Colorado mountain hideout to establish morality, intelligence, and individuality. A female hero Dagny Taggart figures prominently as an executive responsible for transcontinental railroad operations. Her three successive lovers parallel stages in her changing understanding of her own motivations and goals. Economic, antisocialist eutopia.

St. Clair, Margaret (1911–   ). *The Green Queen*. New York: Ace.

With eutopia lurking at its edges, dystopian planet Viridis oozes intrigue. Sexist. Extraterrestrial adventure.

1960–1988

1961

Henderson, Zenna [Chlarson] (1917–   ). *Pilgrimage: The Book of the People*. New York: Doubleday. Reprint, New York: Avon, 1961. Sequel, *The People: No Different Flesh*. New York: Doubleday, 1967.

Episodic, each narrative increases a reader's comprehension of the People of the Group, who emigrated from the planet Home. People can levitate, mind-read, and mind-heal. Having a strong oral tradition, an Assembling of People for recalling the past is the occasion for each episode as one Group member shares a personal experience significant for Group self-identity. Spiritual travel.

1962

Leslee, Jo (–). *It Shall Be Conquered*. Boston: Christopher.
    Present-day interplanetary voyage to unknown planet Maresdon in spaceship captained by a woman. Seven earthlings visit its eutopian society, only vaguely specified, which stresses mental development and exhibits sex equality. Extraterrestrial alternative.
Smith, Evelyn E. (1927–). *The Perfect Planet*. New York: Avalon.
    On Artemis, an all-female society is devoted to physical culture in a satire on concerns about health and beauty. Not feminist, sex-biased, humorous. Extraterrestrial satire.

1963

Roberts [Butts], Jane (1929–1984). *The Rebellers*. New York: Ace.
    In the United States of the twenty-third century, a nightmare "contropolis" of starving human beings exists. Bubonic plague erupts and controls this overpopulation. Cooperation among former antagonists marks a beginning—to live "as part of nature, not apart from nature." Mostly male characters. Future dystopia.

1964

Hotson, Cornelia Hinkley (–). *The Shining East: A Story of Life After Death*. New York: Vantage, 1964 [wr. 1936–50].
    Based upon Swedenborg's "Memorable Relation," the novelette depicts a heaven where people may do what they want, where people cannot be made to act against their own will—whether for good or ill. The heavenly eutopia is a state of mind.
Lawrence, Josephine (1890?–1978). *Not a Cloud in the Sky*. New York: Harcourt.
    A dystopian Tranquil Acres, populated by "our aged" instead of producing satisfied elderly, leads to the formation of a eutopian "rambunctious retired," who win their campaign for irregularity. Not feminist; satiric. Alternative future.

1965

Vale, Rena [Marie] (–). *Beyond the Sealed World*. New York: Paperback Library.

After the Great Destruction, the glasteel civilization run by the Masters of Science arose, in which all is perfectly ordered; those with atavistic endocrine systems are reduced in ovens or banished to the wasteland. Although Daly Ouverture succeeds at great cost in opening the gates between civilization and wasteland, he and his son still look forward to Incaland where science and nature, beauty and health coexist. Ambiguous.

1966

Le Guin, Ursula K[roeber] (1929–   ). *Planet of Exile*. New York: Ace.
    After being stranded for six centuries on Eltanin, human Exiles from Earth learn to work with native Men against a common enemy, the Gaals. Love between a member of each group—native Rolery and Exile Agat—precipitates this cooperation, which permits the transcendence of perceived group differences. Ambiguously utopian; illustrates a process for becoming more utopian.

1967

Le Guin, Ursula K[roeber] (1929–   ). *City of Illusions*. New York: Ace.
    To a future Earth devastated by civil war, Falk-Ramarran—a Colonist from planet Werel—returns to gather information. He finds a divided, dystopian Earth controlled by the "Shing," masters of the lie. Achieving a dual personality permits him to see through illusions foisted upon him. Dystopian future Earth, tempered by individual utopian possibility.

1968

Mannes, Marya (1904–   ). *They*. Garden City, New York: Doubleday.
    A near-future eutopia in which those born before 1925 are segregated from the rest of society—effectively eradicating memory of past individuality. "They"—youthful barbarians, in the view of the exiled five main characters—have violently communized society. Individualistic eutopia of "us."

1969

Carroll, Gladys Hasty (1904–   ). *Man on the Mountain*. Boston: Little, Brown.
    In twenty-first century Great Country, inhabitants are divided among four States according to their ages. Through separation all have become lonely for and suspicious of each other. Explorations of the youngest evoking concern from the eldest will permit reconciliation. Not feminist. Alternative future.
Le Guin, Ursula K[roeber] (1929–   ). *The Left Hand of Darkness*. New York: Walker; 25th Anniv. ed., 1995. Reprint, New York: Ace.
    On the planet Gethen in the distant future, as a visitor from Ekumen,

Genly Ai arrives to accomplish a trade alliance. The unusual feature of Gethens is their ambisexuality, the novel being an early science fiction attempt at imagining alternative gender roles. Extraterrestrial futuristic fantasy; gender experiments.

Lightner [Hopf], Alice M. (1904–   ). *The Day of the Drones*. New York: Norton.

In the future country of Afria, a young black woman, Am Lara, prepares to become its future head. Blacks discover white survivors of nuclear disaster. Future peace requires new civilization integrating whites with blacks. Postcatastrophe alternative future.

1970

Piercy, Marge (1936–   ). *Dance the Eagle to Sleep*. Garden City, N.Y.: Doubleday. Reprint, New York: Fawcett, 1971.

Franklin High School students led by Amer-Indian Corey revolt. Objecting to an insensitive administration, they band together and eventually set up an alternative rural community. Although not feminist, young women begin to recognize gender-role confinement. Communitarian utopia.

Russ, Joanna (1937–   ). *And Chaos Died*. New York: Ace. Reprint, Boston: Gregg/G. K. Hall, 1978.

Several centuries into the future on another planet, a male visitor guided by a female mentor learns that a select group of Earth people have developed ESP. Bisexuality is also common in the Edenic landscape. A dystopian future Earth provides background contrast. Extraterrestrial futuristic fantasy.

Vale, Rena [Marie] (1898–   ). *Taurus Four*. New York: Paperback Library.

In the twenty-third century on planet Taurus Four, Dorian Frank finds himself among a Flower Culture developed from kidnapped hippies, who in their emphasis upon moral and spiritual values win his allegiance. He takes a bride and plans to get help to prevent the planet's colonization by Saurians. Eutopia.

Vale, Rena M[arie] (1898–   ). *The Day After Doomsday. A Fantasy of Time Travel*. New York: Paperback Library.

In an alternative near-future, after a nuclear disaster caused by Sino-American differences, a kidnapped select group, returned to an earlier doomsday, must rebuild a cooperative, egalitarian, life-conserving society.

1971

Alexander, Thea [Plym] (–   ). *2150 A.D.* Tempe, Ariz.: Macro Books.

A Macro Society set in 2150 A.D. and based upon expanded awareness of self and others helps individuals develop capacities only imagined in 1976—for example, telepathy, psychokinesis, and levitation. The novel's chapters alternate between the journal of Jon Lake—left to his friend Karl Johnson, in which Jon records his dream projections into 2150—and the discussions between Jon and Karl about those "dreams." Futuristic romance.

Bryant, Dorothy [M. Calvetti Ungaretti] (1930–   ). *The Comforter.* San Francisco: D. M. Bryant. Reprint, *The Kin of Ata are Waiting for You,* Berkeley: Moon/Random, 1976.

Ata is an alternative world available to whoever chooses to dream of it. It is a world of the spirit, where visions of the moment reveal one's being. Its ideal member is a comforter, who nurtures or heals. Ata symbolizes human possibility through a fantasy world at once communal, pastoral, and feminist. Alternative vision.

Elgin, Suzette Haden (1936–   ). *The Communipaths.* New York: Ace; *Furthest,* Ace, 1971; *At the Seventh Level,* New York: Daw, 1972. Reprint, *Communipath Worlds: Three Complete Novels,* New York: Pocket, 1980.

A eutopian novella, plus two sequels, follows the missions of intelligence agent Coyote Jones on three planets with different societies: heroines in each case demonstrate unusual abilities. One communal eutopia and two dystopias reveal both a feminist social critique of war and sexism, and a feminist vision of human growth and potential. Space travel.

Wetherell, June Pat (–   ). *Blueprint for Yesterday.* New York: Walker.

From 2032 A.D., a heroine searches for her grandfather's secrets with the help of a legacy from her grandmother. Successful, she escapes the United States with her male friend to underground activist Red Rebels headquarters in Delos. Alternative future.

1972

Farca, Marie C. (1935–   ). *Earth.* Garden City, N.Y.: Doubleday. Dystopian sequel: *Complex Man,* Doubleday, 1973.

On a future EARTH—ours or another—a pastoral society lives in self-sufficient ecological balance. A visitor from Earth (possibly our own, as a future dystopian technocracy) arrives to explore, takes away three clones, and also leaves three clones behind. (A sequel permits all six clones to meet on EARTH.) Extraterrestrial futuristic fantasy.

Le Guin, Ursula K[roeber] (1929–   ). *The Word for World Is Forest* in *Again, Dangerous Visions,* edited by Harlan Ellison, Garden City, N.Y.: Doubleday. Reprint, New York: Putnam; New York: Berkley, 1976.

On Altshe called a "paradise planet" where a matriarchy still manages a pastoral, ecologically balanced existence, an invasion of Men destroys and forever changes the society by the introduction of killing; particularly the female Altsheans are Men's targets. Extraterrestrial invasion.

Putney, Susan K. (–   ). *Against Arcturus: A Battleground for Two Empires.* New York: Ace.

On planet Berbidron, Earth children arrive to find a society of immortals—the imaginatively playful aliens, the Sabr—inhabiting a very rich planet. Because humans are the source of a fatal virus, Arcturian humans are expelled from Berbidron, and the heroine-spy, sent by the Earth-New Eden Alliance, gives up return to human society as she gains life forever with the Sabr. Eutopia against dystopia.

1973

[Arnold, June (1926–1982)]. *The Cook & The Carpenter: A Novel by the Carpenter.* Plainfield, Vt.: Daughters, Inc.

Thirteen women and their children live as an intentional community in Texas, with the aim of establishing a school/center to provide alternative health services. Members join and leave the group; differences develop and dissolve; all develop capacity for change. Alternative present; feminist.

Ricci, Barbara Giugnon (–   ). *The Year of the Rats.* New York: Walker.

From 2025–2033, United—the domed capital of future dystopian, technocratic USA—disintegrates as "rats," the savage humans outside, press for food while privileged insiders develop a lethal virus to kill "rats." An accidental epidemic kills insiders save several thousand who exit to Easter Island where an equal number of Russians arrive; together they cooperatively found a new society.

1974

Le Guin, Ursula K[roeber] (1929–   ). *The Dispossessed.* New York: Harper and Row. Reprint, New York: Avon, 1975.

The people of the planet Anarres, the ambiguous Utopia, practice an anarchistic communitarianism. At the novel's center is an atypical male Shevek, a theoretical physicist, the structure of whose story demonstrates the possibility of reconciling contradictory concepts of time—as both linear and circular: the novel completes a circle by ending where it began with the convergence of two linear plot lines. Extraterrestrial alternative.

1975

Benoist, Elizabeth S. (1901–   ). *Doomsday Clock.* San Antonio, Tex.: Naylor.

In 1977, a nuclear attack decimates the earth. A group of friends and stray children descend into a converted mine to await safety from radiation. A dystopian view of the available mode of survival. Borderline: no depiction of society apart from this group.

Coulson, Juanita [Ruth] (1933–   ). *Unto the Last Generation.* Niagara, N.Y.: Laser Books.

By the mid-twenty-first century, resources have become scarce and classes rigidly divided; disasters multiply, including infertility. Eventual cooperation among opposing parties restores necessities to all; cloning becomes a reality as a backup to the few fertile humans discovered to remain. Dystopia.

MacLean, Katherine (1925–   ). *Missing Man*. New York: Putnam/Berkley. (Sections first appeared in *Analog* 1968, 1970, 1971.)

Set about 2000 in New York City, atypical hero George Sanford takes seriously his boyhood oath to help people. He and friend Ahmed try to right and prevent wrongs as residents of various ethnic communes interact. Ambiguous future; psychological concepts central.

Maxwell, Ann [Elizabeth] (1944–   ). *Change*. New York: Pocket.

After a twenty-first century rebellion on Earth, an epidemic of human mutations began that was characterized by paranormal extrasensory powers. Mutants with these powers were called parans. Selena Christian, one such paran, goes to planet Change to develop powers of mindspeech and healing by relating to animals and aliens. Egalitarian romance, heroinic adventure, space colonization.

[Neeper, Carolyn A. (1937–   )], Cary Neeper (pseud.). *A Place Beyond Man*. New York: Scribner's.

Two planets of the near-future contain nonhuman, intelligent and sentient beings, ellls and varoks. Tandra, a scientist from Earth, creates a new family with her daughter, and an elll and a varok, each male. Love permits social construction and universal benefit when expressed across planets and species. Extraterrestrial future fantasy.

Russ, Joanna (1937–   ). *The Female Man*. New York: Bantam. Reprint, Boston: Gregg/G. K. Hall, 1977.

Whileaway, an all-female eutopia, exists ten centuries into the future. The main character is split among four women, each having an identical genotype, but each living in a different time or place. A visitor from Whileaway arrives on presentday Earth, meets two Earth women from different times, and all three encounter a fourth from a time between our present and Whileaway's future. Extraterrestrial Amazonian society.

Smith, Evelyn E. (1927–   ). *Unpopular Planet*. New York: Dell, 1975.

A satire on twentieth century Earth, this future dystopia inverts alternative cultural values to show an eventually depopulated Earth in an Age of Compulsive Nonviolence. Its hero, Nicholas Pigott, finds himself flown from an authoritarian underground Manhattan world of Blue Dragons to Paradise, where he is installed as king. Space adventure; anti-utopia.

Staton, Mary (1945?–   ). *From the Legend of Biel*. New York: Ace.

On planet MC6, an Earth visitor, Howard Scott, dreams of finding the "perfection" he willingly dies to protect from Earth's discovery, but instead births into MC6 society, a sharer of Biel's gene pattern. Her "legend" of possible human development carefully fostered by a mentor constitutes the bulk of the novel. Extra-terrestrial alternative vision.

1976

Bradley, Marion Zimmer (1930–   ). *The Shattered Chain*. New York: DAW.
The Free Amazons enact a eutopian existence for women by providing personal autonomy, home residence, sororal companionship through a system of urban guilds located throughout the planet Darkover. Three diverse and strong women carry the plot—a châtelaine, an intelligence agent, and a Free Amazon. Feminist sword and sorcery.

Butler, Octavia E[stelle] (1947–   ). *Patternmaster*. Garden City, N.Y.: Doubleday.
On future Earth, Clayark disease from another planet causes mutated humans, Clayarks. Extrapsychic capacities enable the Patternists to link together as protection against Clayarks. Each group believes the other to be inhuman. Two brothers fight for political position of Patternmaster, controller of the Pattern. Dystopian quest.

Holland, Cecelia (1943–   ). *Floating Worlds*. New York: Knopf.
Two thousand years into the future, Paula Mendoza—a black, anarchist, interplanetary diplomat—leaves a eutopian commune on Earth to negotiate the best truce possible among dystopian societies on several planets. Space adventure and suspense.

Holly, Joan [Carol] Hunter (1932–   ). *Keeper*. New York: Laser Books.
Within an apathetic people conditioned to survive the stress of overpopulation and fast change, another loving and feeling culture begins to emerge as population decreases and change decelerates: central is the love between a mentally defective child, Peter, and the emotionally sensitive keeper, Frederic Dainig, who cares for him. Near-future USA dystopia.

McCaffrey, Anne [Inez] (1926–   ). *Dragon Song*. New York: Atheneum. Reprint, New York: Bantam, 1977.
On the planet Pern where Terran colonists settled some five generations before, Benden Weyr is a eutopian community where women are effective healers and beneficent rulers. A young signer recovers and her rare gift for music at last receives encouragement. Sword and sorcery.

Piercy, Marge (1936–   ). *Woman on the Edge of Time*. New York: Knopf. Reprint, New York: Fawcett, 1976.
A future eutopian Mattapoisett, Massachusetts, contrasts with present New York City mental institutions. Connie Ramos, a Chicana incarcerated for violence (provoked by the deprivation she has continuously experienced), finds herself periodically in a society, at once communitarian, environmentally aware, bias free, and human potential enhancing—a future compensatory for all the wrongs she has ever known. Alternative vision.

Randall, Marta (–   ). *Islands*. New York: Pyramid Books.
In a far-future interplanetary society, treatments provide immortality and perennial youth, except for now-middle-aged Tia Hamley and one strikingly beautiful male youth. The Immortals cannot stand the sight of

her aging; she separates herself into her various elements and joins the immortality of universal matter. Ambiguous.

Van Scyoc, Sydney J[oyce] (1939–   ). *StarMother*. New York: Putnam/Berkley.

On dystopian Nelding, Jahna arrives from the Service Cadet Corps of Planet Peace to spend two years charged with "molding" six babes during each year. Perfectability and immortality receive an ambiguous twist as Jahna, the StarMother dubbed "sister of the moon, daughter of the sun," discovers what "molding" entails. Future dystopia.

Wilhelm, Kate (1928–   ). *Where Late the Sweet Birds Sang*. New York: Harper and Row. Reprint. New York: Pocket, 1977.

Environmental pollution and radiation waste land and cities; all die save one extended family gathered in a mountain valley where they develop cloning to compensate for sterility. Population decreases to one fertile male and a group of breeder females. Conclusion is stereotypic: a heterosexual couple expecting a child in a world where individuality again predominates. Extraterrestrial futuristic romance.

Yarbro, Chelsea Quinn (1942–   ). *Time of the Fourth Horseman*. Garden City, N.Y.: Doubleday.

In the twenty-first century in southern California, the medical establishment in cahoots with Internal Intelligence has devised a Project for reducing population: random nonimmunization against childhood diseases that are by then eliminated, a practice resulting in a pandemic. Heroine Dr. Natalie Lebbreau acts against this. Future dystopia.

1977

Bradley, Marion Zimmer (1930–   ). *The Forbidden Tower*. New York: DAW.

The emergence through visualization of a previously forbidden Tower of human power for healing establishes this mission and antedates the centrality in later Darkover novels of the Free Amazons. Focus upon realization of utopian goals.

Butler, Octavia E[stelle] (1947–   ). *Mind of My Mind*. Garden City, N.Y.: Doubleday.

Living in contemporary California, Afro-American Mary, a telepath resulting from Doro's breeding plan, keeps together his descendents by training those who are gifted in the care of the others; she preserves the lives of this community by overcoming Doro. Ambiguous.

Ruuth, Marianne (1937–   ). *Outbreak*. New York: Manor Books.

In a domed metropolis an authoritarian council tries to enforce a class system of Primary and Secondary humans. Free Secondaries living in the wilderness outside the dome succeed in bringing the Primary council to negotiate freedom for Secondaries and Primary women either inside or outside the dome. Eutopia emerging within dystopia.

Thompson, Joyce (–   ). *The Blue Chair.* New York: Avon.

In the early twenty-first century, Eve Harmon at 75 discovers unexpected rewards remain: her blue chair as a medium for reliving and recovering past losses, her husband of 50 years as a friend, a younger man as lover, and immortality if she chooses. Eutopian time travel; probably USA.

1978

Bradley, Marion Zimmer (1930–   ). *Ruins of Isis.* New York: Pocket Books.

A scholar-couple from planet University arrives on Isis/Cinderella to study its culture and archeological ruins. They find a Matriarchate, where women dominate and men are slaves. Investigations at the ruins, however, lead to the possibility of an eventual egalitarian society. Dystopia undergoing transformation to eutopia.

Balizet, Carol (–   ). *The Last Seven Years.* Lincoln, Va.: Chosen Books.

Set in Tampa, Florida, 1988–1995, the author sees a future utopia as a Christian heaven on Earth, the last seven years of a polluted, corrupt, and disintegrating world verifying Biblical prophecy. Major actors are male. Sexist. Futuristic religious romance.

Broner, E[sther] M[asserman] (1930–   ). *A Weave of Women.* New York: Holt, Rinehart, Winston. Reprint. New York: Bantam, 1982.

A community of women living in contemporary Jerusalem create rituals affirming women's experience, refuse self-defeat, move from birth through death to life and love. The novel centers first upon one then upon another community woman and her experience. An irreverent—often funny—celebration of womanhood. Alternative present.

Butler, Octavia E[stelle] (1947–   ). *Survivor.* Garden City, N.Y.: Doubleday.

In the near future on another planet, Earth humans called Missionaries, and two enemy groups, Garkohn and Tehkohn, war over their differences and over which will dominate. A love relationship between the brown human heroine Alanna and the blue-furred Teh leader Diut makes concrete the possibility of coexistence, but stubbornly-held religious belief prevents its actualization. Dystopia containing eutopia.

Charnas, Suzy McKee (1939–   ). *Motherlines.* New York: Berkley. Sequel to dystopian *Walk to the End of the World,* New York: Ballantine, 1974. Reprint. Berkley, 1978.

After surviving the Wasting brought about by Holdfast men in *Walk to the End of the World,* the Riding Women tribes and the free fems seek a peaceful coexistence. Protagonist Alldera bears a daughter—who seems likely to start a new motherline—and promises to lead a return to vanquish Holdfast. Amazonian postcatastrophe future.

Le Guin, Ursula K[roeber] (1929–   ). *The Eye of the Heron.* In *Millennial Women,* edited by Virginia Kidd, New York: Delacorte. Reprint. New York: Harper and Row, 1983.

On Victoria planet, two settlements of outcasts from Earth exist in uneasy balance—hierarchical Victoria City and consensual, nonviolent Shantih. The latter permits leadership to women and men—although the former suffer less severe casualties. Inspired by a woman who chose to leave Victoria City, a group from Shantih set out to build a new world in the wilderness. Extraterrestrial alternative.

McIntyre, Vonda [Neel] (1948–   ). *Dreamsnake*. Boston: Houghton Mifflin. Reprint. New York: Dell, 1979.

On postcatastrophe Earth, varied communities exist, one woman-headed tribal group being particularly concerned with human welfare. Future fantasy.

Paul, Barbara [Jeanne] (1931–   ). *An Exercise for Madmen*. New York: Berkley.

On planet Pythia light years from Earth, a future medical research colony discovers its Dionysian underside, upon the arrival of an alien who leads them to indulge in unmitigated pleasure-seeking. The heroine expiates her guilt for welcoming this alien and sacrifices herself to become the brain of a new cyborg that will permit the society to continue existing. Ambiguous.

Randall, Marta (–   ). *Journey*. New York: Pocket.

After twelve years on their planet Aerie, the Kennerin family continue to journey toward creating a world of human interdependence and achievement with the arrival of 200 refugees, whom they rescue from social dissolution on planet New Home. The novel stresses group-defined goals suitable to female and male, nonhuman and human beings. Extraterrestrial future fantasy.

[Sheldon, Alice Hastings (1916–1987)], James Tiptree, Jr. (pseud.). *Up the Walls of the World*. New York: Putnam.

A dystopian present USA is juxtaposed to alien but utopian Tyree where the gender stereotypes we know are reversed or otherwise called into question. Multiple viewpoints enact social pluralism and complexity. A chaotic Destroyer force is humanized into a responsible Saver by a psychically scarred black woman. Ambiguous.

Yarbro, Chelsea Quinn (1942–   ). *False Dawn*. Garden City, N.Y.: Doubleday.

In twenty-first century southern California, Thea and Evan try to find a safe place to live, but none exists. Instead all is pestilence, pollution, or piracy. The possibility of eutopia continually eludes them. Future dystopia.

1979

Carr, Jayge (–   ). *Leviathan's Deep*. Garden City, N.Y.: Doubleday.

On the planet Delyafam, a future society of humanoids exhibits a gender-role reversal with the Noble Lady maintaining a household in which boys serve her. The Delyen noncompetitive, cooperative society struggles to survive against the off-world Terrene, whose technological superiority enables them to subdue inhabitants of planets they visit, but the possibility of equality between Delyen-Terrene individuals exists. Matriarchal future alternative.

[Cherry, Carolyn Janice (1942–   )], C. J. Cherryh (pseud.). *The Fires of Azeroth*. New York: DAW.

Mirrind and Carrhend, two eutopian villages run by elder women and their men, are destroyed in the process of trying to free the world from the limitless power and freedom of the Gates: they permit passage through space and time. The destruction results from the woman Morgaine, who in closing the Gates must sacrifice the villages. Sword and sorcery.

Clayton, Jo (1939–   ). *Maeve: A Novel of the Diadem*. New York: DAW.

On a future planet Maeve, Starwitch Aleytys arrives enroute to finding her son. While there, she uses many unusual talents in the process of saving from control by the Company, two nonhuman populations—the forest cludair and urban ardd. Although once found she had planned to keep her son with her, she realizes he will be happier without her. Disappointed she leaves, but quickly feels excitement about new worlds she will visit. Future fantasy, partial eutopia.

Cox, Joan (1942–   ). *Mind Song*. New York: Avon.

The Terran society of Delpha is eutopian, particularly respecting political and sexual expression. DonEel from Scarsen travels through time and space to discover the nature of the threat to Delpha. He reveals his own and others' capacity for telepathy through space and time, a "mind song of desire" for Eden. Extraterrestrial, interplanetary sword and sorcery.

Eisenstein, Phyllis (1946–   ). *Shadow of Earth*. New York: Dell.

A tale of alternative presents—one our own twentieth-century Chicago, and another in which the Spanish Armada conquered England and Spain explored the new continents; in that alternative, technology has not advanced and "our" land remains a frontier. Themes include increased medical and scientific information, and better conditions for women. Heroine Celia becomes her own person, whose goal is her own growth and not a relationship. Ambiguous utopia.

Elgin, Suzette Haden (1936–   ). *Star-Anchored, Star-Angered*. Garden City, N.Y.: Doubleday.

Coyote Jones, Tri-Galactic Intelligence Service agent, receives orders to investigate the eutopian religious cult, the Shavvies led by Drussa Silver. This female divinity converts Coyote before she is martyred. A blend of detective and science fiction, the book concludes by revealing that the Shavvy Creed, having permeated the multiversities, will in time prevail. Incipient eutopia.

Gearhart, Sally Miller (1931–   ). *The Wanderground*. Watertown, Mass.: Persephone.

The Hill Women roam their Wanderground, located beyond the Dangerland separating them from the City—a pastoral, spiritual, all-female eutopia, where new language and new ritual flourish. The Hill Women live a communal life in tune with flora and fauna around them. Episodes feature the experiences of first one then another member of the group. Amazonian community.

[Gellis, Roberta Leah Jacobs (1927–   )]. Max Daniels (pseud.). *Offworld*. New York: Pocket Books.

On Gorona, offworld from future Earth, an exiled prankster and teacher of battle arts—the multiracial Max—finds himself enlisted to help the Tribe of Enthok, who are nonsexist and classless. He rescues their captured leader Jael from the less principled Tribe of Bolvi. Gorona is populated by tribes of humanoid reptiles. Adventure; preservation of a "good" society.

Killough, [Karen] Lee (1942–   ). *A Voice out of Ramah*. New York: Ballantine.

Six hundred years after escaping from Earth's decadence and violence, emigrants to Marah wonder at the arrival of a Terran ramjet. Its female liaison officer leads the current religious Shepherd—an atypical hero—to expose the Trial, a ritual for adolescent boys, that has held men to 10% of the population. Gender arrangements a central issue. Incipient eutopia.

Lynn, Elizabeth A. (1946–   ). *Watchtower*. New York: Berkley.

In the midst of a sword and sorcery fantasy is eutopian Vanima, a land of summer isolated in mountains, its approach known only to those who have been there. A pacific, pastoral people.

Marinelli, Jean (–   ). *From Blight to Height*. New York: Vantage.

A brief, amateurish eutopia, set in present and near-future United States, depicting the development of a multiethnic society of equals ruled by a male elite and subdivided into self-sufficient Regions of 60,000 people apiece. Alternative future.

Mayhar, Ardath (1930–   ). *How the Gods Wove in Kyrannon*. Garden City, N.Y.: Doubleday.

In the undetermined green world setting of Kyrannon, women and men are warriors for truth, with the spiritual support of the gods and of each other. They tame the Tyrant, Him Who Sits at Lirith, and establish the conditions for peace, love, and justice. Not killing, but force of mind and force of character effect social change. Eutopian sword and sorcery.

Sargent, Pamela (1947?–   ). *The Sudden Star*. New York: Fawcett.

In 2075, the USA has gone awry—trouble coinciding with the sudden appearance of the star Mura in 2000. Disease and disintegration are rampant. A fable of a peach tree and a thorny bush suggests that a better world has already been seeded. Future dystopia.

White, Mary Alice (1920–   ). *The Land of the Possible: A Report of the First Visit to Prire*. New York: Warner.

Charles Aldworth, Ph.D., makes his first visit of one week to seven varying communities in the land of Prire. The Utopia focuses upon governmental, labor, industrial, environmental, economic, and educational arrangements. The society appears strikingly equitable and cooperative. Alternative present.

Wilhelm, Kat[i]e Gertrude (1928–   ). *Juniper Time. A Novel.* New York: Harper and Row.

At the turn of the century, drought has forced the creation of over-crowded Newtowns. Space development continues and the expectation of aliens arriving as saviors seems to move from dream to reality. Linguistic skill of the heroine creates hope; she has learned from Indian people to live in harmony with Earth. Dystopian future on Earth.

Young, Donna J. (–   ). *Retreat: As It Was!* Weatherby Lake, Mo.: Naiad.

A pastoral all-female eutopia on the planet Retreat experiences disruption when visitors from planet Home are attacked and irradiated enroute. Emphasis upon closeness to nature, healing skills, story telling as instruction. Parthenogenetic reproduction; genetic variation through the Ordeal of Sharing. Extraterrestrial Amazonian alternative.

1980

Butler, Octavia E[stelle] (1947–   ). *Wild Seed.* Garden City, N.Y.: Doubleday, 1980.

Doro, the hero of African origin, is some 3700 years old at the beginning of this book. He has the ability to take over the bodies of others. In North America from 1690 to 1840, he has been creating colonies of strong new people from those who are psychically different. He meets his match in the woman Anyanwu, with whom he eventually must compromise. Prequel to *Mind of My Mind.* Ambiguous.

Randall, Marta (–   ). *Dangerous Games.* New York: Pocket.

On Aerie-Kennerin planet, from New Time 1242–46, the Kennerin family led by matriarch Mish struggles against internal and external dangers to maintain their autonomy as a family, as well as their community with extra-human beings the Kasirene, a nonviolent agricultural society. Extraterrestrial future fantasy.

Sargent, Pamela (1947?–   ). *Watchstar.* New York: Pocket.

Heroine Daiya learns during her ordeal of passage on far-future Earth that her agrarian society enforces a group illusion. A visitor to Earth takes her to another world having an infinity of possible ways of being. Daiya chooses to remain on Earth with the hope of teaching the larger mindcraft she now understands. Extraterrestrial futuristic fantasy.

Singer, Rochelle (1939–   ). *The Demeter Flower.* New York: St. Martin's.

Set in California's Sierra foothills about 2020 A.D., the village of Demeter is a pastoral communitarian society of women established during the social breakdown of the 1980s. The arrival of a runaway heterosexual couple rouses the village toward establishing a second village and forces the women to face male treachery. Tea from the seeds of Demeter flowers causes pregnancy. Amazonian communitarian future.

Slonczewski, Joan (1956–   ). *Still Forms on Foxfield.* New York: Ballantine.

In 2133 A.D., representatives from U.N. Interplanetary arrive on Foxfield, a planet where 92 years ago a group of Philadelphia Friends established a First Settlement at Georgeville. The conflict concerns the rights of small groups versus those of a universe. Major characters are women, who have greater endurance and perform better under stress than men. Extraterrestrial futuristic fantasy.

Vinge, Joan [Dennison] (1948–   ). *The Snow Queen.* New York: Dial. Reprint. New York: Dell, 1981.

A dystopian Winter planet Tiamat ruled by Snow Queen Arienrhod is about to undergo, after 150 years, the Change to eutopian Summer. To prevent such evolution, the Queen has cloned herself. A complex plot and large cast of characters—human and nonhuman—demonstrate the uncertainty of achieving ideals. Extraterrestrial fantasy.

Wilson, Merzie (–   ). *Nealites: Doc Genius and Henry the Stud.* New York: Vantage, 1980.

Set mostly in a contemporary courtroom, eutopia for the Black "Tribal People" of Neal County, Louisiana, includes justice before the [white] law and social respect [from whites], legitimacy of all children, [white] acceptance of Black polygamous heritage, [white] acknowledgement of parapsychological events, knowledge of noble African ancestry, and pride in Black men as lovers and fathers. Contemporary USA eutopia.

1981

[Cherry, Carolyn Janice (1942–   )], C. J. Cherryh (pseud.). *Downbelow Station.* New York: DAW.

In the twenty-fourth century on neutral planet Pell, a contest between Earth Company and Union—the latter established by the Beyonder Rebellion—nearly destroys the planet. Survival depends upon the alien Downers, whose safe enclave becomes both a refuge for Pell leadership and a model defusing nonviolent response. Future eutopia enclosed by dystopia.

Elgin, Suzette Haden (1936–   ). *Ozark Fantasy Trilogy.* Book One: *Twelve Fair Kingdoms.* Book Two: *The Grand Jubilee.* Book Three: *And Then There'll Be Fireworks.* Garden City, N.Y.: Doubleday.

On planet Ozark in 3012, Responsible of Brightwater makes a picaresque Quest to visit the twelve kingdoms in order to discover the source of mischief and disorder. Managed by Grannys, Magicians, and the teenaged heroine named Responsible, the kingdoms celebrate their fifth centennial by destroying their confederation, a parodic satire of our present. Only barely do the twelve Kingdoms restore order in time to prevent a conquest by the Garnet Ring of the Out-Cabal. Themes include power of language and trust in maintaining social orderliness. Benevolent but authoritarian utopia.

Holland, Cecelia [Anastasia] (1943–   ). *Home Ground.* New York: Knopf.

A present collective in northern California supports itself on the sale of marijuana. The utopia appears in the ambivalent and painful process of becoming. The heroine remains in the group though the man and young woman who love her leave; she shares pot from her field after a drug bust. Communitarian romance.

Killough, [Karen] Lee (1942–   ). *Aventine*. New York: Ballantine/Del Rey.

A future resort for Beautiful People, Aventine exists at the crossroads of the civilized galaxy. Imagination alone limits entertainment, activities, life itself. Future dystopia, seven related stories.

Lichtenberg, Jacqueline (1942–   ). *Mahogany Trinrose*. "A Sime/Gen Novel." Garden City, New York: Doubleday.

Heroine Aild Ercy Farris sets out to cultivate scientifically the mahogany trinrose so she can extract from it a substance believed magical in its powers over human behavior, although she maintains that magic is not-yet-understood science. This endeavor along with her desire for personal growth leads her to leave the House of Zeor in order to join the Company. Science-fiction fantasy with eutopian implications.

Lynn, Elizabeth A. (1946–   ). *The Sardonyx Net*. New York: Putnam. Reprint. New York: Berkley, 1987.

On Chabad planet, drugs and slavery undergird society, run by four ruling families. The smuggler hero, a young man enslaved to the powerful Yago family, eventually leaves with a vow to find a legal employment. Far future dystopia.

1982

Miesel, Sandra (1941–   ). *Dreamrider*. New York: Ace.

In the early twenty-first century United States, researcher Ria finds she has shamanic powers which she develops under the guidance of aged Kara and the macotter Lute (a human-sized otter); through the medium of dream or trance Ria can time-travel among several alternative pasts and futures. Dystopian frame; approaching-eutopian alternative.

Paxson, Diana L. (–   ). *Lady of Light*. New York: Pocket/Timescape.

In Westria some two centuries after Cataclysm, a new-feudal but ecologically sensitive society has developed. A king goes in search of a queen, who will be "mistress of his heart" and mistress of four Jewels of Power, as well as bear him an heir. Partially eutopian, not feminist, postdisaster future.

Petesch, Natalie L. M. (1924–   ). *Duncan's Colony*. Athens: Swallow/Ohio Univ. Press.

Duncan, a former seminarian, gathers a colony of eight people—four men and four women—to prepare for the coming nuclear holocaust. Colonists break all the rules he has set as they choose individual responses to the fact of their own mortality. A near-past communitarian gathering and disbanding, this novel shows the utopian impulse meaningfully expressed, not in a colony but in social activism.

Salmonson, Jessica Amanda (1952–   ). *The Swordswoman*. New York: Pinnacle Books.

Erin, the swordswoman, moves between Earth and Endsworld, on which she becomes the disciple of centaur Kiron, who teaches her martial arts to use in the service of compassion and according to eutopian principles. Present day, interplanetary sword and sorcery.

Sargent, Pamela (1947?–   ). *The Golden Space.* New York: Simon and Schuster.

After the upheaval of the Transition, new human possibilities develop, including immortality and biological engineering. Two who have lived from before the Transition participate as parents of experimental babies— bisexual of body, extrarational in behavior. Eventually the experimental generation leaves Earth. Postcatastrophe alternative future, science-fictional eutopia.

Webb, Sharon (1936–   ). *Earthchild.* "Earth Song Triad." Reprint. New York: Bantam, 1983.

In a future United States, the discovery of the process Mouat-Gari ensures immortality to those then under fifteen years. During the first five years violence of old against young is common. What results after 99 years is a dystopia. Hero Kurt Kraus decides that immortality must be reversed for human creativity to survive. Medical dystopia, male protagonist.

1983

Bradley, Marion Zimmer (1930–   ). *Thendara House.* New York: DAW.

Thendara House is the residence of one guild of the Order of Renunciates (Free Amazons). Two members experience conflicting loyalties as they seek self- and group-identity. Set on the planet Darkover in an unspecified future, action moves among the Renunciates, Terrans, and Darkovans. Eutopian society for women set within dystopia; second Free Amazon novel.

Calisher, Hortense (1911–   ). *Mysteries of Motion.* Garden City, N.Y.: Doubleday.

On *The Citizen Courier,* six U. S. citizens toward the end of this century believe that they travel toward the first civilian habitat in space. We learn of their past lives and their expectations for this trip. But instead of docking at such a destination, they are left orbiting, perhaps until their deaths, in space. Dystopia, depicting the difficulty of accurately anticipating the outcomes of human plans, the difficulty of creating eutopia.

Carr, Jayge (1940–   ). *Navigator's Sindrome* [sic]. Garden City, N.Y.: Doubleday.

Space adventure involving evil planet Rabelais, where freedom amounts to contractual slavery. Claustrophobic condition called "Navigator's Syndrome" nearly spoils departure plans. Unredeeming dystopia.

[Cherry, Carolyn Janice (1942–   )], C. J. Cherryh (pseud.). *The Dreamstone.* New York: DAW.

The dreamstone permits its wearer to enter Ealdwood, where death and destruction are scarce, where a protectress nurtures growth and uses magical powers. Also the remote mountainous Steading, a refuge for the lost or the chased, is a eutopia existing as an escape (chs. 2, 3). More fantasy than utopia, the book is set in an undetermined past.

Covina, Gina (1952–   ). *The City of Hermits*. Berkeley: Barn Owl Books.

Opening four days before the big Earthquake, this novel manages what most utopias omit—a transformation from before to after. The "city" is one of consciousness rather than place, whose citizens are scattered over the globe. The plot concerns the transition of one group in Guerneville, California, from a Sister Spa collective to nonprofit foundation. Nonracist, nonsexist, environmentally-aware, alternative future.

Gaida, Davida (–   ). *2084*. Chicago: Ringa.

Moving through a time warp, microbiologist Dr. Megan Wendeline discovers that her genetic engineering research to control sex-linked disease has been misused to prevent the births of girls. A dystopia run by a male-dominant Agency in 2084 Southern California permits women to live in brothels or breeding camps, or enslaved to one man; Libras—women with a few supporting men—continue eutopian feminist values of a century ago.

McIntyre, Vonda N. (1948–   ). *Superluminal*. Boston: Houghton Mifflin.

In a future vision of Earth as part of an interplanetary human existence, beings also exist as transitional between animal and human. Superluminal space travel exists in several dimensions; interspecies communication occurs between whales and near-human beings. Heroine Laenea, after surgery that replaces her human heart with a bionic machine, gains full pilot stature. Dystopian future.

Mayhar, Ardath (1930–   ). *Exile on Vlahil*. Garden City, N.Y.: Doubleday.

About one century into the future, the Instrumentality on Earth exiles to uninhabited planets those who refuse mental conditioning. Ila with her computer Companion Alice, which her father has provided, is sentenced to Planet Vlahil, where she finds creatures far more empathic than humans. Two human children also exiled must learn empathy for the creatures of Vlahil. Near-eutopia.

Yarbro, Chelsea Quinn (1942–   ). *Hyacinths*. Garden City, N.Y.: Doubleday.

In the near-future USA, dream research deteriorates from humane efforts to use its symbols as a key to understanding individual psychotic behavior—the "hyacinths that feed the soul"—to commercial Dreamweb, Inc., a travesty of research that drives Dreamers into burnout and psychosis. Dystopian jeremiad.

1984

Bennett, Marcia J[oanne] (1945–   ). *Shadow Singer*. New York: Del Rey/ Ballantine.

In a green world, Singer Poco and Seeker Dahl search the retreat of Dahl's people the Ni-lach, found at last in the Chen-Garry Mountains, an idyllic community. Violent fantasy quest, with glimpse of eutopian green world at end.

Bradley, Marion Zimmer (1930–   ). *City of Sorcery*. New York: DAW.

The complete disappearance on Darkover of the plane of an intelligence scout puzzles, as does her muddled mental state. Resolving the puzzle requires a journey led by Free Amazons in search of the City of Wisdom, residence of the legendary Sisterhood, devoted to fostering goodness. The physical journey becomes a rite of passage into greater self-knowledge. Third Free Amazon novel. Eutopia embedded in dystopia.

Butler, Octavia E[stelle] (1947–   ). *Clay's Ark*. New York: St. Martin's.

In 2021, a virulent extraterrestrial disease organism spreads rapidly and creates havoc throughout the world. It manifests itself through sexual compulsion, sensuous supersensitivity, and superstrength. Offspring are catlike quadrupeds, nonhuman. Nonstereotypic central characters. Dystopian in action, but utopian in pleas for acceptance of difference.

Elgin, Suzette Haden (1936–   ). *Native Tongue*. New York: DAW.

In the United States at the end of the 2200s, a sex-segregated society exists, whose women—especially those relegated to the Barren Houses—develop a women's language which leads to new conditions for all women. A feminist eutopia embedded in dystopia.

Forrest, Katherine V. (–   ). *Daughters of a Coral Dawn*. Tallahassee, Fla.: Naiad.

Minerva narrates a "history" of colony Cybele on continent Femina, planet Maternas, covering 2199–2234, from the colony's initial point when birth rates resulted in an increase in the population of women on Earth, through their interplanetary migration to colony establishment. A lesbian feminist alternative future.

Thompson, Joyce (–   ). *Conscience Place*. Garden City, N.Y.: Doubleday.

The Place practices a eutopian "code" of interaction among the People, genetically defective offspring of parents involved in nuclear accidents. This code makes possible a small, joyously life-affirming community of People who, in contrast to those on the outside, live up to their best possible capacities. Contemporary midwestern USA eutopia.

1985

Bluejay, Jan (–   ). *It's Time: A Nuclear Novel*. Little River, Calif.: Tough Dove Books.

In an undetermined time, groups of women leave the City of Patriarchy eventually to establish their Settlement of Delphi in a forested region. An antinuclear, ecofeminist, antiracist lesbian feminist alternative present/future.

Le Guin, Ursula K[roeber] (1929–   ). *Always Coming Home*. New York: Harper and Row.

The Kesh "might be going to live" in Northern California. The book collects their poetry, history, fiction, folkways, and language. The major narrative, "Stone Telling"—a three-part life history recorded in old age by a woman of the same name—recounts a coming into consciousness and living the practices of a possible Kesh person. The Kesh value appropriate technology, moderate behavior, developed potential, personal autonomy, loyal community. Eutopian imaginary ethnography.

Meluch, R[ebecca] M. (1956–   ). *Jerusalem Fire*. New York: New American Library.

In 5856 after a political and economic collapse had thrown humankind into a 2000-year dark age, hero-rebel-traitor Shad Iliya alias Alihahd—an extraordinary intergalactic captain—attempts to expiate his guilt, cannot, and at the end returns home. Ambiguous utopia, interspecies communication.

Mueller, Ruth. *The Eye of the Child*. Philadelphia: New Society Publishers.

Set in a present or near-future society similar to our own, Mini's child's-eye ecofeminist or Gaian sketch of a sentient Earth at times delights, at times terrifies. Cross-species communication; eutopian vision of unified human and natural worlds.

Reed, Kit (1932–   ). *Fort Privilege*. Garden City, N.Y.: Doubleday.

Set in near-future Manhattan, nearly empty from the exodus of the middle classes, the rich gather for one last gala at the Parkhurst while the masses prepare an attack. Whereas the aged patriarch Abel claims he has tried to be responsible and to share, his daughter Sarah has turned against him and spied for the masses. The patriarchal ideal became a dystopian prison.

1986

Eidus, Janice (–   ). *Faithful Rebecca*. New York: Fiction Collective.

A contemporary women's commune in rural New York not far from New York City doesn't work out after all. Rebecca sees that relationships must occur without disguises, in full self-knowledge. Contemporary USA; antiutopia.

Elgin, Suzette Haden (1936–   ). *Yonder Comes the Other End of Time*. New York: DAW.

A thousand years into the future, Coyote Jones, agent of the Tri-Galactic Federation from Mars Central, visits Planet Ozark, whose ancestors had left Old Earth in disgust at its mess. He finds Grannies and Magicians, led by Responsible of Brightwater, who possesses remarkable telepathic powers, apparently deriving from their faith in her powers. A humorous alternative future that reads like an agrarian fairy tale.

Felice, Cynthia (–   ). *Double Nocturne*. New York: DAW.

After the future Homeworlds wars, Tom Hark and crew travel to the colonies on the planet Islands to repair their governing Artificial Intelligence. He finds three matriarchies—regressive, misanthropic Fox City; medieval

New Penance; and earth-worshipping Selene. Antifeminist, dystopian space adventure.

Finch[-Rayner], Sheila (1935–). *Triad*. New York: Bantam.

Lingster Gia Kennedy, arriving on a new planet Chameleon, analyzes the language of the alien Ents, nicknamed the "fuzzies" by a hostile crew member. Language is shown to create conceptions of a world. Interaction among the primal triads—woman, man, computer; actor, agent, undergoer —leads to increased consciousness of human and alien in an indeterminate future. Ambiguous.

McKay, Claudia (–). *Promise of the Rose Stone*. Norwich, Vt.: New Victoria.

Isa, taken hostage by the Federation, is exiled to sentient planet Olyeve, where she encounters former lover, now Agent Jasa, and meets new lover Cleothe, with whom Isa hopes to return to her mountain village, fulfilling the "promise of the rose stone," a gift to her grandmother passed on to Isa. Ambiguous; promise of eutopia.

Sargent, Pamela (1947?–). *The Shore of Women*. New York: Crown.

Set on Earth after its Destruction and Rebirth, this utopia is the report of chronicler Laissa, who offers narratives from the viewpoints of three characters—herself, her male twin Arvil, and a former female friend Birana. Their viewpoints explore issues of sex and gender in ways that permit no easy conclusions, that insist upon complexity and paradox. Both one-sex and two-sex groups exist. A blend of *The Female Man* and *Woman on the Edge of Time*. Ambiguous.

Sargent, Pamela (1947?–). *Venus of Dreams*. New York: Bantam.
[Vol. 1 of trilogy to cover four generations of one family colonizing Venus]

Six centuries into the future, after numerous Earth wars over resources, Nomarchies controlled by Mukhtars rule the Earth. Eight Cytherian Island colonies exist, preliminary to settling Venus under domes designed to create gradually humanly habitable atmosphere. Risa, the daughter of heroine Iris, and her father are among the first 500 settlers. Alternative societies, called Habitats, also exist. Complex society; an ambiguous utopia exhibiting social change in process.

Slonczewski, Joan (1956–). *Door into Ocean*. New York: Avon.

The peoples residing on the planets Shora and Valedon each separately and somewhat reluctantly decide that the other is in fact human. The plot reveals how their very different definitions of power, freedom, and achievement lead to the near annihilation of one people, but for their fearless capacity to persist. Pacific and communitarian eutopia versus bellicose and commercial dystopia; feminist and ecological issues central.

Snodgrass, Melinda M. (–). *Circuit*. New York: Berkley.

In the late twenty-first century, Cabot Huntington accepts appointment as judge of the Fifteenth Circuit Court of the United States, to preside over the administration of justice in space. He discovers that his real mission is not justice, however, but control of space colonies; to this he rebels and joins the colonists' cause on space station EnerSun I. Not feminist dystopian future; technology central.

Sunlight (–   ). *Womonseed*. Little River, Calif.: Tough Dove.

On Solstice Eve 1999, women of the twenty-year-old community Womonseed—located in a California mountain valley—sit in a campfire circle, each speaking a narrative describing her experience and demonstrating a spiritually transformative technique. Diversely multivoiced. Future, eco-feminist eutopia surrounded by repressive dystopia.

1987

Butler, Octavia E[stelle] (1947–   ). *Dawn*. "Xenogenesis" series. New York: Warner.

On a spaceship run by "repulsive" extraterrestrial Oankali, a black woman, Lilith, is chosen to help train a human group to repopulate an Earth recovered from nuclear destruction after 250 years. Human violence and fear of difference collide with the Oankali desire to crossbreed via their unusual reproductive patterns. Experimental future, posthuman evolution; ambiguous.

Elgin, Suzette Haden (1936–   ). *Native Tongue II: The Judas Rose*. New York: DAW.

In the United States of the late twenty-third century, the women's language Laadan—without men's knowledge—spreads among women via nurses and nuns. Government, academe, and religion as practiced in a patriarchy are the butt of satiric words and actions. An Epilogue reveals an unresolved split between the sexes. Ambiguous utopia.

Goldstein, Lisa (1953–   ). *A Mask for the General*. New York: Bantam.

In 2021 Berkeley, California, ten years after the Collapse of the U.S. government with its takeover by the General, Mary, an epileptic, meets Layla, a maskmaker. Their friendship becomes an asexual bond of love that empowers their confrontation with the General, who in donning a crowmask, breaks his own law against masks. Tightly plotted dystopia containing seeds of eutopia.

1988

Tepper, Sheri S. *The Gate to Women's Country*. New York: Doubleday Foundation Books.

Three hundred years after a "great devastation" killed most of the world's people, the Women's Council rules Women's Country—located in the Pacific Northwest and populated by women, their female children, male children until five years, and male "servitors"—males who at fifteen chose to return to Women's Country after ten years training in a military garrison. A future, ambiguous utopia, inspired by Classical Greece and centering interest upon reproduction.

Index of Authors
(including dual authors, married names, and pseudonyms)

1913a, 1913b, 1913c, 1913d, 1915, 1916, 1920, 1928
Gillmore, 1913
Goldstein, 1987
Graul, 1897
Griffith, 1836

Hale, 1853
Harbert, 1871, 1892
Hastings. *See* Sherwood, 1895
Hawkins, 1902
Henderson, 1961
Henley, 1901
Holland, 1976, 1981
Holly, 1976
Hopf, see Lightner, 1969
Hotson, 1964
Howland, 1874

Irving, 1929
Irwin. *See* Gillmore, 1913

Johnston, 1920
Jones, A., 1956
Jones, A. I., 1892
Jones, L. B., 1916

Kayser, 1922
Killough, 1979, 1981
Kinkaid, 1903
Kirby, 1870
Kirk, E. *See* Ames, 1896
Kirk, E. W. O., 1931
Knapp, 1894
Knox, 1890
Kuttner. *See* Moore, 1957

Lane, 1881
Lawrence, 1964
Lease, 1895
Le Guin, 1966, 1967, 1969, 1972, 1974, 1978, 1985
Leslee, 1962
Lichtenberg, 1981
Lightner, 1969

Livermore, 1891
Lorraine. *See* Wright, 1929, 1930
Lynn, 1979, 1981

McCaffrey, 1976
McCarthy, 1949
McElhiney, 1945
McIntyre, 1978, 1983
McKay, 1986
MacLean, 1975
Maddux, 1957
Mannes, 1968
Marinelli, 1979
Martin, N. P., 1908
Martin, P. M., 1932
Mason, C. A., 1900
Mason, E. L., 1889, 1898
Mason, G.. *See* Meek, 1956; Jones, A., 1956
Mayhar, 1979, 1983
Maxwell, 1975
Mead, 1889
Meek, 1956
Meluch, 1985
Merchant, 1892
Miesel, 1982
Moore, C. L., 1957
Moore, M. L., 1892
Morgan, 1899
Morris, 1938
Mueller, 1985

Neeper, 1975
Norris, 1957

Orpen, 1897
Owen. *See* Snedeker, 1917
Owens. *See* Spotswood, 1935

Paul, 1978
Paxson, 1982
Petesch, 1982
Pettersen, 1924
Phelps, 1868, 1874, 1879, 1883, 1887
Piercy, 1970, 1976

Index of Short Titles

Listed here are titles of all annotated works, including titles of collections that would help the reader in locating a given work. Numerical titles precede alphabetic titles. All titles are located according to the year of first publication as listed in the bibliography, not by book page. Some sequels are discussed under the entry of the first volume in a series: this list is *not* a quick publication reference, but a finding list. Publication information is cited at the beginning of annotation entries.

Life and Labors, 1884
Little Men, 1871
Long Tomorrow, 1955
Lowell Offering, 1841

Maeve, 1979
Mahogany Trinrose, 1981
"Maidstone Comfort," 1912
Man from Mars, 1901
Man on the Mountain, 1969
Manless World, 1891
Man's Rights, 1870
"Martha's Mother," 1910
Mask for the General, 1987
Memoirs of a Millionaire, 1889
Metzerott, 1889
Mildred Carver, U.S.A., 1919
Mind of My Mind, 1977
Mind Song, 1979
Miss Melinda's Opportunity,
    1886
Missing Man, 1975
Mizora, 1881
Modern Fairyland, 1896
"Moon Woman," 1929
Motherlines, 1978
Moving the Mountain, 1911
Mrs. Herndon's Income, 1885
"Mrs. Hines' Money," 1913
Mysteries of Motion, 1983

Native Tongue, 1984
Native Tongue II, 1987
Navigator's Sindrome, 1983
Nealites, 1980
New Aristocracy, 1891
"New Society," 1841
No Borderland, 1938
Not a Cloud in the Sky, 1964

Oasis, 1949
Offworld, 1979
Old Maid's Paradise, 1879
Old-fashioned Girl, 1870
One of "Berrian's" Novels, 1890

"One Thousand Dollars a Day,"
    1894
Other Worlds, 1905
Out of her Sphere, 1871
Outbreak, 1977
Ozark Fantasy Trilogy, 1981

"Page of American History," 1870
Pantaletta, 1882
Papa's Own Girl, 1874
Patternmaster, 1976
People, 1961
Perfect Planet, 1962
Perfect World, 1922
Perfection City, 1897
Pilgrimage, 1961
Pilgrim's Progress in Other Worlds,
    1908
Place Beyond Man, 1975
Planet of Exile, 1966
*Position of Women in the Socialistic
    Utopia*, 1901
Problem of Civilization Solved, 1895
"Proclamation of Inter-
    dependence," 1928
Prohibiting Poverty, 1932
Promise of the Rose Stone, 1986
Pure Causeway, 1899

Rebellers, 1963
Redwood, 1824
Reinstern, 1900
Republic of the Future, 1887
Retreat: As It Was!, 1979
Romance Island, 1906
Rondah, 1887
Ruins of Isis, 1978

Salome Shepard, 1893
San Salvador, 1892
Sardonyx Net, 1981
"Sequel to the Vision of Bangor,"
    1848
Seth Way, 1917
Sex Revolution, 1894

Shadow of Earth, 1979
Shadow Singer, 1984
Shattered Chain, 1976
Shining East, 1964
Shore of Women, 1986
Silent Voice, 1925
Snow Queen, 1980
Some Plant Olive Trees, 1937
Star-Anchored, Star-Angered, 1979
StarMother, 1976
Still Forms on Foxfield, 1980
"Strange Land," 1912
"Sunny Side," 1870
Sudden Star, 1979
Superluminal, 1983
Survivor, 1978
Susanna and Sue, 1909
Sweet Rocket, 1920
Swordswoman, 1982

"Tales of a Great-Grandmother,"
    1891
Taurus Four, 1970
Thendara House, 1983
They, 1968
"Three Hundred Years Hence,"
    1836
Through a Glass Darkly, 1957
Through Gates of Pearl, 1916
Time of the Fourth Horseman, 1976
"Transcendental Wild Oats," 1873
Triad, 1986
Twelve Fair Kingdoms, 1981

Ultimo, 1930
Unpopular Planet, 1975
Unpredictable Adventure, 1935
Unto the Last Generation, 1975
Unveiling a Parallel, 1892

Up the Walls of the World, 1978
"Utopia Interpreted," 1924

Venus, 1924
Venus of Dreams, 1986
Victoria Woodhull Reader, 1870
"Visit to Utopia," 1869
Visitor from Venus, 1949
Voice out of Ramah, 1979
Voices from the Kenduskeag, 1848

Walda, 1902
Walk to the End of the World, 74
Wanderground, 1979
Watchstar, 1980
Watchtower, 1979
Weave of Women, 1978
Wee Lassie, 1902
What Diantha Did, 1910
Where Late the Sweet Birds Sang,
    1976
White City, 1949
Wild Seed, 1980
With Her in Ourland, 1916
Woman of Yesterday, 1900
Woman on the Edge of Time, 1976
"Woman's Utopia," 1907
Woman's Utopia, 1931
Womonseed, 1986
Word for World Is Forest, 1972
Work, 1873
World Above, 1905
World Without Raiment, 1943

Xenogenesis, 1987

Year of the Rats, 1973
Yonder Comes the Other End of Time,
    1986

Notes

Introduction

1. *The Forerunner* 7, no. 11 (1916): 292–93 (chap. 11); reprint, Westport, Conn: Greenwood Press, 1968. All references are to the serialized version. See "Bibliography of Utopian Fiction by United States Women 1836–1988," an annotated finding list arranged by publication date but also indexed by author and title, in *Utopian Studies* 1, no. 1 (1990): 1–58 and reprinted here, pp. 247–304. All titles mentioned in this introduction also appear on this list. A brief update will appear in a forthcoming issue.

2. Charlotte Perkins Gilman, *The Home: Its Work and Influence* (1903; reprint, Urbana: Univ. of Illinois Press, 1972), 277.

3. Frank E. Manuel and Fritzie P. Manuel, *Utopian Thought in the Western World* (Cambridge: Belknap/Harvard Univ. Press, 1982), 23–24.

4. On Jung, see J. E. Cirlot, *A Dictionary of Symbols* (New York: Philosophical Library, 1962), 46–47. Worth recalling is one of the first European utopias to be written by a woman, *The City of Ladies* (1405) by Christine de Pizan. Her city of notable women from history and literature exemplifies Jung's notion as well as answers her era's misogyny.

5. Lee Cullen Khanna, "Women's Worlds: New Directions in Utopian Fiction," *Alternative Futures* 4, nos. 2–3 (1981): 58–59. All utopias by women are not, however, feminist.

6. See Jane Tompkins, *Sensational Designs: The Cultural Work of American Fiction, 1790–1860* (New York: Oxford Univ. Press, 1985); Nina Baym, *Woman's Fiction: A Guide to Novels by and about Women in America, 1820–1870* (Champaign: Univ. of Illinois Press, 1993).

7. Rachel Blau DuPlessis, in "The Feminist Apologues of Lessing, Piercy, and Russ," *Frontiers: A Journal of Women Studies* 4, no. 1 (Spring 1979); my argument is strongly indebted to her definitional section (1–2). For the term *apologue* DuPlessis credits Sheldon Sacks, *Fiction and the Shape of Belief* (Berkeley: Univ. of California Press, 1964), 26; see 7–8n. 2. A later consideration of issues discussed in the article appears in chap. 11, "Kin with Each Other': Speculative Consciousness and Collective Protagonists," in *Writing Beyond the Ending: Narrative Strategies of Twentieth-Century Women's Writers* (Bloomington: Indiana Univ. Press, 1985).

8. Elizabeth Janeway, *Powers of the Weak* (New York: Knopf, 1980), 320.

9. Karl Mannheim, *Ideology and Utopia: An Introduction to the Sociology of Knowledge,*

trans. Louis Wirth and Edward Shils (1929; reprint, New York: Harcourt, Brace, Jovanovich, 1936), 192.

10. Annette Kolodny, "Not-So-Gentle Persuasion: A Theoretical Imperative of Feminist Literary Criticism," in *Feminist Literary Criticism* (Research Triangle Park, N.C.: National Humanities Center, 1981), 7; see also Leah Fritz, *Dreamers and Dealers: An Intimate Appraisal of the Women's Movement* (Boston: Beacon Press, 1979), especially chap. 10.

11. On the concept of "infinite revolution," see Philip E. Wegner, "On Zamyatin's *We:* A Critical Map of Utopia's 'Possible Worlds,' " *Utopian Studies* 4, no. 2 (1994): 94–116; on "unfinalizability" and Bakhtin, see M. M. Bakhtin, *Problems of Dostoevsky's Poetics* (Minneapolis: Univ. of Minnesota Press, 1984), 166, and also Michael Gardiner, "Bakhtin's Carnival: Utopia as Critique," *Utopian Studies* 3, no. 2 (1992): 21–49.

12. Annette Kolodny in *The Land Before Her: Fantasy and Experience of the American Frontiers, 1630–1860* (Chapel Hill: Univ. of North Carolina Press, 1984) discusses additional imaginative texts that reveal longings similar to those emerging in women's utopias.

13. For a discussion of the woman as outsider, see Virginia Woolf, *Three Guineas* (1938; reprint, New York: Harbinger, 1966); Vivian Gornick, "Woman as Outsider" in *Woman in Sexist Society* (1971; reprint, New York: New American Library, 1972), 126–44.

14. Elizabeth Stuart Phelps, "Victurae Salutamus" (Latin: "we women, who are about to attain our goal, call upon you"; for the translation, I thank Emily J. Puder Farley, my mother and a Latin scholar), *Songs of the Silent World and Other Poems* (Boston: Houghton, Mifflin, 1885), 99.

15. A 1971 feminist utopia is strikingly similar; see Dorothy Bryant, *The Kin of Ata Are Waiting for You*. On language, see Eric Partridge, *Origins: A Short Etymological Dictionary of Modern English* (New York: Macmillan, 1959), 140, 166. On dreaming, see Ann Faraday, *Dream Power* (1972; New York: Berkley Medallion, 1973), 297–98, and G. William Domhoff, *The Mystique of Dreams: A Search for Utopia Through Senoi Dream Theory* (Berkeley: Univ. of California Press, 1986). For a study of Aboriginal Australian women's Dreamtime ritual and practice, see Diane Bell, *Daughters of the Dreaming* (Sydney: George Allen and Unwin, 1983).

16. For a recent discussion of Ernst Bloch's concept of "not yet," see Ruth Levitas, *The Concept of Utopia* (Syracuse: Syracuse Univ. Press. 1990), 86–88. *Utopian Studies* 1, no. 2 (1990) contains five "Featured Articles on Ernst Bloch."

17. Marge Piercy, *Circles on the Water* (New York: Knopf, 1982), 116–17.

18. For a discussion of predominantly male authors, see Kenneth M. Roemer, *The Obsolete Necessity: America in Utopian Writings, 1888–1900* (Kent, Ohio: Kent State Univ. Press, 1976). Of the sample of 154 works, only 14 (less than 10 percent) are by women; hence, generalizations summarize men's views far more than women's views.

19. Numbers are deliberately approximate; each scholar categorizes texts slightly differently. For this reason, I believe that providing estimates of sample sizes is in fact more accurate than precise numbers that can only be inexact.

20. *Elizabeth Cady Stanton/Susan B. Anthony: Correspondence, Writing, Speeches,* ed. Ellen Carol DuBois (New York: Schocken, 1981), 56. And for a recent hypothesis stressing the impact of sex ratio in a society upon women's status in dyadic relationships, see Marcia Guttentag and Paul E. Secord, *Too Many Women? The Sex Ratio Question* (Beverly Hills, Calif.: Sage, 1983), especially chaps. 1, 6, 9.

21. Olive Banks, *Faces of Feminism: A Study of Feminism as a Social Movement* (New York: St. Martin's Press, 1981), especially chaps. 1 and 13. For an historical overview of the present, see Hester Eisenstein, *Contemporary Feminist Thought* (Boston: G. K. Hall, 1983), whose discussion addresses three areas of freedom, the political, the economic, and

the sexual (xvi). A useful recent anthology is Maggie Humm, ed., *Modern Feminisms: Political, Literary, Cultural* (New York: Columbia Univ. Press, 1992).

In this Introduction, by *feminist* I shall mean "favoring women's rights and valuing that which is female." *Anti-feminist* will thus mean "anti-female." And *sexist,* by analogy to racist, will mean "sex-biased or accepting gender-role stereotyping." People of either sex may be sexist toward their own or the other sex.

22. For example, see Susan Faludi, *Backlash: The Undeclared War Against American Women* (New York: Crown, 1991) and Naomi Wolf, *Fire with Fire: The New Female Power and How It Will Change the Twenty-First Century* (New York: Random House, 1993).

23. Those utopias that I have called "feminist" show several characteristics. They provide a critique of women's status, offer alternative ways of being female, recommend reforms benefiting women, place women centrally in the plot, and show either sex atypically. Other discussions of some of the texts or ideas to be discussed appear in Jean Pfaelzer, "A State of One's Own: Feminism as Ideology in American Utopias, 1880–1915," *Extrapolation* 24, no. 4 (1983): 311–28; Jill K. Conway, "Utopian Dream or Dystopian Nightmare? Nineteenth-Century Ideas about Equality," *Proceedings of the American Antiquarian Society,* 96 (1986): 285–94; Nan Bowman Albinski, *Women's Utopias in 19th and 20th Century Fiction* (London: Routledge, 1988); Carol A. Kolmerten, *Women in Utopia: The Ideology of Gender in American Owenite Communities* (Bloomington: Indiana Univ. Press, 1990); Angelika Bammer, *Partial Visions: Feminism and Utopianism in the 1970s* (New York: Routledge, 1991), specifically chap. 2 "Utopia and/as Ideology: Feminist Utopias in Nineteenth-Century America"; and *Women in Spiritual and Communitarian Societies in the United States,* ed. Wendy E. Chmielewski, Louis J. Kerna, and Marlyn Klee-Hartzell (Syracuse: Syracuse Univ. Press, 1993). In the context of archetypes, see Carol Pearson and Katherine Pope, *The Female Hero in American and British Literature* (New York: Bowker, 1981), chap. 8; and Annis Pratt, *Archetypal Patterns in Women's Fiction* (Bloomington: Indiana Univ. Press, 1981), chap. 8.

24. For a historical overview and documents concerning then-contemporary activism, see Eleanor Flexner, *Century of Struggle: The Woman's Rights Movement in the United States* (New York: Atheneum, 1973), and Anne Firor Scott and Andrew MacKay Scott, eds., *One Half the People: The Fight for Women's Suffrage* (Urbana: Univ. of Illinois Press, 1982).

25. For a popular cross-disciplinary survey, see Marilyn Ferguson, *The Aquarian Conspiracy: Personal and Social Transformation in the 1980s* (Los Angeles: J. P. Tarcher, 1980). And see Fritjof Capra, *The Turning Point: Science, Society, and the Rising Culture* (New York: Simon and Schuster, 1982); Robert T. Francoeur, "Religious Reactions to Alternative Lifestyles" in *Contemporary Families and Alternative Lifestyles: Handbook on Research and Theory,* ed. Eleanor D. Macklin and Roger H. Rubin (Beverly Hills, Calif.: Sage, 1983), 371–99; Elise Boulding, *Building a Global Civic Culture: Education for an Interdependent World* (New York: Teachers College Press/Columbia Univ., 1988).

26. Mary Griffith, "Women" in *Our Neighborhood; or, Letters on Horticulture and Natural Phenomena: Interspersed with Opinions on Domestic and Moral Economy* (New York: E. Bliss, 1831), 246–83; Margaret Fuller [Ossoli], "The Great Lawsuit. Man versus Men. Woman versus Women." *The Dial* 4, no. 1 (July 1843): 1–47 (reprint, *The Feminist Papers,* ed. Alice S. Rossi, [New York: Columbia Univ. Press, 1973]), later revised as *Woman in the Nineteenth Century* (1845).

27. In two novels, Alcott shows women's cooperative ventures succeeding: four young women in *An Old-fashioned Girl* who share rooms and the heterogeneous community of women who conclude *Work.* See Louisa May Alcott, *An Old-fashioned Girl* (Boston:

Roberts, 1870), chap. 13: "The Sunny Side"; *Work: A Story of Experience* (1873; New York: Schocken, 1977), chap. 20, both chapters included in *Alternative Alcott,* ed. Elaine Showalter (New Brunswick, N.J.: Rutgers Univ. Press, 1988).

28. For background, see J. E. Lovelock, *Gaia: A New Look at Life on Earth* (London: Oxford Univ. Press, 1979); Carolyn Merchant, *The Death of Nature: Women, Ecology, and the Scientific Revolution* (San Francisco: Harper and Row, 1980); Sandra Harding and Merill B. Hintikka, eds., *Discovering Reality: Feminist Perspectives on Epistemology, Metaphysics, Methodology, and Philosophy of Science* (Boston: D. Reidel, 1983); and Valerie Andrews, *A Passion for This Earth: Exploring a New Partnership of Man, Woman and Nature* (New York: HarperCollins, 1990).

29. For background see, Barbara Welter, "Anti-Intellectualism and the American Woman, 1800–1860," in *Dimity Convictions: The American Woman in the Nineteenth Century* (Athens: Ohio Univ. Press, 1976), 71–82; Julia Ward Howe, ed., *Sex and Education* (1874; reprint, New York: Arno, 1972), a collection of articles responding to Dr. Edward H. Clarke, *Sex in Education* (1873). Utopian author Elizabeth Stuart Phelps contributed chapter 7 to this volume, an essay in which she asserted that the end-of-education illnesses, reported by Dr. Clarke and others to be caused by overexertion in school, might better be attributed to the ending of such stimulation. Also timely is Phelps's 1871 essay "The 'True Woman,' " reprinted in *The Story of Avis,* ed. Carol Farley Kessler (New Brunswick, N.J.: Rutgers Univ. Press, 1992). And see Carroll Smith-Rosenberg, *Disorderly Conduct: Visions of Gender in Victorian America* (New York: Oxford Univ. Press, 1985).

30. Charlotte Perkins Gilman, *Moving the Mountain* (1911; reprint, Westport, Conn: Greenwood, 1968); "The Waste of Private Housekeeping," *Annals of the American Academy of Political and Social Science* (July 1913): 91–95; *What Diantha Did* (New York: Charlton, 1910).

31. See Khanna, note 5 above; Pearson and Pope, (1981), note 23 above. For two 1970s examples, see Dorothy Bryant, *The Kin of Ata Are Waiting for You* (1971; reprint, Berkeley: Moon/Random, 1976) and Marge Piercy, *Woman on the Edge of Time* (New York: Knopf, 1976).

32. See Rosemary Radford Ruether and Rosemary Skinner Keller, eds., *Women and Religion in America: A Documentary History,* Vols. 1: *The Nineteenth Century,* and 3: *1900– 1968* (New York: Harper and Row, 1981, 1986); and Judith Plaskow and Carol P. Christ, eds., *Weaving the Visions: New Patterns in Feminist Spirituality* (San Francisco: HarperCollins, 1989).

33. For examples, see John Kenneth Galbraith, "The Economics of the American Housewife," *Atlantic* 232 (Aug. 1973): 78–83; Marilyn Waring, *If Women Counted: A New Feminist Economics* (San Francisco: HarperSanFrancisco, 1990); Dolores Hayden, *The Grand Domestic Revolution: A History of Feminist Designs for American Homes, Neighborhoods, and Cities* (Cambridge, Mass.: MIT Press, 1981) and *Redesigning the American Dream: The Future of Housing, Work, and Family Life* (New York: Norton, 1984); Eleanor Leacock, "History, Development, and the Division of Labor by Sex: Implications for Organization," *Signs: Journal of Women in Culture and Society* 7 (1981): 474–91; Bettina Berch, *The Endless Day: The Political Economy of Women and Work* (New York: Harcourt Brace Jovanovich, 1982); Susan Strasser, *Never Done: A History of American Housework* (New York: Pantheon, 1982); and Felice Schwartz, *Breaking with Tradition: Women and Work, the New Facts of Life* (New York: Warner, 1992).

34. Jessie Bernard, "The Paradox of the Happy Marriage," in *Woman in Sexist Society: Studies in Power and Powerlessness,* eds. Vivian Gornick and Barbara K. Moran (1971; reprint, New York: New American Library, 1972), 145–62; and for the nineteenth-cen-

tury, see William Leach, *True Love and Perfect Union: The Feminist Reform of Sex and Society* (New York: Basic Books, 1980).

35. Quoted by June Sochen, *Movers and Shakers: American Women Thinkers and Activists, 1900–1970* (New York: Quadrangle/New York Times, 1973), 100.

36. See Sochen above, especially chap. 3 on 1920–1940; Elizabeth Janeway, *Man's World, Woman's Place: A Study in Social Mythology* (New York: William Morrow, 1971).

37. Lois Banner, *Women in Modern America: A Brief History,* 2d ed. (New York: Harcourt Brace Jovanovich, 1984); Nancy F. Cott, *The Grounding of Modern Feminism* (New Haven: Yale Univ. Press, 1987); and William Chafe, *The Paradox of Change: American Women in the Twentieth Century* (New York: Oxford Univ. Press, 1991).

38. Elaine Showalter, "Feminist Criticism in the Wilderness," 261–62, and Annette Kolodny, "A Map for Rereading or, Gender and the Interpretation of Literary Texts," 61, n. 26, both reprinted in *The New Feminist Criticism: Essays on Women, Literature and Theory,* ed. Elaine Showalter (New York: Pantheon, 1985). See also Nina Auerbach, *Communities of Women: An Idea in Fiction* (Cambridge; Mass.: Harvard Univ. Press, 1978); Sandra M. Gilbert and Susan Gubar, *No Man's Land: The Place of the Woman Writer in the Twentieth Century,* Vols. 1 and 2 (New Haven: Yale Univ. Press, 1987, 1989). On female culture, see Jessie Bernard, *The Female World* (New York: Free Press/Macmillan, 1981); Anne Wilson Schaef, *Women's Reality: An Emerging Female System in the White Male Society* (Minneapolis: Winston, 1981); Carol Gilligan, *In a Different Voice: Psychological Theories and Women's Development* (Cambridge, Mass.: Harvard Univ. Press, 1982), chap. 6; and Mary Field Belenky, Blythe McVicker Clinchy, Nancy Rule Goldberger, and Jill Mattuck Tarule, *Women's Ways of Knowing: The Development of Self, Voice, and Mind* (New York: Basic Books, 1986). On theory, see Elizabeth Kamarck Minnich, *Transforming Knowledge* (Philadelphia: Temple Univ. Press, 1990), and Robyn R. Warhol and Diane Price Herndl, eds., *Feminisms: An Anthology of Literary Theory and Criticism* (New Brunswick, N.J.: Rutgers Univ. Press, 1991). On separatist utopias, see Pratt, note 22 above, chap. 6; and Kristine J. Anderson, "The Great Divorce: Fictions of Feminist Desire" in *Feminism, Utopia, and Narrative,* ed. Libby Falk Jones and Sarah Webster Goodwin (Knoxville: Univ. of Tennessee Press 1990). Also a reminder: although this study looks only at women, feminist writing by men has its own tradition, an early example being Charles Brockden Brown, *Alcuin* (1798), and a more recent, Ernest Callenbach, *Ecotopia* (1975).

39. Quoted by Robin Morgan, *The Anatomy of Freedom: Feminism, Physics, and Global Politics* (New York: Doubleday/Anchor, 1982), 83.

40. See Phelps, note 14 above.

Selections

1. *Man's Rights; or, How Would You Like It*

1. The Irish woman's name Bridget was then nearly synonymous with housemaid. Over a million Irish had left their country because of absentee landlordism and famine resulting from a potato blight, so that by 1870, Irish constituted the largest group of immigrants in the United States, and hence a large labor supply.

2. *Tout ensemble,* Fr. for "whole effect."

3. *Ad libitum,* Lat. for "in accordance with one's wishes"; colloq., *ad lib.*

4. portemonnaies, Fr.; literally, "carry money," or "change purse"

5. "Lords of creation" was an expression frequently used satirically in nineteenth-century writing by women. A case in point is the 1837 verse written by the gifted abolition-

ist poet, Maria Weston Chapman (1806–1885), in response to the infamous pastoral letter which New England clergy wrote objecting to the fact that the Grimké sisters—Sarah, (1792–1873), and Angelina (1805–1879)—advocated the abolition of slavery before "mixed" audiences attended by both women and men. Weston called her verse "The Times That Try Men's Souls" and signed it, "The Lords of Creation":

> Confusion has seized us and all things go wrong,
>   The women have leaped from "their spheres,". . . .
> So freely they move in their chosen ellipse,
>   The "Lords of Creation" do fear an eclipse.

6. From a "widow's mite," the "very little" she may have been left by her husband: laws did not require him to leave more than a third of his estate, if that. Thus a "mite-society" would try to help destitute widows, as the sewing-society would sew for the needy. These were volunteer benevolent societies.

7. In 1871, Elizabeth Stuart Phelps would write a series of articles for *The Independent,* many reprinted in *The Woman's Journal,* in which she discussed women's rights and wrongs. See Carol Farley Kessler, *Elizabeth Stuart Phelps* (Boston: G. K. Hall, 1982), 44–52.

8. A "Grecian bend," as explained by Cridge in Dream Number Six, is as follows: "beneath every coat-tail was a Grecian bend, which caused said caudalities [coat-tails] to project at an angle of forty-five degrees" (33).

9. Two and a half decades into the future, Elizabeth Cady Stanton would prepare *The Woman's Bible* (1895, 1898; Reprint, Seattle: Coalition Task Force on Women and Religion, 1974), including passages from the Old and New Testaments concerning women, with commentary by women trained in religious doctrine. The project was considered so radical that Susan B. Anthony was unable to prevent the 1896 NAWSA (National American Women's Suffrage Association) Convention from passing a Bible Resolution disassociating NAWSA from Stanton's *Bible,* much to the dismay of Charlotte Perkins Stetson (Gilman).

10. See note 5.

11. She refers to Robert Burns (1759–1796), a Scottish poet, popular for his dialect poems about the life of common folk. The poem quoted, inaccurately, is "Green Grow the Rashes, O" (written 1784). The fifth and final stanza, including the correct lines, reads:

> Auld nature swears, the lovely dears
> Her noblest work she classes, O:
> Her prentice han' she try'd on man,
> An' then she made the lasses, O.

(Biologically in nature, a male fetus develops from initial femaleness.) In "The Twa Dogs" (1786), Burns uses the expression "lords o' creation."

12. Whilom = "formerly," a literary term from Middle English.

13. *Venus de Medici,* a statue of Venus, the Roman goddess of love and beauty, a Hellenistic statue (1st century A.D.) possibly an approximation of a work by the Classical Greek sculptor Praxiteles—Aphrodite of Cnidus (3d-2d century A.D.), owned by the Medici, a powerful Renaissance family in Florence, Italy.

14. Cridge spells characters' names inconsistently.

15. Expressions from German: *der Teufel* = the devil, *was ist?* = what's this?; from French: *sacre tonnerre* = sacred thunder, *place aux dames* = position allocated to women.

16. *revenons à nos moutons* = French expression, literally, "let's return to our sheep," signifying "let's get back to our subject," from a farce, *Pierre Pathelin,* in which a judge requests a witness whose testimony is off the topic to return to it.

17. Magdalen asylums were reform or correctional institutions for prostitutes, or Magdalens, as they were then called, after the New Testament Mary Magdalen.

18. Colors may well refer to race ("Black" and "white"), and to the colors associated with the armies of the recent Civil War between the states ("blue" with the Union army, and "gray," the Confederate).

19. In the postbellum United States, especially in New England, many so-called "superfluous" women existed, because of the large death toll on Civil War battlefields to husbands and engaged men, and because of westward migration. See Harriet H[anson] Robinson in her *Massachusetts in the Women Suffrage Movement: A General, Political, Legal, and Legislative History from 1774–1881* (Boston: Roberts, 1881), and Carl Degler, *At Odds: Women and the Family in America from the Revolution to the Present* (New York: Oxford, 1980) esp. 151–65.

2. "A Dream Within a Dream"

1. Epictetus, a Greek slave who lived in Rome from A.D. ca. 55 to ca. 135, believed in Stoicism, a philosophy asserting that the ethical goal of life is to live in accord with nature, this being achieved through consistent rational action.

2. *The Independent* was a nineteenth-century magazine of the arts, literature, and social issues, having an editorial view influenced by the doctrine of the protestant congregational denomination, which places authority in the church congregation as opposed to the clergy, who serve at the congregation's pleasure. Congregational is low church as compared with high-church Episcopal (sometimes called Anglican), whose English-language practices are very close to those of Roman Catholicism.

3. The Park Street Church still stands at the corner of Tremont Street in Boston, originally of Trinitarian congregational denomination in protest to the upstart Unitarian movement (though Unitarians later inhabited the premises). Built in 1809, abolitionist William Lloyd Garrison (1805–79), first spoke out publicly here in 1829.

3. *Papa's Own Girl*

1. Spermacity—also spermaceti; spindly candles made from a waxy substance obtained from whales' oil.

2. Fr.: now I know nothing about it.

4. "A Divided Republic: An Allegory of the Future"

1. *The Strike of a Sex* (New York: G. W. Dillingham, 1890) by George Noyes Miller (1845–1904)—educated at the Oneida Community in New York state and a cousin of its founder, John Humphrey Noyes, inspired *A Sex Revolution,* 1894, by Lois Waisbrooker (1826–1909), (reprint, Philadelphia: New Society Publishers, 1985). Both imagine women separating from men: in Miller's book Sisterhood leads to a "Great Woman's Strike" for the "right to the perfect ownership to her own person" while in Waisbrooker's, the narrator, after falling asleep reading *The Strike of a Sex,* dreams that women refuse to

follow men's lead into war and are allotted five years to show the superiority of Mother Love as a guiding principle for government.

2. George Franklin Edmunds (1828–1919), a Radical Republican Senator from Vermont between 1866 and 1891, was responsible for the Tucker-Edmunds Act of 1887 outlawing polygamy and aimed primarily at Utah Mormons. George Graham Vest (1830–1904), a member of the Confederate Congress between 1862 and 1865 and a Democratic Senator from Missouri between 1879 and 1903, was notorious for also fearing the Negro vote. Neither Senator supported women's causes. Both feared being de-sexed.

3. Biblical sources in Judg. 11.1–12.7. 1Sam.12.11; Heb. 11.32: Jephtha (Gk.: Jephthae), a judge of Israel, vowed to God to sacrifice the first person to see him upon his return from military victory; that person was his daughter, the cost of his vow.

4. William A. Hammond, M.D., was the author of *Sexual Impotence in the Male and Female* (Detroit, 1887), and a former surgeon general of the United States Army.

5. Carl Schurz (1829–1906), a university-educated German immigrant, was a reformer in the areas of abolition, government corruption, civil service, Indian Affairs, but not women's rights.

6. John Boyle O'Reilly (1844–90), was an Irish patriot, author and editor, and leader of Irish-Americans, who resided in Massachusetts.

7. Victorian literature, Howells had stated, must contain nothing offensive to the eyes of chaste young women. See his "What Should Girls Read?" in *Harper's Bazar* 36 (Nov. 1902): 956–60. Likewise, James' depiction of his women characters' defection to stereotype over innovation expressed his misogyny. *The Bostonians,* 1886, demonstrates the defeat of feminist purpose. For further discussions, see Judith Fetterley [chap. 4] in *The Resisting Reader: A Feminist Approach to American Fiction* (Bloomington: Indiana Univ. Press, 1978), and Alfred Habegger, "James and Howells as Sissies," Chapter 7 in *Gender, Fantasy, and Realism in American Literature* (New York: Columbia Univ. Press, 1982).

8. The Rev. Morgan Dix (1827–1908), was the rector of New York City's Episcopal Trinity Church.

9. Henry Bergh (1811–88), founded the American Society for the Prevention of Cruelty to Animals as well as organizing a Society for the Prevention of Cruelty to Children.

10. John Lawrence Sullivan (1858–1918), popular and successful boxer and lecturer on temperence, never ran for President, for which he would have had no experience.

11. General Montgomery Blair (1813–83), "served" against the Seminole Indians in 1836, then left the army for a career in law and politics. He argued on behalf of Dred Scott before the Supreme Court in 1857, and was U.S. Postmaster General from 1861 to 1864.

12. See note 2; John James Ingalls (1833–1900), was a Republican Senator from Kansas between 1872 and 1891.

13. Dry Tortugas are an island group off south Florida, west of Key West. One of the islands is the site of Fort Jefferson National Monument.

14. I was unable to identify "a female Buddenseck."

5. "A Feminine Iconoclast"

1. The Harvard Annex informally offered courses to women who passed specific examinations in 1879. In 1882, it was officially named and organized as the Society for the Collegiate Instruction of Women, the precursor of today's Radcliffe College, formally established in 1893. Since 1963 Radcliffe students have been awarded Harvard degrees as one faculty instructs both Radcliffe and Harvard students.

2. *The Dawn* was a periodical published by the Society of Christian Socialists from 15 May 1889 (1.1) to March 1896 (8.2). Abreast of current publications concerning women, Ford calls attention to this magazine, which by November 1889 had existed at most for six months.

3. See selection 4, note 10, for Sullivan identity. The Massachusetts boxer, called the "Great John L.," knocked out Paddy Ryan in 1882 for the world heavyweight championship, which he held until 1892.

8. "A Woman's Utopia"

1. The comment forecasts discussions on the responsibility of literature that Gilman would later publish: "Masculine Literature," *The Forerunner* 1, no. 3 1.3 (1910):18–22, and especially "The Effects of Literature upon the Mind," *The Forerunner* 3, no. 5 (1912):133–39.

2. Bayonne, New Jersey, and Port Richmond, Staten Island in New York City, face each other across the Kill (channel) Van Kull.

3. The Chautauqua movement originated in the 1870s at Lake Chautauqua, New York, where Episcopal Methodist summer camp meetings had been held. Religious education was extended to include lectures, concerts, and plays. An annual adult summer school was established, and *The Chautauquan* published from 1880 to 1914. Other communities in the United States copied this plan, and "chautauqua" became a generic term for a summer lecture series or educational program. The R.G.U. ("argue") Club exemplifies this sort of program.

4. Gilman subscribed to Fabian evolutionary socialist thought, rather than Marxist revolutionary socialism. Here she likely means developing concern not for one's own welfare, but for that of the whole society, a communal, communitarian, or community-oriented concern. Her view restates that of John Adams (1735–1826) writing to Mercy Otis Warren (1728–1814): "Passion for the public good . . . must be Superiour to all private Passions" (16 Apr. 1776; see Cohen, 482).

5. John Bunyan (1628–88), published the completed *Pilgrim's Progress* in 1684, an allegory in the form of a dream vision of the hero, Christian, who undergoes various trials and temptations passing through the country of Beulah, en route to the Celestial City. The book has provided metaphors common in utopian writing and in reference to utopian reform. For example, both Louisa May Alcott and Kate Douglas Wiggin, among many others, refer to *Pilgrim's Progress* in their writing.

6. Charles M. Sheldon (1857–1946), wrote his 1896 bestseller *In His Steps* to depict how a minister could practice the Social Gospel by following in the footsteps of Jesus. He was educated at Andover Theological Seminary during the time that the father of Elizabeth Stuart Phelps sat on the faculty. Her 1895 *A Singular Life* also depicts the life of a minister practicing a Social Gospel.

7. Cotton Mather (1663–1728), was an eminent Puritan divine, noted especially for his *Magnalia Christi Americana,* 1702, a history of New England in which Mather emphasizes the workings of God's Providence so as to reveal the purity of American religion as compared with the depravity of European. His sermons on the evil that witches could effect was one factor supporting the Salem witchcraft trials of 1692.

8. Babylon was once located south of Baghdad, Iraq, near the Euphrates River, its Gardens having been one of the Seven Wonders of the Ancient World, its people devoted to materialism and pleasure.

9. *A Cityless and Countryless World: An Outline of Practical Co-Operative Individualism,*

an 1893 utopia by Henry Oelrich (Holstein, Iowa: Gilmore and Oelrich; reprint, New York: Arno, 1971), who wrote several additional utopias. Gilman was favorably impressed by this book, set on Mars, four of whose central chapters focus upon "sex relations." A major premise of the utopia is the interrelationship of all facets of any society: "a change in sex-relations is accompanied with a corresponding change in dress, food, dwellings, education, modes of travel, amusements, individual freedom, in the manner of rearing offspring, and in countless other ways" (8–9). As the novel's title suggests, parks, farms, residences, and workplaces are interspersed. Martian society was communal and lacked nuclear families; instead, people lived in complexes of one thousand, each with a private room.

10. Alexander Dowie (1847–1907), preacher and religious enthusiast, founded Zion City, Illinois, in 1901. He controlled all of the town's industry and business. A financial scandal resulted from his autocratic means of gathering funds to pay his debts.

11. The expression "negro problem" reveals Gilman's racism: she blames "negroes" for causing a problem rather than understanding that deep-seated prejudice and racism hem in all people of color living in the United States. The problem is in fact a "white" problem —the problem of having a racist mindset.

12. Whiteberg appears to be an Anglicized version of the German "Weissberg". Gilman became increasingly xenophobic and eventually suggested that a future downfall of the USA would be caused by a too-liberal immigration policy. The melting pot has "great dangers," she is reported as having claimed in a 1924 lecture (Schlesinger, Gilman Collection, Box 23, Folder 294).

13. Again Gilman's partial silence regarding origins. Might a household joining Russian and German be Jewish in religion? This was a period of substantial Jewish immigration; throughout the nineteenth-century German Jews emigrated and pogroms ("like thunder") continued in Russia, one of the worst occurring in 1905, with persecution continuing through 1907. Gilman in other writings expresses anti-Semitic views.

14. Thomas Robert Malthus (1766–1834), English economist, theorized that populations increase faster than their means of subsistence and must be checked by will, if not by disaster. Theodore Roosevelt (1858–1919), twenty-sixth President of the United States from 1901 to 1909, supported many Progressive initiatives.

15. Gilman alludes to the eugenics movement, then strong, which agitated for planned human breeding to improve human stock. Obviously those needing improving were not the advocates of improvement; those "others"—lower class, less educated, perhaps immigrant—needed such controls. Again Gilman misses the veiled elitist or racial slurs implicit in her position.

9. Five Generations Hence

1. Caucasian, a term no longer used scientifically, formerly designated a human racial group characterized by very light to brown skin color and straight to wavy hair, inhabiting Europe, north Africa, west Asia and India. The term now refers to inhabitants, languages, or cultures of the Caucasus region, located between the Black and Caspian seas, including Russia, Georgia, Azerbaijan, and Armenia.

2. The Biblical Ham, the son of Noah, is considered to be the original ancestor of the Egyptians, the Nubians, and the Canaanites, the peoples of color. The Ethiopians would also be believed to trace ancestry back to Ham.

3. Canaan is the ancient name for the general region later called Palestine, metaphorically a land of plenty, a utopia.

10. *Seth Way: A Romance of the New Harmony Community*

1. Note by Columbine Way: fictional daughter of Seth Way and narrator of the account.

You can see these marriage lines in the files of the *New Harmony Gazette* in our Public Library [author's note].

11. *Mildred Carver, U.S.A.*

1. Victrola is the RCA (Radio Corporation of America) Victor brand, one of the earliest, of phonograph or record player.

2. Washington Square, in New York City's Greenwich Village. The residence described suggests The Row, built in 1831–33 at the intersection of Fifth Avenue, Numbers 1–13 Washington Square North. It was one of the first examples of controlled urban design, all houses having red brick fronts with white marble basement stories, steps, porches, and trim.

3. Tode Hill Road (also spelled Todt, the Dutch word for death), on Staten Island, at 409.2 feet, the highest point on the eastern seaboard south of Maine. It passes Moravian Cemetery, location of Vanderbilt Family Mausolea, burial site of Cornelius Vanderbilt, upperclass descendent of Dutch ancestors.

4. "White"—imagery suggesting racism by implication. "Whiteness" as "purity," "goodness," "decency," by implication allocates to "blackness" the opposites, racism likely unintentional on the part of the speaker, but nonetheless revealing underlying cultural attitudes and bias regarding "whiteness" and "blackness."

5. Torexo Park is the location of the Catskill Mountains summer mansion of the Carver family and the Van Arsdale summer cottage, where Mildred and Nick had fallen in love.

12. *A Visitor from Venus*

1. GI stands for "*g*eneral" or "*g*overnmental *i*ssue," the official supplies issued to enlisted men in the US army, a name especially current during World War II, and which came to apply to the men themselves to whom the goods were issued. Then, of course, only men served in the army.

2. WAC is an acronym for *W*omen's *A*rmy *C*orps. During World War II, volunteer corps for women were also affiliated with the other three divisions of the military services: WASP for *W*omen *A*irforce *S*ervice *P*ilots, which antedated the WAF for *W*omen in the Air Force; WAVES for *W*omen *A*ccepted for *V*olunteer *E*mergency *S*ervice (navy); and WMs. for *W*omen *M*arines.

3. Marilyn Ferguson, in *The Aquarian Conspiracy: Personal and Social Transformation in the 1980s* (Los Angeles: Tarcher, 1980), discusses what she calls "autarchy" or "government by the self," a concept similar to the Venusian practice of "government from within." The character of a society, she explains, emerges from the character of its people, also a Chinese Confucian concept. Ferguson stresses the correlative of freedom—responsibility. In the chapter called "Right Power," Ferguson argues that "power over one's life is seen as a birthright, not a luxury" (192).

4. Short alludes to the very realistic adaptation of H. G. Wells' *The War of the Worlds* (1898) written and read over the airwaves by Orson Welles (1915–1985) in 1938. Terrified listeners believed that the United States had actually been invaded by Martians.

5. See note 3 for discussion of autarchy.

6. From the New Testament (King James Version, 1611), Revelation 19:15: "And out of his mouth goeth a sharp sword, that with it he should smite the nations: and he shall rule them with a rod of iron: and he treadeth the winepress of the fierceness and wrath of Almighty God." This same verse is echoed in the 1861 Civil War song, "The Battle Hymn of the Republic" by Julia Ward Howe (1819–1910), poet, abolitionist, feminist: "Mine eyes have seen the glory of the coming of the Lord;/ He is trampling out the vintage where the grapes of wrath are stored;/ He hath loosed the fateful lightening of His terrible swift sword:/ His Truth is marching on."

7. Victor-Marie Hugo (1802–85), a prolific French poet, novelist, and dramatist, was a central figure in the Romantic movement. After the European rebellions of 1848, he became politically active on behalf of republican government. His writing became visionary.

8. See, for one such example in the New Testament (King James Version, 1611), John 15:26: "But when the Comforter is come, whom I will send unto you from the Father, even the spirit of truth, which proceedeth from the Father, he shall testify of me."

9. From the New Testament, First Epistle of Paul the Apostle to the Corinthians, 13:4–5; the King James Version uses "charity" where modern translations are more likely to use "love."

References

Bibliography, Definition, Tradition

Boulding, Elise. "Building Utopias in History." In *Towards a Just World Peace,* edited by R. B. J. Walker and Saul H. Mendlovitz, 213–34. Guilford, Eng: Butterworths, 1987.

Golffing, Francis, and Barbara Gibbs. *Possibility: An Essay in Utopian Vision.* New York: Peter Lang, 1991.

Goodwin, Barbara. *Social Science and Utopia.* Brighton, Eng.: Harvester, 1978.

Jameson, Fredric. *The Political Unconscious: Narrative as a Socially Symbolic Act.* London: Methuen, 1981.

Kessler, Carol Farley. "Bibliography of Utopian Fiction by United States Women 1836–1988." *Utopian Studies* 1, no. 1 (1990): 1–58.

———. "Notes Toward a Bibliography: Women's Utopian Writing." *Legacy: A Journal of Nineteenth-Century American Women Writers* 2, no. 2 (1985): 67–71.

Levitas, Ruth. *The Concept of Utopia.* Syracuse: Syracuse Univ. Press, 1990.

Lewis, Arthur O. "The Utopian Dream." In *Directions in Literary Criticism: Contemporary Approaches to Literature,* edited by Stanley Weintraub and Philip Young, 192–200. University Park: Pennsylvania State Univ. Press, 1973.

———. *Utopian Literature in The Pennsylvania State University Libraries: A Selected Bibliography.* Bibliographical Series, No. 9. University Park: Pennsylvania State Univ. Libraries, 1984.

Manuel, Frank E., and Fritzie P. Manuel. *Utopian Thought in the Western World.* Cambridge, Mass.: Harvard Univ. Press, 1979.

Mead, Margaret. "Towards More Vivid Utopias." *Science* 126, no. 3280 (8 Nov. 1957): 957–61.

Negley, Glenn, and J. Max Patrick, eds. *An Anthology of Imaginary Societies.* New York: Henry Schuman, 1952.

Nicolls, P., ed. *Science Fiction Encyclopedia.* New York: Doubleday, 1979.

Patai, Daphne. "British and American Utopias by Women (1836–1979): An Annotated Bibliography." *Alternative Futures: The Journal of Utopian Studies* 4, nos. 2–3 (Spring/Summer 1981): 184–206.

317

Roemer, Kenneth M. *The Obsolete Necessity: America in Utopian Writings, 1888–1900*. Kent, Ohio: Kent State Univ. Press, 1976. Bibliography of Primary Sources, 186–209.

Sargent, Lyman Tower. *British and American Utopian Literature 1516–1985: An Annotated Bibliography*. New York: Garland, 1988.

Suvin, Darko. "Defining the Literary Genre of Utopia: Some Historical Semantics, Some Genealogy, a Proposal, and a Plea." *Studies in the Literary Imagination* (1972): 121–45.

———. "SF Theory: Internal and External Delimitation and Utopia (Summary)." *Extrapolation* 19, no. 1 (1977): 13–15.

Williams, Raymond. "Utopia and Science Fiction." *Science-Fiction Studies* 5 (1975): 203–14.

Selected Critical References

Albinski, Nan Bowman. "Utopia Reconsidered: Women Novelists and Nineteenth-Century Utopian Visions." *Signs: Journal of Women in Culture and Society* 13, no. 4 (1988): 830–41.

———. *Women's Utopias in Nineteenth and Twentieth Century Fiction*. London: Routledge, 1988.

Alternative Futures: The Journal of Utopian Studies 4, nos. 2–3 (Spring/Summer 1981): "Women and the Future."

Barr, Marleen S. *Alien to Femininity: Speculative Fiction and Feminist Theory*. Contributions to the Study of Science Fiction and Fantasy, no. 27. Westport, Conn.: Greenwood, 1987.

———. *Feminist Fabulation: Space/Postmodern Fiction*. Iowa City: Univ. Press of Iowa, 1992.

———, ed. *Future Females: A Critical Anthology*. Bowling Green, Ohio: Bowling Green State Univ. Popular Culture Press, 1981.

———. *Lost in Space: Probing Feminist Science Fiction and Beyond*. Chapel Hill: Univ. of North Carolina Press, 1993.

Barr, Marleen S., and Nicholas Smith, eds. *Women and Utopia: Critical Interpretations*. Lanham, Md.: Univ. Press of America, 1983.

Bartkowski, Frances. *Feminist Utopias*. Lincoln: Univ. of Nebraska Press, 1989.

Baruch, Elaine Hoffman. " 'A Natural and Necessary Monster': Women in Utopia." *Alternative Futures: The Journal of Utopian Studies* 2, no. 1 (1979): 29–48.

Conway, Jill K. "Utopian Dream or Dystopian Nightmare? Nineteenth-Century Ideas about Equality." *Proceedings of the American Antiquarian Society* 96 (1986): 285–94.

———. "Women Reformers and American Culture, 1870–1930." *Journal of Social History* 5 (Winter 1971–72): 164–77.

Cott, Nancy F. *The Grounding of Modern Feminism*. New Haven: Yale Univ. Press, 1987.

Cranny-Francis, Anne. *Feminist Fiction: Feminist Uses of Generic Fiction*. New York: St. Martin's, 1990.

Donawerth, Jane, and Carol A. Kolmerten, eds. *Utopian and Science Fiction by Women: Worlds of Difference*. Syracuse: Syracuse Univ. Press, 1994.

DuPlessis, Rachel Blau. *Writing Beyond the Ending: Narrative Strategies of Twentieth-Century Women Writers*. Bloomington: Indiana Univ. Press, 1985.

Eisenstein, Hester. *Contemporary Feminist Thought*. Boston: G. K. Hall, 1983.

Eisler, Riane. *The Chalice and the Blade: Our History, Our Future*. New York: Harper and Row, 1988.

Freibert, Lucy. "World Views in Utopian Novels by Women." *Journal of Popular Culture* 17 (1983): 49–60.

Frontiers: A Journal of Women Studies 2, no. 3 (Fall 1977): "Fantasy and Futures."

Giele, Janet Zollinger. *Women and the Future: Changing Sex Roles in Modern America*. New York: Free Press/Macmillan, 1978.

Gubar, Susan. "Feminism and Utopia." *Science-Fiction Studies* 13 (1986): 79–83.

———. "*She* in *Herland*." In *Coordinates: Placing Science Fiction and Fantasy*, edited by George E. Slusser, Eric S. Rabkin, and Robert Scholes, 139–49. Carbondale: Southern Illinois Univ. Press, 1983.

Hayden, Dolores. *The Grand Domestic Revolution: A History of Feminist Designs for American Homes, Neighborhoods, and Cities*. Cambridge, Mass.: MIT Press, 1981.

———. *Redesigning the American Dream: The Future of Housing, Work, and Family Life*. New York: Norton, 1984.

Heresies: A Feminist Publication on Art & Politics 3, no. 3 (1981). No. 11: "Making Room: Women and Architecture."

Heresies: A Feminist Publication on Art & Politics 4, no. 1 (1981). No. 13: "Feminism & Ecology: Earthkeeping/Earthshaking."

Huckle, Patricia. "Women in Utopias." In *The Utopian Vision: Seven Essays on the Quincentennial of Sir Thomas More*, edited by E. D. S. Sullivan, 115–36. San Diego: San Diego State Univ. Press, 1983.

Jaggar, Alison K., and Susan R. Bordo, eds. *Gender/Body/Knowledge: Feminist Reconstructions of Being and Knowing*. New Brunswick, N.J.: Rutgers Univ. Press, 1989.

Jones, Libby, and Sarah Goodwin, eds. *Feminism, Utopia, and Narrative*. Tennessee Studies in Literature, no. 32. Nashville: Univ. of Tennessee Press, 1990.

Kaplan, Barbara M. "Women and Sexuality in Utopian Fiction." Ph.D. diss., New York University, 1977.

Kessler, Carol Farley. *Charlotte Perkins Gilman: Her Progress Toward Utopia*. Syracuse: Syracuse Univ. Press, 1995.

Khanna, Lee Cullen. "Frontiers of the Imagination: Women's Worlds." *Women's Studies International Forum* 7, no.2 (1984): 97–102.

Kolmerten, Carol. *Women in Utopia: The Ideology of Gender in the American Owenite Communities*. Bloomington: Indiana Univ. Press, 1990.

Kolodny, Annette. *The Land Before Her: Fantasy and Experience of the American Frontiers, 1630–1860*. Chapel Hill: Univ. of North Carolina Press, 1984.

Lane, Ann J. Introduction to *Herland: A Lost Feminist Utopia*, by Charlotte Perkins Gilman, v–xxiv. New York: Pantheon, 1979.

Leach, William. *True Love and Perfect Union: The Feminist Reform of Sex and Society*. New York: Basic Books, 1980.

Lefanu, Sarah. *Feminism and Science Fiction*. Bloomington: Indiana Univ. Press, 1989.

Le Guin, Ursula. *Dancing at the Edge of the World: Thoughts on Words, Women, Places*. New York: Grove, 1989.

————. "Is Gender Necessary?" In *Aurora: Beyond Equality,* edited by Vonda N. McIntyre and Susan Janice Anderson, 130–39. New York: Fawcett, 1976.

McAllister, Pam. "Women in the Lead: Waisbrooker's Way to Peace." Introduction to *A Sex Revolution,* by Lois Waisbrooker, 1–46. Philadelphia: New Society Publishers, 1985.

Mellor, Anne K. "On Feminist Utopias." *Women's Studies* 9, no. 3 (1982): 241–62.

Merchant, Carolyn. *The Death of Nature: Women, Ecology, and the Scientific Revolution*. San Francisco: Harper and Row, 1980.

Moylan, Tom. *Demand the Impossible: Science Fiction and the Utopian Imagination*. New York: Methuen, 1986.

Palumbo, Donald, ed. *Erotic Universe: Sexuality and Fantastic Literature*. Contributions to the Study of Science Fiction and Fantasy, no. 18. Section III, "Feminist Views," 165–231. Westport, Conn.: Greenwood, 1986.

Patai, Daphne. "When Women Rule: Defamiliarization in the Sex-Role Reversal Utopia." *Extrapolation* 23, no. 1 (1982): 56–89.

Pezzuoli, Giovanna. "Prisoner in Utopia." In *Theory and Practice of Feminist Literary Criticism,* edited by Gabriela Mora and Karen S. Van Hooft, 36–43. Ypsilanti, Mich.: Bilingual Press, 1982.

Pfaelzer, Jean. "A State of One's Own: Feminism as Ideology in American Utopias, 1880–1915." *Extrapolation* 24, no. 4 (1983): 311–28.

Pratt, Annis. *Archetypal Patterns in Women's Fiction*. Bloomington: Univ. of Indiana Press, 1981.

Quest: A Feminist Quarterly 2, no. 1 (Summer 1975): "Women and the Future."

Quissell, Barbara C. "The New World That Eve Made: Feminist Utopias by Nineteenth-Century Women." In *America as Utopia,* edited by Kenneth M. Roemer, 148-74. New York: Franklin, 1981.

Roberts, Robin. "The Female Alien: Pulp Science Fiction's Legacy to Feminists." *Journal of Popular Culture* 21, no. 2 (1987): 33–52.

————. *A New Species: Gender and Science in Science Fiction*. Urbana: Univ. of Illinois Press, 1993.

Rohrlich, Ruby, and Elaine Hoffman Baruch, eds. *Women in Search of Utopia: Mavericks and Mythmakers*. New York: Schocken, 1984.

Rosinsky, Natalie M. *Feminist Futures: Contemporary Women's Speculative Fiction*. Studies in Speculative Fiction, no. 1. Ann Arbor, Mich.:UMI Research Press, 1984.

Rothschild, Joan, ed. *Machina Ex Dea: Feminist Perspectives on Technology*. Elmsford, N.Y.: Pergamon, 1983.

Ruppert, Peter. *Reader in a Strange Land: The Activity of Reading Literary Utopias*. Athens: Univ. of Georgia Press, 1986.

Sargent, Pamela, ed. *More Women of Wonder*. New York: Vintage, 1976.
————. *The New Women of Wonder*. New York: Vintage, 1978.
————. *Women of Wonder*. New York: Vintage, 1975.
Shinn, Thelma J. *Worlds Within Women: Myth and Mythmaking in Fantastic Litera-ture by Women*. Contributions to the Study of Science Fiction and Fantasy, no. 22. Westport, Conn.: Greenwood, 1986.
Smith-Rosenberg, Carroll. *Disorderly Conduct: Visions of Gender in Victorian America*. New York: Oxford Univ. Press, 1985.
Staicar, Tom, ed. *The Feminine Eye: Science Fiction and the Women Who Write It*. New York: Ungar, 1982.
Stimpson, Catharine R. "Feminisms and Utopia." In *Utopian Studies III,* edited by Michael S. Cummings and Nicholas D. Smith, 1–5. Lanham, Md.: Univ. Press of America, 1991.
Suvin, Darko. *Metamorphoses of Science Fiction: On the Poetics and History of a Literary Genre*. New Haven: Yale Univ. Press, 1975.
Tompkins, Jane. *Sensational Designs: The Cultural Work of American Fiction, 1790–1860*. New York: Oxford, 1985.
Tripp, Maggie, ed. *Woman in the Year 2000*. New York: Arbor House, 1974.
Waugh, Patricia. *Feminist Fictions: Revisiting the Postmodern*. London: Routledge, 1989.
Williams, Lynn F. "Great Country for Men and Dogs, but Tough on Women and Mules: Sex and Status in Recent Science Fiction Utopias." In *Women World-walkers: New Dimensions of Science Fiction and Fantasy,* edited by Jane B. Weedman, 223–36. Lubbock: Texas Tech Press, 1985.
Women's Studies 14, no. 2 (1987): "Feminism Faces the Fantastic."
Women's Studies International Forum 7, no. 2 (1984): "Oh Well, Orwell—Big Sister Is Watching Herself: Feminist Science Fiction in 1984," edited by Marleen S. Barr.
Women's Studies International Quarterly 4, no. 1 (1981): "Women in Futures Re-search."

Works Cited
(in Introduction and Editorial Notes)

Albinski, Nan Bowman. *Women's Utopias in Nineteenth and Twentieth Century Fiction*. London: Routledge, 1988.
Alcott, Louisa May. *Alternative Alcott*. Edited by Elaine Showalter. New Bruns-wick, N.J.: Rutgers Univ. Press, 1988.
————. "The Sunny Side." Chap. 13 of *An Old-Fashioned Girl*. Boston: Roberts, 1870.
————. *Work: A Story of Experience*. 1873. Reprint, New York: Schocken, 1977.
Andrews, Valerie. *A Passion for This Earth: Exploring a New Partnership of Man, Woman & Nature*. New York: HarperCollins, 1990.
Auerbach, Nina. *Communities of Women: An Idea in Fiction*. Cambridge, Mass.: Harvard Univ. Press, 1978.

Bakhtin, M. M. *Problems of Dostoevsky's Poetics*. Edited and translated by Caryl Emerson Minneapolis: Univ. of Minnesota Press, 1984.

Bammer, Angelika. *Partial Visions: Feminism and Utopianism in the 1970s*. New York: Routledge, 1991.

Banks, Olive. *Faces of Feminism: A Study of Feminism as a Social Movement*. New York: St. Martin's, 1981.

Banner, Lois. *Women in Modern America: A Brief History*. 2d ed. New York: Harcourt Brace Jovanovich, 1984.

Baym, Nina. *Woman's Fiction: A Guide to Novels By and About Women in America, 1820–1870*. 2d ed. Champaign: Univ. of Illinois Press, 1993.

Belenky, Mary Field, Blythe McVicker Clinchy, Nancy Rule Goldberger, and Jill Mattuck Tarule. *Women's Ways of Knowing: The Development of Self, Voice, and Mind*. New York: Basic Books, 1986.

Bell, Diane. *Daughters of the Dreaming*. Sydney: George Allen and Unwin, 1983.

Berch, Bettina. *The Endless Day: The Political Economy of Women and Work*. New York: Harcourt Brace Jovanovich, 1982.

Bernard, Jessie. *The Female World*. New York: Free Press/Macmillan, 1981.

———. "The Paradox of the Happy Marriage." In *Woman in Sexist Society: Studies in Power and Powerlessness*, edited by Vivian Gornick and Barbara K. Moran, 145–62. Reprint, New York: New American Library, 1972.

Bloch, Ernst. *The Principle of Hope*. Translated by Neville Plaice, Stephen Plaice, and Paul Knight. 3 vols. Cambridge; Mass.: MIT Press, 1986.

———. Special issue. *Utopian Studies* 1, no. 2 (1990): 1–95.

Boulding, Elise. *Building a Global Civic Culture: Education for an Interdependent World*. New York: Teachers College Press/Columbia Univ., 1988.

Bryant, Dorothy. *The Kin of Ata Are Waiting for You*. Berkeley, Calif.: Moon/Random, 1971.

Capra, Fritjof. *The Turning Point: Science, Society, and the Rising Culture*. New York: Simon and Schuster, 1982.

Chafe, William. *The Paradox of Change: American Women in the Twentieth Century*. New York: Oxford Univ. Press, 1991.

Chmielewski, Wendy E., Louis J. Kern, and Marlyn Klee-Hartzell, eds. *Women in Spiritual and Communitarian Societies in the United States*. Syracuse: Syracuse Univ. Press, 1993.

Cirlot, J. E. *A Dictionary of Symbols*. New York: Philosophical Library, 1962.

Cohen, Lester H. "Mercy Otis Warren: The Politics of Language and the Aesthetics of Self." *American Quarterly* 35, no. 5 (1983): 481–98.

Cott, Nancy F. *The Grounding of Modern Feminism*. New Haven: Yale Univ. Press, 1987.

Degler, Carl. *At Odds: Women and the Family in America from the Revolution to the Present*. New York: Oxford Univ. Press, 1980.

Domhoff, G. William. *The Mystique of Dreams: A Search for Utopia through Senoi Dream Theory*. Berkeley: Univ. of California Press, 1986.

DuBois, Ellen Carol, ed. *Elizabeth Cady Stanton/Susan B. Anthony: Correspondence, Writing, Speeches*. New York: Schocken, 1981.

DuPlessis, Rachel Blau. "The Feminist Apologues of Lessing, Piercy, and Russ." *Frontiers: A Journal of Women Studies* 4, no. 1 (Spring 1979): 1–8.

Eisenstein, Hester. *Contemporary Feminist Thought.* Boston: G. K. Hall, 1983.

Faludi, Susan. *Backlash: The Undeclared War Against American Women.* New York: Crown, 1991.

Faraday, Ann. *Dream Power.* 1972. Reprint, New York: Berkley Medallion, 1973.

Ferguson, Marilyn. *The Aquarian Conspiracy: Personal and Social Transformation in the 1980s.* Los Angeles: J. P. Tarcher, 1980.

Fetterley, Judith, *The Resisting Reader: A Feminist Approach to American Fiction.* Bloomington: Indiana Univ. Press, 1978.

Flexner, Eleanor. *Century of Struggle: The Woman's Rights Movement in the United States.* New York: Atheneum, 1973.

Francoeur, Robert T. "Religious Reactions to Alternative Lifestyles." In *Contemporary Families and Alternative Lifestyles: Handbook on Research and Theory,* edited by Eleanor D. Macklin and Roger H. Rubin, 371–99. Beverly Hills, Calif.: Sage, 1983.

Fritz, Leah. *Dreamers and Dealers: An Intimate Appraisal of the Women's Movement.* Boston: Beacon, 1979.

Fuller [Ossoli], Margaret. "The Great Lawsuit. Man versus Men. Woman versus Women." 1843. Reprinted in *The Feminist Papers,* edited by Alice S. Rossi, 158–82. New York: Bantam, 1974.

Galbraith, John Kenneth. "The Economics of the American Housewife." *Atlantic* 232 (Aug. 1973): 78–83.

Gardiner, Michael. "Bakhtin's Carnival: Utopia as Critique." *Utopian Studies* 3, no. 2 (1992): 21–49.

Giele, Janet Zollinger. *Women and the Future: Changing Sex Roles in Modern America.* New York: Free Press/Macmillan, 1978.

Gilbert, Sandra M., and Susan Gubar. *No Man's Land: The Place of the Woman Writer in the Twentieth Century.* Volumes 1 and 2. New Haven: Yale Univ. Press, 1987, 1989.

Gilligan, Carol. *In a Different Voice: Psychological Theories and Women's Development.* Cambridge, Mass.: Harvard Univ. Press, 1982.

Gilman, Charlotte Perkins. "The Effects of Literature upon the Mind." *The Forerunner* 3, no. 5 (1912): 133–39.

———. *The Home: Its Work and Influence.* 1903. Reprint, Urbana: Univ. of Illinois Press, 1972.

———. "Masculine Literature." *Forerunner* 1, no. 3 (1910): 18–22.

———. *Moving the Mountain.* 1911. Reprint, Westport, Conn.: Greenwood, 1968.

———. "The Waste of Private Housekeeping." *Annals of the American Academy of Political and Social Science* (July 1913): 91–95.

———. *What Diantha Did.* New York: Charlton, 1910.

———. *With Her in Ourland.* Chapter 11. *Forerunner* 7, no. 11 (1916): 292–93. Reprint (entire work), Westport, Conn.: Greenwood, 1968.

Gornick, Vivian. "Woman as Outsider." In *Woman in Sexist Society: Studies in Power and Powerlessness,* edited by Vivian Gornick and Barbara K. Moran, 126–44. Reprint, New York: New American Library, 1972.

Griffith, Mary. *Our Neighborhood; or, Letters on Horticulture and Natural Phenomena: Interspersed with Opinions on Domestic and Moral Economy.* New York: E. Bliss, 1831.

Guttentag, Marcia, and Paul E. Secord. *Too Many Women? The Sex Ratio Question.* Beverly Hills, Calif: Sage, 1983.

Habegger, Alfred. *Gender, Fantasy, and Realism in American Literature.* New York: Columbia Univ. Press, 1982.

Hayden, Dolores. *The Grand Domestic Revolution: A History of Feminist Designs for American Homes, Neighborhoods, and Cities.* Cambridge, Mass.: MIT Press, 1981.

———. *Redesigning the American Dream: The Future of Housing, Work, and Family Life.* New York: Norton, 1984.

Harding, Sandra, and Merill B. Hintikka, eds. *Discovering Reality: Feminist Perspectives on Epistemology, Metaphysics, Methodology, and Philosophy of Science.* Boston: D. Reidel, 1983.

Howe, Julia Ward, ed. *Sex and Education.* 1874. Reprint. New York: Arno, 1972.

Howells, William Dean. "What Should Girls Read?" *Harper's Bazar* 36 (Nov. 1902): 956–60.

Humm, Maggie, ed. *Modern Feminisms: Political, Literary, Cultural.* New York: Columbia Univ. Press, 1992.

Janeway, Elizabeth. *Man's World, Woman's Place: A Study in Social Mythology.* New York: William Morrow, 1971.

———. *Powers of the Weak.* New York: Knopf, 1980.

Jones, Libby Falk, and Sarah Webster Goodwin, eds. *Feminism, Utopia, and Narrative.* Tennessee Studies in Literature, no. 32. Knoxville: Univ. of Tennessee Press, 1990.

Kessler, Carol Farley. *Elizabeth Stuart Phelps.* Boston: G. K. Hall, 1982.

Khanna, Lee Cullen. "Women's Worlds: New Directions in Utopian Fiction." *Alternative Futures: The Journal of Utopian Studies* 4, no. 2–3 (1981): 47–60.

Kolmerten, Carol A. *Women in Utopia: The Ideology of Gender in the American Owenite Communties.* Bloomington: Indiana Univ. Press, 1990.

Kolodny, Annette. *The Land Before Her: Fantasy and Experience of the American Frontiers, 1630–1860.* Chapel Hill: Univ. of North Carolina Press, 1984.

———. "A Map for Rereading or, Gender and the Interpretation of Literary Texts." In *The New Feminist Criticism: Essays on Women, Literature and Theory,* edited by Elaine Showalter, 46–62. New York: Pantheon, 1985.

———. "Not-So-Gentle Persuasion: A Theoretical Imperative of Feminist Literary Criticism." In *Feminist Literary Criticism,* Working Paper no. 3, 3–20. Research Triangle Park, N.C.: National Humanities Center, 1981.

Leach, William. *True Love and Perfect Union: The Feminist Reform of Sex and Society.* New York: Basic Books, 1980.

Leacock, Eleanor. "History, Development, and the Division of Labor by Sex: Implications for Organization." *Signs: Journal of Women in Culture and Society* 7 (1981): 474–91.

Lovelock, J. E. *Gaia: A New Look at Life on Earth.* Oxford: Oxford Univ. Press, 1979.

Mannheim, Karl. *Ideology and Utopia: An Introduction to the Sociology of Knowledge.* 1929. Translated by Louis Wirth and Edward Shils. New York: Harcourt, Brace, Jovanovich, 1936.

Merchant, Carolyn. *The Death of Nature: Women, Ecology, and the Scientific Revolution.* San Francisco: Harper and Row, 1980.

Miller, George Noyes. *The Strike of a Sex.* New York: G. W. Dillingham, 1890.

Minnich, Elizabeth Kamarck. *Transforming Knowledge.* Philadelphia: Temple Univ. Press, 1990.

Morgan, Robin. *The Anatomy of Freedom: Feminism, Physics, and Global Politics.* New York: Anchor/Doubleday, 1982.

Oelrich, Henry. *A Cityless and Countryless World: An Outline of Practical Co-Operative Individualism.* Holstein, Iowa: Gilmore and Oelrich, 1893. Reprint, New York: Arno, 1971.

Partridge, Eric. *Origins: A Short Etymological Dictionary of Modern English.* New York: Macmillan, 1959.

Pearson, Carol, and Katherine Pope. *The Female Hero in American and British Literature.* New York: Bowker, 1981.

Pfaelzer, Jean. "A State of One's Own: Feminism as Ideology in American Utopias, 1880–1915." *Extrapolation* 24, no. 4 (1983): 311–28.

Phelps [Ward], Elizabeth Stuart. *A Singular Life.* Boston: Houghton, Mifflin, 1895.

———. "The 'True Woman.' " 1871. Reprinted in *The Story of Avis,* edited by Carol Farley Kessler, 269–72. New Brunswick, N.J.: Rutgers Univ. Press, 1992.

———. "Victurae Salutamus." In *Songs of the Silent World and Other Poems,* 99. Boston: Houghton, Mifflin, 1885.

Piercy, Marge. *Circles on the Water.* New York: Knopf, 1982.

———. *Woman on the Edge of Time.* New York: Knopf, 1976.

Pizan, Christine de. *The Book of the City of Ladies.* 1405. Translated by Earl Jeffrey Richards. New York: Persea Books, 1982.

Plaskow, Judith, and Carol P. Christ, eds. *Weaving the Visions: New Patterns in Feminist Spirituality.* San Francisco: HarperCollins, 1989.

Pratt, Annis. *Archetypal Patterns in Women's Fiction.* Bloomington: Indiana Univ. Press, 1981.

Robinson, Harriet H[anson]. *Massachusetts in the Women Suffrage Movement: A General, Political, Legal, and Legislative History from 1774–1881.* Boston: Roberts, 1881.

Ruether, Rosemary Radford, and Rosemary Skinner Keller, eds. *Women and Religion in America: A Documentary History.* Vols. 1: *The Nineteenth Century,* and 3: *1900–1968.* New York: Harper and Row, 1981, 1986.

Sacks, Sheldon. *Fiction and the Shape of Belief.* Berkeley: Univ. of California Press, 1964.

Schaef, Anne Wilson. *Women's Reality: An Emerging Female System in the White Male Society.* Minneapolis: Winston, 1981.

Schwartz, Felice. *Breaking with Tradition: Women and Work, the New Facts of Life.* New York: Warner, 1992.

Scott, Anne Firor, and Andrew MacKay Scott, eds. *One Half the People: The Fight for Women's Suffrage.* Urbana: Univ. of Illinois Press, 1982.

Showalter, Elaine. "Feminist Criticism in the Wilderness." In *The New Feminist Criticism: Essays on Women, Literature and Theory,* edited by Elaine Showalter, 243–70. New York: Pantheon, 1985.

Sochen, June. *Movers and Shakers: American Women Thinkers and Activists, 1900–1970.* New York: Quadrangle/New York Times, 1973.

Stanton, Elizabeth Cady, ed. *The Woman's Bible.* 1895, 1898. Reprint, Seattle: Coalition Task Force on Women and Religion, 1974.

Strasser, Susan. *Never Done: A History of American Housework.* New York: Pantheon, 1982.

Tompkins, Jane. *Sensational Designs: The Cultural Work of American Fiction, 1790–1860.* New York: Oxford Univ. Press, 1985.

Waisbrooker, Lois. *A Sex Revolution.* 1894. Reprint, with an introduction by Pam McAllister, Philadelphia: New Society Publishers, 1985.

Warhol, Robyn R., and Diane Price Herndl, eds. *Feminisms: An Anthology of Literary Theory and Criticism.* New Brunswick, N.J.: Rutgers Univ. Press, 1991.

Waring, Marilyn. *If Women Counted: A New Feminist Economics.* San Francisco: HarperSanFrancisco, 1990.

Wegner, Philip E. "On Zamyatin's *We:* A Critical Map of Utopia's 'Possible Worlds.' " *Utopian Studies* 4, no. 2 (1994): 94–116.

Welter, Barbara. "Anti-Intellectualism and the American Woman, 1800–1860." In *Dimity Convictions: The American Woman in the Nineteenth Century.* Athens: Ohio Univ. Press, 1976.

Wolf, Naomi. *Fire with Fire: The New Female Power and How It Will Change the Twenty-First Century.* New York: Random House, 1993.

Woolf, Virginia. *Three Guineas.* 1938. Reprint, New York: Harbinger, 1966.

Utopianism and Communitarianism
Lyman Tower Sargent and Gregory Claeys, *Series Editors*

This series offers historical and contemporary analyses of utopian literature, communal studies, utopian social theory, broad themes such as the treatment of women in these traditions, and new editions of fictional works of lasting value for both a general and scholarly audience.

Other titles in the series include: